EARLY PRAISE FOR *GIRLS' NIGHT OUT*

"*Girls' Night Out* is a heart-stopper of a thriller, rippling with suspense from its opening pages. But it's also much more: Liz Fenton and Lisa Steinke plumb the intricacies of female friendship with skill and depth and heart. It's a deeply satisfying read, and one you won't want to miss."
—Megan Abbott, national bestselling author of *You Will Know Me*

"It's trouble in paradise for three best friends struggling to make amends in the latest thriller from the dynamic writing duo of Liz Fenton and Lisa Steinke. *Girls' Night Out* is a chilling page-turner full of secrets and hostility that will leave readers shocked again and again . . . and again. I loved it."
—Mary Kubica, *New York Times* bestselling author of *The Good Girl* and *Every Last Lie*

"A wild ride into a high-powered girls' trip to Mexico. Suspense at its best. Liz and Lisa have taken their writing partnership to a new level!"
—Kaira Rouda, *USA Today* bestselling author of *Best Day Ever*

"This suspenseful novel is full of twists and turns and makes clever use of chronology. It will make you think twice about going on a girls' night out!"
—Jane Corry, bestselling a : *Wife* and od Sisters*

"In *Girls' Night Out*, Liz Fe ers on a suspenseful international tou s best and worst. As enviable fun takes a turn thr spicion toward pure fear, you'll find out just how wrong a trip to paradise can go."
—Jessica Strawser, author of *Almost Missed You* and *Not That I Could Tell*

PRAISE FOR *THE GOOD WIDOW*

A *PUBLISHERS WEEKLY* BEST SUMMER BOOKS 2017 SELECTION, MYSTERY/THRILLER

"Fenton and Steinke deliver a complicated tale of love, loss, intrigue, and disaster . . . This drama keeps the pages turning with shocking twists until the bitter end. A great read; recommended for admirers of Jennifer Weiner and Rainbow Rowell."

—*Library Journal*

"Fans of Joy Fielding will appreciate the story's fast pacing and sympathetic main character . . . [a] solid psychological thriller . . ."

—*Publishers Weekly*

"Fenton and Steinke's talent for domestic drama comes through . . . For readers who enjoy suspense writers like Nicci French."

—*Booklist*

"A fantastic thriller that will keep you on your toes . . ."

—PopSugar

"Accomplished authors Liz Fenton and Lisa Steinke make their suspense debut with great skill and assurance in this enthralling novel of marital secrets and lies, grief and revelation. *The Good Widow* led me along a winding, treacherous road and made a sharp, startling turn that I didn't see coming. Unputdownable!"

—A. J. Banner, #1 Amazon bestselling author of *The Good Neighbor* and *The Twilight Wife*

"Liz Fenton's and Lisa Steinke's *The Good Widow* begins by asking what you would do if your spouse died in a place he wasn't supposed to be in with a woman he wasn't supposed to be with. What follows is a gut-wrenching thriller, sometimes heartbreaking, sometimes darkly funny, but always a page-turner. And as you read it late into the night you'll look over at the person in bed next to you and wonder how well you really know him. A wild, skillfully written ride!"

—David Bell, author of *Since She Went Away*

"An irresistible and twisty page-turner, *The Good Widow* should come with a delicious warning: This is not the story you think it is."

—Deb Caletti, author of *He's Gone*

"*The Good Widow* is both heartrending and suspenseful, deftly navigating Jacks's mourning and the loss of her less-than-perfect marriage. The writing is sharp and evocative, the Hawaiian setting is spectacular, and the ending was a wonderful, twisty surprise. A quintessential summer beach read!"

—Kate Moretti, *New York Times* bestselling author of *The Vanishing Year*

"*The Good Widow* is a fresh take on your worst nightmare—your husband dies and he isn't where, or with whom, he said he was. I ripped through these pages to see where Fenton and Steinke would take me, which ended up being somewhere unexpected in the best kind of way. You will not be sorry you read this!"

—Catherine McKenzie, bestselling author of *Fractured* and *Hidden*

GIRLS'
NIGHT
OUT

GIRLS' NIGHT OUT

A NOVEL

LIZ FENTON & LISA STEINKE

LAKE UNION
PUBLISHING

Text copyright © 2018 by Liz Fenton & Lisa Steinke
All rights reserved.

Published by Lake Union Publishing, Seattle

www.apub.com

Amazon, the Amazon logo, and Lake Union Publishing are trademarks of Amazon.com, Inc., or its affiliates.

ISBN-13: 9781503902565
ISBN-10: 1503902560

Cover design by Faceout Studio, Lindy Martin

Printed in the United States of America

To best friends everywhere—hang on to each other.

"It's all very well to tell us to forgive our enemies; our enemies can never hurt us very much. But oh, what about forgiving our friends?"

—Willa Cather, *My Mortal Enemy*

CHAPTER ONE

THE DAY AFTER
NATALIE

Waves lapped against the shore. It sounded as if the sea were breathing. *In and out. In and out.* Between the whitecaps breaking against the sand, there was a pause, almost as if the ocean were inhaling and preparing to release another breath. *In and out. In and out.*

Natalie was in a haze, falling somewhere between sleep and semi-consciousness, about to let herself dip back into a deep lull, when she felt a breeze tickle her bare arms. Had they left the door to their hotel room ajar last night? She opened her eyes, expecting to see her suitcase parked in the corner, her espadrilles sitting next to the sliding glass door, her purse resting on the ledge behind her. Her passport, extra pesos, and wedding ring locked away in the safe. She'd spy Ashley's brown curls poking out from beneath the sheets next to her, their clothes and shoes from the night before left in a forgotten pile on the floor.

Squinting, Natalie attempted to adjust to the semidarkness, the only light coming from the rising sun, still resting on the ocean, about to make its way into the sky.

She shot upright.

She was outside. On the beach. Lying under one of the hotel's rustic cabanas. She craned her neck—a sharp pain jolting her as she tried to turn it—expecting to see Ashley, or possibly Lauren, next to her, but all the chairs were empty. She swallowed, her throat dry. As she swung her legs over the side of the chaise, her wet dress clung to her. When she pulled at it, sand fell from the hem. She stood slowly as her head spun, noticing her calves were also caked. She paused, took a deep breath, and attempted to get her bearings.

"Ashley? Lauren?" she called, even though she could see the beach was desolate, save for a stray dog running near the surf, his ribs visible through his fur. It felt like a dream.

Was it?

Her stomach fluttered, worry starting to build as she thought of having slept out here, alone, overnight. The things that could have happened to her. Ben would not be happy if he ever found out. After all the lectures he'd given her about Mexico—the things that could happen to women traveling alone—she couldn't let him know. Taking a quick inventory of her body, running her hands over it, she decided nothing seemed off, other than a throbbing behind her temples that rocketed through her skull every time she moved. Her legs felt heavy as she began to walk the narrow path that led to the hotel, stumbling slightly up the wooden steps, passing the rustic cottages and hoping no one would take notice of her. What would they think? *That poor almost-forty-year-old woman who drank like she was half her age, then woke up outside.* She shuddered. That wasn't her. Not by a long shot. She hurried up the stairs toward her room, clinging to the railing, bile swirling in her stomach.

She hoped Ashley would know why she'd slept outside—why she hadn't made it the three hundred yards to their room. That she'd fill in the gaping hole in her memory. She imagined her friend's eyes narrowing as she took in Natalie's sandy legs, the way her crossbody purse was still secured lightly on her chest. (Thank God it was still there!) Then she'd play back the night in detail, filling in all the blank spots Natalie couldn't. Ashley would tell her not to worry. Natalie would worry anyway.

Natalie tried to conjure what she could from the night before—their girls' night out. She recalled getting ready. Putting on the black dress with the floral embroidery that she'd purchased from a street vendor in downtown Tulum, the dress that now hung heavy on her. She recalled going out to dinner—to that restaurant with the wooden tables—what was it called? She strained until the thought finally came—Hartwood! Yes, that was it. She recalled Ashley ordering Patrón, Natalie protesting weakly before finally giving in. Despite her policy against doing tequila shots because they would only lead to no good—she could name a dozen possibilities—Ashley's big brown eyes had won her over when the small handblown glasses were set on the table next to a plate of limes. Ashley's body had been angled just slightly away from Lauren, and her request was clear. *Please. Have fun with me. We need this.*

And Ashley had been right. They'd needed it.

Natalie had grabbed the glass and tossed it back, the burn of the tequila in her throat making her feel both invigorated and a little bit dangerous. As her chest warmed and her eyes stung, she was struck with a feeling that anything could happen.

But what *had* happened?

Natalie yanked on the sliding glass door of her hotel room, but it was locked. Digging inside her purse, she found the oversize key chain with the room key dangling from it and unlocked the door, pulling it open quietly so as to not wake Ashley, who was most definitely not a morning person—especially after a night of heavy drinking. Natalie planned to slip under the duvet and drift back to sleep, getting the answers she needed about the night from Ashley once she woke up.

But Ashley wasn't in the room.

Natalie's eyes darted around the suite. The king-size bed was made, the white comforter pulled taut in that way only housekeeping could do, and the pillows embroidered with bluebirds and flowers were perfectly positioned.

Where was Ashley?

Shuffling toward the bathroom, confusion and fear mixing together in the pit of her stomach, she scanned the room for something that would jog her memory. Had Ashley told her where she was going and Natalie had forgotten? Towels from their showers were hanging on the wooden ladder leaning against the wall, Natalie's cream one-piece bathing suit and black cover-up dangling from a hook by the closet, Ashley's workout clothes strewn about the room. Natalie's makeup bag and toiletries were arranged neatly, Ashley's splayed across the counter. She saw a flash of the two of them putting on makeup in tandem. Ashley telling Natalie how the lavender eye shadow complemented her green eyes. They'd sipped margaritas and made jokes about how big their hair was thanks to the humidity. Natalie had given up and pushed her red bob back with a headband while Ashley kept at it, trying in vain to use the BloBrush to tame her curls. She could hear Ashley's feathery laugh as she had surveyed herself in the large steel-framed mirror, then gave her reflection the middle finger. Ashley pivoted on her heel toward the door. "I guess even this thing has its limits," she'd joked, holding up the bright pink hot brush Natalie had designed. "I give up. Let's get out of here!"

But had that been last night? Or another night? Her mind felt like a dull pencil, her thoughts lacking the sharp edges they needed.

Natalie's skin pricked as she felt around in her purse to make sure her wallet was still inside. Her breathing slowed when she pulled it out and found her driver's license, credit card, and pesos tucked into the billfold. Her cell phone was still where she'd forgotten it last night—charging on the shelf behind the bed. That detail came through so clearly—but not much else. Why? Her instinct had been to go back and get it—in case Ben, Meg, or Lucy needed her. Meg had just gotten her first cell phone and seemed intent on being able to reach Natalie whenever she wanted. She'd text her from the school bus, band practice, even the living room when Nat was just in the kitchen. Natalie didn't know if it was the newness of the phone or if Meg had a sincere desire to connect with her mother. She hoped it was the latter. She had begun to miss her girls terribly, and the ache to see them throbbed in the pit of her stomach. But Ashley had convinced her not to go back for the phone, saying that any of her family members could find Nat through her or Lauren.

She studied the blank screen now. They hadn't called or texted, and neither had Ashley or Lauren. She quickly dialed Ashley, but it went straight to voice mail. *Hi, you've reached Ashley Green with BloMe, Inc. Please leave your name and number, and I'll get back to you as soon as possible.* She hung up, wishing she had Marco's number—Ashley was probably with him. They'd spent nearly every day of their trip with the good-looking local, but Natalie had never thought to ask for his contact info. She tried Ashley once more and heard her message again. Concern started to rise inside her—Ashley's phone was always on; Nat couldn't remember the last time she'd heard Ashley's outgoing message. Once, Natalie had called her at 2:00 a.m. in a panic, wondering if Ashley had mailed the tax extension request for BloMe, and Ashley had answered.

Natalie sent a text now.

Where are you, Ashley?

CHAPTER TWO

FOUR DAYS BEFORE
ASHLEY

Ashley sat in the bar of the boutique hotel, admiring the gorgeous tiled light fixtures hanging from the high ceiling above, the colorful Mexican plates displayed on shelves, the framed chalkboard on the wall indicating live music later that night. Being in Tulum made her feel so far away from her five-bedroom mid-century modern house in Santa Monica, with its floor-to-ceiling windows facing west, and sleek but slightly uncomfortable gray furniture. With its closets full of more shoes than she could ever wear—the garage boasting designer cars and every toy and gadget her two daughters could ever want—its backyard home to a pool and hot tub she hadn't so much as dipped a toe in for months.

She stole a glance at her two friends sitting next to her at the well-worn wood table, feeling both incredibly calm and anxious. Lately Ashley had swung between the emotional highs and the lows easily, unable to find her baseline. The day she'd impulsively hit "Send" on the email inviting Lauren and Natalie on this trip to Mexico and insisting on paying for it? *High.* Now, as she sat, tired from her 4:00 a.m. wake-up alarm and sweaty from the wall of wet heat that greeted them at the Cancún airport, her oldest friends with their expectant faces staring back at her? *Low.*

"This place is gorgeous," Ashley said, inhaling the warm salty air. She knew she should say something deeper, but the words were caught in her throat, or maybe her heart. Where would she start? With Lauren and their terrible fight a year ago? With Natalie and the recent offer from Revlon to buy their company—creating tension within their friendship and business partnership? Or say nothing at all?

"It really is," Natalie agreed, playing with the straw in her margarita.

Lauren stared out at the ocean, her eyes sad.

"Let's toast," Ashley said, a nervous pit in her stomach. She needed this trip to work—for her friends to see that she was trying to reconnect with them. Especially Lauren, whom she'd barely seen in the last year. Lauren and Natalie obligingly held up their glasses. "To old friends." Ashley smiled.

"How are we forty?" Lauren broke her silence, pushing a strand of her long, dark hair away from her face, exposing her youthful ivory skin.

"If I'm doing my math correctly, I'd say you're the only one at this table who can check the new box on forms," Natalie said, her lips drawn up but her tone unreadable. "We're still clinging to thirty-nine over here." She pointed at Ashley.

Lauren smiled, but it faded quickly.

"Well, you might be the oldest, but you look the youngest!" Ashley reached over and clinked her glass against Lauren's. "You could pass for thirty." She was flattering her, her voice throaty.

Lauren threw a nod and a seemingly genuine smile her way, and Ashley felt a spark of hope that the muscle memory of their friendship did still exist. Because this was it—her Hail Mary, her mea culpa. She'd sold them hard in her email invitation—calling attention to the beauty of the resort, the fun things they could do together in the Yucatán Peninsula. But she'd avoided mentioning the real reason. Had she worried deep down that if she'd revealed her true intentions, they would have declined?

"I know people always say this, but it really does seem like yesterday that we were in college," Natalie interjected, twisting her wedding ring.

Ashley studied her friend, her choppy red hair, small green eyes, petite nose, and could still see her standing in the quad on campus with yet another petition for Ashley to sign, her passion dripping from each word as she made her pitch. Over the years Natalie had slowly stopped going to bat for the things that were important to her. Ashley sighed. When the Revlon offer came in last month, she recognized the Natalie from twenty years ago, the one who didn't take no for an answer. Why she had resurfaced now?

"Does it?" Lauren said, her eyes thoughtful. "It feels like a long time ago to me." She looked away.

Ashley followed her gaze across the courtyard toward the clear blue Caribbean Sea. Lauren had been so different from anyone Ashley had met at Harvey Mudd, a small private college east of Los Angeles. She wore flannels and Birkenstocks and didn't seem worried about trying to fit in. Ashley cared too much. She sat in the dorm bathroom every morning applying her makeup and styling her hair until she was satisfied it looked perfect.

"You really didn't care what people thought of you," Ashley said, then caught Lauren's confused expression. "No, I mean it in a good way—you dressed like you were going to a Grateful Dead concert every day while the rest of us were trying to copy the girls in the J.Crew ads."

Lauren laughed finally, that familiar slightly high-pitched giggle Ashley would recognize anywhere, and she let out the breath she'd been holding.

"And look at me now," Lauren went on, tugging at her gray and yellow sundress, which hung gracefully to her knees. "I've come a long way." She finished her margarita, her cheeks flushing. She looked quizzically at Ashley. "And so have you! I saw your little purchase on Instagram last week."

"Not so little," Natalie muttered, before taking a long sip of her cocktail.

Ashley blushed. It had seemed like such a great idea at the time to buy that Porsche convertible. She'd seen one pull up next to her as she sat in traffic on Santa Monica Boulevard and immediately envied the blonde behind the steering wheel as she sang along with the radio. Ashley convinced herself that her life would be better if she were driving the Porsche instead of her Volvo—that she'd start belting out songs when she drove to work. That she'd be happier, somehow. "I probably shouldn't have posted that," she said, glancing at Natalie, thinking back to how her eyes had flashed when she first saw the onyx sports car in the parking garage at work. *Why didn't you tell me?* she'd asked.

Ashley had just shrugged, avoiding the real answer: *I had no idea I was going to buy it when I rolled out of bed this morning.*

Lauren waved her hand. "Life is short; do what you want, and post what you damn well please. It can all be over like *that*," she said, snapping her fingers for effect.

Natalie looked down and played with her napkin. Ashley nodded and swallowed hard before finding her voice.

"You're right, Laur. I'm glad we're still friends after all this time. And that we're all here together now. We've let too much time go by." She met Lauren's gaze. Did she replay the argument they'd had last year in the same detail Ashley did? Ashley still woke up in the middle of the night, her body covered in a layer of sweat, wondering whether she'd done the right thing. She couldn't go back and change anything. But the truth was, if given the chance, she wouldn't anyway.

"You seem so sentimental, Ash, not your usual style," Lauren said, and flagged the bartender.

Was she joking or serious? Ashley couldn't tell. Even though she supposed it was true—if she listed her own personality traits, that one would not make the cut. Still, it hurt a little to hear it out loud.

"I agree," Natalie said, elbowing Ashley. "Where's the woman who chastised me just last week for saving my kids' artwork?"

"I still stand by that logic. Total waste of space!" Ashley insisted, laughing, but surprised by her mounting insecurity. So she wasn't someone who saved mementos. That was okay, wasn't it?

"Aww, if I had kids, I'd save that stuff too," Lauren said wistfully, and bumped Natalie's shoulder.

Ashley couldn't seem to crack Lauren's shell, as if the shadow of their fight last year lurked in the background of their conversation. But Natalie was connecting with her so easily.

She thought of the jeweled framed picture of the three of them she kept on her desk at work. Lauren, her hair piled neatly on top of her head, her dark eyes shining. Natalie, her long, wavy red hair a contrast to the stark bob she wore today. Lauren and Natalie bookending Ashley in the middle, her thick chestnut hair slick and straight. It had been that photo that sparked the idea for this trip. She'd stared at it while on a conference call with the buyer at Costco, feeling desperate for a moment like that again. The way they'd come together so easily, their smiles wide and open. The way they'd inhabited each other, their bonds uncomplicated. She'd hung up the phone and Googled the words *spiritual, renewal, Mexico*. Tulum, a small beach town, had come up instantly in her search, its ancient ruins and mystical cenotes making it sound like a perfect fit. She'd shot off the email to Lauren and Natalie before she could change her mind, the high that came along with the split-second decision making her feel delirious. But much like the spontaneous purchase of the Porsche, it wore off harshly once reality set in.

"I'm just . . . I don't know . . . happy you both came," Ashley finally mustered weakly, watching her friends' faces, hoping they'd agree with her, that they'd say they were happy too.

Before anyone could respond, the bartender, who'd introduced himself as José, walked up and asked if they'd all like another round.

Ashley gave two thumbs up. Her glass was already empty. She needed another drink to help temper her nerves.

"I would love another," Lauren said eagerly, and Ashley exhaled sharply in relief.

"I'm fine for now," Natalie said.

Ashley pulled a face. "Don't listen to her. She'll take another," she said, pointing to Nat's glass. Natalie didn't respond—just pressed her lips together the way she did when she was trying to keep herself from saying something. Nat wasn't a big drinker, but Ashley knew that for them to put their inhibitions aside, to relax around each other again, she needed to push her. Just a little.

"Excellent." José clapped his hands together. "My jalapeño mezcal margaritas really are the best. A little sweet and a little spicy, just like me." He winked, then glanced at Lauren, his chiseled cheekbones becoming more defined when he spoke.

"Can't wait," Lauren said, her cheeks flushing—from the alcohol or José, Ashley couldn't be sure. *Well, that's interesting.*

"I'll pass for now, but I'm sure they're delicious," Natalie said.

This wasn't one of their obligatory happy hours they attended with clients. This was a vacation to Mexico. One they needed. Couldn't Natalie see that?

"Come on, for me?" Ashley puffed out her lower lip in a pout. She tried to gauge how Natalie *really* felt about being here. She'd said yes immediately, but that was often her way—to be agreeable. The truth was, their underlying issues had been simmering for some time, and this reunion already felt as if it were heading down the wrong path. She wanted to say: *Drink with me. Take my side. I miss you. Let's pretend Revlon never called. That we never got that offer. At least for the next five days. Let's be the friends we used to be.* But the words wouldn't come. She hoped that once they settled in, had a few drinks, and became more comfortable around each other, the words would slide off her tongue.

"Fine," Natalie finally said, rolling her eyes. "I'll even pay." She handed her card to José. "Keep it open."

"Yay! Nat's going to get drunk!" Ashley knew a second drink wasn't going to fix them, but it was a good start.

"Two drinks don't equal inebriation!" Natalie corrected. "But they are pretty damn good."

"You can't have only two—nobody can," Ashley said. "Or maybe that's just me." She caught José's eye, who grinned before walking to the bar.

"So, how's the BloBrush doing?" Lauren asked.

Ashley glanced at Natalie but couldn't read her expression, so she pushed on.

"It's good. Actually, we got an offer—Revlon wants to buy it," Ashley said.

"Really? Wow!" Lauren held up her glass. Ashley quickly toasted, but Natalie didn't. "Isn't this good news?"

"Depends on who you ask," Natalie said, and Ashley noticed her shoulders were tensing. Ashley didn't want this to lead to an argument. They'd already had too many about this issue.

"It is good news. I think we'd both agree on that." Ashley didn't look at Natalie this time. "But what we don't see eye-to-eye on is what to do—sell it or not," she added, then quickly finished her thought, "but we're going to figure it out soon. And whatever happens, happens."

"Is that what we're doing? Leaving it up to chance?" Natalie laughed sharply, but Ashley felt her stomach knot again. "We need to be resolute. This is our business."

"The business you want to get rid of?" Ashley's eyes flared. And just like that, they were at it again. She glanced at Lauren, who was frowning. She knew she should pull back, table it, change the subject, anything. But this topic was a hot button for her, and she almost couldn't control herself.

"That's not fair," Natalie said, glaring at her. Lauren nodded slightly in agreement, which made Ashley feel a spike of betrayal.

She leaned in. "We built BloMe from the ground up, for *eight* years. You invented the damn thing. And now you just want to kiss it all goodbye? To a huge company that's going to do who knows what with it?"

Natalie gritted her teeth. "It's a lot of money. Life-changing money. And it's not like Revlon is going to buy it and destroy it!"

"They are going to bring their own people in after six months. Let everyone go, even the people who have been with us from the very start, when we were working out of your garage!" Ashley shook her head. "So we don't know they won't destroy it. And none of us will be there to do anything about it." She couldn't stop herself from catching Lauren's eye as she said the words. She'd already made this argument to Natalie ad nauseam, to no avail. Certainly Lauren could see the logic?

Natalie rubbed the back of her neck. "Arthur has told Revlon we'd want a clause in the contract that each of our employees gets a year of severance."

Ashley studied Natalie. She looked worn out. "It's not about money."

"Maybe not for you!" Natalie snapped, and then took a deep breath before speaking again. "All I'm saying is that Tricia from marketing isn't going to become homeless if we sell. We've discussed complete transparency. Everyone will be compensated and be given plenty of time to find something new."

Ashley paused before replying, surprised again at the urgency in Natalie's eyes, in her voice, whenever she talked about selling. Something Ashley hadn't seen before when it came to their business. Usually, even if she didn't agree, Natalie acquiesced to Ashley. Why was she choosing now to take a stand? She was about to ask her, but Lauren spoke before she could.

"Hey, guys. Calm down. I didn't mean to start something. I was just curious." She looked back and forth at them, confusion etched in the knot in her brow.

Ashley wanted to tell Lauren she and Nat were fine. They could all be fine. But what could she say? Because none of them were fine at all.

"It's okay. Ashley shouldn't have gotten into it here." Natalie tightened her lips again and Lauren gave her a look, as if to say, *No, she really shouldn't have.* "What about you?" Natalie turned toward Lauren. "Are you back at work?"

"No, I haven't felt up to it yet. Between Geoff's estate and his life insurance, I'm going to be fine," she said, her eyes sad. "But lately I've been thinking about going back to school. I still want to teach."

"You should," Natalie said. "Geoff would have wanted you to."

Lauren scoffed. "Come on, now. We all know that isn't true."

Ashley froze, not sure what to say. She agreed with Lauren—Geoff would not have liked that at all, but she sure as hell wasn't going to say it. And was that a smirk on Natalie's face?

"Three jalapeño mezcal margaritas," José said, setting them down on the table, and they all picked them up and drank fervently. Even Natalie.

"Let's change the subject," Lauren said, her voice tight. "How are your husbands? I saw Ben at my birthday party last month and we caught up briefly. It was good to see him—I'm glad you all came." She made strong eye contact with Natalie, and Ashley felt like she caught some subtext in her expression—because Ben had gone and Jason hadn't.

"Ben was happy to see you after so long," Natalie said before Ashley could get a word in. "And so was I—thanks again for the invite. It was a great party. That chocolate fountain was amazing."

"Wasn't it? I had so many dipped strawberries I thought I was going to puke afterward."

"So did I." Natalie laughed. She paused. "But it was nice to see you smiling again."

"Thank you," Lauren said. "It felt good to have something to smile about."

Their conversation had fallen into a perfect rhythm, like a tennis ball flying back and forth over the net. Ashley tried and failed to recall when she'd ever felt like a third wheel with them. Typically, she would be the one directing the conversation. "Jason was sorry he couldn't be there," she interjected, not meeting Natalie's gaze because she knew the real story—that Jason had refused to attend when the invitation came in, telling Ashley she shouldn't go either. Not after how Lauren had treated her. But she wouldn't have missed Lauren's fortieth. She'd been relieved to be invited. And she'd also enjoyed the chocolate fountain. But she wasn't going to say it now—that moment had passed.

"That's okay," Lauren said, but Ashley felt like she wasn't okay with it at all. "How is he?"

Ashley took a long pause. When she'd planned this trip, she envisioned them reminiscing, bantering easily, like they had so many times before. She'd imagined leaning in and whispering the secret that she'd held for so long. It always sat perched on the tip of her tongue—when Natalie lamented how little time she and Ben spent together. When Ashley thought of the pain Lauren had been through, both before and after Geoff's death. But instead she felt as if she was on the defensive, no longer the conduit between her two closest friends. She made the quick decision to pare back her confession.

"He's good, but . . ." She chose her next words carefully. What she could and couldn't say about why their marriage had fallen apart. She gulped half of her margarita and spit out the words. "He's good, but our marriage is not. I'm thinking of leaving him. It's why I wanted to come here. To think."

She'd said it. And she couldn't take it back now.

"What? Are you kidding?" Natalie said, clearly shocked.

Ashley hadn't told her anything about it. She'd kept it bottled up for so long that whenever she was with Natalie and she asked about him or brought him up, Ashley could convince herself that her problems with Jason didn't exist. They simply lived deep inside of her and came out when they were at home, behind closed doors.

Ashley shook her head. "I'm serious."

"I had no idea," Natalie said, her voice high, her eyes narrowed. "We work side by side every day. We've talked about him, but you never mentioned it. We all had that barbecue a couple of weeks ago. Nothing seemed off."

"I know." But it was—it was all so very off. As Jason flipped the hamburgers, his back rigid. When they'd argued in the car on the way over, in hushed voices, their daughters oblivious, plugged into their iPads.

Lauren kept her eyes trained on Ashley but said nothing.

"So you were pretending?" Natalie pressed.

"Yes and no." She hoped Lauren might step in. Ashley knew she could relate.

"Why didn't you tell me?" Natalie asked, frowning.

Because you love him. I love him. This is Jason. The guy who helped us move all the furniture into our first office space because we couldn't afford to hire movers. The one who called you after I had Hannah to tell you every detail because you were stuck in traffic on the 405.

Ashley's eyes filled with tears. She had wanted to confide in Natalie so many times, but she couldn't bring herself to do it. Part of her hoped it would get better. Part of her was curious whether she could tolerate it if it didn't.

"I wanted to, but if I said it out loud, that would make it real. Then I'd have to deal with it. Keeping it inside was easier." She blew out a deep breath, even a partial confession lifting a large weight from her shoulders. Regardless of their issues, these were the people she wanted to share this with.

Lauren finally spoke. "I'm sorry."

"Thank you," Ashley said.

"Are you going to try counseling?" Natalie asked.

They were so far beyond couple's therapy at this point, Ashley was sure that would never help them. But she knew why Natalie was suggesting it, why she wanted them to work it out. They sometimes joked that she liked Jason more than she liked Ashley.

But Natalie had no idea what she was talking about. Who he really was.

"I don't think he'd go. And honestly, I don't know if I want to," Ashley said.

"Sometimes it just is what it is, no matter how much you want it to be something else," Lauren said, more to herself than anyone else, picking up a menu and staring blankly at it. As she had so many times

16

this past year, Ashley yearned to be inside her head. To see where her battle lines were drawn.

"Anyway, enough about that," Ashley said, trying to hide the disappointment she felt that Lauren hadn't said more. "Jason is a big part of why I wanted to be here with you two. I've got some soul-searching to do."

She didn't miss the look that passed between Natalie and Lauren.

"Excuse me." José stood next to their table and turned to Natalie. "I'm sorry, miss, but your credit card was declined."

"What? That's impossible. Try it again," Natalie said, her cheeks brightening.

"I ran it three times. Do you have another?" José looked away, as if embarrassed for her.

"It's okay, charge it to my room," Ashley said quickly.

"No, I wanted to pay for it," Natalie said.

"Next time." Ashley waved her off as José walked off to rebill the charges.

"You know what, I forgot to call my bank to let them know I'd be out of the country. They probably declined the charges because they think it's fraud," Natalie reasoned.

"That's probably it," Lauren reassured her. "You can call them later."

"I will." Natalie smiled, Ashley noticing it didn't quite reach her eyes. Natalie hated failing at anything, even if it was just a credit card charge. She was the one who still prepped for their business meetings as if they were final exams, making notecards until her eyes were blurry.

A tall man with thick black hair and green eyes appeared at their table. "I'm Ishmael. Your rooms are ready. Sorry for the wait."

"No problem," Ashley said, relieved for the interruption. She needed time to regroup.

"I have two suites." He looked between them. "Who is sharing?"

Ashley sent a guilty glance in Lauren's direction. "There are only eight bungalows in this hotel and only two were left when I booked. I thought I could sweet-talk a third room, but no luck . . . yet."

"We are still fully booked," Ishmael said sheepishly.

"No worries, but if there are any cancellations, I'll be your first call, yes?" Ashley laid her fingers on his forearm and he blushed.

"Yes, of course."

"So, Laur, I figured Nat and I could share because we practically live together at work anyway and there's only one big bed, and your room is actually closer to the ocean than ours." Ashley smiled brightly as she said the words. She had considered putting herself with Lauren, to accelerate their reconciliation, but she worried it might be too much, too soon. And even though things between her and Natalie were strained, they'd worked through conflict before. They could certainly handle sharing a room for a few days.

Lauren tilted her head slightly, her face blank. "Thank you—that sounds nice," she said softly as they grabbed their drinks and followed Ishmael out of the bar. He introduced them to Maria, another hotel employee, a short young woman with chocolate-brown hair twisted into two braids.

"I'll take you to your room," Maria said. "It's this way."

Lauren began to follow her but turned back. "Meet up later?" she asked.

"Of course. I want to throw my stuff down, maybe take a quick shower. But then we'll hit the beach!" Ashley said, trying not to focus on the expression on Lauren's face—it looked like she thought she and Natalie were abandoning her. This trip was not supposed to pull them apart. It was meant to bring them back together.

She watched Lauren walk toward her room and then followed Natalie's tall frame to their bungalow, stopping to wash her bare feet in the wash-basin at the base of the stairs—which Ishmael had called a *lavapie*—and decided maybe the trip hadn't started off on exactly the right foot. But it was just the first day. There was still time to rediscover the smiling women from the framed picture. They hadn't veered so far off the path.

Had they?

CHAPTER THREE

Four Days Before
Natalie

Ashley dropped her purse on a chair and looked around their suite. "Wow, this is gorgeous! Even better than the pictures online." She walked over to the sliding glass door and pulled it open, a warm breeze blowing in.

Natalie sent off a quick text to Ben. Credit card declined. Do we need to talk?

She sighed, hoping it was a mistake but knowing in her heart it wasn't. She set her phone facedown on the table and took in the room, trying not to let what had happened distract her. There was a king-size bed draped with a white sheer canopy. A balcony with an ocean view. Beautiful beveled glass faux windows lined the hallway to the bathroom. Ben would love it here. She couldn't recall the last time they'd gone on vacation; he had been supportive of her long hours building and maintaining the business for years, but as the girls had gotten older he had started to resent it, more of the family responsibilities falling on him. Natalie was often so tired when she got home that she couldn't so much as read the girls a bedtime story. If they were even still awake. If she and Ashley didn't sell the business, she honestly didn't know when her family would be able to travel together again, to become a cohesive unit once more.

"So, you and Lauren seemed pretty chummy back there." Ashley pressed her lips flat.

Natalie took a deep breath, knowing what was coming. The dynamic among the three of them had always been a careful balance of closeness and conflict—something as simple as a look or a remark tipping them to one side or the other. "Yeah, we were catching up. Wasn't that the plan?"

"Right. We were *all* supposed to be doing that."

Natalie cocked her head. "You confuse me, Ash. You bring us all here to bond, and then an hour in you're doing that thing again."

"What thing?"

"Oh, come on—whenever the three of us are together, you have to dominate the discussion and everyone's attention, or else." She tried to keep her voice even, knowing how easily this conversation could go sideways.

"Or else what?" Ashley put her hands on her hips. Her expression was one Natalie could only describe as absolute confusion—which was baffling. This had always been their setup. Part of the reason this last year without Lauren in their lives as much had been easier in so many ways.

"Or else this." Natalie waved her hand back and forth between them.

Ashley gave Natalie a long look, but said nothing.

"You know I'm right," Natalie teased.

Ashley sat on the chair next to her. "You're not wrong," she managed.

They both smiled.

"That's a good start," Natalie said after a few moments. "Admitting someone's *not wrong.*"

"It just felt like you guys were teaming up, agreeing about every-thing. And that I couldn't say anything right." Ashley frowned, then held up a finger. "And before you call me on it, I already know I'm being a little childish."

Despite the fact Ashley had evolved from the nineteen-year-old girl Natalie had met in her biology class at Harvey Mudd to an entrepreneur who was married with two daughters, in many ways she was still that college girl. She craved attention like you yearn for water to quench your thirst. And she was still used to getting her way—sweet-talking friends or colleagues to sway them to her ideas just as she had done with teachers, getting them to extend a deadline for an assignment as easily as she could put one foot in front of the other and walk.

"Can I ask you something?" Natalie said gently.

"Sure," Ashley said.

"I thought you wanted this—her, here. The three of us together again."

"I did—I do."

"I feel bad for Lauren," Natalie said, the words out before she realized—the margaritas she'd had earlier were emboldening her. They were delicious, not to mention they eased her tension, and she could already tell her usual two-drink limit would not be standard in Mexico for both those reasons.

"Why?" Ashley asked, twirling the end of her hair around her finger.

Did Ash really not get why? They'd barely seen Lauren after what happened at the funeral nearly a year ago. She studied Ashley's face—her soft brown waves that highlighted her high cheekbones, her nose that was just a little too big but somehow worked with her wide-set brown eyes.

"I guess I was trying to make her feel comfortable. Letting her know I was ready to move past it."

"But what happened last year is about me too—I was also there. I was also hurt."

"And so was I," Natalie said, trying to keep her voice neutral. But the truth was, she hated thinking about that night, still pushing down the guilt about her part in it.

"So you can see how giving her all of your attention could come across like you're taking her side."

"You know I wasn't doing that."

"But she might think you were." Ashley sighed.

"I know that." Natalie selected her next words with care. "But *you* invited her here. Don't you think that, in itself, is giving her the impression you're not still holding on to everything?"

"I do want to get past it, I really do, and I think I tried to go there a couple of times, didn't I?"

"Well, you talked about Jason." Natalie was treading carefully. But she was surprised that had been Ashley's reason for coming here. *To figure things out.*

"And old friends!" Ashley said. "I tried!"

"Did you?" Natalie asked gently.

Ashley shrugged. "I thought I did. But maybe not. I just didn't think I should come right out with what happened at the funeral."

"That's not what I'm saying. Just give her some time," Natalie said. "And maybe I overcompensated, tried too hard with her earlier. I didn't intend to make you feel left out."

"But one of us always is." Ashley bit her lip.

"True—we need to figure that out. We're almost middle-aged!" Natalie said, wondering if they ever would. At a J. Lo concert they'd gone to many years ago, there had been two seats together and the other was one row up. Both Lauren and Natalie obviously wanted to sit with Ashley, but in the end Ashley had taken the lone seat. Nat would never know whether it was because she was being selfless, avoiding conflict, or wanting to flirt with the group of cute boys in the next seats. All she knew for sure was that three was a difficult number when it came to friendship.

"I think I messed up with the room thing."

Natalie gave her a sympathetic look. "You didn't really think coming to Mexico was all we'd have to do and then poof, we're all put back together?" she said.

"No, I don't know. I just couldn't seem to connect with her. It's never been that hard before."

"This one's going to take more than batting your eyelashes." Natalie smirked.

"Hey." Ashley laughed, jabbing her in the arm.

Natalie raised her eyebrows. "Truth hurts?"

Ashley pushed her again playfully, then opened her suitcase and started rifling through it, mumbling something about a bikini.

Natalie flipped over her phone——no response from Ben. She let out a long exhale. She knew the news wasn't going to be good when she heard from him. "Hey, can we talk more about Jason?" she asked hesitantly.

Ashley's back stiffened, her movements slowing as she searched for her bathing suit. "What else do you want to know?"

"I'm just wondering, now that we're alone, why you didn't say anything. Come to me."

"It's complicated," Ashley said, still not turning around. "Like I said, talking about it would have made it real, you know? Denial really can be a beautiful place to live."

Natalie couldn't imagine what could be so bad between them. When Jason had bought Ashley a blender for a recent birthday, she'd gone ballistic. Natalie sent her smoothie recipes for more than a month—it was their own little inside joke. But how long ago was that? Over a year ago, for sure.

Ashley pulled a white two-piece bathing suit from the suitcase and turned around, sitting on the floor. She spoke again while Natalie was still thinking. "It's been a long time coming. You know, building slowly."

"I'm sorry."

"We fight. A lot." Ashley's eyes were steely.

"Ben and I fight too," Natalie said, thinking of their last one. Just before she left for Tulum—Ben pushing her to make Ashley change her mind about the offer. *You need to make her understand you want out. The girls need you. I need you. We need this.*

"Not like we do." Ashley looked down.

"Everyone thinks that, right? We've both been married a long time. What's it going to be for you? Twelve years? Fourteen for me? It's normal to have issues." Natalie wasn't sure if she was trying to convince Ashley or herself. "It's why selling the company could be good for us—for our families. Maybe with the pressure off, you guys could figure it out."

"Nat, please . . ."

Natalie held up her hands. "Okay."

Ashley gave her a thoughtful once-over. "So what if I do this: What if I promise to give the Revlon offer some more consideration on this vacation?"

"You'd do that?" Natalie asked, feeling a rush of hope. She'd never known Ash to so much as sleep on something. She routinely made quick decisions, declaring that her impulsiveness was her secret sauce.

"I want you to know that I want to be better. I know I've been hard to deal with, but I'm really trying." She shifted on the floor. "It might not seem like it yet, but I am."

"Okay," Natalie said, swallowing her surprise. She hadn't heard Ashley talk like this before—it was refreshing. Hopeful, even.

"I want to take a quick shower, and then let's hit the beach with Lauren. Maybe I can sweet-talk José into making us three of his specialty margaritas and get him to throw in an extra splash of mezcal—that is, if you're ready for another one?"

Natalie smiled. "Why not? And I'm sure you'll have no problem convincing him."

"You seem to think these lashes have magical powers." Ashley blinked rapidly for effect.

"Don't they? I still can't believe you were able to get us reservations at Hartwood for our last night here. I mean, it's *you*, so I can, but still, I'm impressed," Natalie said. The hip restaurant in Tulum owned by two former Brooklynites booked out months in advance. Ashley had called just a couple of days ago and charmed the host into squeezing them in. Natalie had leaned against the doorjamb of Ashley's office as she pleaded her case in a slight southern drawl (she tended to manifest one when needed), explaining she was bringing her girlfriends to Mexico, even admitting she'd had a falling-out with one of them and that this dinner was going to be her apology, then letting out a high-pitched squeal when she got the reservation. "I'm giving you the biggest kiss when I get there!" she'd exclaimed, and winked at Natalie, as if to say, *There's no way in hell that's happening.* That was the thing with Ashley—she'd say just about anything to convince you of something. The trick was distinguishing the facts from the bullshit.

Ashley shrugged. "It's just what I do. We can't all be engineering geniuses. Some of us have to hustle." She swatted Natalie on the butt with a striped towel. Ashley peeled off her leggings, T-shirt, bra, and panties and turned on the shower. She stood there naked, sticking her fingers under the water. "It's ice cold."

"Ishmael warned us that the water takes a while to heat up. You're always so damn impatient!"

"But you love me anyway!" Ashley sang as she stepped in.

Natalie ignored her last comment, walking out to their lanai, spying Lauren across the courtyard on her balcony. She was leaning against the bamboo railing, waving her hands as she spoke animatedly on her cell phone. Who was she talking to? Her mom? A boyfriend, perhaps? Natalie felt a pang of embarrassment for how little she knew about Lauren's current life. As she watched her, she hoped she'd find out on this trip.

Her phone buzzed. Ben.

Sorry about the credit card. Let's talk live about it. Any news on your side???

Not yet.

There was no answer she could give Ben other than that she'd convinced Ashley to sell. They'd gone round and round about cutting back her hours—which she'd attempted before, with disastrous results. She'd once taken the week of spring break off to clear her head and be with her girls, but Ashley had called her so many times, needing help with payroll, wanting to know where she could find the patents, and having a meltdown over the new sales rep who wasn't quite pulling her weight, that Natalie had come back in after two days. While Ashley was the face and the creative mind, Natalie was the one who handled all the shit—all the behind-the-scenes things that kept the company running and that Ashley didn't want to do. That's why the offer from Revlon had been a godsend. Natalie would get the one thing she wanted most—her freedom.

The only thing standing in the way of that?

Ashley.

CHAPTER FOUR

THE DAY AFTER
NATALIE

Natalie sat on the edge of the bed, her wet dress hanging heavy on her body, clinging to her legs. She dialed Lauren but the call went straight to voice mail, and she found herself staring at the screen, trancelike. Still no text or call back from Ashley. Her adrenaline spiked. If she wasn't in Lauren's room, she had to be with Marco, but it felt strange that Natalie couldn't locate her. She always knew where to find Ashley, the way she always knew where her daughters were.

A shiver passed through her. Once, several years ago, she'd heard a small gurgling sound coming from the baby monitor. She'd run to her daughter's room, fumbling around in the dark until she discovered there was a small circular thread that had poked free from the soothing aquarium that hung on the side of the crib. It had somehow gotten wrapped around Lucy's neck. Natalie quickly released her from it, her heart pounding, the fear of what could have happened intertwining with the relief she'd felt that Lucy was safe. It still surprised her how much she thought of that night, how much energy her mind still spent on what could have happened, and she felt that same consciousness strike her hard now.

She'd find Ashley. Hopefully in Lauren's room. Then they could all have a laugh about how Natalie was finally the one who'd drunk so much she blacked out. She opened the door and headed across the courtyard, pushing to evoke more of her memory. How had she ended up sleeping on that beach chair, and why was she wet? But she could only grab snippets of scenes from the night before—being at dinner at Hartwood, taking shots, drinking red wine and more red wine, then changing locations—going to La Cantina, a bar downtown, and dancing to "Brown Eyed Girl." It was like she was trying to recall a dream. She knew it was in there somewhere, but the details wouldn't take shape. What had happened to wipe her memory away? A pit formed in her stomach—a physical alert that felt like a warning.

She hurried up the steps to Lauren's suite, where the curtains on the sliding glass door were pulled shut. She knocked lightly, then harder. What if Lauren wasn't here either? She tried not to think about the research she'd done after Ben's lecture, scrolling through the travel warnings on the Department of State website. She'd fallen into a rabbit hole that night, clicking from one article to the next, ending up on one from Reuters that said there were thirty thousand people missing in Mexico who had disappeared under suspicious circumstances. Almost one thousand mass graves had been found, fifteen hundred corpses, only half of them identified. Natalie found it alarming how much violence occurred in the very same place tourists flocked to in droves.

Finally she heard the latch and her pulse slowed slightly. Lauren opened the door, blinking rapidly. "Hey."

Natalie's eyes darted around the room, her gaze falling on the closed bathroom door. "Is Ash here?"

Lauren shook her head. "Why, what's going on?"

She felt that twinge in her gut again. Where was Ashley? She frowned, her mind spinning with explanations. But there was something unsettling about that—the not knowing. She raked her fingers through her hair, feeling some sand granules shake out. "I don't know where she is," she said, the weight of Ben's words to her before she left for Tulum sinking in. *Be careful. It's Mexico. Stay together.*

Had they stayed together?

"She's probably with Marco." Lauren rolled her eyes.

Marco. The thought stirred her anger. If Ashley was with him and didn't tell them—didn't bother to so much as text—Natalie wasn't sure what she'd say to her when she did come back.

"Have you called her?"

Natalie swallowed her sigh. Of course she'd called her. A dozen times. She nodded. "Can you try her, please?" she requested, a sliver of her worried that Ashley might be ignoring her calls because they'd argued last night.

Lauren picked up her phone. "Why is your dress wet?" She looked her over.

Natalie touched the fabric. "I don't know. I woke up down on the beach."

"What? You?" Lauren smirked.

"I hardly remember anything from last night," she said, her voice small.

"Why not? You weren't that drunk, were you?" Lauren studied her.

"I guess I had more than I usually do, so maybe it hit me harder than I thought?" Natalie sat on the bed, checking her phone again. Still no response.

"I'm just getting voice mail," Lauren said. "I'll send her a text in case she's in a bad cell spot." She typed something on her phone. "So what do you remember?"

"Just parts. Like I know we had tequila shots and lots of red wine at dinner, right?"

"And pork ribs and mahi-mahi. Ashley was doing her annoying picky food thing. She talked the waiter into going next door to get some goat cheese for her beet salad when they told her they'd run out." She shook her head.

"I remember that." Natalie recalled watching Ashley touch the server's hand lightly as she made her request. *Is there any way you could find some goat cheese for me?* In the past, Natalie would have made a funny comment about how Ashley could convince anyone of anything. She may have even retold that story from the early years of BloBrush, when Ashley had sat in the QVC lobby for hours until she won over the cranky receptionist with the colorful tattoo sleeves, who ended up getting Ash five minutes with the woman who decided which products went on air. Natalie teased her about how cocky she'd been as she'd packed her oversize bag that morning, filling it with granola, bottled water, and magazines. *I'm not leaving until I talk to someone, Nat.* Nat would say that part in the nasally voice she used to imitate her, the one that always made Ashley laugh. But she didn't do any of that last night. Instead, she'd stared at Ashley as she slowly chewed her beet salad with pine nuts and pondered how she'd ever thought it was funny that Ashley manipulated people everywhere she went—that it was so ingrained in who she was that even Natalie wasn't sure she could tell the sincere from the fake anymore.

"I guarantee you she's in Marco's bed right now." Lauren pursed her lips. "You saw them last night on the dance floor—he was all over her."

Natalie sighed, recalling how he'd crashed their girls' night, monopolized Ashley's attention.

"Do you recall that part?" Lauren asked. "'Brown Eyed Girl' came on and you three were dancing—well, after Ashley pretty much dragged you out there."

"I do," Natalie said. She saw herself in a sea of bodies, awkwardly moving her feet left and right like a teenage boy at his first dance, singing along, laughing as she heard her awful pitch. Amazed that she was actually singing. She didn't even sing alone in the shower! She had once. She'd belted out Beyoncé's "Crazy in Love" and Ben had walked in, making a joke that thank God she had a day job to fall back on.

The digital clock on the bedside table said 6:52 a.m. "Anything from Ash?"

"No. You?"

"Nothing. We need to go find Marco. I can't believe we didn't get his number."

"Well, it wasn't like we wanted to keep in touch," Lauren said dryly.

Natalie stood up. Suddenly something occurred to her. "Do you think my blackout is from more than drinking too much? Do you think I could have been drugged?" She wrapped her arms around herself, the thought making her feel nauseous. She'd never blacked out, not once, and the idea that she could lose a piece of herself was terrifying.

Lauren looked at her. "Maybe, but when?"

"I don't know—at La Cantina? Things are pretty clear up until that point."

"I guess it's possible, but that's a scary thought."

Natalie chewed on her lower lip. "I know."

"Are you okay? Do you think anything happened to you?" Lauren looked her over.

"It doesn't feel like anything did . . ." Natalie trailed off. Could someone have raped her—or tried to? She didn't think so, but the mere idea of it sent a chill up her back.

"Okay, good. Let's go find her." Lauren went to the closet and changed into yoga pants and a T-shirt. "Of course this is how we have to spend our last morning. Tracking her down," she huffed as she grabbed her tennis shoes off the floor.

Natalie bristled slightly at her agitation. "It's okay," she offered.

Lauren gave her a funny look. "What's the last thing you remember from last night?"

"What?"

"You guys left me at La Cantina. You went with Marco. Took a cab somewhere."

"Why didn't you go with us?" Natalie asked, shifting uncomfortably.

31

Lauren pulled her hair back into a ponytail. "I said I didn't want to."

"The night was bad, wasn't it?"

"It was a disaster, in my opinion." Lauren sighed. "Ashley asked me to go somewhere with her so we could talk. She said the three of us could all go bond on the beach." She studied herself in the mirror. "I said no. I was just over it."

Natalie squeezed her eyes shut. How could her mind have erased something so important happening between her two friends? She remembered being in the bathroom, two women recognizing them from their popular YouTube videos. She also had the sense she'd argued with Ashley while in there. But what had they had been fighting about? *Revlon,* a voice inside her head whispered. But was she just assuming that, or was it an actual memory?

"Well, when we find her, you guys can talk it out," Natalie said.

"I'm over trying to talk things out with her. I think I'm done. And I told her as much." Lauren looked like she was going to say more but didn't.

"Really?" Natalie was shocked by the finality in Lauren's voice. She couldn't say she was surprised Lauren felt that way after the last five days. But she also hadn't known Ashley to reach out like that—to be the bigger person. If Ashley was trying, why couldn't Lauren have tried too? Shouldn't you try as many times as it took?

"Really," Lauren said, her face impassive.

"And even in the light of day you still feel the same?"

"I think so, yes. It's just been so difficult, Nat. Friendship shouldn't be this hard."

She was right. Friendship with Ashley was often difficult. But did that mean it wasn't worth it?

"So, nothing after dancing? Just a blank slate?" Lauren asked.

A memory broke the surface. The bathroom at La Cantina. She saw her reflection in the mirror, her eye makeup smudged. She and Ashley were arguing. About Revlon. Ashley still adamant about not selling. But she remembered them trying their best to put it aside and drinking more alcohol to make the night bearable. Ashley pulling her out on the dance floor. The details were hazy, but they were there. Natalie drew her eyebrows together.

"Just bits and pieces from La Cantina. Then I woke up out there." Natalie pointed in the direction of the hotel's private beach, her stomach twisting. "I'm trying not to panic, but this is Mexico. I won't be able to relax until we can confirm she's with Marco."

"I think she's okay. That girl always lands on her feet." Lauren's voice was confident, but her eyes flashed something conflicting. Doubt? "I'm going to call her again." She put her phone on speaker.

Natalie willed it to ring, for Ashley to answer. But it went straight to voice mail again. Maybe Ashley was just upset about last night and went somewhere to cool down. "Do you think her phone is off because of what you said to her?" Natalie asked.

"Don't put this on me. You were pissed at her too." Lauren crossed her arms over her chest, then looked away. But Natalie caught her expression before she did—she was worried.

"I'm not," Natalie said, not wanting to put Lauren on the defensive. "But *if* that's it—and I'm not saying it's your fault—it would be a good thing. It would mean she was okay."

"I have no idea, Nat. Ashley could be screwing Marco right now and not even thinking of us. Do you really think we're at the top of her mind right now? We didn't seem to be during this entire trip."

Natalie thought about this. "You're right, but it sounds like she tried to connect with you last night."

"Once it was too late. Once I was done. She had a year."

Natalie pinched her lips together. She hated how much tension there was. It had practically swallowed them whole. But even more than that, she hated the guilt she still felt about her part in the argument a year ago. That she could have done more to defuse Lauren and she didn't. "I wish we hadn't left with him."

"Like you were going to stay. Have you ever chosen me over her?" she asked matter-of-factly.

Natalie looked away, rubbing her temples, feeling bad she'd taken off and left Lauren behind, even if she had told Ashley to leave without her. She was struck by how easily the three of them went from bad to worse in such a short amount of time.

"I'm sorry," Natalie said. "I wish I knew why I left you."

Lauren waved her off. "Don't worry about it."

"How could we all be so stupid?" Natalie asked. "You staying by yourself. Us going off and leaving you. Not even getting Marco's number. This is Mexico!"

The lyrics from the Van Morrison song played in her mind. Ashley had grabbed her elbow and tugged her. Both of them setting their drinks on an empty table by the bar. Ashley's white tank top glowing under the lights.

Natalie swallowed. Ashley had been their brown-eyed girl.

And now she was gone.

CHAPTER FIVE

Four Days Before
Lauren

Lauren sat on the edge of the king-size bed and sent a text to Annie, a friend she'd met in her grief group about ten months ago. Lauren was so grateful for her, for the way she'd plucked her from the very lowest valley of sadness when she'd found her crying outside the entrance to the church, unable to go inside. But even though she'd made a new friend, there was still a big part of her that missed Ashley and Natalie too. They'd been the closest people in her life before Geoff's death. And now she weighed whether it could ever be the same again. If she ever wouldn't feel like a third wheel when the three of them were together.

> Hi from the odd man out in Tulum. They are sharing a room and gave me my own.

She added a sad-face emoji.

She saw the little gray dots indicating Annie was already writing back. She was always there. Always available. That's how friends were supposed to be, right?

Wedge yourself back in there! Don't let them leave you out. And look at it this way—now you can walk around naked!

Lauren smiled, despite how she was feeling—like she was thirteen years old sitting alone at the cafeteria lunch table. She considered whether the hotel was really sold out or if she'd somehow convinced Ishmael to lie. She supposed she couldn't entirely blame Ash if she'd done that. Their friendship had been basically nonexistent ever since the moment Geoff dropped dead in front of her, clutching his chest in disbelief before his head crashed on their cream-colored Italian travertine tile. She could barely remember calling 911 after he collapsed, the ride to the hospital, the doctor coming out to tell her he was so very sorry, going home alone that night. Her mom driving her to a funeral home, helping her pick out the coffin—did she want steel or wood, bronze or copper? And then suddenly she was putting on her shapeless black dress and riding in the back of a town car to the cemetery.

Her phone pinged. Another text from Annie.

I know you're still sitting there feeling sorry for yourself. Get your bathing suit on and invite them down to the beach.

Lauren sent a thumbs-up emoji and obediently walked to her suitcase and pulled out her red bikini. The same one she'd worn on her honeymoon. She rubbed the fabric between her fingers, recollecting how Geoff had eyeballed her when she'd put it on, how he'd thrown her on the bed, where they'd stayed all day, never making it to the pool. She stopped herself. Her therapist said it wasn't healthy to only remember the good days. Because there had been so many terrible ones.

She picked up her cell phone, walked outside, and dialed Annie, speaking quickly when she answered on the first ring.

"Hey," Lauren said.

"So, you're not having fun?" Annie asked.

"Not yet. We've had a couple of drinks together, and it's already tense."

"Girl, you're in paradise! What are you doing?"

"I may have been a bit cold to Ashley."

"Why?"

"I don't know! I thought I was okay coming on this trip, but when I saw her at the airport I felt sick all over again, and I couldn't really shake it after that." She recalled the way Ashley had bounded toward her at the gate, Natalie in tow. Like nothing had happened. Lauren bit her lip. "I guess I worry if I play along, if I act like we're all fine, then it makes what she did okay." She paused. "And it makes me feel disloyal to Geoff, in a weird way."

"Did Ashley bring him up?"

"No," Lauren said. "But she did say she was seriously thinking about leaving her husband, Jason, which made me start thinking about Geoff. What if I'd seen the signs earlier?"

Annie paused. "You couldn't have known. People like Geoff are masters of manipulation. Look what he did with your mom."

"Right," Lauren said, thinking of the way he'd swooped in to save the day when her mom was going to lose her apartment and Geoff had secretly called the landlord and paid her rent for the next year. At the time Lauren had been blinded by his generosity—especially because it had been after only six months of dating. But later she'd seen it for what it really was—a power move. "But maybe if I'd finished school, made more of my life, I would have never needed his help in the first place."

"You tried to go back to school," Annie huffed. Lauren knew why. They'd had this same conversation the week before. And the week before that.

Lauren bowed her head, feeling ashamed. "I let him talk me out of that too," she said, remembering how he'd reacted when she'd told him she'd decided to go back to get her teaching degree. He told her no. It had not felt like she had a choice.

"Are you surprised about Jason and Ashley?" Annie asked.

"I am," Lauren said. "I mean, I never thought they were perfect—but maybe I was so caught up in my own drama that I didn't notice theirs. Or maybe things started to fall apart in the last year? I think she would have said something to me had it been going on when we were still close." She hoped that was true, anyway. "And then there's this whole thing going on between her and Nat about selling their company." She filled Annie in on what she knew about the Revlon offer, leaving out the tension she'd felt between Ashley and Natalie. It had surprised her, really. She'd seen them argue before, but this was different. She got the sense this deal had high stakes for both of them.

"Anyway, I'm sitting there, my stomach twisting, feeling stupid because I thought she invited us here to make peace with me. But of course, it's all about Ashley. She came here to *think*. For 'soul-searching.'"

"The two don't have to be mutually exclusive. She can want to figure herself out and make peace with you as well."

"You really believe that?" Lauren asked, hopeful. "Why not lead with that then?"

"Well, you were being cold to her, right?" Annie asked.

Lauren thought about the way she'd purposefully sided with Natalie whenever she could. It had made her feel powerful, like she was sending a message to Ashley. *You're going to have to work harder for my forgiveness.* "I suppose I could have been nicer."

"Okay then. So maybe she wants to settle in with you first," Annie reasoned. "That's what I'd do anyway. It sounds like she has a lot going on."

"She does. But is it bad that I still want to be a priority? It's so simple. Two words: 'I'm sorry.'"

"Did you apologize to her?"

"No," Lauren said heavily. "I know how this is going to sound. But I wanted her to say it first. Like it would mean more if she did."

"Well, maybe she was thinking the same thing about you," Annie said. "Because from the story you've told me, you both could stand to apologize."

"You know, I really hate you sometimes," Lauren said sarcastically. "It's irritating how rational you are."

"Hey, if all else fails, have a margarita. Margaritas fix everything."

Lauren didn't laugh. She still couldn't get there.

"After thinking about it, I don't know if I'm ready to put on my bikini and drink with them," she said. "I thought I was better than this. That I was beginning to move on."

She heard Annie inhale, and Lauren imagined her tapping her fingers on the vintage desk in her office. Annie was a ghostwriter and had written several memoirs of celebrities and sports stars. She had this magical way of sitting with someone and seeing right through them. Lauren both loved and hated this about her. It made it hard to hide when she didn't want to face the truth.

"Where is the anger focused? On Geoff? Ashley? Or yourself?"

Lauren stared out at the coastline. It was humid, and a trickle of sweat had begun to glide down her back.

"All of the above. You know that," she said irritably.

"I know it's complicated," Annie started.

"You think?" Lauren laughed bitterly. "I never know who I'm angrier with—Ashley, for forcing my hand, or myself for getting involved with him in the first place. And then not leaving."

She heard Annie sigh softly on the other end. This wasn't the first time they'd had this conversation. Annie understood the boundaries of what she could and couldn't say. She got that when people died, it was easy to change who they'd been while alive. Annie's husband's death had been the opposite of Lauren's husband—a slow and painful death from brain cancer. Annie had been thinking about leaving him before his diagnosis—he could be selfish and childish, and she was ready to be on her own. They'd been together sixteen years and she wanted to get out while she still had some good years left. She'd admitted once, after several glasses of rosé, that she sometimes felt like she was robbed of those years. The ones where she could have become someone else entirely. Now she was just Matthew Gordon's widow.

"You know why. He swooped in and saved the day."

Lauren nodded, hating herself for needing to be saved.

"This is why I was worried about you going to Tulum. There's so much baggage," Annie finally said. "But I do want you to work it out with them. I do. The real question is, Do you want to? Because if you don't, you might as well get on the next plane home."

Lauren bit her lower lip, conjuring up Ashley's words from a year ago. *You deserve better. I'm just trying to protect you. You have choices here.* "Would you believe me if I told you that I really do want to get past this?" Lauren asked Annie while leaning against the railing of the balcony, quickly wiping away a lone tear.

"I would. I know I'm really super awesome and everything," Annie said, and Lauren chuckled. "But I'm your death person."

"No—" she began to argue.

"It's okay," Annie interrupted. "I'm glad to be the person who gets that side of you. But you also owe it to yourself to reconnect with the person you were before all this happened. And maybe you need Ashley and Natalie to help you do that."

"But that person was weak. I don't want to reconnect with her."

"But she's still a part of you. And to resolve this, you have to deal with her. With what happened."

Lauren knew her logic made sense. But in many ways she'd been on pause since Geoff's funeral, when she'd lost her shit on Ashley in the coatroom while being poked in the back with a Burberry umbrella. Ironically, it had all begun with the words Lauren had wanted to hear from her so badly today. *I'm sorry.*

Lauren tugged herself out of the painful memory. Why couldn't she forgive Ashley? Had she become addicted to how the anger felt, how it slid into the small chasms of her budding happiness, crushing it? Maybe. But the only thing she knew for sure was that saying she wanted to forgive Ashley and actually forgiving her were two totally different things.

"You still there?" Annie asked.

"Sorry, yes, I am. I was just thinking about the funeral. And yes, I really am going to try to get over this."

"You promise?"

"I do," Lauren said, and felt a weight lift in her chest as she said the words. "Enough about me—how are you?"

"Same. I'm still trying to decide if I should join Match.com. It just feels so . . ."

"Weird?"

"Yeah, strange. 'I'm Annie. I like strawberry daiquiris and romantic comedies.'"

"You hate both of those things."

"But isn't that the point—to lie?" Annie chuckled. "No one wants to hear that I actually prefer whiskey and slasher movies, do they?"

"Knock, knock?" José, the hot bartender from the restaurant, appeared at the top of the stairs. "Complimentary margarita," he said, holding a thick glass with blue trim, a ring of salt on its rim, and a lime. Just the way she'd ordered it at the bar.

"I've got to run," Lauren said, smiling at José. "I'll keep you posted, okay? And hey, I think you should join Match—and write an *honest* profile. Who knows, maybe the right guy will show up with a bottle of Jack Daniel's and *Saw II*! Just be open. That's all I'm saying."

"Advice you could take yourself," Annie admonished gently.

"Touché," Lauren said before hanging up and turning to the handsome man on her balcony. "How did you know that was exactly what I needed?" She took the margarita off the tray.

José's lips curled upward, his white teeth a stark contrast against his caramel skin. "I aim to please," he said, and raised an eyebrow. "Do you and your friends have plans tonight?"

Lauren held up her drink. "More of these. That's my game plan anyway."

"Well, this is Tulum. Margaritas at every turn."

She noticed the way his eyes trailed over her, pausing on her legs, which were her best asset. Small and firm and strong.

"I already know I'm going to like yours the best." She looked him over, imagined running her hands across his body. "We're going to hang out on the beach. Can I request you make our drinks and hand-deliver them?" she said brazenly.

"I wish—but I have a second job I work at tonight." He glanced at his watch. "But I'm off my shift here right now. And have an hour before I have to be at my next gig . . ." He peered toward the open slider behind her.

She thought of her therapist. They'd made so much progress. This would be a setback.

Her phone buzzed. She saw it was a text from Natalie to meet her and Ash on the beach for drinks. She felt a surge of hope.

"Well, a lot can be accomplished in an hour," Lauren said as she slipped into her room and beckoned him inside, deciding that she would only let it happen the one time.

CHAPTER SIX

FOUR DAYS BEFORE
ASHLEY

"You have to admit this is paradise," Ashley said, surveying the drink menu as they sat in a cabana on their hotel's private beach. The sky was streaked with faint clouds, the late-afternoon sunlight shimmering on the tips of the waves.

"Amazing," Natalie agreed, exhaling loudly.

"Oh look, there's a drink called the Pink Flamingo." Lauren giggled. "How cute; I'm going to try that. It's made with grapefruit juice, lime, and vodka."

Natalie peered at Lauren over her menu. "You're glowing."

Ashley had noticed it too—Lauren's ivory skin was tinged with a rosy sheen that hadn't been there earlier.

"Am I?" Lauren asked, twirling the jade necklace Ashley had rarely seen her without. Her mother had given it to her as a gift; it had been hers when she immigrated from Korea. "Must be the sun—you know me, I'm fair, so a little goes a long way." She grinned.

For the first time since they arrived, Ashley saw all of her teeth. She suspected the glow and the giddiness was from more than the sun, but she wasn't going to push to find out. If she told Lauren she seemed lighter, friendlier, happier, it would suggest that she hadn't been those things earlier. And Ashley was just happy she seemed happy.

They all ordered Pink Flamingos when Emmanuel, who'd said he'd just started his shift, came by.

"He's not nearly as cute as José," Ashley said when he walked away. She recalled his brown eyes framed by thick black lashes. His dimple when he smiled. "I think José might have a little thing for you, actually." She looked at Lauren. "He was checking you out earlier."

"I doubt that." Lauren waved her off, but Ashley noticed a sparkle in her eye.

"This place is so peaceful," Natalie said, reclining in her chair. "Can we stay here forever?"

"I know," Lauren said. "I was on my balcony earlier, staring out at the Caribbean. I don't think I've been anywhere so beautiful."

"I saw you!" Natalie grabbed her arm. "You were talking to someone . . ."

"Yeah, that was my friend Annie," Lauren said, putting her sunglasses on.

"Annie?" Ashley asked, trying to recall if Lauren had ever mentioned her. "How do you know her?"

"She's my death friend."

"Your what?" Natalie frowned.

"What's a death friend?" Ashley scrunched up her nose. "A good thing, I hope?"

"It is. She is. She gave herself that label, and it just kind of stuck. It's our way of adding humor to an otherwise grim situation, if that makes any sense."

"I get it," Ashley said in an attempt to connect, even though she didn't really understand.

"I met her in my grief group," Lauren said.

"Oh, I didn't realize you went to . . . ," Ashley started. She tried to picture it—Lauren sitting in a circle with other people, their collective sadness spilling out and pooling on the linoleum floor.

"It's okay—it's not something I usually talk about. You know?" Lauren said lightly. "Anyway, her husband died of cancer, so she gets what I'm going through. I don't know what I would have done without her."

"That's so great," Natalie said sincerely. "I would love to meet her sometime."

"Me too," Ashley said brightly, trying to separate her conflicting feelings—she was happy that Lauren hadn't been alone, but she also registered a healthy dose of fear that she'd been replaced by someone who understood a part of her that Ashley could not.

"Oh, you guys would love her. She's hilarious. She has so many stories—she ghostwrites celebrity memoirs."

"Three Pink Flamingos," Emmanuel said, handing each woman her drink carefully.

"Thank you," Ashley said, taking a sip. It was tart.

"Oh my God!" Lauren said, staring at her phone. "Guess what just popped up in my TimeHop?"

"What?" Natalie and Ashley said in unison and then laughed.

"Jinx." Ashley pointed at Natalie. "You owe me a Coke."

"Four years ago today was the viewing party," Lauren said.

"No way! Let me see that." Ashley swiped the phone out of her hand and studied a picture of a group of people standing in front of the flat-screen TV on the wall in Ashley's living room, Natalie and Ashley in the middle, their arms wrapped around each other so tight it was hard to tell where one ended and the other began.

Ashley couldn't believe it had been four years since their episode aired on *Shark Tank*. Since their company went from being on the cusp of something to being huge. They'd practiced for months, hoping to get their pitch just right—Ashley could still recite it. She leaned toward

Natalie's chaise. "So, Sharks, which one of you is ready to take the cry out of blow-dry?"

Natalie's eyes brightened. "That was a great line."

The set had been so much smaller than it looked on TV when Ashley and Natalie walked out of those double doors, arms linked. "Hello. I'm Ashley Green and this is Natalie Sanders, and we're seeking 500,000 dollars for a 10 percent equity stake in our company, BloMe." Ashley paused as the Sharks laughed at their company name, glancing over at Natalie, who looked nervous. Ashley had tried to catch Natalie's eye to wink at her, but she couldn't.

"We are always on the quest to achieve the perfect blowout at home. But no matter how hard we try, we end up quitting midway through, our arms tired from holding the blow-dryer and the brush—or if we do finish the job, it looks frizzy and amateurish when we're done. And that's where this comes in. The BloBrush." Ashley held the brush out in front of her. "It's a cordless blow-dryer and brush in one and will give you a sleek, salon-quality blow-dry that lasts for several days. And will save you many tears of frustration. So tell me, Sharks, which one of you is ready to take the cry out of blow-dry?"

"Remember we had that drinking game at the party? Every time you said 'blow,' we drank," Lauren said as she sipped her pink drink.

"We drank a lot," Ashley said. "In fact, I'll drink to that now."

"Drinking to drinking. I love it," Lauren said, her tone relaxed.

Finally, Ashley thought. "Remember the tutorial, Nat? Trying to figure out how to show them how the BloBrush worked? I think that was harder than designing it."

Natalie's eyes grew wide. "Yeah, *you* worked really hard on that design."

Ashley gave her a look, that old feeling of inferiority tickling her. Natalie had been the one to think of and then design the BloBrush, and it had always made Ashley slightly uneasy. Sure, she'd been a huge part of its success as well, her tenacity and natural moxie getting them into big-box stores and developing BloMe as a brand, rather than just a product. But still, she hadn't *invented* it.

"I'm kidding," Natalie sang a moment later, but Ashley wondered whether she really was. Natalie always overlooked that it had been Ashley who'd won over the Sharks.

"The BloBrush speaks for itself." Ashley had pushed "Play" on the remote control she'd been holding as she made eye contact with Mr. Wonderful, who looked at her, humor dancing in his eyes. Clearly hair products were not his area of expertise. "Just watch this video. You put a section of your hair on the brush, press this button, hold it for a couple of seconds, then let it go. As you can see, each finished piece is perfect." The video started to speed up as Ashley finished her hair, and then spun around to show the finished result. "We patented a special rechargeable battery that is like nothing else out there—it gives the blow-dryer the heat and power you need so you don't have to be plugged into an outlet." She'd paused to show them the battery.

Once negotiations had begun, all of the Sharks made an offer, but they each wanted at least 20 percent and Ashley was adamant they'd take no more than 10 percent. Their bottom line had been they would leave with an investor; their top choice was Lori Greiner. But the Sharks wouldn't budge. And neither would Ashley.

"My jaw dropped when you guys walked away," Lauren said.

It had been a spur-of-the-moment decision—one Ashley hadn't consulted Natalie about. And for that she still felt bad. Even though it had all worked out, she should have asked to speak to Natalie privately first. She knew this.

"Yeah—we weren't allowed to tell anyone what happened," Ashley said, glancing at Natalie, thinking about the tension between them for months between the taping and the airing. Ashley questioning herself. Natalie questioning Ashley. Ashley hoping she'd been right.

"We all had bets. I thought you were going to end up with Lori," Lauren said.

"So did I," Natalie said dryly, finishing her drink.

Ashley tried to read her. To recall the last time they'd talked about what happened. It had been years, for sure. On the way home from the taping, Nat had been livid Ash hadn't consulted her before she told everyone no. But Ashley had explained that she had a gut feeling about BloBrush. That they were going to be uber successful—without the help of the Sharks. To trust her. And she'd been right.

"I actually did too," Ashley said. "But she wanted too much equity. I'm glad we didn't take an investor. Think about how much money we've made as a result."

"That's very true." Natalie clinked her empty glass against hers.

"Did you guys ever talk to any of the Sharks again?" Lauren asked, sipping her drink.

"Not really, but we saw Lori backstage in the greenroom at QVC and she couldn't have been nicer."

"Yeah, she told us she used the BloBrush every day and was still sad she didn't get to invest."

"She called us 'the ones that got away' as she walked out of the greenroom," Ashley mused, grinning at the memory. "But look, we got on QVC anyway, and we didn't need her help after all."

"True. But I wonder what she would have said about the Revlon offer," Natalie said.

Ashley shrugged, slightly annoyed. "I don't know, but I'm happy we don't have to worry about it. It's hard enough trying to decide with only two people. And look at us now, successful with a popular YouTube channel—did you see we're up to a million followers?"

Natalie gave her a look like she hadn't.

"Anyway, you two YouTube superstars, enough about work, let's get another round," Lauren said, setting her empty glass on the table. She flagged Emmanuel. Ashley sent her a grateful smile.

"Spoken by the only person at the table with no job," Natalie said.

Ashley watched Lauren's face, terrified she might take offense to Nat's comment. But to her relief, she laughed.

"If the life insurance payout fits . . . ," Lauren said, but Ashley wasn't sure whether she should laugh too. So far Geoff had felt like an untouchable subject. She glanced at Natalie—who also looked dumbfounded.

"Ladies, come on! Annie would be rolling on the floor over that one!"

"To death friends," Ashley said, holding up her glass.

"To death friends," Lauren and Natalie repeated.

The buzz of the alcohol radiated through Ashley's body. This was good—they were joking, laughing, enjoying the blurriness that came with the drinking. The way it made things close seem far away, how it made the gap between them shrink from a canyon to a crevice.

Ashley took a deep sip of her drink and prayed it would be that easy.

CHAPTER SEVEN

THE DAY AFTER
NATALIE

Natalie stopped by her room to change out of her wet dress while Lauren waited. She tossed it on the countertop, shuddering as more sand fell out of it. She'd never wear it again.

They jogged over to the front desk and called out to Maria. The front-desk attendant looked up at the sound of her name, her two thick braids falling forward over her shoulders. "How was your girls' night?" she asked. "I only saw you come back before my shift ended." She looked at Lauren. "But, Natalie, I didn't see you or Ashley, so I was a little worried. I'm so happy to see you are well."

I'm not! Natalie wanted to say.

"That's why we're here. We don't know where Ashley is. Have you seen her this morning?" Natalie held her breath.

"No," Maria said.

"So not since we all left last night?" Natalie tried again.

"Not since then."

"Why did you say you were worried when you didn't see us come back?"

"It's a small hotel, so I naturally keep track of everyone—but I'm always nervous when women travel alone, especially when they are drinking. But Tulum is safe—you've seen the guards at the entrance to the town."

The day they'd arrived, a guard with a machine gun strapped across his torso had met them when their cab had turned down the road toward their hotel. Her chest tightened as she digested the rest of Maria's words. *I worry when women travel alone, especially when they are drinking.* Natalie clearly hadn't been thinking about safety last night.

"So you came back without Ashley?" Maria asked.

Natalie thought about what she'd had to drink. A margarita or two when they got ready. The shot at Hartwood. Then wine. The dry pinot noir helping temper her annoyance with Ashley. And when they arrived at La Cantina, there were more shots. Mojitos. Then what? Had that been when she was drugged?

Natalie looked up to find Maria watching her. "I don't remember coming back here—I think maybe someone put something in my drink?"

Maria widened her eyes, but didn't say more. Instead she asked if she should call the police.

"The police?" Natalie asked. "But you said Tulum is safe."

"We need to find Marco first," Lauren interrupted.

"Right," Natalie said, trying to breathe. Praying that Ashley was with him. No matter the reason. At least she'd be safe.

"Marco?" Maria asked.

"He's someone we hung out with this week," Natalie said.

"Did he ever come here to the hotel?" Maria asked.

Natalie glanced around the lobby. Why hadn't he? As she thought back, he always had wanted to meet elsewhere. Had there been a reason for that? "He owns the juice bar down the road," she offered.

Maria frowned. "Tropical Kiss?"

"Yes," the women said in unison.

"I haven't been there, but I thought the owner was a man named René."

Natalie shrugged. "I don't know; maybe it changed owners recently. We should head over there now." She looked at Lauren.

"Will you talk to the staff here—see if anyone has seen Ashley, or saw anything last night or this morning?" Lauren asked Maria.

Natalie picked up a pen off the desk and wrote down her cell phone number. "Please call me if you hear anything. Or if she comes back."

"Of course. I'm sure you're going to find her," Maria said, but she didn't look convinced.

A chill worked its way through Natalie, and she rubbed her arms.

They headed to the beach cruisers, and Natalie unlocked the lime-green bike she rode to yoga the morning after they'd arrived. Lauren got on the bubblegum-pink bike Ashley had ridden. They pedaled silently to Tropical Kiss, Natalie praying they'd find Ashley. Her stomach constricted as they pulled up to the juice bar. It didn't appear to be open. They stopped their bikes and got off. Natalie squinted at the door, looking for the business hours. Twisting the doorknob, she was surprised to find it unlocked. She pushed it inward, a bell hanging from the door dinging. "Hello?"

She heard movement from a back room. An older woman with strawberry blonde hair swept into a messy ponytail emerged, wiping her hands on her apron, a pair of eyeglasses hanging from a chain around her neck. "We're not open yet . . ."

"We're looking for the owner," Natalie said.

"René?"

"No. Marco."

"René is the owner. He's been in Mexico City for the past couple of weeks."

Natalie stiffened. "But do you know Marco? He does work here, right? He made us smoothie bowls . . ."

"There is a Marco who works here; he's been here a few months, but he's definitely *not* the owner," she said, rolling her eyes so subtly Natalie almost missed it.

What else had Marco lied about? "Do you know where he lives?" She looked at Lauren. "Or his last name?"

"May I ask who you are?" the woman said, then extended her hand. "I'm Jeanie."

"I'm Natalie and this is Lauren. We are looking for our friend Ashley, and think she might be with him. We haven't heard from her since last night."

Jeanie surveyed them for a moment. "You didn't get this from me." She walked over to the desk, pulled out a book, copied something down on a piece of paper, and handed it to Natalie.

Natalie read the paper. It was an address with the name Marco Smith next to it. Smith? Her temples pounded. "Thank you," she said to Jeanie.

"I hope you find your friend."

Natalie thought she picked up on a hesitancy in Jeanie's voice, but she didn't trust her instincts just then.

"Do you recognize the address?" Lauren asked as they got on their bikes. "Do you think you might have gone there after you guys left La Cantina?"

"I have no idea," Natalie said. "Why do you think he lied about being the owner?"

"He was probably just trying to impress Ash. After she told him about your company, he might have felt being a juice bar employee wouldn't be enough."

"And Smith?" She pointed to the name scrawled on the paper. "Do we think that's his real last name?"

Lauren paused. "It's possible. I know he said he was born here, but his father could have been American."

Natalie nodded, but she wasn't sure what to think. In the time they'd spent with him, Marco had been in a perpetual good mood, acting like he was some sort of spiritual counselor. He loved his dog, always petting him and kissing his head. Any outsider looking in would think he was a nice guy. And objectively he'd done nothing to make Natalie feel otherwise. But looking back, there had always been something that was bothering her. She'd chalked it up to the annoying way he doted on Ashley, and his subsequent invasion of their girl time, but what if it had been something more?

I'm going with you. Natalie heard her own voice. She strained to push through the wall that stood between her and her memory. What was said after that? She stared at Marco's address scribbled on the tiny piece of paper. Had they all gone there together? "Did Marco say anything to you before we left?" Natalie asked.

"No." Lauren dragged her hands through her hair. "I wasn't very nice to him."

Natalie sighed, wondering again what exact chain of events had led to Ashley's disappearance. If Lauren had been nicer to him, would Marco have wanted to leave? Or would they have stayed and danced until the bar closed? Natalie was sure there were things she could have done differently too—if only her memory would unlock those details.

"I shouldn't have talked to him. Maybe I offended him or pissed him off?"

"We can't do this. Question everything. We'll drive ourselves crazy," Natalie said—even though she'd just been doing the very same thing.

"You're right. I'm sure she's fine," Lauren said. "This is *Ashley* we're talking about. You know she likes to walk the line on predictability."

Natalie nodded. But she wasn't so sure. It had been hours since they'd heard from her. The Ashley she knew would have at least sent a text by now.

"But"—Lauren pulled out her phone—"I'm still going to call the airline. Even if she showed up right now, we'd never make the flight." She held the phone up to her ear and muttered, "Dammit, Ashley."

Natalie tried Ashley again. Voice mail. She sent another text. Are you okay? She'd never missed a flight before. In fact, Natalie could count on one hand the number of times Ash had been late. Ten minutes early, even.

Lauren walked back over. "I canceled them for now. We can rebook once we find her."

Natalie pulled up Google Maps on her phone and typed in Marco's address. "It's 1.2 miles from here," Natalie said, pushing her bike forward and starting to pedal. "The faster we get there—"

"The faster we can find her and get the hell back home," Lauren said as she swung her leg over the worn leather seat of her bike.

Natalie hoped she was right. That the biggest travesty of the day would be canceling and rebooking their flights.

As they made their way down the bumpy road, she struggled to push aside the negative thoughts that kept trying to take over her consciousness. What if Ashley wasn't at Marco's? What if he opened the door, much the way Lauren had, groggy from sleep, with no clue where to find Ashley? That possibility sent jolts of fear through Natalie as she followed Google's commands toward the mysterious address. It was as if the edge of her mind were a cliff, and she was teetering there with two choices: 1. Stay put and hope the memories come back. 2. Take the plunge and pray she was prepared for what she might discover. As she pedaled forward, she already knew the only choice was the second one.

She just hoped it was the right one.

CHAPTER EIGHT

Three Days Before
Ashley

The warm wind whipped through Ashley's hair as she navigated her pink beach cruiser down the narrow, bumpy, puddle-filled road to yoga class. To her right, huge palms crowded together, running the length of the street. To her left, a mix of tourists and locals were sitting in front of coffee stands. Shop owners were hanging dresses and staging their merchandise to entice customers.

The road was still slick with the rain from the morning. Luckily it had passed before they'd started riding. Ashley glanced back to make sure Lauren and Natalie weren't too far behind, just as her front wheel hit a pothole. She swerved and braked quickly so she wouldn't crash. God, how long had it been since she'd ridden a bike? Like, a real bike, not one in a spin class? She leaned into her handlebars, breathed in the fresh salt air as she directed the ancient cruiser, her bag bobbing up and down in the straw basket, her calves burning and her breathing shallow after only the first half-mile. Her legs felt like they were working much harder than when she ran on the beach back home. She wiped her face with the back of her hand. Her tank top was already soaked with sweat and they hadn't yet stepped foot in the yoga class Lauren had talked them into last night—after too many mezcal margaritas on the beach.

They'd stretched out on the chaise longues, their conversation steering clear of any major land-mine topics that might send them in reverse. Marriage. The funeral. The last year. Revlon. Lauren had loosened up, her earlier cool demeanor toward Ashley no longer there. She'd even opened up a little about Annie, a new friend she'd met. It had been fun—and they'd laughed about old times.

But tension was layered underneath the surface of their laughter, at least for Ashley. Her laughter was a little too loud when Lauren told that story about the time they'd bungee jumped in tandem and Ashley's screams almost broke her eardrum, her smile just a bit forced as she tried to recapture the feeling they'd once shared. As if that would transform them back into the girls who had taken a literal leap of faith together, their fates intertwined.

Then Lauren had banged on their door at 7:30 sharp this morning, a mug of steaming coffee in her hand, a mention of already having taken a long walk on the beach. Ashley had wanted to skip, but Natalie had told her to get her ass up, that it would be good for them to exercise—and to spend time doing something Lauren wanted to do. You could always count on her to do the right thing, a trait that Ashley swung between appreciating and resenting. Especially lately. Because of Revlon. Because Nat's version of the right thing was not in line with Ashley's. And she wasn't sure how to bridge the gap.

Lauren pedaled past Ashley, pumping her legs hard, as if she were trying to escape. Ashley often worried there was a part of her that would always keep her distance, their deep divide becoming a scar that would never quite fade away.

It's your fault he's dead.

Last night as they watched the sunset together, Ashley convinced herself Lauren hadn't meant the words she'd shouted at her after the funeral. As the darkness set in and they continued to drink and reminisce, she'd told herself everything was going to be okay. But this morning she wasn't as confident.

They tethered their bikes to the wood rack at the hotel where the yoga class was offered, Natalie shaking Ashley's lock to make sure it was secure. "Come on, Nat," Ashley said. "Even *I* can figure this out."

"Oh, I know," Natalie said, not even aware how often she second-guessed Ashley.

Had it now become a habit? At work it was commonplace. Ashley would draft an email and Natalie would rewrite most of it. And it had eventually bled over into other aspects of their lives. Like the ancient bike lock.

"How do you look so fresh-faced after drinking all those margaritas last night?" Ashley asked Lauren as they made their way down the dirt path, Natalie having gone ahead to find the restroom. Ashley had always been shocked that such a tiny woman could handle so much alcohol without getting sick. In college, Lauren could shotgun more beers than a lot of the fraternity guys.

Lauren shrugged. "I drank a lot of bottled water before bed. Plus, my tolerance is higher now—I've had a lot of wine this year," she said, looking away.

Ashley knew she meant since Geoff died. She wanted to say something—to reach out to her and make their tension disappear like it had seemed to last night. But had that only been because of the alcohol? She was afraid to say the wrong thing—again—to push her even further away. So she simply smiled at her. But Lauren had already turned, kicking off her flip-flops outside the studio, a stucco building with a thatched roof. She bent down and petted a golden dog with a shiny coat that was lying in the shade. Ashley immediately noticed the glaring difference between him and most dogs she'd seen running around Tulum. He had a full body and thick fur. He was healthy. They walked inside and grabbed mats, blankets, and blocks from the back of the room.

As Ashley rolled out her mat, she mulled over how long it would take for the quiet easiness of her friendship with Lauren to return. She had naively hoped it would be instantaneous. Of course, that wasn't how life worked. But Ashley was trying so hard. Didn't that count for something? She sighed.

"Are you okay?"

Ashley turned toward the voice belonging to a good-looking man with dark hair that fell long around his ears. His eyes were brown with flecks of gold.

"Sorry, I didn't realize that was so loud."

"Well, if you need to clear your head, you came to the right place," he said as he set two blocks next to his mat. "Lyssa teaches the best classes." He gestured toward a young woman in the front of the room who was doing a backbend. "You'll be sigh-less in no time." He gave Ashley a thumbs-up.

She took in his coffee-colored skin and his toned arms and legs. He looked like he could rock climb or windsurf with ease.

"How long have you been visiting?" Ashley asked.

"I'm not. I live here." He stretched his arms over his head. "I was born in Mexico, but lived in the States until a year ago, when I came back to Tulum for a yoga retreat and never left."

"People really do that?" Ashley asked. Something tugged at her stomach when she thought of going back home. Of facing Jason.

"People really do that," the man repeated. "I did that. It was pretty easy, actually."

"Why?" she asked, then backpedaled when she saw his face. "Sorry, that's probably too personal."

"No, no. It's okay. I wish I had some big exciting story for you, but I don't. I just wanted to try a different life."

Try a different life. Ashley would have shaken her head at that idea not that long ago, but lately she found herself questioning almost every decision she'd made—except for agreeing to start BloMe, Inc. with Nat. The decision that kept her up at night the most was the one to marry Jason. What if she hadn't? Of course, she didn't regret having her daughters. But she'd often secretly fantasized what it might feel like to be single again. What if she did sell the company, like Natalie wanted so badly, took her half of the money, and started over somewhere? She'd promised Natalie she'd give selling more thought, but deep down she worried she'd never be able to let it go.

"Did your family come with you?" Ashley asked, glancing discreetly at his finger to see if he was wearing a ring.

"I'm not married. No kids. It's just me. And my dog, Spencer. You might have seen him out front—the yellow Lab—he was a stray that I took in when I got here. He's a big fan of carne asada; it helped get him back to his fighting weight."

"Isn't it the best?" Ashley said. "I get it all the time where I'm from—although I'm sure it's much better here. Do you put cilantro in it?" She wrinkled her nose.

"Of course we do! They are street tacos. You can't have them without it! Don't tell me you're a hater?"

"Guilty as charged. I just like my food a certain way, that's all."

"I can respect that, but cilantro, really?"

"The struggle is real," she said, grinning.

"Where are you from?"

"SoCal."

"What part?"

"LA—Santa Monica. Ever been?"

He shook his head. "Never been to California, if you can believe that. When I was in the States I was in Texas, mostly. Austin."

"Well, I guess now that you're living here, why would you go anywhere else?" Ashley smiled, picturing her house nestled on a hill that bordered the Pacific Palisades. It was large—over seven thousand square feet. Did they really need that much space? She rarely entertained. She didn't utilize the formal dining room. The chef's pantry. When she was home, which wasn't often, she was in one of three places: her bedroom, the balcony off her bedroom, or the kitchen. Her girls were the same—hibernating in their rooms or going down to graze the refrigerator and pantry. Ashley's meager attempts to draw them into conversation often fell flat. And she didn't see much of Jason when he was home—especially not lately. She found it easier to avoid him; if they didn't communicate, there was less chance they'd fight.

"You're zoning out over there," the man said.

"Oh, sorry," Ashley said. "I was just thinking about home."

"All good things, I hope?"

"I'm not so sure right now." Ashley surprised herself by telling this perfect stranger the truth. But there was something about his warm eyes that invited her to share. She looked over to where Natalie and Lauren had set up their mats—side by side toward the front of the room. Sometimes it was easier to talk to people who didn't know anything about you.

"Is that why you're here?"

"Partly, yes. And also for them." Ashley pointed to Natalie and Lauren. She lowered her voice. "We've been friends for a long time, but things are kind of in flux. And when I read about Tulum, about the energy, the spirituality, it seemed like the perfect place."

"You chose very wisely. It is believed that sixty-six million years ago, an asteroid struck right here in Tulum. It produced an intense energy that is still here and has created a magical aura. There is so much opportunity to look within and to find the answers you seek. They are so much clearer down here."

"Wow, that's crazy about the asteroid. I had no idea."

"You will see. You will feel so much while you're here. And if you allow your mind to be still, the answers will come."

"I hope you're right. I need clarity. I need a sign that will point me in the right direction. Not just with my home life and my friends, but also my work life." Ashley stopped herself. "I'm sorry, I'm rambling."

"What do you do for work?"

"My friend, the redhead." Natalie nodded in Nat's direction. "She and I own a company called BloMe." She paused, letting the name register.

61

He smirked, but didn't comment.

"We sell hot brushes."

"What are hot brushes?"

Ashley looked at his hair—hanging over his eyes, but she still guessed he never used a blow-dryer. "Nothing you'd ever use!"

"Is that a compliment?" His tone was light.

"Yes. Our target audience is female."

"I'm Marco." He held out his hand.

"Ashley," she said, shaking it. It was strong and warm. She held on for a beat longer.

"Well, Ashley, it's very nice to meet you. I'm also a business owner."

"Oh? What do you do?"

"I own a smoothie bowl place down the road. It's called Tropical Kiss."

"Awesome. Can I ask you something then, business owner to business owner?"

"Sure," Marco said, doing a forward fold over his outstretched legs.

"If someone offered you a lot of money to buy it, would you sell?"

Marco looked at Ashley for a few moments. "I would."

"Why?"

"Because everything must end—even the good things. I would see it as a sign that it was time for me to move on."

"Really? You think it's that simple?" Ashley asked, perplexed. Wondering whether she was missing something when it came to thinking about selling the company. Was she overlooking an opportunity?

Marco adjusted his yoga mat. "Down here it is. It's easier to see the universe's will. Maybe not so much in LA—too many distractions."

Ashley contemplated the breakneck speed with which she lived her life. How all her thoughts seemed to merge together into a giant knot that seemed impossible to untangle. She'd always reasoned it was just who she was, but what if it was her environment?

"But the universe hasn't sent anyone to purchase my store, so for now I'm still the owner. Bring your friends by after class, and I'll make you each an amazing smoothie bowl. On the house. If my blending skills can't bring you and your friends closer again, I'm not sure what can." He smiled easily, like it was something he did often.

Ashley felt that familiar buzzing deep inside her when a new distraction came into focus. She was often restless, especially lately. It could be a TV show she'd binge-watch or a genre of books she'd read until she grew sick of it. Anything she could throw herself into so she could temporarily forget how much pain she was often in. Over the last year she'd debated having an affair. There had certainly been opportunities, yet no matter how terrible Jason had been to her, she couldn't justify it. But she'd come here to get some space from her relationship—did that mean she should explore what it would feel like to be with someone else?

"Think of the life we could have with that money, Ash," Jason had said to her the night before she left for Tulum. He'd stepped into her dressing room and sat on a velvet bench, his large torso dwarfing it. His gray eyes looked tired as he ran his fingers through his black hair speckled with gray. The gray was new—just within the last six months. Ashley didn't think it was a coincidence that it had sprouted about the same time his investors had started complaining about the restaurant's terrible numbers. It hadn't been profitable in almost a year.

"I guess I'm just surprised Natalie is so willing to walk away from the company. From me," Ashley said—her stomach had dropped when she realized how excited Natalie was to sell. To abandon something that had become the backbone of their friendship.

"Maybe you've finally worn her out, Ash. She's probably dying to get away."

His comment stung, but she kept her face neutral. "That isn't true, and you know it."

63

Jason shook his head and let out a cold laugh. "You've been taking advantage of your friendship with her for years. Working her to death—"

"We both work hard because we love this company," Ashley interjected, feeling her cheeks grow red. "I'm not her boss."

"You sure act like it."

"What?"

"I've heard her try to talk to you about how tired she is. At the barbecue she had a couple of weeks ago, she said she was burned out. And you know what you said?"

Ashley did know what she'd said, but she shook her head anyway.

"That she should take a spa day." Jason sneered. "*You* love this company, Ash. It borders on unhealthy. The only difference? It doesn't really bother me when you're gone all those hours. But Ben, he gives a shit."

"Wow, that was harsh," Ashley said. And even though she knew they were well past the point of missing each other or caring if they went to sleep alone, it still hurt.

"It's not like you don't feel the same way." He gave her a look, challenging her to argue. "Natalie wants more in her life."

Ashley's body tensed. "How the hell do you know that?"

"How the hell do you *not know* that? It's fucking obvious to everyone except the one person who claims to be her best friend!" Jason gave her a look of something Ashley could only describe as disgust. "Maybe it's time you stopped being so selfish."

Even though she understood he was being cruel, there was some truth to his words. That Natalie struggled to find the balance between BloMe and the rest of her life. And Ashley didn't. Because it wasn't like she had a happy or productive marriage to worry about. And her daughters were so busy with a billion activities, they hardly noticed when she wasn't home. At least that's what Ashley told herself. So why, just because Natalie needed more family time, did it mean they had to sell the company?

She thought about the things she wanted moving forward. A life without Jason, without the constant arguing, would be at the very top of the list. Hannah and Abby were the two things that kept her from leaving—her love for them making her feel helpless. But was she really doing them any favors by remaining married to a man who felt he hadn't reached his true potential, who was enraged that his wife had eclipsed his dreams by succeeding in her own?

Jason's intolerance of Ashley hadn't happened overnight—in the beginning it had been a condescending remark here, a dagger stare there, but it eventually took on a distinct shape.

"Why do I have to sell my company for everyone else to have the life they want? Including *you*." Ashley pulled a bathing suit cover-up off the hanger and held it. "Because your restaurant is bleeding money?" She watched as his face lost some color. "Oh, you thought I didn't know?"

Jason started to say something, but Ashley cut him off. "You want me to sell something very successful—arguably on the edge of even greater success—and bail you out. Again." She paused to let her words sink in. This wouldn't be the first time he'd taken her money. She'd given him a hundred grand a few years ago, to save his restaurant. He'd gone over budget on a remodel and wasn't sure how he was going to pay the contractors *and* the staff. And of course he'd never recouped the money. Because he couldn't. He'd never climbed out of the red again.

"You are the most selfish person I've ever met, Ash. You know what? Don't sell. Maybe we should get divorced, *finally*. This isn't working and hasn't been for a while. Then you'll really know what losing your money feels like. Or half of it, anyway. You can just work yourself to death and end up alone. Married to that fucking company of yours."

She'd looked away and said nothing. Because he wasn't completely wrong. She'd contemplated more than once that she loved BloMe much more than she loved her husband. She would pretty much do anything to protect it.

Ashley took in Marco's relaxed posture, his open demeanor. "A smoothie bowl sounds delicious," she finally said. "Do you have dairy free?" She cracked a smile.

Marco leaned across his mat. "I hope you won't take this the wrong way, but there is something about you. You have an amazing energy—it shines through your beautiful brown eyes. I can just tell, you are a very good person, even if you don't like cilantro," he said, smiling at his own joke. "Sorry, is that too forward?"

Ashley grinned. "Not at all. And thank you for saying that. Although I'm not sure many people would agree with you," she said, directing a look at Lauren.

Marco looked perplexed. "What? Why?" He leaned even closer. "I have to tell you; I am rarely wrong about these things. People often lie, but their energies are the universe's way of knowing the truth."

"Well, in that case, I have a few people I'd like you to lay that wisdom upon," Ashley said, laughing. She couldn't tell if he was full of shit or not. But his faith in her character was comforting.

"It would be my pleasure," he said as the class began and he settled into his Downward-Facing Dog easily.

Ashley watched him for a moment before she joined, contemplating how he'd known the exact words she'd needed to hear.

CHAPTER NINE

THREE DAYS BEFORE
LAUREN

The yoga teacher took her position in front of the class. Lauren tried to pay attention to her instructions, but she couldn't stop watching Ashley and the man she was talking to. He was ruggedly handsome, his dark hair swept across his forehead, his sculpted jaw covered in stubble. Ashley leaned toward him and flipped her hair, her dark-gray Lululemon yoga pants hugging her in all the right places. Lauren strained to hear their conversation—but she couldn't make out any words. Just laughter.

Lauren had always marveled at Ashley's ability to draw people to her without even trying. She'd noticed the man watching Ashley before they spoke. She saw him choose the spot next to her, rolling out his mat as he kept one eye on her. She knew the man hadn't noticed Ashley only because she was classically beautiful, but also because of the energy she emitted.

She'd been in awe at the first frat party Ashley had taken her to, watching as people came up to her one after the next, all talking as if they were her best friend. Lauren had felt initially out of place as she glanced around at the students playing beer pong, rings from the bottom of the Solo cups covering the surface of the Ping-Pong table. She'd hunched her shoulders slightly as she realized how differently she was dressed from the other girls, all wearing high-waisted jeans and bodysuit tops, Lauren in a flannel shirt and leggings. But as the night went on, Lauren started to feel better. Almost as if Ashley's self-assuredness were rubbing off on her. She'd always felt it was one of Ashley's best qualities. But today, widowed and forty, Lauren was envious. She couldn't make a connection with a man unless she was buzzed and he was a stranger—like José. (She still wasn't sure what she was going to do when she saw him next—something she hadn't considered when she'd pulled him into her hotel room.) But usually her sexual needs were met by men she found on Tinder, her inhibitions blunted by the ability to simply swipe and type. To connect with another person physically—bodies intertwined, chests pressed together, limbs locked. She feared if she started an actual relationship, she'd lose control again. In bed was the only place she felt like she was in charge. She didn't want to give that up.

"Take a deep breath in through your nose, and let it out through your nose," the instructor said. She was a lithe redhead and sat cross-legged in front of them. Lauren tugged at her loose-fitting top, thankful it was covering the extra weight she'd gained around her middle since Geoff died. Her small frame didn't leave many places for her to hide the results of her binge drinking. Calorie-rich red wine had been her choice for many months. She spied Ashley's toned body as she glanced over at her again, her posture perfect as she stood at the head of her mat. Lauren listened to the instructor's smooth voice as she asked them to focus on their intention for the hour.

Lauren already knew what hers should be: forgiveness. Her therapist had told her that. She should come on this trip so she could forgive and hopefully be forgiven.

Last night, after the mezcal margaritas on the beach, she was sure she could do it. In fact, she'd almost turned to Ashley and said it. But in the end she'd held her tongue, not wanting to have the conversation in front of Natalie. Not wanting her to be a part of it. Wanting it to be something she and Ashley shared privately.

But there was no such thing as something special between her and Ashley.

Years ago, Ashley had called Lauren and said she had an extra ticket to Pearl Jam. Did Lauren want to go? Hell, yeah, she did. Never thinking to ask why Ashley had that ticket. They'd drunk endless draft beers and danced next to their seats to "Jeremy" and "Alive." Months later Natalie casually mentioned she and Ashley had had a fight the night before and that was why she hadn't gone. Lauren's heart had sunk. Would she always be second choice?

Maybe Ashley had decided she wanted their friendship to be nothing more than nights like the concert or even last night—fueled by liquor and giggling, no serious talk. Lauren hoped not, because she'd come to realize since being here that she really missed her. The Ashley who listened to her cry into her pinot grigio just days before meeting Geoff, sobbing because she was the only one not married out of the three of them. Would she ever meet someone? Ashley had given her a long look and said, *You are beautiful and smart and any man would be lucky to have you. It will happen when you least expect it.* And the next week Geoff had walked into the coffee shop where she was working, ordered a tall dark-roast coffee, and asked her out.

It was almost as if Ashley and Geoff were now congruent thoughts. When she'd first seen Ashley at LAX, she'd immediately pictured Geoff's sheet-white face before he clutched his chest and fell over. Lauren had to launch into a story about her bag tumbling down the escalator just to cover her frazzled expression and mask that the hugs she gave both Natalie and Ashley were so stilted. Annie had told her a million times that she had to stop associating Geoff's death with Ashley, but it was so much easier said than done. Even though her mind was ready to do that, her heart wouldn't seem to allow it.

Lauren took a deep breath and tried to block out the image of Geoff lying on the marble floor as she clasped his hand, waiting for the paramedics. The instructor began to guide them through Vinyasa. Lauren flowed from Plank to Chaturanga into Upward-Facing Dog and then into Downward-Facing Dog and repeated this several times. She'd tried yoga for the first time a few months ago, at Annie's insistence. She'd convinced her it was a great outlet to release her emotions. And even though Lauren scoffed and made Annie promise to buy her a bottle of Meiomi pinot noir if she hated the class, Annie turned out to be right. Lauren was surprised by how it took her mind off everything; all she had to do was concentrate on her breath.

The class slowly got harder, and before she knew it Lauren's face was dripping with sweat. She looked over at Natalie, whose body was shaking as she tried to hold Tree pose. Lauren watched as she furrowed her brow, concentrating hard to not fall over. She met Lauren's eyes and gave her a look as if to say, *You know me. I will get this right. I will not give up.* The teacher then contorted her body into Crane, an incredibly challenging pose, and Natalie followed suit, twisting her figure to match the teacher's. Lauren was impressed.

Just when her mind and body were in an absolute place of Zen— that *hallelujah, maybe she could forgive*—she heard Ashley squeal. Lauren lost control over her own pose and looked over and saw that Ashley had toppled on top of the man she'd been talking to at the beginning of class. Ashley giggled hard until the teacher shot her a warning look. Lauren tried not to laugh, but she couldn't hold back. She released a huge cackle and the teacher also gave her a death stare. Lauren's and Ashley's eyes met in the mirror and Ashley flashed a smile, which Lauren returned. Maybe forgiveness would be possible and maybe they could be the friends they once were—or maybe even better ones? Different friends. But good friends all the same. Because as easy as it was to say she was sorry and explain herself when she role-played the conversation with Annie, she knew real life was unpredictable. That Ashley was unpredictable. And if Lauren didn't time the conversation right, it might have a bad outcome. They could end up right back where they'd been a year ago.

After class, Lauren saw Ashley and the man talking outside, the yellow Lab she'd seen earlier now at his feet. She and Natalie walked up.

"Lauren and Nat, this is Marco," Ashley said, then petted the dog's head. "And Spencer."

Lauren ran her fingers through the dog's soft blond fur. "I met this beauty before class."

"Nice to meet you," Marco said to Lauren and Natalie.

"You too," they chimed.

"So that was pretty funny in there. I thought we were all going to get kicked out," Ashley said, taking a long drink from her water bottle.

"Lyssa takes her classes *very* seriously." Marco rolled his eyes.

"No shit," Ash said. "I can't help it if I can't stay balanced! Isn't yoga supposed to be about peace? By the way she glared at me, you'd think I'd stolen her firstborn."

"She gave me the same look—I thought I was going to turn to stone." Lauren laughed.

"So, I'll see you at Tropical Kiss?" Marco said, and Ashley nodded. "I'll make you a smoothie bowl that will change your life." He winked as he unhooked the leash that was connecting his dog to the tree.

Lauren rolled her eyes. This guy seemed like a real player.

"I bet you will." Ashley tucked a strand of hair that had slipped from her ponytail behind her ear.

"And after, I hope you guys will allow me to show you around Tulum. I know a private beach that's incredible."

"That would be amazing," Ashley said, her eyes shining.

Lauren was curious whether Ashley was just being nice or intended to take him up on his offer. She hoped it was the former. Last night had been fun; they'd fallen into an easy familiarity, laughing about old times as the margaritas kept flowing. Lauren wanted to stay on that path—wanted more of *that* Ashley. When she woke up this morning, she'd felt her guard go back up, the one that protected her from getting hurt by Ashley again. Because it was so like her to do something like this—attach herself to a random person—her need for attention almost like a drug. And if she brought this man into their vacation, Lauren would lose faith in Ashley again, and she knew that her wall would stay up.

After Marco was out of earshot, Natalie leaned toward Ashley and asked the very question Lauren had been wanting to know. "So—what's his story? And do you really want to hang out with him?" she asked, raising her eyebrows.

Ashley shrugged. "He was born in Mexico and lived in the States most of his life. Moved to Tulum a little over a year ago and says it's been the best thing he ever did. Said this is the perfect place to figure things out."

"So is that the plan? To figure out things with him by your side?" Natalie asked.

Lauren waited expectantly. *Please say no,* she thought. *Please say you were just flirting, but the three of us are going to hang out today like we did last night.*

But before Ashley could answer, her phone started ringing. "It's the girls!" she said. "They're FaceTiming me—I can't believe it! I usually have to call them!" She answered, then turned her phone toward Nat and Lauren briefly, and Lauren caught sight of their faces. Hannah's had thinned, the baby cheeks now gone, her brown eyes framed by long dark lashes. And Abby. She still had the freckles dotting her nose and full pink lips like her mom.

"Hi!" Nat called out to them before Ashley turned the phone back around.

Lauren wanted to say hi too, but she felt awkward. She hadn't seen Hannah and Abby in almost a year. Did they remember her? She knew that sounded ridiculous—of course they did; they were too old to have completely forgotten. She'd been Aunt Lauren since they were born. And just two years ago she'd spent the summer with them. Ashley had been in a bind, with her nanny backing out at the last minute. She'd called Lauren in a panic—could she help out? Ashley had squealed when Lauren said that she could, Lauren grimacing slightly at the thought of telling Geoff. He wouldn't like that she'd committed herself to something else for the next two months, but whatever the consequences, it would be worth it to spend the summer with Ashley's girls, who were seven and nine—such cute ages! Abby was starting to read on her own; Hannah had been obsessed with her American Girl doll. Lauren didn't have kids of her own, and the thought had brought a familiar twinge. She'd held their hands as they strolled down Third Street Promenade in Santa Monica, letting ice cream melt onto their fingers until they became sticky. Of all her regrets from that day in the coat closet, the fact that her anger with Ashley kept her from the girls was the biggest one.

But what had Ashley told them a year ago—when Lauren had all but disappeared?

Ashley walked toward the beach to talk. Lauren watched her pointing the phone at the ocean, heard her telling Hannah and Abby about how warm it was—and that she planned to go swimming at a private beach later. Then Ashley came over and turned the phone toward Natalie. "Say hi to Aunt Nat!" Lauren listened as Natalie chatted with them about their dance classes. Lauren didn't know they'd started hip-hop. How had she let it go for so long? How had she not reconciled, if only for the girls? Natalie said goodbye and gave the phone back to Ashley. She heard the girls ask if she wanted to talk to Dad. Lauren didn't miss the look on Ashley's face—it was clear she did not. "Sure," she said, then walked away to where Lauren couldn't hear her anymore.

"The girls sound good," Lauren said to Nat while they waited.

"They are. I saw them a couple of weeks ago and Hannah was playing me Selena Gomez songs on her phone. And Abbs, well, she is a voracious reader. She just finished the Harry Potter series."

"Wow," Lauren said. Her eyes started to water, and she grabbed her towel and wiped them.

"You okay?" Nat asked her.

"Yeah, I just feel bad about not seeing them or your girls for so long. Although I do appreciate your invite to Meg's band recital."

"I know," Natalie said. "I wish there had been more opportunities. I just didn't know."

"It's okay. I also could've tried harder."

"We all could have tried harder. But we'll figure it out. That's why Ash brought us here, right?"

"Is it?" Lauren asked, knowing she was moving into uncharted territory. Ashley was usually a subject that they steered clear of when they were alone together. And Lauren couldn't recall the last time they had been.

Natalie frowned. "Ash definitely wants to make things better between all of us—between you guys. Why are you unsure? Is it because you don't?"

Ashley walked up before Lauren could answer. "So, you guys ready for some smoothie bowls? I have no idea what they are, but they sound amazing."

"Hannah and Abby sound so much older all of a sudden," Lauren said.

Ashley lowered her gaze. "I'm sorry I didn't have you talk to them. It's just I didn't know if it would be awkward since they haven't seen you in a while. I thought maybe when we got back, you could come over?"

Lauren regarded her to see whether she meant it. Or if she was just saying it to cover herself. "Sure," she said, wanting to feel hopeful, trying to grasp onto the way she'd felt the night before on the beach. That they could be okay again.

"Good, then it's a date," Ashley said, looping her arm through Lauren's as they all walked to the bike racks.

~

They pulled up to Tropical Kiss a little while later, their sore legs making the journey back toward the hotel seem much longer, and propped their bikes against the side of the restaurant.

"Ladies, you made it!" Marco said, gesturing toward a group of empty tables. "You can sit wherever you like. We're not busy—off-season, you know. I'm the only one here—I'll be serving you."

Lauren felt bad for him. Off-season or not, business must really be slow if the owner couldn't afford to have even one employee come in and help. No wonder he'd invited them—he was probably desperate to make some pesos. As he handed them menus, Marco's shirtsleeve slid up his arm, revealing a nice biceps muscle. Lauren bet he had a six-pack under there too. Maybe it wouldn't be so bad to go to that private beach with him, if only to see that body of his?

"Okay, so everyone wants to know—what the hell is a smoothie bowl?" Ashley asked.

Marco smirked. "It's like a smoothie, but in a bowl with fruit and other delicious toppings."

"So you don't drink it, you spoon it?"

"Yep. I'm surprised you guys haven't heard of them—I think they started in LA?" Marco raised his eyebrows.

"We don't get out much." Ashley's eyes danced. She shot Natalie a look before shutting her menu. "There are just too many choices here. I'm overwhelmed. What do you recommend?"

"Our most popular is the acai berry bowl," Marco suggested.

"I'll have that," Ashley said.

"We can make it with coconut yogurt." Marco gave her a private look.

"I'll have the same," Lauren said, catching his eye and grinning. She had to admit he was handsome. José had been a lot of fun the afternoon before, but she liked the way she could see the outline of Marco's pectoral muscles under his T-shirt. If Ashley was going to be insistent on keeping him around, Lauren was at least going to get something out of it.

Her sexual appetite had taken a strange turn in the last six months, after the fog began to lift from Geoff's death. She knew being promiscuous was self-destructive and, in the case of last week, when she'd met a thirty-six-year-old named Randy in a questionable motel in Hollywood, dangerous. But while that might be true, there was no arguing the way these encounters made her feel: *alive*. For that small amount of time she wasn't a widow who had blown up her own life and may or may not have been a factor in her husband's death. She was just a girl wearing great lingerie, being fucked by whomever she chose. For those brief moments she felt something other than grief, guilt, or anger, and concentrated only on what was right in front of her. Or at least that was the theory her stony-faced therapist had voiced, right after he'd concluded that Lauren had a sex addiction.

That had been hard to hear.

"I'm getting the coco bowl with spirulina and dates," Natalie said.

"Bold choice," Marco said, nodding.

"She's tricky, that one." Ashley picked up a spoon and pointed it at Natalie. "Just when you think she's going to get a boring plain yogurt with granola, she ups her game."

Natalie laughed lightly. They watched as Marco started making the order. Ashley held up her phone to capture him, and he blocked his face. "I hate having my picture taken," he said from behind the bar, then patted his flat stomach. "Don't you know the camera adds ten pounds?"

Lauren sauntered up to the counter and leaned in seductively. "So what's the secret to your smoothie bowls?"

Marco looked up from slicing a mango, its juice spilling out on the cutting board. He pointed his knife at it. "The fruit. It must be supple."

Lauren raised her eyebrows. "Supple fruit, huh?" She lowered her eyes flirtatiously. "And where do you find it?"

Marco frowned, confused. "Oh, we don't source our own fruit. They deliver it fresh each day."

Lauren took a slight step back. "Of course. That makes sense."

Marco slid a bowl toward her. "Would you mind taking that over to Ashley? I'm dying to know what she thinks."

Lauren tried to mask her disappointment. Of course he only had eyes for Ashley. Why had she expected anything to have changed in the last year? Ashley had always been the brightest star in the group, the friend who breathed fresh air into any room she walked into, the one who always got what she wanted. Lauren felt that familiar pit of insecurity in her stomach—that she'd always be in Ashley's shadow.

"Sure thing," she said, grabbing the bowl and setting it down in front of Ashley.

This was going to be a long day.

～

"Wow," Ashley said an hour later when they arrived at the secret beach with Marco. She dropped her bag on the sand and walked toward the turquoise water. "I thought the beach just off our hotel was amazing. But this, it's breathtaking."

"It's one of Tulum's best-kept secrets," Marco said, tossing a Frisbee toward the ocean, Spencer bounding across the sand to fetch it.

"Well, after the effort it took to get here, I'm shocked there are no other human beings on this beach," Natalie said sarcastically.

Lauren laughed at Natalie's comment—the trek in had been ridiculous. She'd also been annoyed that he'd asked them to meet at Tropical Kiss, instead of picking them up at the hotel. Then even more agitated as they piled into Marco's old Nissan Sentra, she and Natalie and the dog wedged together in the back. She hadn't wanted to spend the day with a complete stranger, but she didn't want to seem like a bitch by bringing it up. So she'd stayed silent as Marco started driving south of their hotel. It had taken about a half hour to reach the nature preserve. Marco paid a few pesos and they parked. But that was just the beginning. They had to hike for what seemed like forever through dense jungle to get to the sand.

"It is pretty, but I probably could've done without the bushwhacking," Lauren said. They'd gotten through the forest using thick sticks to push back the plants and brush. Lauren reached down and scratched her leg, sure she had a million mosquito bites.

Lauren looked at Natalie, who knotted her eyebrows while scratching at her own calf. Their eyes met and it was clear Natalie was just as annoyed as she was. Lauren felt slightly ashamed by the comfort she found in that.

"The water is so calm," Ashley said, taking off her cover-up before wading in. Lauren watched as Marco tore off his shirt, revealing the well-defined abs and muscular back she'd suspected would be under it, as he dove in confidently. Lauren peeled her dress off and followed, the cool water soothing her hot and itchy skin.

"See over there?" Marco pointed. "There's a barrier reef made up of over eighty-four species of coral, including brain coral, which can be up to seven meters in diameter. That's what keeps the water calm and protected."

"I feel so clearheaded out here," Ashley said, splashing some water on Natalie, who flinched as she made her way into the ocean.

"Stop it!" she squealed. "I don't want to get my hair wet!"

Ashley spread her arms out. "But don't you feel it? It's like the water is vibrating."

"Many people feel like they are closest to God in the water," Marco said serenely.

"Whatever," Lauren muttered, and dove under, coming back up quickly and slicking her hair back behind her ears. "I do feel better, though. I will give you that."

"Have you ever come up with an amazing idea or a solution to a problem while in the bathtub or shower?" Marco asked, looking at Lauren.

"Not that I can recollect," Lauren said, floating on her back, kicking lightly to move farther out into the ocean, deciding she'd had enough of Marco and his theories for one day. He'd already gone on and on about some asteroid that had apparently hit Tulum sixty-six million years ago. When she came upright again, she heard Ashley declaring that she'd thought of the BloBrush tagline, *Blow (on) me*, while shampooing her hair.

Marco's eyes twinkled. "That's clever."

"Thanks," Ashley said. "Maybe if I stay in this ocean long enough I'll think of a way to solve *all* of my problems."

Lauren turned to see Natalie's reaction. She was still quietly registering irritation.

When Lauren and Natalie headed toward the beach, Marco and Ashley stayed in the ocean, drifting to the left, the current pulling them away while locked in conversation. Soon they were so far down that Lauren could barely make them out.

"This isn't how I saw the trip going," Lauren said finally.

Natalie rolled her eyes as she got up to rearrange her towel. "Me either. Do you think we need to be worried about that?" She cocked her head in the direction of the two specks that were Ashley and Marco.

"You would know better than me," Lauren said, pulling her hat lower on her face. She'd promised Annie she'd be careful not to get burned, Annie having lectured her once when they'd gone to the pool and Lauren hadn't reapplied sunscreen after swimming. It was sweet how much she cared. Ashley used to encourage Lauren to use tanning oil and would wake her up only after her skin was flaming red.

"I think we should keep an eye on it," Natalie said, her tone surprising Lauren. "Because, let's face it, she doesn't always know what's best for her, does she?" Before Lauren could answer, Natalie reached into her bag, pulling out a bottle of sunscreen. "Your shoulders are getting a little pink. You'd better reapply."

"Thanks." Lauren took it from her and squirted the liquid into her hands. "You know, it's been really nice to spend some time with you on this trip."

"It has, hasn't it?" Natalie said, pushing her sunglasses onto her head. "I'm sorry it took so long. I've thought of you so often."

"Then why didn't you call?" Lauren asked, not unkindly. She'd spent so much time wondering. Questioning why she hadn't picked up the phone either.

Natalie adjusted her sundress nervously. "That's a good question. You were so upset at the funeral. I just thought maybe it was easier to let you cool off. But then one month turned into two, which became a year. And here we are," she said sadly.

Lauren understood. She had told herself she'd be ready to forgive, and then the feeling would come and go. Annie had finally pointed out that the person she was most upset with was never coming back: Geoff.

Geoff had been constantly at odds with himself—the light within him at war with the dark. Stuck between the person he was, a man whose temper flared hot and hard, and the person he strived to be, a caring and peaceful husband. That had been the most difficult thing to accept: that the hope Geoff could change, a notion Lauren had clung to for years, would now never come to fruition. That all of Lauren's bruises would fade, as would the memory of how she got each one, a twist of an arm, a push into a wall, a hurl onto the hard floor. Yes, she understood that the notion was crazy that a controlling, physically abusive man could change. But it was the one thing that had kept Lauren going until his death.

She looked at Natalie. Sweet Natalie, who had always revered Ashley as much as Lauren did. Until now. Now the axis of power seemed to be tilted, and it felt odd. They'd wrapped so much of themselves around Ashley for so long—did they have a strong enough friendship to stand on its own?

"It's okay," Lauren said. "We have right now. So let's make the best of it."

CHAPTER TEN

The Day After
Natalie

As Natalie made her way up the concrete steps to apartment 4, which according to the slip of paper in her hand was Marco's place, she felt a sense of déjà vu. She gripped the wooden railing to steady herself and looked up at the heavy cedar beams and thatched roof, hoping it meant her memory was coming back. She closed her eyes and willed those thoughts that were just beyond the periphery of her mind to present themselves. But when she stopped climbing the stairs, Lauren, who was right behind her, bumped into her, and she lost her concentration.

"Sorry," Lauren said. "Are you okay?" she added when Natalie didn't move.

Natalie started up the steps again. "I just thought I was remembering something."

"Did you?" Lauren asked.

Natalie looked at her over her shoulder. "Not really—only that I think I've been here before. I feel like I've walked up these stairs. It's so strange having that feeling but no memory to attach to it." She sighed, so tired of fighting against herself. Maybe if she stopped pushing so hard, her memories would return.

"It will come back," Lauren said, squeezing her arm.

Natalie didn't answer or agree; she just kept moving upward, rubbing her temples. Her memories were gone, but her instincts were still there—it was a strange sensation. And something deep inside her was telling her that remembering might not mean good things. That remembering might be very bad.

She stopped and turned to Lauren. "I really hope she's here."

Lauren bit her lip. "I do too."

At the top of the stairs was a pale green door with an orange number 4 painted on the front. Natalie knocked, then found the doorbell and pressed that too. Once, twice, three times.

No answer.

A pit formed in her stomach. "Marco?" There was a small window to the side of the door, and she cupped her hands and looked in. "There's hardly anything in there," she said, small waves of panic hitting her. "Just a couch, a table, a lamp. It looks like he cleared his place out. Fuck."

Lauren squeezed in next to Natalie to see for herself. "I just got the chills." She rubbed her arms. "This can't be good."

Natalie's heart was racing. If Ashley wasn't here . . . if Marco was gone . . . they might have to start saying what they hadn't been—that it was possible something bad might have happened. Natalie jiggled the doorknob. It was unlocked. Would this be breaking and entering? She didn't care. "I'm going in," she said before she could lose her nerve. She pushed the door open and it swung wide, settling against the wall. The women stood on the threshold and looked around.

"I don't understand," Lauren said. "Is there any chance this isn't his place? That we have the wrong address? He lied about owning Tropical Kiss, so maybe he lied about where he lived?"

Natalie surveyed the room. There were nails in the walls where pictures once hung. In the kitchen only a refrigerator remained, humming quietly. A dog bowl half filled with water sat on the floor. Some cupboards were still open, revealing a cup here, a plate there. There was a lone spatula next to the sink. "No, this is it," she said quietly, goose bumps sprouting on her skin. "I've been in here." She wanted to crumple to the floor and unravel completely. To scream into the worn carpeting.

Where are you, Ashley?

The musty smell was familiar to Natalie. A mix of marijuana and incense. She could almost feel herself sinking into the ratty chenille couch that remained in the room. She touched the arm of the sofa. "Marco?" Natalie called again, her voice echoing in the empty apartment. She stepped forward slowly and Lauren followed. She crossed through the living room and walked down the hallway, which led to a bedroom. There was a futon against the far wall, a bath towel in the corner. "Ashley?" she said, even though it was clear she wasn't going to respond. That she wasn't here.

Lauren looked into the bathroom. "There's nothing but a shower curtain and a bottle of shampoo." She walked quickly into the bedroom. "Nothing in the closet either." Lauren turned around. "Okay, I'm really getting freaked out here," she said, her voice trembling. "If you were here with Ashley just last night—it's nine in the morning now, so maybe nine hours ago—how is this place practically vacant? And why?" She looked at Natalie. "Are you sure you were in *this* apartment?"

Natalie rubbed her hand over her forehead, covered with sweat from the humidity. "I was," she said, then added, "I think."

"You need to be sure," Lauren said sharply, adding a moment later, "Sorry, I didn't mean to snap."

But Natalie couldn't be completely sure. The only thing she knew for certain was that Ashley was gone. "I can't be positive, but I think I was," she said, glancing around again, noticing a trash can in the corner. She looked inside: three Corona bottles, one of them half full. Had they been drinking them last night?

"This is getting really scary," Lauren said. "I was feeling more hopeful at the hotel, but now I'm getting worried, Nat. What if Marco took her? Did something terrible? Do you think that's possible?"

Natalie rubbed her face. "I don't know, but I have a bad feeling."

Lauren sighed. "This is my fault."

Natalie's heart sank. "It's not. You couldn't have known." But she wished, now more than ever, that Lauren had told Ashley that they could all go somewhere and talk. That she hadn't been so damn stubborn—hadn't told her she was done. And Natalie also wished she hadn't fought so much with Ashley. That she hadn't pushed her so hard about Revlon.

A thought suddenly nagged at her: What if nothing bad *had* happened? What if Ashley took off with Marco because she wanted to—because of the Revlon deal, to ensure it didn't happen? Would Ashley go to such lengths to prevent the sale of BloMe?

She was about to ask Lauren her opinion when her cell phone rang. They both jumped slightly at the sound. "It's the hotel," Natalie said and put the call on speaker. "Hello?"

"Natalie, it's Maria."

Natalie sucked in a breath, her heart beating hard. "Did Ashley come back?" she asked, saying a silent prayer.

"No, I'm sorry. But two of the hotel guests heard someone last night by the ocean. I think you'd better come back here right away."

CHAPTER ELEVEN

Two Days Before
Natalie

"Have you guys ever thought about getting your chakras cleared?" Marco doused his scrambled eggs with hot sauce. They'd met him for breakfast at Ziggy's, a restaurant with tables in the sand and white linen daybeds with brightly striped pillows to lie on while sipping mimosas. They'd landed a table in the shade after Ashley tilted her chin at the young host as she made a bad joke about getting boob sweat if she sat in the sun.

"What's Spanish for 'boob sweat'?" she'd asked, her bubbling laughter carrying through the restaurant. A man in a flowered Tommy Bahama shirt glanced over, admiring Ashley's legs in her pale pink shorts romper, looking away sheepishly only when his wife hissed his name.

Natalie had rolled her eyes, seeing it for what it was—a piece of Ash's persona that she turned on and off, like a spotlight in the dark. It was always on when she wanted something—like the table. The host, clearly charmed, had led them down the beach to a shaded area in the sand, Ashley winking at Natalie as they sat down. Natalie watched her as she pulled her napkin out and set it carefully on her lap, wondering when her charm had bled into manipulation.

"Get our what-whats?" Ashley squinted at Marco now.

"Chakras, you know, like auras," he replied.

Natalie took a drink of her coffee, hoping the caffeine would help numb her frustration. They'd spent the entire day with Marco yesterday, and his talk of crystals, spirituality, and the ancient Mayan civilization was beginning to grate on her. This morning Natalie had asked Ashley why she was insisting on seeing him again, but Ashley had blown her off. *It's just breakfast. Recommended by a local! Think of him as a tour guide.* Now, as he suggested yet another activity, she felt her annoyance bubble.

Ashley outlined her body with her hands. "I know mine's pretty dirty." She winked, then took a bite of her egg whites.

"It's part massage, part therapy. And believe me, it's life changing. I literally had a conversation with God when I did it for the first time. I cried afterward." Marco looked up at the sky, contemplative.

Natalie suppressed an eye roll, sure that his suggestion was just another ploy to spend more time with Ashley. She looked over at Lauren to see how she felt about hanging out with Marco—again—but her face was hard to read. Why were they both so unwilling to let Ashley know how annoyed they were? Even more to the point, why couldn't they talk to each other about it? They danced around it yesterday, like a hot fire to which they didn't want to get close. But they had a right to go there. It wasn't just Ashley's vacation—it was theirs too. "Will you be joining us?" Natalie asked, trying to keep her voice even.

"I don't want to impose—" Marco began.

"You wouldn't be imposing!" Ashley exchanged a knowing look with Marco, then looked over at Natalie as if daring her to argue.

"I've heard about this chakra clearing," Lauren said, surprising Natalie. "When I went to Sedona a few months back with my friend Annie." She took a bite of her omelet, a gleam in her eye, clearly remembering a fun time. Natalie wondered what else Annie had shared with Lauren in her and Ashley's absence.

"And?" Natalie asked.

"And it's going to be great," Ashley answered before Lauren could. "It involves a massage, so I'm in." Natalie watched Marco place his hand on Ashley's knee and squeeze, then pull it away quickly as if he knew it could be there only a split second before he would be crossing a line. But as far as Natalie was concerned, he already had. He would never do that if Jason were here. She studied his dark brown eyes as he listened to Ashley talk, wondering what she was witnessing. Flirtation or something more?

Ashley had a bad habit of leading men on unintentionally. Natalie had watched her effortlessly wrap them around her finger, whether it was the rotund FedEx guy wearing Coke-bottle glasses or the incredibly handsome head of publicity at QVC. She sometimes seemed like a heat-seeking missile for others, as if absorbing their energy made her more powerful. Was that all this was with Marco? Or was Ashley feeling something for him?

"I was asking Lauren," Natalie said to Ashley, her tone sharper than she intended. She had planned to keep her annoyance inside, to talk to Ashley about it privately after breakfast.

"Geez, what's gotten into you?" Ashley asked, spooning some raw sugar into her coffee.

Natalie tried to swallow her irritation, looking away, focusing on a couple on the daybed closest to them. She was feeding him strawberries from her champagne glass. Corny, for sure, but Natalie still felt a pang. When was the last time she and Ben had even cuddled? The last month and a half had put their marriage to the test—leaving her speculating whether they'd get through it.

"It gets rid of your negative energy. Out with the bad, in with the good. Emotional stress and negativity can build up and block good things from coming your way," Lauren said.

"That's exactly right," Marco said. "Open chakras help the positive energy flow to you more easily."

Natalie narrowed her eyes and subtly shook her head at him.

"What?" Ashley asked her, not missing a beat.

"Nothing." She looked down at her huevos rancheros, pushing them around on her plate.

"Why do you have that look on your face?"

"Fine." She set her fork down. "I just think it all sounds a little hokey. Why don't we do something else, like paddleboarding?"

"Paddleboarding?" Ashley scowled as if Natalie had suggested a root canal. "We can do that at home."

"See!" Marco said, waving his hand in the air. "This is exactly why I think you all should do this. Clear that negative energy out of your friendships. Isn't that why you came here?" He looked at Ashley, who gave him a crisp nod in return.

What had Ashley told Marco? They'd been out in the water alone yesterday. Had they been talking about her? Lauren?

She threw a look to Lauren, who raised an eyebrow.

Marco picked up his cell phone. "Should I make us some appointments? I'm friends with the owner. He'll fit us all in; I'm sure of it."

"I'm in. God knows I could use some answers!" Ashley declared.

"Maybe He holds the answers you seek," Marco said, placing his hand over Ashley's. Natalie cringed.

"Maybe," Ashley said.

Lauren caught Natalie's eye again. Natalie wondered if she was thinking the same thing. Ashley had clearly confided in him. About them.

Marco moved his hand to Ashley's back possessively. Natalie waited for Ashley to lean forward, to inch away, to do anything to dissuade him. But when she didn't, something inside her snapped.

"Can I talk to you for a minute?" Natalie said to Ashley. "Privately."

"Sure," Ashley said as she got up from the table, smiling at Marco as if they were sharing an inside joke.

"Will you excuse us?" Natalie said to Lauren and Marco, but she didn't wait for an answer. She headed down to the water and Ashley followed.

"What's going on?" Natalie asked when they were several yards away.

"What do you mean?"

"Between you and Marco?"

"Nothing."

"Come on."

"I swear—nothing."

"Then why are you letting him be so handsy?"

"'Handsy'?"

"Don't play dumb. Would you let him touch you like that if Jason were sitting there?"

"Of course not," Ashley said.

"Then don't go down this road."

"Why do you care so much? This—whatever it is—does not impact you."

"Doesn't it? I thought you were here to connect with me and Lauren, not with some guy you just met."

"We've had plenty of alone time," Ashley argued, clenching her jaw. "The first night on the beach, yoga . . ."

"We've barely been able to take a breath without him right there, spewing some mystical wisdom!" Natalie sighed heavily, glancing back at the table where he was reclined in his seat, his hands clasped behind his head as he gazed at the sky.

"He's nice. He's shown us around." Ashley put her hands on her hips. "I don't get what the problem is."

"That's not all this is, and you know it." Natalie threw up her hands in frustration. "He was touching your knee, your lower back."

Ashley pinched her lips. "It's nothing. A little harmless flirtation. Calm down."

Natalie turned toward the water, collecting her thoughts. Finally she said what was really bothering her. "Why is he acting like you've told him things?"

"Because I have. I needed someone to talk to."

"But you don't know him." Natalie felt a burning in her chest—wondering again when they had drifted so far apart that they'd stopped talking about the things that mattered most. About the feelings they concealed from nearly everyone else but shared with each other. When they'd both had newborns, they'd sit for hours and talk about everything from C-section stitches to sex drive to fears they'd screw up their kids. Lately, they felt more like acquaintances making small talk at the grocery store.

"Maybe that's exactly why he's easy to confide in." Ashley looked down at her bare feet.

Natalie wanted to ask her, *Why aren't you confiding in me? Really?* She opened her mouth to say it, but Ashley cut her off. "Why do you care what I tell him, anyway?" She crossed her arms defiantly.

Natalie felt her anger start to brim, but she pushed it down. "I thought this trip was about all of *us*." As she spoke the words, she realized just how much she was hoping to fly home at the end of the week with a happy ending. With Lauren. For her and Ashley. For their company. And ultimately for her and Ben. Until Marco had stepped in and uprooted their dynamic, she hadn't understood how much she'd been counting on it. "How are we supposed to reconnect if he's always here?"

Ashley's eyes softened. "You still feel like we aren't connected?"

Natalie dug her toes into the sand. "Look at things from my perspective—finding out about you and Jason, telling me and Lauren together like I'm not your best friend? Like there weren't a million opportunities to tell me before we came here? What am I supposed to think?" She watched Ashley twitch slightly at her confession. "*I'm* supposed to be your closest friend, and right now I feel like I barely know you. So yes, I'm here to reconnect. I want to be here for you. I'm here to see if we can find some common ground about Revlon. And sure, I'm hoping we can turn Lauren into someone we know again, rather than the polite stranger she's become. But most of all, I'm here because you asked me to be."

Ashley rubbed her lips with her forefinger. "I want all those things too. Can't you see that?"

"If that's true, then why spend all this time with Marco? Why confide in him and not us—*me*?"

"It's not like I planned it. We were in the water, and the wind was blowing. It was so peaceful, you know? I felt calm for the first time in a long time. When he asked me about my life, it just spilled out."

"Don't you get it? He's probably telling you everything you want to hear so he can get you into bed," Natalie said, unable to contain her frustration any longer. "Don't be so naive!"

"God, Nat," Ashley said. "Did it ever occur to you that he just wants to be helpful? Why are you so personally offended that I told him things? This isn't about you!"

"You really can't see it?" Natalie said. "You think that he just wants to be besties?"

"What's going on with you?" Ashley asked wearily. "It feels like all we ever do lately is fight."

Natalie's eyes narrowed as she stared out at the brilliant blue water, examining what it was that was bringing all these conflicted feelings about Ashley to the surface. Was it the location—that they were somewhere remote where there was nowhere to turn and nothing to distract her from her aggravation like when she was at work, when she could close her office door, put on her headphones, and lose herself in a manufacturing contract? Or was it simply timing? That this trip had directly coincided with her hitting her breaking point? "Maybe I'm just tired of how selfish you can be, Ash. We have to wait on giving an answer on the offer because of *you*. We have to fly to Mexico because *you* have things to work out. And now we have to get our chakras cleared with"—she pointed toward Marco—"some guy *you* are making us hang out with!"

Ashley looked as if she'd been slapped—her face registering shock, then sadness, then anger. "I'm done with this conversation. If you don't want to get the damn massage, then go paddleboarding. I don't give a shit! But don't you dare put this all on me. It's not fair, and you know it."

Natalie watched as Ashley walked back toward the table where Marco and Lauren were still sitting—Lauren's nose buried in her phone, Marco staring up at the cloudless sky. Ashley sat down and scooted her chair closer to Marco, glancing back defiantly at Natalie. A shiver ran through Natalie. Yes, Ashley could be a little unpredictable, even crazy at times. But in all the time she'd known Ash, Natalie had always felt like she had a handle on Ashley's sometimes erratic behavior, almost as if she were holding firmly on to the reins of a headstrong Thoroughbred.

But since the moment they'd received their offer from Revlon, she'd been trying to push off the feeling that maybe she didn't know Ashley at all. That the anger she'd just flashed was merely a preview of what lay ahead.

CHAPTER TWELVE

THE DAY AFTER
NATALIE

Natalie's heartbeat banged in her ears. Sweat soaked her back as she pedaled. She glanced behind her—Lauren was red-faced but keeping pace. After Maria's call they hadn't said a word to each other; they had a silent understanding to get on their bikes and race back to the hotel. Natalie's legs felt like rubber, but her adrenaline pressed her forward.

She thought about what Maria had said. That guests of the hotel had heard someone in the water last night. There had been an urgency in the front desk attendant's voice. Natalie could still see the sand caked on her legs and feel her wet dress clinging to her body. Was there a connection between what the guests heard and Natalie sleeping on the beach? Something had started to nag at her gut in Marco's apartment.

What if Natalie had something to do with what had happened to Ashley?

She pedaled faster in an attempt to jiggle the memory free, but her mind was thick. She knew there was something there—just out of reach. Her heart continued to pound, her mouth dry. It was so hot. She prayed. *Please let Ashley be okay.*

Lauren rode up beside her. "We're almost there." She pushed her damp hair away from her face.

Natalie only nodded. She didn't trust herself to speak. If she did, she might scream.

They laid their beach cruisers on their sides in front of the hotel and hurried up the steps, where they spotted Maria standing with a young couple. The woman was petite, her blond hair piled high on top of her head, aviators perched in front of her topknot. She had a tote bag slung over her shoulder with *Beach Hair Don't Care* stitched on the side. Next to her stood a man with a baseball cap turned backward, his board shorts slung low on his hips, a rolled-up towel under his arm. Natalie hadn't seen them before—were they the guests Maria had called about? From the way they were looking at her, she was pretty sure she had her answer.

"Natalie, Lauren," Maria said, motioning them over. "This is Scarlett and her husband, Henry. They're the ones I called about. They think they heard someone in the ocean last night."

Natalie rubbed her sweaty palms on her shorts before shaking their hands. Lauren did the same. The only sound was their labored breathing from the hot and humid bike journey.

Finally Scarlett spoke. "We are staying in that room there." She pointed. "Last night, we were on our balcony, and we heard a woman's voice."

Natalie had a fluttery feeling in her stomach. Had it been Ashley?

"It was late, and we'd drunk quite a bit—we'd just gotten back from La Zebra," Henry said, wrapping his arm around his wife protectively. "So we didn't make anything of it—at first."

"Yeah—like Henry said, there was laughing and some screaming, but we thought it was all good, you know? Like maybe the woman was a honeymooner, like us. Out there with her husband, having a good time." Scarlett shared a secret smile with Henry, the way people did when they were still in the throes of early love. When a marriage still had that new-car scent.

"But then the screams turned into crying," Henry said. Natalie's heart started to race, not sure where he was going with the story, frightened of what he was going to say next. She held her breath. "We listened for a minute—not sure what we were overhearing—and then it stopped. We figured we should go down to the water and check to make sure nothing was wrong. But when we went out to the balcony and looked, it was pitch-black, and we didn't see or hear anyone."

"What time was it?" Natalie asked, thinking hard. Had she and Ashley and Marco gone to the hotel's beach? Was that why she'd woken up there? Had Natalie been the one screaming? Had it been Ashley? Her heart pounded as she cataloged all the reasons either of them would have been yelling in the ocean in the middle of the night. Natalie thought about the way her chest clenched each time Ben asked if she'd convinced Ashley to be reasonable about Revlon. Each time she thought about not selling. Being stuck there.

"That's the thing, we don't know. We didn't even think to look at the clock," Scarlett said, her cheeks flushing.

"We got back to our room at one. So it was after that," Henry added, and squeezed his wife's hand.

"We figured we'd been mistaken. But if it was your friend out there and something was wrong, and we were too lazy to walk down to the beach . . . We are so sorry. We'd had so many margaritas." Scarlett's lower lip quivered.

"It's okay—you couldn't have known," Lauren said, then widened her eyes at Natalie, most likely thinking about the fact she'd woken up in her wet dress this morning. That she'd slept on the beach. Was she making the same assumptions Natalie was?

Natalie felt heat rush through her. Fear now taking over as she tried to make sense of everything. She pressed her thumbs to her temples. Would she ever get her memory back?

"Don't you think it's time to call the police?" Maria asked.

Natalie's entire body tensed as she looked at Maria's pinched expression. Her gut told her it was time, but her heart wasn't ready. Calling the police would take this search for Ashley into a whole different stratosphere. It would make her disappearance *real*. But it had been too many hours since they'd seen her. Or could remember seeing her. They probably should have already called. Natalie hoped she wouldn't regret that later.

She looked at Lauren.

"We should call them," Lauren said, her eyes filling with tears.

"I agree," Natalie said, trying to hold her emotion back. If she started crying now, she might never stop.

"Thank you for talking with us," Maria said. She asked the couple whether they'd be willing to tell the police what they knew, and they agreed. They mumbled more apologies and asked to be updated on Ashley before walking away.

"I need to call Jason too," Natalie said. Her mind immediately went to what Ashley had confided. Had the problems in their marriage propelled her to run off with Marco? To want to escape her own life? "I probably should have called him first thing, but I didn't think . . ."

Lauren smiled at her sadly. "It's okay. We're doing our best. Alarm bells didn't go off at first because it's Ashley. You know what I was just thinking about? When she went camping on the Kern River with that guy she'd just met—she called from a pay phone that night."

"And made us come get her the next morning at that Jack in the Box," Natalie said. She remembered answering the phone in their dorm room, Ashley giggling and telling her his name in case she didn't show up for class the next day. *But I will*, she said before hanging up.

"But she called," Lauren continued. "That's what's different about this time. We haven't heard from her. That's the part that makes me sick to my stomach."

When they'd picked her up at the fast-food restaurant, Ashley had regaled them with stories about white-water rafting and sleeping in a tent, Natalie trying not to burst her bubble by reminding her she didn't know the guy at all. What if he'd raped her? Or worse? Part of her had always felt Ashley was immortal—maybe because of how she tended to make spontaneous and often careless decisions but always came out okay.

"Do you think Ashley might have left with Marco and she just hasn't called yet because she's not thinking about how scared we might be?" Natalie asked hopefully. "Because I could see her doing that."

Lauren sighed. "I don't know. If things are really as bad as she said they are with Jason, it's possible she took off, and who knows when or if we will hear from her."

"She'd never leave Hannah and Abby," Nat said, looking down. "Right?"

"I have no idea, Nat. Of course she loves them, but a bad marriage can make you do strange things. Especially once it's out in the open." Lauren averted her eyes for a moment. "You get messy, desperate even. If that's even why she left. Maybe she took off because of how I treated her."

"Maybe she's just somewhere cooling off," Natalie said, but she knew it wasn't likely, because Marco had cleaned his place out. It felt final—whatever it was.

"I don't know what to think." Lauren stared down at her feet. "I just wish I could go back and change what I said to her at La Cantina."

"I wish I could change a lot of things too," Natalie said, especially wishing they hadn't argued so much. That she hadn't been so pushy about Revlon. Because now that Ashley had disappeared, that deal was slipping away. She hated that this thought followed the last. But she couldn't help it.

Lauren smiled sadly and said she was going to get them some coffee. Natalie looked over and saw Maria on the phone, presumably with the police. She pressed Jason's name on her cell and waited. Her heartbeat raced again as she tried to gather the words to say to him. To tell him Ashley had disappeared in Mexico. That she couldn't remember anything of significance to help find her. She put her head in her hands and waited for him to answer, scared shitless to tell him his wife had gone missing on her watch.

"Hey, Nat, what's up?" Jason asked casually. He always answered the phone this way, saying a person's name before they could speak. But still, she wasn't prepared. The sound of his voice made it more real.

"Jason—" Her voice shook. She paused.

"Hello?"

"I'm here," she spoke slowly. "Have you talked to Ashley?"

"Is everything okay? You don't sound good."

"Have you talked to her today, by chance?" She held her breath. Maybe she had contacted him—told him where she was. Called the girls?

"No—but she texted me last night. It was around midnight here. Why?"

That would have been 2:00 a.m. in Tulum. Lauren said they'd left La Cantina at 11:30 p.m., so she'd texted him after that. Maybe from Marco's place? She hoped she told him something—gave him a clue that would help them find her.

"What did she write to you?"

"It was just a bunch of emojis. Hands in prayer, a sad face with a tear, and an ocean wave. I didn't see the message until this morning. And she hasn't written back. Why? What's going on?"

Natalie took a deep breath. "We don't know where she is."

"What?" His tone startled Natalie.

"I woke up this morning around six thirty and she wasn't in our hotel room or in Lauren's. And we've been looking, but we can't find her."

"And you're just calling me? That was three hours ago," he said, his voice rising.

"I know, I'm sorry. We thought we'd find her."

"When was the last time you saw her?"

"I'm not sure. Most of the night is a blur." Natalie squeezed the bridge of her nose.

"What?" He spoke sharply, and Natalie felt sharp pricks run up and down her arms.

"I think I may have been drugged," Natalie said, releasing a long breath.

She could hear Jason exhale. "Just tell me everything you know from beginning to end—please," he said, his words measured.

She filled him in on what she could. She left out Marco, for now. That could wait. There was so much they still didn't know.

"Have you called the police?" Jason asked when she finished.

"Yes, they should be here soon." She could see Maria talking to Lauren by the front desk.

"Soon?" Jason snickered. "You're in Mexico, Nat. I'll probably get there before they do. I'm going to try to get on the next flight out."

Natalie waited for him to say more, but she could only hear his deep breathing on the other end. "Hey, you still there?"

"I'm here, Nat. This is just not the call you want to get—*ever*."

Natalie wanted to say, *This is also not the call you want to make— ever.* Especially when she couldn't even be sure when the last time she saw Ashley was. A thought started gnawing at her insides. What if her mind was protecting her from the devastation of her own memories?

Jason sighed. "That thing you told me about a woman screaming in the water, that scares the shit out of me."

"They said they couldn't be sure what they heard," Natalie tried, even though it scared her too. She should tell Jason that she'd woken up at the beach, but she held back. She didn't want to make him mad, because it would only lead to more questions she couldn't answer right now. She'd tell him when he got here—maybe she'd have figured out what had happened by then.

"Listen, we are going to find her. We will," he said, his voice strong. "And when I get there, I'll take over and deal with the police. But until then, tell them she's a minor celebrity in the US. Actually, don't even say minor. Just that she's been on TV, well-known. Otherwise they could sit on it, ignore it even."

She pondered whether he could be right. If they would get Maria's call and the message would end up in a stack of missing persons reports that would simply collect dust. She thought of Ben again, whom she also needed to call. She was dreading that one too—would he say, *What were you thinking? How could you not remember?* "Okay," she finally said.

"I need to go—I'll call my mom," he said, then stopped. "Oh God, the girls." Fear finally crept into his voice, replacing the earlier anger.

"Like you said, we're going to find her. We have to."

"You're right. Let's stay positive. Okay, I will be there as fast as I possibly can." She could hear him scrambling and imagined him fumbling for his laptop, desperate to find the fastest route there. "I'll text you as soon as I land in Cancún."

Natalie stared at her cell phone after they said goodbye, the screen saver a picture of her daughters. Lucy had her arm slung over Meg's shoulder in that awkward way kids do when their parents tell them that's how they have to pose. But she loved it because Ben had photobombed them, his grin filling the background.

All he had ever wanted was for them to spend more time together— to not let the company she'd built take over their lives. But it had. It had seeped into every crack, every facet of her day, every interaction. It had gotten to the point where Natalie was reticent to tell Ben even the good news that was still coming in after the offer, like when *People* had called wanting to do a feature. That had happened only last week, and Natalie had been excited. What a way to go out before they sold, she'd thought. But she knew Ben would mistake her excitement over a magazine she'd been a loyal subscriber to for years as a sign she wasn't steadfast enough in her conviction to sell. Even though there was nothing she wanted more. She didn't want to lose him.

How far would she go to make sure she didn't?

CHAPTER THIRTEEN

TWO DAYS BEFORE
ASHLEY

"Let's get out of here," Ashley said to Marco, digging into her purse and pulling out a wad of pesos, tossing them on the table, still fuming at Natalie's words. Was that why she'd been siding with Lauren practically since the minute they'd landed? Because all of a sudden she was pissed about their dynamic—the same one they'd had for years? They'd busted their asses to get BloBrush off the ground, spent more nights than Ashley could count in the early days worrying about making payroll—whether their hard work and the investment of everything they had would pay off. It infuriated Ashley. How was it they could battle through those hard times with their friendship intact, only to have it slip away from them now?

Marco grabbed the money and handed it back to her and pulled several stiff pesos from his own wallet. "That should cover everyone," he said.

Ashley smiled at Marco, then looked at Lauren. "Do you want to come with us?"

"What's going on, Ash?" Lauren asked. "What are you and Nat arguing about? The offer?"

"No, actually." She sighed as she looked toward where Nat was still standing on the beach, her back to them, her choppy red hair blowing in the breeze. "It's complicated. Let's just say I can't deal with Natalie's judgments right now." She gave Marco a look. Ashley had discussed Natalie with him yesterday—her inability to see why Ashley didn't want to let go of the company. Her complaint that she should have told Natalie about Jason *first*. Ashley almost didn't recognize Nat anymore. Where was her supportive and loyal best friend?

"Please don't leave," Lauren said. "Stay here. I'm sure you guys can work it out."

"So is that a no?" Ashley asked curtly, then softened when she saw Lauren's face. This wasn't her fault. "Sorry, I didn't mean to be short. I just really need some new scenery."

"It's okay. But please stay. I don't think *anyone* should leave right now," Lauren said, giving Marco a look.

Ashley's heart was pounding. She was hurt and pissed all at the same time. "Well, I need some space to clear my head." She grabbed Marco's upper arm.

"I'll take you wherever you want to go," he said.

"Anywhere but here," Ashley said.

"Consider it done."

They started to walk away, and Ashley turned around. "I'm sorry, Lauren. It's not about you. I won't be gone long." She looked at Marco, knowing in her heart she should stay but also not sure what she'd say to Natalie if she did. She was afraid she'd make things even worse. "Maybe we can go to the beach later or do that chakra-clearing thing?" she added hopefully.

Lauren gave her an empty stare, and Ashley swallowed the guilt that rose up in her throat.

"What happened back there?" Marco asked when they'd made their way down the beach.

"Can we just walk for a bit?" Ashley said. She didn't speak again until she could no longer see Ziggy's in the distance.

"Natalie is upset with me," she finally said.

"About what?"

"Honestly?"

"Of course."

"A lot of things," she said, thinking of Natalie's harsh words, the way her nose had scrunched up as she said them, as if Ashley had let her down. "But mostly you."

"Ah," he said.

"You're not surprised?"

Marco shook his head. "Let me guess. You're hanging out with me too much."

"Something like that," Ashley said, pulling the rubber band off her wrist and twisting her hair into a ponytail.

"How do *you* feel?" Marco asked.

"About what?"

"Hanging out with me?"

Ashley's cheeks warmed, and a small butterfly bounced around her insides. But why? Sure, he was a good-looking guy, but not any more handsome than half the men in Santa Monica. Maybe it was his eyes, the way they locked into hers when she spoke. Jason only half listened. She'd ask him to bring her DayQuil, and he'd show up with NyQuil. She'd explain her schedule, and he'd still blow her phone up the next day, irritated and wondering where she was. But Marco listened, recalling every detail. And he had this really interesting way of peering into the world—it made Ashley look and think about things differently. Like earlier, when he mentioned talking to God. If anyone else had said that, she would have laughed in their face. Thought they were nuts. But when Marco said it, she believed him. It made her want to talk to God too.

"I like the way you think about things," she said, looking away. "I came here to get some answers, and for some reason I feel like maybe you're the one to give them to me. Is that crazy?"

"No," Marco said slowly. "I don't think that's crazy at all. The universe tends to bring people together for a reason."

Ashley walked toward the ocean and pulled her sandals off, wading in to her knees. Marco followed her. She turned toward him. "But I don't even know you."

"Well, then get to know me."

Ashley blushed, and asked the first question that came to her mind. "Why aren't you married?"

Marco chuckled. "Why *are* you married?"

"Seriously," Ashley said, dragging her foot through the sand beneath the clear water. "Look, a crab!" She pointed, but it was gone before Marco turned.

"I'll answer you, if you tell me first. Why did you get married?" Marco asked.

Ashley had met Jason when she was twenty-seven years old, working as an assistant at a public relations firm in Westwood. He'd come in for a meeting, wanting help generating buzz for his first food truck. He was tall—six-foot-four. He had the body of an athlete—probably a former high school or college football player, Ashley had guessed. His black hair was buzzed, making his round dark-gray eyes look bigger. He'd worn a white button-down shirt, rolled up to the elbows, and dark jeans. Ashley had been taking notes in the meeting and looked up when her boss told Jason the amount of the retainer. Jason could barely disguise his shock, meeting Ashley's eyes across the table. She'd felt her heart flutter. Jason had quickly wrapped up the meeting after that, citing a need to be somewhere else. But Ashley knew it was because he couldn't afford it—shit, hardly anyone could manage their astronomical fees. It was the conundrum of flailing businesses. They needed publicity but didn't have the money to get it. Ashley's wheels had started turning immediately with ideas for how to help him, and when her boss was at lunch she'd slyly photocopied his card so she could contact him later. She had a plan—she'd offer to quit the assistant job and work for him for a fraction of the fee her boss had mentioned.

Ashley had called Jason a few days later. He'd hired her. She'd quit her job, much to Natalie's chagrin. They'd started dating almost immediately—also a concern to Nat, who was a little self-righteous in that way you can be when you've found *the one*. She'd dated Ben for two years before he popped the question, and she'd taken a full twelve months to plan the wedding. Their courtship had been very by the book, Natalie not taking any chances, wanting to make sure he was the right guy. She'd practically followed a checklist from one of those bridal magazines on how to vet a man. Even though Ashley had been thrilled for her, she knew she'd never be like that. She didn't follow the rules; she followed her gut.

And if she wanted to date her boss, she would. She and Jason worked together side by side twelve to fifteen hours a day, spending most of their time inside the twenty-foot-by-four-foot truck. Ashley started off doing the PR and soon found herself with her hands in every aspect of the business. Ashley quickly fell for him, deciding if she could spend that amount of time in such tight quarters with someone and not be bored or even annoyed by him, it had to mean something. Plus, there was no mistaking the attraction between them. He had been kind when he didn't have to be. He had been agile and smart with his business. And he loved Ashley's ideas. They'd sit on the curb, their backs against the truck, drinking beers late at night, and she'd fire them off. He'd just laugh, telling her not to break his bank.

A year later Ashley got his food truck on the cover of *Los Angeles Magazine*. And that's when everything changed—not just for his business, but for them. They'd been out to dinner, celebrating, and he'd asked her to marry him. She'd started to laugh, but then saw his face. He was serious. But she was still so young. Sure, she loved him. More than any other man she'd dated long-term, but was she ready to commit? She honestly hadn't given it much serious thought before that night. They'd certainly never discussed it. Maybe it was the overpriced bottle of Chianti they were drinking. Or the way his eyes were almost pleading.

Or the fact that Natalie and Ben seemed so happily married, well after the honeymoon years. But she'd heard herself saying yes.

"I loved him," she finally said. "He was different back then." She turned to face Marco. "Sometimes I think I broke him. That maybe I wasn't supportive enough or that my success with the BloBrush somehow overshadowed us. I worry that he changed because of me."

Marco laid his hand on her shoulder. "Sometimes people don't reveal their true selves until life gets a little tough. And you guys were young, right?"

"I was twenty-eight. I guess you're right. Can we really know anything at that age?"

"And now you're what, forty?"

"Hey." She swatted him. "I'm thirty-nine. At least for two more months."

"Okay, so you're thirty-nine, and are you happy? If you could go back, would you do it again?"

"That's complicated."

"That sounds like a no."

"Well, for one, I have two daughters. I would never change that."

"Of course. But if you went back in time, your life would be totally different."

"Spoken like someone who doesn't have kids," Ashley said. Hannah was about to turn eleven and was a fifth grader but was already talking about middle school. Almost overnight her face had lost its baby-like roundness and was now thinned and angular. She was wearing her hair long and parted down the middle and had convinced Ashley to let her dye the ends pink. And were her legs getting longer or her shorts getting shorter or both? She was the more independent, spirited, and savvy of her daughters—the one Ashley already predicted she'd have to keep an eye on as she got older. Probably because she was more like Ashley than her younger daughter, Abby. Abbs was almost nine and had just started third grade. She had one adult front tooth and the other was halfway grown in. Her hair was cut in a sweet bob, and she cared far more about her American Girl dolls and her books than anything electronic. She seemed intent on staying a child. When they'd called yesterday, it had felt so good to hear from them.

If she hadn't married Jason, they wouldn't exist. And even though motherhood hadn't been something she adapted to instantly—in fact, in many ways she was still adjusting to it, often feeling like she got it wrong far more than she got it right—she was still their mom.

A couple of months back, after one too many times of her daughters pointing out that she rarely attended their school parties, the ones that took place in the middle of the workday—she'd usually just send the napkins and plates she'd committed to via email, pushing away the stab of guilt as she tucked them into Hannah's cherry-red backpack—she'd volunteered for the next one, a 2:00 p.m. Valentine's Day extravaganza. She'd signed up for the items she usually couldn't accommodate—things that could melt. As she lugged the cartons of cotton-candy ice cream up the stairs to the classroom, it seeped out, staining her ivory silk blouse. As soon as she arrived her phone began to blow up—the manufacturer had received some faulty wiring, and it was going to delay their first shipment to Costco. They had finally agreed, after eighteen months of Ashley practically stalking the buyer, to stock BloBrush in 250 stores as a trial, and now that deal was in jeopardy. Ashley had cringed as she hid in the corner of the classroom, hissing orders into the phone, trying to ignore the way the other moms looked at her—and the disappointed look on Hannah's face.

It was the last time her daughter had asked her to come. Later that night, after she'd apologized profusely to Hannah, she sank into a hot bath, burying the notion that she was more emotionally attached to her company than to her family. Telling herself repeatedly that when push came to shove, she'd choose them. But she wondered if that were true—because she often felt so alone despite her full house.

She looked at Marco. "Do you ever get lonely?"

"Sometimes," he said.

"But how old are you? Thirty-two? Three?"

"I'm thirty-seven."

"Really?" Ashley looked him over. "Well, the Yucatán Peninsula looks good on you."

Marco smiled. "Life doesn't have to be hard or complicated. You don't have to settle for where you've ended up. From what you've told me about Jason, it doesn't sound good between you guys."

"It's not," she confessed, thinking of the way her chest hollowed when Jason threatened divorce the night before she'd left for Tulum. Yes, she knew the right thing was to leave him. But it was the actual leaving part that scared the shit out of her.

"So then why stay? And before you say for your daughters, what about what *you* need?"

"I don't know. I feel so upside down. My marriage is falling apart. I could lose my company. My friendships are on fragile ground."

"So then take a leave of absence."

"From work?"

"From your life. Walk away. Make a fresh start."

"You sound like Natalie," Ashley said.

"What do you mean?"

Ashley told Marco about the Revlon offer. "Natalie thinks we should sell. I don't. It's why she's upset with me."

"Ah, so this explains your question at the yoga studio."

Ashley nodded.

"So why don't you want to sell?" Marco asked.

Ashley paused before answering, thinking about all the reasons why not. "If I leave Jason, I'll be giving up so much—my marriage, half of my time with the girls, my house, my assets. BloMe will be all I have. I can't give that up too."

"But maybe that's exactly what you need to do. Give up all your safety nets and see what lies beneath. Discover who you really are. And if you sell, it sounds like you'll have the money to do that."

"Maybe," Ashley said. "But money isn't going to buy my happiness. It's not that simple."

Marco shook his head hard. "This isn't about money. It's about starting over. And that might mean walking away from the company you've built. And your life as you know it." He turned and faced her. "And maybe some of your friendships too."

Ashley bent over and ran her hand through the water, taking notice of her wedding ring. How it sparkled under the sunlight. Could she really walk away from Jason? From her family as she knew it? Or was she just feeling buoyed by her surroundings—by the distance between them? "I feel stupid for thinking that coming to a beautiful place would be enough to make everything better. That Googling 'renewal and Mexico' would help me." She pointed back toward the restaurant, where she could almost make out Natalie and Lauren sitting at the table. "That being with my oldest friends would bring me comfort, you know? But it's almost made things worse. It feels like our friendships are collapsing underneath all the layers—that our foundation isn't strong enough to support us anymore."

Marco looked at her thoughtfully. "Maybe you've just outgrown each other."

Ashley stared out to the edges of the sea. So still, so calm, and she wished she could absorb its quiet energy. Had Lauren moved on emotionally? Had their separation over the past year created too many cracks in their foundation? And Natalie. Had they just tired of smoothing out the other's rough edges? Were they too close to see that they didn't fit anymore?

"Maybe," Ashley said, his words stinging. Even if they were broken, those friendships were a part of her identity. If she gave them up, would she still recognize herself?

"Here's a thought," she started. "I could agree to sell the company and *we* could run off together—go live in some little corner of Mexico where no one could ever find us again," she said, scooping up some water and flicking it at him. She bet Marco would never tell her she was a terrible mom. A bad friend.

Marco stepped closer, his eyes bright. "Wouldn't be the worst idea in the world."

Ashley stepped back instinctively. She'd been joking, but the way Marco had latched on to the idea made her a bit vexed. "Come on, let's go get something to eat—maybe the carne asada you were bragging about. I barely had two bites of egg whites before Natalie went off on me."

Her phone buzzed in her pocket. Jason. She frowned at his message. **We need to talk.**

"You don't look very happy," Marco said, peering at the screen over her shoulder.

Ashley pulled it away quickly, irked.

"Oh! Got something to hide, do we—who is it?"

"No one I feel like talking to," she said quickly, throwing her phone in her purse.

"You're a terrible liar," Marco said and poked her lightly, and she laughed despite her earlier irritation.

"Not always," Ashley said mysteriously and stuck her tongue out at him. She tried to ascertain the last time she'd been playful with Jason, but she couldn't. There was something about Marco that both centered her and made her feel a little off-balance, her emotions flying up and down like a child on a seesaw.

~

"You're right, this is amazing," Ashley said later as a piece of carne asada fell out of her mouth and hit the dirty sidewalk. "Sorry . . . it's just so good. I barely even taste the cilantro!"

"I told you—best carne asada in Tulum. Make that Mexico," Marco said, taking a giant bite of his burrito. "And I'm very proud of you that you didn't ask them to pull it out. That would have been embarrassing."

Ashley forked more meat into a corn tortilla, topped it with hot sauce, and took a bite. She finished chewing. "You were right. I thought we had good Mexican steak at home because we're so close to the border. But this is like nothing I've ever tasted. It melts in your mouth."

"Stick with me; I'll show you all the secrets of Mexico," Marco said, taking his last bite and wiping his mouth with a napkin.

Ashley set her taco down and took a swig of her Corona, thinking about her next words. "I'd love that, but I do need to be with my friends too. It's why we're here."

"I get it. Four's a crowd?"

"I think we're nearing that territory, yes. Natalie is already irritated. She thinks something's going on with us!" Ashley huffed.

"Isn't it?" Marco said, his eyes locked on hers.

"Marco, I'm married," Ashley said quietly as her stomach swirled, wondering if she was even allowed to use that as a defense after telling him how unhappy she was with Jason.

"It doesn't seem like a happy marriage."

"Can we change the subject? I'm so tired of thinking about Jason," Ashley said and tried to ignore the pinch of anxiety in her gut. Like she had said too much, taken too much of a stand. "Know a good place to get some flan? I've been craving it since I got here."

"You're avoiding." Marco smiled.

"Hey, it's what I do. I avoid talking about anything heavy. I always have. I asked Nat and Lauren to come here, and then I've been too chickenshit to actually talk to them about our issues."

"You mean what happened at the funeral?" Marco asked, referencing what Ashley had told him when they'd taken a walk alone on the beach yesterday.

"Yes. The first day we were here, Lauren just seemed so standoffish."

111

"Not what you expected?"

Ashley played with the beaded bracelet on her wrist. "This may sound stupid, but I wanted it to be easy. We've been friends for so long, you know?" She swallowed to push back the tears that she felt rising up. "I'd hoped that inviting her here was enough of an olive branch."

"You figured because she accepted the invitation, she was ready to move forward," Marco said, grazing his hand across her arm.

"Exactly!" Ashley exclaimed. "I hadn't thought about it that way, but you're right." Marco had lasered in on what had really been bothering her: how Lauren's cold demeanor had felt like a punch to the gut and had essentially capsized the dynamic of their trip. And even when they had drinks on the beach and they'd had fun, was it only because they hadn't talked about anything significant? She worried that once they tried, it would be a disaster. Especially after the fight she'd just had with Natalie. She was quickly starting to lose hope, to fear that she might leave here feeling worse than she did when she'd arrived.

"You can only do so much. At some point, Lauren has to forgive you, or maybe you should move on," Marco said thoughtfully. "If she's truly your friend, she should understand you didn't mean to hurt her. And Natalie, she needs to look past herself. To give you some grace. Don't you deserve that?"

Ashley pondered his words. Their issues weren't as simple as Marco had framed them. She was still desperate to find the right words to make Lauren understand she'd never meant to hurt her—to make Natalie see why she hadn't confided in her. "That's a very Zen approach," she said, careful to keep the sarcasm out of her voice, knowing he was only trying to help. That he cared.

"Being here makes it easy to be that way. This life." He spread his arms out. "This land has so much spirituality. We aren't far from where the Maya started it all—Chichén Itzá."

"Chichén Itzá?"

"Don't tell me you've never heard of the Mayan ruins?"

"I haven't." Ashley felt dumb, bracing herself for Marco to call her on it. She looked at him, realizing that, of course, he wasn't going to do that. That was Jason's territory, and it wasn't normal.

"They're about two hours from here, and many consider them to be the eighth wonder of the world." He leaned in. "It's a spiritual beacon."

"That sounds amazing. I've heard you mention the Maya. How do you know so much about their history?"

"I've been to Chichén Itzá multiple times, and I've read every book on the Maya that I could get my hands on. Ashley, you must go there," he said, his voice quickening with excitement. "I'll take you."

Ashley took another sip of her beer. "Thank you, but I think maybe my friends and I should go—just the three of us," she pushed back. "It sounds like the perfect place for me to talk to Lauren. To get back on track with Natalie. After all, that's why we're here."

"You're right—that would be a wonderful place to resolve your conflicts. To strip away everything and remind yourselves why you all became friends in the first place. It doesn't sound like the chakra thing is happening." He smirked. "I should stay back anyway—I have a bunch of bookkeeping to get done at work. And if you want, I can set you up with a private tour. To climb El Castillo."

"That would be great," Ashley said, relieved that he wasn't upset. She had thought he had been a little bit pushy but now realized it was just his passion for Chichén Itzá.

"You don't understand. People aren't allowed to climb it anymore. This tour, it would be after hours. But in my opinion, it's the only true way to feel the power of the Maya."

"Like we'd be the only people there? Is that legal?"

Marco smiled. "Not really. But trust me, it's worth the risk to be able to climb that pyramid."

Ashley pondered his suggestion. It didn't worry her to skirt the rules a little, but she knew it would be hard to convince Natalie. She wouldn't even park in a red zone to drop off her kids at dance class. "You really think it would help?"

"I do. It is sacred up there. I try to go often, just to center myself. Maybe you'll find the balance you're seeking too."

Ashley clapped her hands. "Okay, we are totally doing that. I'm in!" She looked at Marco. "Thank you."

"For what?" Marco asked.

"For everything," Ashley said.

Marco grabbed her arm and pulled her in close. "Ashley," he whispered. "Do you feel what's going on here?"

Ashley's heart jumped. Because she did. But was it really something? Or was she just so unhappy with Jason that it made Marco seem more appealing than he really was, simply because he was the polar opposite? "I do. But I need to be careful."

"With what?" His mouth was so close to hers. It would be so easy for her to lean in and touch her lips to his.

"With my heart. And with yours," Ashley said, pulling back slightly. Her mind was so crowded right now—puzzled by Lauren, frustrated by Natalie, furious with Jason. Adding Marco into that mix, as tempting as it sounded, would make things more complicated. And she had all the complications she could handle at the moment. "We should go."

Marco looked down at his hands. Ashley pushed her chair back and stood. "Come on," she said, holding out her hand to him. "This isn't a no. It's a *not right now*. Okay? I need to think."

"Just don't wait too long," he said, taking her hand in his as they walked out to the dirt parking lot where his dusty car sat.

She followed him, wondering whether he might hold the answers she was seeking.

CHAPTER FOURTEEN

TWO DAYS BEFORE
NATALIE

"I can't believe she left with him." Natalie watched Marco and Ashley walk down the beach until their figures disappeared into the horizon.

"She just needs to cool off," Lauren said. "She's obviously going through something."

Natalie sighed. She wished she could snap her fingers and have the Revlon offer figured out, wipe the funeral argument from their minds. She knew all of this weighed heavily on Ashley. But why was she turning to Marco instead of them? It made Natalie wonder whether there was more going on that she wasn't telling them.

"Why didn't you go with them?" Nat asked.

Lauren hesitated briefly. "I didn't want to leave you by yourself."

"Really?" Natalie smiled.

"Don't look so surprised—you're my friend too. Always have been."

"I know," Natalie said sheepishly. "It's just—"

"You think my loyalty is to Ash."

"Isn't it?" Natalie asked as she pulled up the currency exchange app on her phone and made sure Marco had left enough money. She had to admit that when Lauren told her he'd paid, she'd been surprised. A part of her had speculated that he might be clinging to Ashley because of her celebrity, her money.

"It's complicated," Lauren said, then paused briefly. "Especially after Geoff's death. I can't believe it's gone on for this long. That we were both so stubborn."

"I'm sorry that it has. That we *all* were stubborn," Natalie said, thinking back to the funeral, how Ashley was in a fit of tears as they drove back to Natalie's house. Natalie had been shaking as she held the steering wheel, playing back the argument in the coat closet, trying to reason how Lauren could believe Ashley was responsible for Geoff's death. She knew it had to be the grief talking, but she had been so venomous. It was hard for Natalie to reconcile that behavior with the Lauren she'd always known. She and Ashley had sat on Natalie's back patio that night, drinking wine until Ashley's eyelids started to droop—Natalie tucking her in to the guest bed so she could sleep it off. What had struck Natalie was that Ashley hadn't been angry with Lauren at all.

"Maybe if I'd just kept my mouth shut, Geoff would still be here," Ashley had said, her words garbled. "I think she might be right. That it's my fault."

Natalie had shaken her head hard. "No. That's crazy. It is not your fault!"

"I'm going to call her and apologize," Ashley had said, as if she hadn't heard Natalie.

"That's the chardonnay talking!" Natalie had argued. For some reason she felt adamant that Ashley not give in. She'd even talked her out of it again the next morning, once she'd sobered up.

At the time she'd chalked it up to indignation, because rationally there was no way Ashley was responsible. But maybe Natalie had just wanted to have Ashley to herself. It was a dark thought that hibernated within her, revealing itself only when she lay between slumber and wakefulness.

"You know," Lauren began, "I thought for a long time that I didn't need you guys. I told myself I was okay. But being here"—she waved her hand toward the beach—"has made me realize that I do."

"It hasn't exactly been pretty," Natalie said, thinking about her words to Ashley down on the beach. The way her face had fallen when she accused her of being selfish.

Lauren motioned for more coffee and waited patiently as the server poured the dark liquid into their ceramic mugs before commenting. "Has it ever been, though? There was that fight you and Ash got in at Jake's wedding. What the hell were you even arguing about anyway?"

Natalie cringed at the memory. "We were drunk," she said. "One of the many reasons I'm not a big drinker. All I remember was being angry at her after she said something about me dating him—right in front of his mom. Such poor taste. I wanted to pull all that beautiful chestnut hair out of her head!"

Lauren chuckled. "Thank God I was there to intervene."

Natalie swirled a spoon in her coffee until the creamer blended in. She could already feel her earlier anger at Ashley dissipating. "Isn't it weird? How you can be so mad, and then it can all fade away? Like it never happened?"

"If you're lucky, that's how it goes. The situation with Geoff wasn't quite the same."

"Oh no, I wasn't comparing—" Natalie backtracked.

"It's okay," Lauren interrupted. "I know you weren't. I think my point is that the worst thing we can do is romanticize what we all had. We had conflict before, like people do. And we have it now. The question is, Do we want to be the kind of people who get over it?"

"That's a tough question," Natalie said a few moments later.

"You bet your ass it is," Lauren said.

Natalie wished she could see her eyes behind her dark sunglasses.

"Do you still romanticize your relationship with Geoff?" Natalie asked, and held her breath slightly. Sometimes Natalie felt like she did that with Ashley. That she clung so hard to their long history that she had lost the ability to be objective about their current relationship.

Lauren waited a beat before answering. "Of course. I mean, I haven't forgotten the abuse." She turned and faced Natalie. "You can't. But he was so much more than that, you know? Like the way he tiptoed around in the early morning when he left for work. He'd come in and kiss me lightly before leaving, whispering that he loved me." Lauren wiped a tear that slid out from under her sunglasses. "And for some reason that's the thing I miss about him most. Those mornings. I'd give almost anything to have one more."

Natalie reached over and grabbed her hand, and to her surprise Lauren squeezed it tight, forming a bridge between their chairs. "I'm sorry," she said.

"So am I," Lauren said softly, and they sat there like that, holding hands in silence, until Natalie's phone began to vibrate.

"Thank you for talking to me about this, for trusting me," Natalie said. They'd never discussed Geoff before, not like this. Natalie felt hopeful that they'd broken through the emotional barrier that had been between them since his funeral. She glanced at the screen. "It's the kids," she said, "but I can call them back later."

"No, take it," Lauren insisted. "I'm okay."

Natalie stared at the phone ringing.

"Really!" Lauren reiterated. "Go talk to your family."

Natalie nodded and grabbed her phone off the table, walking away to answer it.

"Hi, honey!" Natalie said, grinning at the image of Meg, her hair tied into two French braids, a white satin headband in her hair. She would be turning eleven in a few months, and Natalie could sense that time was beginning to speed up. Soon she'd ditch the little-girl hair accessories and want to shop for bralettes. The milestone moments she'd be posting on Facebook flashed through her mind. Meg's first day of middle school, of high school, getting her driver's license, homecoming dances, her college acceptance letter, senior prom, high school gradua-tion. Then, just like that, she'd be gone. Time Natalie could never get back.

"Hey, Mom," she said, and Natalie could see she was sitting in her bedroom, on her blue and white striped comforter. "Are you having fun?"

"I am, but I miss you guys! What are you up to today?"

Natalie listened as Meg detailed every single thing she'd done since waking up. How Lucy had barged in at 6:32 a.m. and woken her up. How Ben had made French toast, the kind with the bananas that she loved. Then Lucy popped in, her red hair twisted into two messy braids—an obvious attempt at copying her sister—arguing that it had actually been 6:35 a.m. Natalie smiled as they sparred with each other about the time, Lucy finally relenting and running off to grab a picture she'd drawn, to show Natalie. Meg was just starting to tell her about a new book she was reading when Natalie saw Ben come into the frame.

"Hi!" he said, easing the phone away from Meg.

"Hey," Natalie said. She could see he hadn't shaved since she'd left, the gray and brown stubble fighting for space on his chin, his nutmeg eyes looking tired.

"So, what's the word?" Ben asked, and Natalie's heart dropped—she knew he wasn't inquiring how white the sand was, whether the water was as warm as they'd read, or if she'd enjoyed the ceviche. He was ask-ing about the Revlon offer—again. He had left Meg's room and was now in theirs. She saw their unmade California king in the background, Ben never so much as pulling up the duvet most mornings. "Did you get her drunk and have her sign the agreement?" He laughed, an empty sound that made Natalie feel uneasy.

"We just got here," she said, attempting to keep the annoyance out of her voice. "It's not going to happen overnight. But it will happen. Just trust me, I've got this. But you have to let me handle it in my own way."

"Okay," he said, but it came out sounding like a challenge. "But I don't understand—why can't you just tell her what's *really* going on?"

"Because I'm embarrassed!" she said, finally losing her patience. "I feel like an idiot."

"But I'm the one who screwed up—made the bad investment—lost everything. Not you."

"You don't get it. That's the humiliating part. Telling her my husband gambled away all of our money."

"Not gambled—invested," Ben said, his eyes bloodshot. He clearly hadn't been sleeping. And neither had she, lying in bed, the stress of their finances weighing so hard on her chest she could barely breathe. But she was good at compartmentalizing her feelings. And in the light of day, she could manage the stress of their financial situation much better simply by not thinking about it. Talking to Ben about it never helped. She avoided it, but he always found a way to work it into their conversations.

"Don't do that. You don't get to do that."

"Fine," he said quietly. She knew she was kicking him while he was down, but she was so angry at him. It was as if she couldn't control her emotions. She swung between being furious and trying to be understanding. He hadn't gone to the casino. He thought the app he was investing in was solid. And had it worked out and he'd come to her with the opposite news, would she still have been pissed he'd gone behind her back?

"I'm sorry about the credit card," he said.

"Did the bill not get paid? Or, God, have we maxed that one out too?" Natalie cringed, thinking of the conversation they'd had six weeks ago when he'd told her what he'd done. He'd sat her down and confessed that he'd made some terrible investments. That he'd gambled with their savings, the girls' college funds, and lost. It had gutted Natalie, who still drove her old reliable Toyota Prius. She had sacrificed so much to make it—to succeed. When they'd built the business she'd cleared out her

401(k), bought her clothes on sale, scouring the internet for deals when they had to make a purchase like a washing machine. And to this day, she still lived as if they didn't have the kind of money they did. And now Ben had taken away her opportunity to eventually enjoy any of it. He'd sobbed, telling her they had sixty days—maybe ninety if they didn't pay certain bills—before their checking account was empty. She'd only seen him cry like that one other time—when his father died. Natalie had lain in bed that night, her gut twisting. What would become of them?

"It's over the limit," he finally said. She heard the defeat in his voice, saw it in his eyes. "If we skip a house payment or two, even three, it will buy us more time. I did some research. The bank won't come after us for a while."

"I'm not going to squat in my own home!" Natalie started breathing heavily. Were they really having this conversation?

Ben rubbed his eyes. "I'm sorry. I don't know what I was thinking."

"You weren't, obviously," Natalie said sharply, feeling angry that she actually used to love the way Ben took risks. It had been one of the things that had initially attracted her to him—the opposite of her own personality.

"Listen," Ben said. "If you can just convince Ashley to sell, all of these problems go away. If you would just tell her—"

"We've already been over this," Natalie interrupted. "I'm not telling her what you did." They'd been so excited when the offer from Revlon had come in, just days after Ben's admission. It had felt like a sign as they'd jumped up and down in their bedroom, screaming with joy. But that feeling had quickly dissipated once Natalie had realized Ashley would most likely never sell. Ben didn't understand why she couldn't confess their missteps. Why she wouldn't let Ashley swoop in and save the day, the same woman who purchased an $80,000 car on her lunch break because she felt like it. Natalie had always been the one who saved her money, who didn't let her impulses sway her. She was embarrassed to her core that Ben had put them in this position.

No. She was going to convince Ashley another way.

"Natalie—"

Natalie snapped. "Stop. I'll figure it out. That's the whole reason I came here, isn't it? To bail you out?"

He shook his head. "I know. I screwed up. I don't know how many more times I can say I'm sorry at this point."

"You're right." Natalie sighed. She hadn't had sex with him since he'd told her. She couldn't so much as kiss him. She felt betrayed, like he'd been unfaithful. She questioned why he'd hid it from her for so long. Had he lied about other things too? She didn't know if she'd ever be able to trust him again. Or what would happen to their marriage. But for now, she was focused on getting Ashley to sell so she didn't lose everything.

Especially not her house. If they didn't sell, she'd have to give up the two-story craftsman with the blue door, which sat only a few blocks from the beach. When they'd bought the fixer-upper that they'd slowly renovated over several years, Natalie had been pregnant with Meg. She'd imagined packing up the bright red Radio Flyer wagon she'd had her eye on and spending long days lying on the sand with her growing family. She could count on one hand how many times that had happened, BloMe launching the year after Lucy was born, the daily stresses of their startup inhaling all the small moments she'd hoped for. That house marked who she'd wanted to be as a mother. Giving it up, letting go of the pencil marks in the closet that measured the girls' height as they grew up, would be like handing over the keys to the life she *really* wanted.

"I know you don't like this option, but we could transfer them to public school sooner."

"No. It will crush them," Natalie said. "This isn't their fault."

"I'll tell them it's mine." Ben ran a hand through his thick hair.

"Like that will make it any better," Natalie shot back.

"We can still find our way out of this. You just need to stay focused."

"*I* need to stay focused?" Natalie said sharply. "Why is fixing *your* mistake suddenly my problem?"

"Because we don't have another option."

"Because of *you*. Why are you pushing me so hard? I feel like I can't breathe." She clenched her teeth together so she didn't completely lose her temper. But she was close to saying hurtful things she couldn't take back.

"You're right, I'm sorry," he said softly, staring off at something in the distance.

She knew he was embarrassed, humiliated, and frightened. And even though unleashing her anger on him right now might make her feel better for a few seconds, it wasn't going to bring their money back. "Look, I've had a hard enough time processing what's happened. And now there is so much pressure on *me* to fix it. I will fix it. Just let me take care of it my way. Please."

She hated that selling had become their only way out. Not because she didn't want out, because she did, but that it had become so desperate. And she didn't want to have the same argument again—that keeping her job wasn't enough to fix this . . . her annual salary wouldn't make much of a dent. That taking money out from the company had to be approved by Ashley because she'd also have to take the same amount. And both of them withdrawing that much wasn't even possible. Their company couldn't afford that big a hit.

"I shouldn't have been so pushy. I just hate that I've done this to us, and I can't solve it."

She pushed back the tears that were threatening to fall. "I'm going to get her to change her mind."

She hung up the phone and raised her head to the sky, a dark storm cloud making its way toward her from the east. "What if I can't convince her?" she whispered to herself. She almost always let Ashley have her way. She could count on one hand the number of times she'd put her foot down about something at work. Would Ashley understand it was Natalie's turn to get her way? She stood there until the ominous cloud was directly overhead, and let her tears mix with the rain it brought, finally composing herself and walking back to where Lauren sat, as if the world she'd built wasn't crumbling.

~

Later, after Natalie composed herself in the bathroom, she and Lauren walked back to their hotel and made themselves comfortable on the beach chairs under the thatched umbrellas, a stack of tabloid magazines and a half-empty pitcher of piña coladas between them. Natalie sat, rereading the same article, her conversation with Ben replaying in her mind. She had thought she'd have more time to figure everything out.

Ashley walked up, kicking up sand from under her flip-flops.

"Hey," she said, and sat at the end of Natalie's beach chair, Natalie shifting slightly to make room. She wondered again if she really could convince her. When Ashley made her mind up about something, that was usually it. Would Natalie finally playing her *I never ask you to do anything for me* card be enough?

"Hey," Natalie said, matching her tone.

Lauren lowered her sunglasses and said nothing.

"I'm sorry. I know Marco has been around a lot, and I get why you're annoyed." Ashley looked at Natalie. "And you probably are too," she said to Lauren.

Natalie frowned slightly, unsure how to respond. She felt exhausted by her own problems. The one with Ashley felt far away. But she needed to push herself to be here in this moment. To focus on their friendship. That was going to be the key to solving her financial problems.

"Thanks for saying that," Lauren finally said, glancing over at Natalie. "He's nice, but he was kind of getting on my nerves."

"Yes, thank you," Natalie echoed, wondering if her words sounded as flimsy as they felt.

If they did, Ashley didn't seem to notice. "I have an idea. Have you guys ever heard of Chichén Itzá?" she asked, speaking rapidly.

"I've read about it," Lauren said. "It's supposed to be amazing."

"I'm happy to hear you say that, because I set up a private tour for us tomorrow. We'll get up close and personal with the Mayan ruins!" she exclaimed. "It's going to be awesome. Just what we need."

"How did you find out about it?" Natalie asked, even though she already knew the answer. Marco.

"Does it matter?" Ashley said, her tone sharp, but she quickly softened. "If you're asking if Marco is coming, the answer is no. This is my way of saying sorry for not being a good friend. Before now and on this trip," she added, shooting a quick look at Lauren, who gave her a small smile in return. "Please? Will you guys come?"

"I'm in," Lauren said. "I'm a sucker for ancient civilizations that disappeared mysteriously!"

"Nat?" Ashley grabbed her leg. "I'm sorry, okay? Can we just move on?"

Ashley's eyes sparkled with anticipation. Natalie knew she needed to let it go—so she could get back on the right footing with Ashley, to help her realize that selling was the best thing for both of them. She forced a smile, not unlike the one she'd plastered on for the last six weeks. She could do this. Be the Natalie Ashley wanted her to be. "Yes," she said. "On one condition."

"What?" Ashley said, her eyes darkening, apprehensive.

"You buy the next round of piña coladas," Natalie deadpanned, and Lauren and Ashley giggled loudly, causing the older couple next to them to look over with interest.

"That, I can do," Ashley said, heading toward the bar. "I'll be right back!"

Lauren and Natalie sat in silence for a few beats.

"You okay?" Lauren asked Natalie.

"Sure? Why do you ask?" Natalie lied. She knew Ben's call had rattled her and it showed.

Lauren cocked her head. "You've seemed a little off since you took that phone call."

Natalie peered at Lauren. How good it would feel to unload her problems, to relieve some of the pressure that had built up inside her chest. Maybe she could even help her convince Ash to sell? But no. Even though Lauren's anger toward Ashley was clearly still lingering, her loyalty had always been to Ash. Natalie didn't blame her, because she was often the same way. She'd just have to rely on herself—and hope she had it in her to change Ashley's mind.

She turned to Lauren and lied once more. "I promise, everything is fine."

CHAPTER FIFTEEN

ONE DAY BEFORE
LAUREN

"That's our ride," Ashley said, pointing to a black SUV parked in front of the hotel. "I was planning to rent a car, but Marco nixed it." She lowered her voice. "He said corrupt cops are notorious for pulling over American tourists and demanding huge sums of money or threatening jail time. So he hired a driver for us. Wasn't that sweet?"

Lauren caught Natalie's eye. She was so relieved he wasn't coming today, she'd secretly low-fived Natalie when they were getting coffee in the restaurant earlier. They both smiled at the memory now.

As they rode down the two-lane highway toward Chichén Itzá, Lauren settled into her seat for the two-hour drive and stared out the window, taking in the thatch-roofed houses—wondering how the seemingly weak structures survived the hot, humid rainstorms that seemed common here. She also wondered how the roadside merchants peddling handmade statues and jewelry made a living wage. So much poverty, yet she hadn't met one person who didn't seem happy, who didn't greet her with a smile and a seemingly open heart. From where did their optimism stem? Back home, Lauren's morning sometimes went off the rails if someone cut her off on the 405 freeway. That realization shamed her as they crossed through small towns and joyful children kicked soccer balls into rusted goals on desolate dirt-caked fields.

"Look at that poor little guy," Ashley said, pointing to a malnour-ished dog lying on the side of the road. "So many homeless pups. I wish we could take them all home."

"It is really sad. That one is missing a tail," Lauren said, pointing to a black-and-white mutt. "I read that Mexico doesn't have a shelter system like in the US. The dogs have no place to go." She thought of Marco's dog, Spencer. How he'd rescued him. That had been a nice thing to do—maybe she should focus more on the kindness in people and stop being so skeptical.

"It breaks my heart. Maybe I'll adopt a dog when I get back home," Ashley said more to herself than to them, as if she didn't believe she'd actually do it.

"So I did some reading about Chichén Itzá and El Castillo last night after you fell asleep," Natalie said, ignoring her declaration.

"And?" Ashley asked.

To Lauren, Ashley's tone sounded accusatory. She wondered what things were like in their hotel room. There was no escaping each other in their king-size bed.

"Well, for one, are you aware they closed El Castillo to the public in 2006 after an eighty-year-old woman fell off the steps and died?"

"I'm sure it was just because she was old, right?" Lauren said.

"Apparently her fall was the last straw, as there had also been inci-dents of people vandalizing it. They don't let anyone up those stairs anymore—or inside." She gave Ashley a worried look.

"Hence the private VIP tour," Ashley said. "I'm sure our guide will make sure we don't fall off," she joked, then continued when Natalie didn't respond with more than wide eyes. "This is going to be an amaz-ing experience. When the ruins close at dusk, our guide will show us around the ruins and explain the mysterious history of the Mayan people. At the end we'll climb to the top of El Castillo. Think about it—this is like getting access to the Vatican secret archives or Club 33 at Disneyland." Ashley spoke rapidly, and Lauren asked herself, not for the first time, why it was so important to her that they visit Chichén Itzá. She'd been talking about it nonstop since yesterday.

"Well, as amazing as it sounds, have you forgotten we're both CEOs of a pretty well-known company? What if we get caught? The media would have a field day." Natalie chewed on her lower lip.

"I doubt that we'll get caught. I think the Mexican police are pretty busy with the drug war that's going on," Ashley said.

Lauren watched Natalie's reaction to what Ashley had said. She sensed that Natalie was on the verge of initiating a debate. She was obviously uneasy about the climb, but Lauren knew Ashley was unlikely to give that much weight and back down from her position. Lauren decided to step in, hoping she could be the tiebreaker. "I think Natalie brings up a good point," Lauren said, and Natalie smiled at her gratefully. It felt a little foreign to take Nat's side against Ashley. But something had shifted yesterday. Ashley's alliance with Marco had inadvertently brought Lauren and Natalie closer together, which felt good.

Ashley pretended to pout, then looked at Natalie. "Fine. I do see your point."

Natalie's face changed quickly from strain to relief. "I really appreciate you setting it up, but I'm going to skip the part where we climb. Is that okay? I'll be able to keep watch, just in case," she said. "But the tour sounds amazing."

"Always doing the right thing. It can drive me nuts, but I suppose it's who you are." Ashley smiled.

"You have a love-hate relationship with my rule-follower side." Natalie poked her in the arm.

"Right now I kind of hate on her, but it's all good." She laughed, then turned to Lauren. "What about you?"

"An illegal climb to the top of a restricted monument? I'm definitely game! If I've learned one thing this year, it's that life is short," Lauren deadpanned. Then she caught sight of Ashley's and Natalie's faces. It was clear they didn't know how to respond to a joke Annie would have cackled at. As she laid her head against the window and drifted off to sleep, she hoped that one day soon the three of them would be in sync again.

❧

Two hours later, Lauren opened her eyes as the car turned down a long driveway. She immediately noticed the silence in the car. Natalie was reading something on her phone, and Ashley was staring out the window. She wondered if they'd talked at all while she'd slept. She hoped they had, but there was tension in the air.

The driver dropped them off at Villas Arqueológicas, a hotel just outside of Chichén Itzá. Felipe, a stout man with a thin mustache that tipped up at the ends, found them as dusk was approaching and quickly explained that they would be cutting through the jungle that connected to the back of the ruins. "You'll need to be quiet," he said. "We have to pay the security guards when we get to the back entrance."

Ashley reached into her bag and drew out a stack of pesos, counting them quickly. Felipe took the stack from her and deposited it into his fanny pack in one swift motion.

Two stoic men stood guard behind the ruins and gave a slight nod of recognition when Felipe's profile became clear. They spoke in rapid Spanish, Lauren picking up only a few words. *Señoritas. Dinero. Subir.* Women. Money. To climb.

After a dramatic pause, the men pulled back the thick rope that balanced the battered wood "Closed" sign, waving them in with their guns. Lauren tried not to look at their weapons, but they were so ominous, almost taking over their lithe uniformed bodies.

The women walked past tentatively, finally breaking stride as they came into a clearing, Felipe pointing out El Castillo, which was dazzling in the fading light. Lauren felt a shiver slice through her body as the pyramid came into view. She couldn't be sure whether it was a confirmation that they were on the right path or a warning to leave.

Felipe turned to them, tightened his fanny pack, and smiled for the first time. "Are you ladies ready for a life-changing experience?"

Lauren walked behind the others as Felipe started talking about the ruins. She took in the majestic view of the ancient Mayan city that stretched out before her. She held out her hand and let the vibration in the air penetrate it. Felipe explained that the Mayan culture was one of deep religion and human sacrifice, and if you concentrated, you could feel their spirits. Lauren could definitely feel their energy. She had so many questions about who they were—why so many of them had chosen death.

Geoff hadn't chosen death. It had struck him quick as lightning. Ashley and Lauren were the bolts that killed him. Ashley, who had stumbled upon Lauren's deepest secret, that Geoff was physically abusive. And Lauren, who had let herself be convinced by Ashley to leave him, adamant there was no other choice. But there had been no choosing for Geoff. One minute he was there, in their foyer, as Lauren announced she was leaving, and then he was gone. Leaving her first, in the most final way. Intellectually, she understood they hadn't killed him. But in her darkest moments, the small tendrils of guilt still haunted her.

"This is the observatory, also referred to as El Caracol, or the snail, because of the sprawling spiral staircase located within the tower. It is aligned with the movement of Venus," Felipe said, gesturing toward a pyramid. "The Maya were incredibly gifted astrologers. The staircase here in front"—he pointed—"faces west and is where Venus and El Caracol connect perfectly. At summer solstice sunrise and winter solstice sunset, the northeast and southwest corners align."

"Wow," Natalie said, stepping closer to the pyramid. "How could they have ever known that?"

"The Maya were very advanced for their time," Felipe mused. "It's why Chichén Itzá, and El Castillo in particular, is thought to be the eighth wonder of the world."

"Yet no one knows why they just disappeared?" Natalie asked, frowning. "Their civilization was just wiped out?"

"There are many theories. Great floods, civil wars, even aliens. Although that's more of a conspiracy theory." Felipe walked ahead. "Other structures of Chichén Itzá include the Temples of the Jaguar, the Temple of the Warriors, and the Great Ball Court, and all have significance to Mayan mythology." Felipe paused. "Do you know what cenotes are?"

"Sinkholes?" Ashley responded. "I heard some people at our hotel talking about them."

"It is true that cenotes are natural sinkholes that result from the collapse of limestone bedrock that exposes the groundwater underneath. But they are also very spiritual. They are mouths that opened into the underworld. For example, the Sacred Cenote, not far from where we are standing now, is believed to have received many human offerings."

"Really?" Ashley asked.

"*Sí,*" Felipe said. "The Maya believed it was an honor to be sacrificed." He turned to face Lauren, holding her gaze.

She felt tingles through her entire body. Had Geoff ultimately been sacrificed for her own freedom? She glanced at Ashley, her face scrunched up as Felipe spoke. It was the same look she'd worn when she met Geoff, as she silently calculated his power suit and dark hair, peppered with gray. The same look she'd tried to hide when Lauren showed up for brunch in the brand-new silver Audi he'd purchased, which Lauren had paid for with the bruises hidden under her lilac wrap sweater. She was upset with Ashley for so many reasons, but the hardest thing to swallow was that it was likely she had known all along who Geoff really was.

"They did not fear death the way people do today. They saw it as an opportunity for passage to the underworld. Where they could begin again. According to many people who have studied the symbols carved into the walls of the Great Ball Court, where I will take you next, it was interpreted as a positive to be the loser of those games. The team captain would sacrifice himself to the gods—getting beheaded, his skull then thrown into the Sacred Cenote. They say there are thousands of skulls at the bottom and also gold, carved jade, pottery, flint—offerings from the Maya." Felipe paused, seemingly for effect. "There's also a cenote that was discovered under El Castillo."

"Wow," Lauren said, looking toward the bottom of the pyramid then over at Ashley, who smiled.

"It's so overwhelming—in a good way," Natalie said, looping her arm through Lauren's.

Lauren walked with Natalie over to Ashley and wrapped her free arm around Ashley's. "Now we're all joined," she said.

"Just how I want it," Ashley said, and rested her head on Lauren's shoulder briefly.

Felipe continued his tour and the women shared a silent smile at his lack of understanding of their moment. "They found the cenote in 2009, and they are planning an excavation," Felipe said. "They are quite certain that the cenote is over one hundred feet long and sixty-five feet deep." He started to walk and motioned for them to join him. "Come, now I will show you the Great Ball Court."

They walked in silence, finally arriving at a grass court surrounded by huge limestone walls, a large ring high above on each side.

"So the Maya played this ball game on that court hoping to lose, hoping to die?" Lauren asked after Felipe explained the ancient ball game, her mind gravitating toward Geoff again. At the hospital, when she'd said goodbye to him, she'd been numb. At the funeral she'd felt almost as if she were acting the part of the widow—her true feelings of grief just beyond reach, blocked by her irrational anger. But here, surrounded by the spirits of hundreds of thousands of people, she felt him. She felt connected, the conflicted feelings she'd often experienced while he was alive filling her thoughts. How he swung from affection to anger in the blink of an eye, the very smallest things setting him off. Lauren had often felt as if she were walking a tightrope—one small deviance and she'd get badly hurt. She truly hoped he was settled now—that his death had ultimately brought him peace. In life, it had eluded him.

"Don't think I didn't see the way you were looking at him," Geoff had said one night as Lauren set her red clutch on the kitchen counter and began to peel off her jacket. His voice was low and deep, often the prelude to his rage. She didn't have to ask who he was talking about—the server at dinner had winked at her when he'd placed her petite filet with béarnaise sauce on the table. She hadn't needed to look at Geoff to know there would be consequences either. She barely made a sound when he slammed her against the taupe wall of their living room, curling into the fetal position as he kicked her.

The next day she'd winced when Ashley touched her arm, and her secret had come spilling out, like a milk carton crashing onto the kitchen floor. Ashley had bundled Lauren into her car and driven her to her house, refusing to let her leave until she agreed to end things with Geoff. They'd walked down to the beach and sat on the sand, Ashley holding her tight as she cried. Promising her she could stay with her as long she liked. Promising that she deserved better. Promising it would all be okay.

She didn't keep those promises.

Their fight at Geoff's funeral was ugly, the three of them shoved into the coat check, Lauren broken and desperate to place blame. Standing just inches from Ashley's face.

You killed him. You are the reason he's dead.

Ashley exploding with tears as she defended herself. *He was hurting you. I was trying to help you. Save you from a monster.*

Natalie coming to Ashley's defense. *Calm down. You can't really believe she's responsible. I would have tried to help you too, if I'd known.*

Neither of them understood how you could both love and fear someone, how you could wish to be free but then lament your freedom.

I'll never forgive you.

The words had escaped Lauren before she could take them back. Anger raged inside of her, and she pointed at the door. *I don't need friends like you. Leave. And don't come back.*

So they had, hesitating slightly at the door, Lauren finally exhaling when it clicked shut. Lauren studied Ashley and Natalie now, standing close, their arms crossed over their chests, almost as if they had planned it. Last year, they'd all come to a crossroads, and Lauren had taken a sharp right turn, away from them. She could sense that she was in a similar place now. Walking a fine line between moving forward or falling back.

Felipe shook his head at Lauren's speculation about the Mayan warriors. "It's hard to say if they were hoping to lose so they could be sacrificed. There are just as many who have looked at those same carvings on the walls and have interpreted them differently—believing that it was actually the winner who was sacrificed. That it was a great honor."

"So who should we believe?" Lauren asked.

"Like anything in life, it is up to you. Your thoughts are your own."

"Why did they presume that the underworld was better than this one?" Lauren asked tentatively. People had told her over and over how Geoff was in a better place now. Maybe this visit to Chichén Itzá would give her proof.

"The Maya were deeply religious. In their eyes, it was a great honor to die for their gods. Their faith was everything," Felipe said simply, and looked at Lauren, offering her a sympathetic smile, as if he knew she had lost her faith somewhere.

"They really thought dying was better than living?" Ashley asked, staring at the carved walls.

"Yes, their belief in the afterlife was that powerful." He tilted his head to the east. "We must keep moving. It's getting dark."

Lauren followed the group to the base of the north side of El Castillo and tried to concentrate on Felipe's voice as he explained the significance behind its dimensions. "It is believed the pyramid was built around 800 AD. It has ninety-one steps on each of its four sides. There are ninety-one days between each annual solar cycle—winter solstice, spring equinox, summer solstice, and fall equinox. So, if you take the four cycles per year, which is ninety-one times four, that equals three hundred and sixty-four days. Then you add the top step."

"That makes it three-hundred sixty-five. It matches up to our calendar," Natalie said, and Felipe nodded.

"*Sí*. And what's also quite amazing is the alignment of the pyramid is such that in the late afternoon of March 21, the low sun casts a shadow resembling a wriggling snake. Thousands of people come during the spring equinox each year to watch the feathered serpent god appear to crawl down the side of the pyramid and illuminate one of the serpent heads at the bottom."

"That's unbelievable," Ashley said, reaching out to touch the serpent's head.

"Also, you'll see that there are nine levels of El Castillo. One for each level of the afterlife that a person has to traverse to achieve exaltation or euphoria," Felipe continued.

Lauren heard Ashley suck in a deep breath next to her, as if she was going to say something. Lauren waited, but she remained silent.

"It's stunning," Lauren said after a beat. The pyramid was massive. She listened as Felipe explained that the structure was as tall as a ten-story building—and made from tens of thousands of limestone blocks that the Maya carried in on their backs. Concealed beneath it was another pyramid that El Castillo was built on top of. She craned her neck—the stairs leading to the top were so steep that she had to walk backward to take them in. At the base of the staircase were twin serpent heads carved from limestone that appeared to guard the bottom of the stairs. Lauren touched the rough stone of one of the serpent's heads, across its eye and over its nose, imagining the men who'd painstakingly carved it, believing that it would protect their people. She was grateful she was getting the chance to climb to the top of the pyramid. She couldn't wait to look out over the entire city, absorbing as much of its energy as she could. She wished she could bottle this feeling—take it home with her. It made her feel strong. Like she might finally conquer her own demons.

"Before we climb to the top of El Castillo, there is one more thing I must show you." Felipe stood still. "The quetzal was an important part of Mayan culture. Its feathers, along with jade, were among the most precious commodities. The Maya believed the quetzal's emerald-green tail feathers were more valuable than gold. The bird also had a distinctive chirp. If you stand right here at the base of the stairs of the pyramid, you can make the same sound." Felipe looked up then clapped his hands together, and the tone of a bird's trill echoed loudly.

"That's amazing!" Natalie said.

"Come." Felipe beckoned them. "You try."

Lauren stood quietly while Ashley and then Natalie clapped their hands and were rewarded with the same note. "Now you," Felipe said, pointing at Lauren.

Lauren pulled her purse onto her shoulder and clapped, the chirping echo that followed much louder than the others. She felt her skin prick slightly.

Felipe studied her for a moment. "Very good—the gods would approve. Are you all ready to climb?"

Lauren turned to Natalie. "Will you reconsider coming? I really think we should all do it together," she pleaded, grabbing her arm. "I'm feeling the love here," she added shyly. "I want you to be part of it too."

Natalie drew Lauren in for a hug. "I'm so happy this place is opening your heart," she said, and pulled back to face her. "But I just can't. I'm scared of heights on my best day, and the whole illegal part of it is freaking me out. I'm sorry." She looked over at Ashley, who was watching them, her mouth hovering between a smile and a frown. "It will be good for you two to do it together."

Ashley nodded and looked at Lauren hopefully.

"Just you and me, then?" she said, pointing at Ashley, her heart feeling lighter than it had in months. She felt *hope*. Hope she could find a path back to her friendships. That she could carve a route back to herself. "Let's do this."

"I'll wait for you over there." Natalie pointed to a patch of grass nearby. "Please be careful. Those steps are really steep and narrow."

"She's right," Felipe said. "We must be mindful. The stones are not only thousands of years old, but they are shallow and worn, and you must climb them carefully. I suggest you get down like this." He pushed his fanny pack around to his back and knelt. Placing his hands on the steps above him, he showed them how to crawl up the stairs. "You must respect El Castillo. This is why they stopped letting tourists ascend this pyramid—because, even before the woman died, people were defacing it with graffiti." He shook his head at the memory. "You are lucky to be here—with me—now. Don't forget that," he said firmly, then turned to Natalie. "And please know that your friends will not get into trouble. I only do this for very select people. And you were brought to me through a source I trust. So, if you want to change your mind—"

"No, that's okay. I'm better here with my two feet planted firmly on the ground," Natalie said primly.

Lauren could feel the pull of thousands of years of spirits buzzing around her—she hoped it would guide her to find the strength to forgive Ashley. Maybe it was a good sign that they were going up without Natalie. As much as she would have liked for her to experience it with them, maybe she and Ash were meant to come to a resolution in this sacred place. But as she glanced up to the top, the stairs appearing so much steeper now, she was gripped with fear.

"You okay?" Ashley sidled up to Lauren and grabbed her elbow, propelling her gently toward the first step. "All this talk about death . . ." Ashley didn't finish her sentence. She didn't have to.

Lauren dropped down, her knee finding a groove in the weathered stone. She looked up. It appeared as if there were more than the ninety-one steps Felipe had mentioned. She glanced at Ashley, who still stood steadfast beside her. "I'm scared," she said before she could stop herself from being honest. But as she said the words, she realized it wasn't the pyramid she feared. She was terrified she'd never be able to move on from what had happened. That she could never get past the fact that Ashley had pushed her to confront Geoff, and that he had died because of it.

Ashley's eyes were warm.

Lauren blinked, and suddenly she saw the girl she'd met years before, the one who'd seen something special in her. She couldn't help herself; she smiled. Maybe she could clear the hurdles of their friendship. Maybe today was the day they would do it.

"Don't worry," Ashley said. "I'll be right by your side the whole way up. Come on." She extended her hand and Lauren reached greedily for it, letting the past slip away silently as they began their trek.

They climbed like that the entire way up, clinging to each other and to the impossibly tiny steps, neither of them speaking, but understanding each other perfectly all the same. Lauren gasped as she came up the last few stairs, the night air still humid and hot, making it harder to catch her breath.

"Harder than it looks, no?" Felipe said, and held out his hand to help her up.

"It really is—thank you," Lauren said, gripping his palm, then reaching down to help Ashley. "You can see for miles!" she said as she took in the view of the vast evergreen jungle that stretched out before them.

"Follow me around the top of the temple and I will show you all of the structures we toured on the ground. They look even more spectacular from up here." Felipe started walking. "Over there is the Group of a Thousand Columns." He pointed to the large structure. They stopped and took it in, then continued walking. "There is the Platform of Venus. And then over there is the High Priest's Grave."

Lauren drew in a deep breath, her heartbeat finally resting after the climb. She couldn't believe an entire civilization had once lived here. She looked over at Ashley, who was watching her, her eyes thoughtful. "Do you feel it?" she asked Lauren. "The energy? Makes me realize that life . . ." She paused, as if unsure to continue.

"Is short?" Lauren filled in.

Ashley nodded. "Yes, and it also makes me believe we can get through this. Me and you."

Lauren smiled. "Maybe we can."

Felipe interrupted their conversation. "This is the largest entrance to the high temple, where it is believed many religious ceremonies were performed, and we will go in there in a moment." He motioned toward a doorway, then turned. "And you can't see it from here, but out through the jungle there is the Sacred Cenote."

"Where the bodies are buried," Ashley said as she angled her phone so she could take a selfie.

"The skulls are, yes," Felipe said, then looked over at Ashley. "I'd rather you not take pictures. It's disrespectful."

Ashley brought her arms down to her sides, frowning. Lauren laughed. Ashley and her selfies. How she loved them.

"Some people believe that if you disrespect the Maya, you do so at your own peril," Felipe continued.

"I did read that," Ashley said thoughtfully. "But I thought it was more if you took something from here?"

"It's hard to say, and I like to be extra cautious with my tours. Other guides—the ones less informed about the deep history—let people do things like jump in front of El Castillo so they are airborne with the temple behind them. But I choose to respect the grounds. There have been several incidents, like you mentioned, of people stealing from the temple. One man from Ohio took just a small pebble from this structure home to America with him. I read on the internet that he claims to be cursed—said terrible things have happened to him since he left here—he lost his job, his house . . ."

"So no souvenirs for us then?" Ashley joked, slipping her phone into her back pocket.

Felipe smiled ruefully. "No, not today. At least not from up here." He walked toward the edge and motioned for them to join him. "Below us are the chambers that were discovered in the pyramid under this one. Inside they found a chacmool, which is a statue that represents human sacrifice, and a jaguar throne." He pulled a book from his fanny pack, flipped it open, and showed them pictures.

Lauren took in the eerie eyes of the jaguar and felt a shiver pass through her.

"As I mentioned, this entire structure—and everything under it—is very spiritual. Follow me," Felipe said, then walked inside.

Ashley followed.

Lauren hesitated.

"Are you all right?" Ashley asked, turning around.

Lauren felt that energy again. She was frozen in place as she stared at the opening to the temple—the doorway flanked by two upright bodies of snakes carved into the stone. She touched one of the snake carvings and hoped she could find her own redemption.

She was tired of living in contradictions, swinging like a pendulum between love and anger, between wanting to rebuild her old friendships and wanting to tear them down to the studs.

CHAPTER SIXTEEN

ONE DAY BEFORE
ASHLEY

"Are you sure this is okay?" Lauren asked Felipe as they entered the temple.

"Yes, come," Felipe said, and Lauren walked inside.

"What's that?" Ashley said, pointing to a low stone table with haunting faces carved into its thick legs.

"That is a sacrificial table." Felipe walked up behind her quickly.

"Did they actually . . ." Lauren trailed off.

"Yes," Felipe said. "Many have died up here."

Ashley crouched down, fingering the limestone beneath her feet, imagining the sacrifices that had taken place here—the pictured warriors, sweaty from their ball court victory below, bowing their heads to the mighty shamans who stood tall, mystical, and magical. Still, she just couldn't comprehend how the Maya had *chosen* death. How they viewed it as their salvation.

She stood up, stealing a quick glance at Lauren, who seemed deep in thought. She wondered if Lauren was thinking of Geoff. That there had been no salvation for him.

"El Castillo is centuries old. So many people were sacrificed here. It's sacred," Felipe said.

Ashley touched Lauren's shoulder. "You okay?" she asked, her voice soft, praying Lauren would let her in—the climb up the narrow pyramid steps had left her hopeful.

"It's hard being here. I can't stop thinking about him." Lauren's eyes were empty as she said it, and Ashley felt a dull ache in her chest, the same one that had throbbed behind her rib cage at Geoff's funeral, when Lauren had blamed her for his death. Was she blaming her now?

"I hate what's happened to you. To us," Ashley said faintly. She'd finally found the courage to start telling Lauren how she felt. Words she wished she'd said to her the moment she'd seen her at the crowded terminal at LAX.

Lauren looked toward the sky. Ashley followed her gaze, noticing that the clouds were moving quickly above, one looking like it was chasing another. She prayed Lauren would say she hated what had happened to them too.

Finally she turned toward Ashley. "Why did you have to push me so hard?"

Ashley didn't want to relive that horrible fight in the coat check. She wanted it to be easy—to skip ahead to the forgiveness part. She took a deep breath. "You were getting hurt—badly hurt. I was worried about you. I did what any friend would do. I wanted you out of the situation. I wanted it to stop, and so did you. Right?"

"He was getting better; it was happening less. He would have changed, eventually."

Ashley got the impression it wasn't the first time she'd said those words. That somewhere along the way, Lauren had convinced herself of this.

She stepped closer to Lauren. "Do you hear yourself?" she said, not unkindly.

"You don't think it's possible he could have changed?"

Ashley hesitated, understanding that Lauren desperately needed Ash to agree with her—to tell her Geoff *could* have stopped hitting her. But she couldn't, no matter how badly she wanted to deflate their problems. "No," she said quietly.

"But what if you're wrong?"

"He almost broke your arm the week before he died. When I saw you at lunch, you jumped when I barely touched it! Lying to me and saying you fell before finally admitting what was really going on. What was I supposed to do? Wait until he did worse?" Ashley's voice began to rise. "I was *not* going to let that happen."

"You overstepped. And I never should have listened to you." Lauren's cheeks reddened. "I wish it had been me, not him."

Ashley's face tightened. "But that's what you aren't getting. If you'd allowed things to continue or I hadn't helped, it *would* have been you!"

"If I hadn't confronted him, he'd still be alive," Lauren said, unyielding, and Ashley could almost see all the goodwill they'd built earlier fade away. "I always thought you knew everything. Maybe because you prance around like you own the world. It made me blind," she spit, her face hard.

Ashley felt like she'd been punched in the gut. She watched Felipe quickly retreat to the other side of the temple to give them space, clearly uncomfortable with the direction the conversation had turned. "Is that what you really think of me?" Her voice had lost its tension, like an old rubber band. She had thought she was doing the right thing. Why couldn't Lauren see that?

"Just look at how you've behaved on this trip," Lauren continued. "Spending so much time with a perfect stranger when you supposedly came here to be with us."

"We're together now. And I had hoped we could get past what happened." Ashley couldn't explain why she'd gravitated toward Marco. Why she'd turned to him as a confidant instead of Lauren and Natalie. Everything was upside down.

"You know what the worst part is, Ash? I actually thought you'd have gained some perspective after a year."

The accusation hit her hard, and she felt her knees begin to shake slightly, realizing that Lauren's anger toward her was still deeply embedded. Understanding that she might never be able to change that. "I'm sorry your life hasn't turned out the way you thought it would. But I will *not* apologize for encouraging you to leave the man who was hurting you. You can blame me for a lot of things. We all know I'm not perfect. But you can't blame me for Geoff hitting you. And for having a bad heart."

"It wasn't that bad," Lauren said loudly, her voice thick.

"Goddammit, Lauren! Yes, it was! They said his two main coronary arteries were completely blocked. He would have eventually had a heart attack, regardless of whether you confronted him. How can you not get that? You listened to me because you knew in your heart you should. You knew how bad it was. You were scared. Maybe the person you're really mad at is him."

Lauren started to cry, and Ashley felt her own tears threaten to spill over. The last thing she wanted to do was cause Lauren more pain. How would they ever find their way out of this toxic cul-de-sac?

Ashley softened and tried again. "I know you loved him," she said. And she did know. She knew exactly what it was like to love someone that you shouldn't. To stay when you should run. "And I know there were good times. Maybe even more than the bad. Believe me, I get it."

"How could you possibly understand anything?" Lauren wiped her tears away.

Ashley swallowed hard. "I need to tell you something," she said, her voice breaking. She had to tell someone before it consumed her, the same way it had with Lauren. "I'm hoping it will help you understand why I was so adamant. Why I wanted to help you get out of your marriage. To stand up for yourself. No one knows, not even Natalie."

"What is it?" Lauren asked, sniffling as she tried to regain her breath.

"I didn't tell you guys everything the other day. I didn't explain why my marriage is falling apart." Her heart started pounding and she put her hand over it. "Jason yells at me and puts me down. A lot. He calls me stupid. Tells me I'm an awful person. That I'm an idiot, a dumbass, a bitch; you name it, he's got a word for it." A sob escaped her throat, and Lauren's face went slack as she absorbed her words. Ashley hadn't realized how hard it would be to release the truth. To finally stand up and be honest about what her life really looked like. She understood now why Lauren had hidden her secrets deep.

Ashley took a breath. "And he came at me. Just once."

"Wait, what?" Lauren interrupted. "Are you saying Jason hit you?"

"No, he never hit me. Just pushed me. But still, I fell pretty hard. It was in the early days of BloMe and we were arguing about some super expensive shoes I'd bought. They were my first pair of Prada, I think?" she said more to herself than Lauren. "Anyway, we'd just secured a meeting with Sephora, and I wanted to celebrate. He lost his temper. Pushed me up against the dresser in our bedroom and I fell back and slid to the floor. He came this close"—she used her fingers to illustrate—"to my face, his fists up. And God, Lauren, I don't think I've ever been so scared in my life. I told him the next day that I'd take the kids and walk out the door if he ever touched me like that again." It had felt surreal to see Jason's rage peak. How underneath her bravado, she'd been terrified she'd somehow made him like that.

Lauren stood still, much like the statues that surrounded them. Ashley pushed on with her story, now feeling desperate to let it spill onto the floor of the ancient pyramid, to be brave like the Mayan warriors. In this moment, she could almost understand their fearlessness, the ability to let the gods decide their fate.

"And he never laid a hand on me again. But he still makes me feel small in other ways. Especially since the Revlon offer came in. He's so damn angry I won't sell and bail his restaurant out of debt again." Ashley's voice cracked as she said the last words. "He tells me constantly that I'm a terrible mother. That he never should have married me. I convince myself they're just words. That they can't hurt me." Her eyes filled with tears. "But it breaks me a little bit every day. And now I'm terrified that I won't be able to put myself back together. I try so hard to seem strong. But I feel so weak."

Lauren began to cry again, and Ashley reached out to grab her hand, grasping it tightly. "And maybe when I realized how bad things were for you, I thought, I can't help myself, but I can help her. You didn't have kids . . ." Her voice caught, but she pressed forward. "And I couldn't let you live with that fear any longer. I didn't want you to feel small. You deserve better. We both do." Ashley finished and stared at Lauren, her eyes wide. She had laid her heart open, much like Ashley envisioned the warriors who'd once been sacrificed in this temple had. It was just for a moment, but she felt empowered. The truth was out there now, for better or for worse.

"Why haven't you left him already? You told us you were thinking about it, but you didn't sound sure." Lauren sniffled loudly, but Ashley thought she'd heard something off in her tone—anger? She reflected on the moment Lauren had confided Geoff's abuse. Ashley had been touched by a myriad of emotions: shock, sadness, indignity, and yes, of course, an uncontrollable anger with Geoff. But Lauren's angry tone seemed directed at Ashley.

She paused, suddenly acutely aware that she needed to be careful with her words. "I told myself that I could handle it—put up with it until the girls were a bit older." She stopped and studied Lauren's face, her expression now reading skepticism. Or was she just imagining it? She pressed on anyway. "But now, I don't know anymore."

"It's not as easy as it looks, is it? Walking away?" Lauren said.

"No, it's not. But I never said it was," Ashley said, more curtly than she intended, her frustration growing. Where was the *I'm sorry*? The *I understand*?

"So I was your project because you were too weak to leave your own marriage? Because hitting is worse than yelling? Because you have kids and I don't?" Lauren sounded tired. She glared at Ashley.

"What? No," Ashley said, finally understanding why Lauren hadn't comforted her. She was pissed. "I mean, the kid part makes everything more complicated."

"You have no fucking clue what you are talking about. Just because we didn't have kids didn't mean it would be any easier to leave. How could you be so myopic?"

Lauren's words stung and Ashley dropped her chin. "I guess it was because I've always thought that if I didn't have Hannah and Abby, I would have left Jason years ago." And it was true—her daughters had been the anchor that had kept her in her marriage. But now, with a few days away to think, she was recalculating that decision.

"Still not the same," Lauren said, her words like daggers. Ashley flinched. This was not going at all how she had thought it would. She had imagined connecting with Lauren over their shared experience, but it was clear she had grossly misjudged the situation.

"Look, here's the thing," Ashley tried to reason. "I'm not making excuses for Jason, but he has never laid a hand on me since that one night. Not even close. He was under a ton of pressure—he'd just gotten a terrible review in the *Los Angeles Times* and his dad was not doing well. He snapped. My situation is different. Geoff controlled you and abused you, no matter what was going on in his own life. He talked you out of having kids! Of getting your teaching degree! At least I was living the life I wanted to lead. If Jason had ever touched me again, I would've been out the door."

"Do you hear yourself, Ash? You *are* making excuses. The same ones I used to make. That you told me *I* had to stop making! You're a hypocrite. And don't you dare try to convince yourself otherwise."

Ashley felt stricken, dizzy with the realization that Lauren was right, that she'd pushed Lauren to leave to assuage her own guilt for staying.

She'd focused so much on pushing away the accusations surrounding Geoff's death that she never really evaluated how it mirrored her own life. Sure, it had been the right thing to encourage Lauren to leave, but to do it without revealing her own secrets? Cowardly.

She turned and impulsively stepped on the sacrificial table before Lauren could speak again, wanting her to understand. She was sorry. So sorry. Felipe called out from several feet away, and he hurried toward them, waving his hands.

Ashley ignored him, raising her arms toward the sky, feeling desperate. "You know what? I *am* a hypocrite! I should have packed my shit and left the first time Jason told me I was an imbecile who rode on Natalie's coattails. I couldn't see it at the time. But you're right. I should have told you."

"You know what I'm not hearing you say? 'I'm sorry,'" Lauren yelled. "Why are you incapable of giving me the apology I deserve? Why is it always about you?"

Tears streamed down Ashley's cheeks. "I'm fucking sorry, okay? If I could go back and change that I didn't tell you, I would. I'm so sorry every time you look at me. In every glance, I see how much you hate me. How much you blame me for his death." Ashley wiped her eyes. "But I'm *not sorry* I didn't just look the other way and let Geoff continue to hurt you, just because of my own secrets. And you know what? I'm not sorry he's gone. You are better off without him, even if you can't see it. And maybe I'll be better off without Jason too."

"But you know what the difference is?" Lauren yelled. "You get to decide! You took that away from me. And I don't know if I can ever forgive you for that."

Ashley deflated at her assertion. She'd laid everything out on the table, *literally*, and it wasn't enough.

Felipe lost his balance as he reached her, and stretched his arm out to steady himself on the wall. "You need to get off—" he began to say, eyes wild. But before he could finish his thought, they saw the flash of lightning, the thunder following quickly after, the sky opening up and crying hot, angry tears.

Ashley jumped off, slipping slightly as she tried to catch her footing. They were shielded by the top of the temple, but the storm was still ominous and threatening. Loud and attacking. As if it were directly responding to their argument. "Is this normal? For a storm like this to come out of nowhere?" Ashley asked, peering out the doorway.

"Yes, it rains like this quite often here. But you should not have stood on the sacrificial table. You may have angered the gods." The rain slowed to a hard, steady drizzle. He gestured toward the entrance of the temple. "We should go."

Ashley looked imploringly at Lauren. "I was just trying to make you listen—"

"You didn't think, Ash," Lauren said. "That's your problem. You don't think about anyone but yourself."

Ashley looked at the table but stayed silent. Everything that could have been said, had been. There were no more words to say.

"Ladies," Felipe warned as he glanced at the sky nervously. "We shouldn't stay up here during this storm. The rain is slowing. We need to go now."

"Please. Just one more minute," Ashley said, then stepped closer to Lauren. "I'm sorry for how I handled things. Why can't you just forgive me?"

"Maybe it's not enough anymore, Ash," Lauren said. Then she turned toward Felipe. "I agree with you. We need to go." She looked back at Ashley. "Come on. This is over."

Ashley let the finality of Lauren's words sink deep into her soul as she followed, each of them carefully crawling backward down the ancient steps, which had been wiped clean by the rainstorm.

CHAPTER SEVENTEEN

THE DAY AFTER
LAUREN

Lauren watched Natalie stare at her phone, her brow furrowed. How did you tell your best friend's husband not only that his wife had disappeared but also that you couldn't remember most of the night you spent with her? That she'd gone missing on your watch? Lauren couldn't figure out how that had happened. Natalie was convinced she was drugged, but why had she made it back to the hotel safely while Ash was nowhere to be found? As the day wore on and they were no closer to answers, that little voice in Lauren's head kept asking, *Does Natalie really not remember . . . or is she hiding something?*

Before this trip Lauren would have never questioned Natalie this way, but it was as if the curtain had been pulled back to reveal a friendship and partnership between Natalie and Ashley that was far from as perfect as Lauren once believed.

"Hey," Natalie said, sliding her phone into her pocket as she walked over to Lauren. "Jason's on his way."

"What did he say?" Lauren asked, wondering what it would be like to see him now that she knew how he treated Ashley. Ashley hadn't had to see Geoff again after Lauren had revealed his abuse. And honestly, Lauren envied that. When she saw Jason she was going to have to fake it, to bury her anger toward him for the way he treated Ash. And that would not be easy for her to do. It also felt wrong—like she was letting him get away with it. It felt disloyal to Ashley. She realized suddenly that it wasn't Ashley's arrogance or pushiness that made her so adamant that Lauren leave Geoff. It was her loyalty. How had she not seen that before? She studied Natalie, wondering how she was going to handle her feelings about Jason when she saw him face-to-face.

"He's mad that I didn't call him sooner, which only makes me feel worse. I've handled all of this so wrong."

"No, you haven't. How does anyone know how to act in this situation?"

Natalie paused. "I think Ben would have been upset with Ash if the roles were reversed."

"Are you defending him?" Lauren frowned.

"Not for verbally abusing our best friend, no. But he's her husband. We have to respect that." Natalie sighed. "Look, I know this hits close to home for you—"

"Please don't do that," Lauren said.

"Okay. Then can we stay focused on finding Ashley? When Jason gets here we're going to have to put what we know aside. It won't help anything to be mad at him. Can you do that?"

Lauren bit her lip. Of course all of this hit a little too close to home. But they needed to find Ashley. "It won't be easy, but I can do it. Had he heard from her?" Lauren asked.

"Last night she texted him some emojis at around two in the morning, our time. But that's it."

"Which emojis?"

"He said it was hands in prayer, a sad face with a tear, and a wave. I have no idea what it means and neither does he."

"I don't either. But come on, using emojis as a Dear John letter? Not even Ash would do that."

"I know," Natalie said, sounding defeated. "So if she wasn't saying goodbye, what was she saying?"

"I don't know. Those emojis could mean a million things."

Lauren pulled up the emojis on her phone. "Hands praying, you said?"

Natalie nodded.

"That could be asking for help." Lauren found the wave. "And a wave, that could mean she was in trouble near water of some kind. Or maybe she was just drunk. She used to send me random emojis all the time. Like a fire truck, and those girls with bunny ears."

"Wait, maybe the couple . . . maybe they did hear her," Natalie said. "Maybe she was out in the ocean and something did happen."

"If that's the case, could you have been with her?" Lauren asked carefully. "You were soaking wet." There. She'd finally asked her the question that had been weighing heavily on her mind. She felt relieved but also terrible once she saw the distraught look on Natalie's face.

"I don't know," Natalie said, her voice trembling. "But if you're trying to imply I would have hurt her in the water . . ."

"I'm not," Lauren said quickly. It wasn't as if she believed Natalie was capable of purposely hurting Ash. But Ashley was gone, and Natalie's memory along with her. "I just want to find her."

"That's what I want too." Natalie's face went slack. "There's just nothing when I force it. Nothing after La Cantina."

Lauren looked at her, trying to mask her thoughts. Ashley had sent a water emoji. A couple heard a woman screaming in the water. Natalie woke up wet—just a few feet from the ocean.

"Why are you looking at me like that? You don't believe me, do you?" Natalie's voice was a few octaves higher than it had been earlier. She seemed nervous. Why?

"I didn't say that, but to find her, we need to be honest and tell each other everything." She leaned in. "You know you can tell me anything, right? Even if it's really bad. I can handle it. I want to help you. Help Ashley."

"I have told you everything!" Natalie yelled, and a woman grabbing a paperback from the loaner library in the lobby looked over.

"Okay, okay, I'm sorry if I came on too strong," Lauren apologized, surprised at Natalie's vehemence. Had she ever spoken to Lauren like that? No. But then again, these were extraordinary circumstances. "Sit down, please."

Natalie slumped on the sofa next to Lauren. "I promise I don't know anything else," she said, then turned abruptly. "But what about you? Did you really come back here after La Cantina? Or are you lying to me?"

"What? No, I'm not lying," Lauren said, startled. Of course she'd come back to the hotel. But maybe Natalie was picking up on that gap in what she'd told her and the truth.

"How does it feel to be accused? Pretty bad, right?" Natalie's eyes were wet.

"It feels awful." Lauren chewed her lip, debating how much to reveal. But if she was demanding that Natalie tell her everything, then she needed to reciprocate. "Okay. I did come back here, but I didn't go straight to sleep." She stopped, suddenly unsure whether she could say the next words out loud. Her therapist had encouraged it, but she hadn't told anyone yet.

Natalie's eyes widened. "Did you see me? Ash?"

"No, I just want to be completely honest with you," Lauren said, pressing forward—not just to gain Natalie's trust, but to gauge her reaction. If Natalie was understanding, it would help Lauren believe that her addiction didn't define her. She detailed how she'd hooked up with José the bartender the first day they'd arrived and then again last night, after coming back from La Cantina. She'd taken a cab and had planned to go straight to her room and sleep. The night had exhausted her. But as she'd passed the bar, he was wiping it down. "Drink?" he'd said, his eyes twinkling. She couldn't resist. She knew he could take her mind off everything. "Why not?" she'd said. And after two margaritas they'd sneaked to her bungalow. "And it's not just something that I've done here—I'm on Tinder and I hook up with people back home. A lot," Lauren said. "I'm in therapy. For addiction."

Natalie looked stunned. "I don't know what to say."

"It's okay. I'm just coming to terms with it myself."

"I'm so sorry I pushed you like that. If you weren't ready to say anything about it and I forced you, I feel so bad."

"It's all right. Really. I'm getting help but it's going to be a process."

Natalie gave her an empathetic look but didn't say more. Lauren was grateful for that. That she wasn't pressing for more information or giving her unsolicited advice. That she was being the kind of friend she needed right now. Helping more than she could know.

"Can we be on the same side here?" Natalie finally said.

"Yes," Lauren said, but her gut was still unsure. She had a strong feeling there was a lot more to the story.

They sat for a few minutes without speaking.

Natalie finally broke the silence. "So, I'm still thinking about the emoji thing again. Why wouldn't she text 911 or something if she was in trouble? Why be so cryptic?"

"Maybe she didn't want Marco to know she was on to him," Lauren said.

"Do you think he may have kidnapped her? Or worse?" Natalie sat up.

"I have no idea. But at this point I don't think we can rule anything, *or anyone*, out. We just need to do whatever we can to find Ashley."

CHAPTER EIGHTEEN

THE DAY AFTER
NATALIE

Natalie and Lauren sat side-by-side in silence, both contemplating Lauren's words: they had to find Ashley. Natalie continued to analyze the emojis Ashley had sent Jason—hands in prayer, a wave, a sad face with a tear—feeling like she was trying to understand one of Meg's texts to her friends. It would never happen. Because the emojis could mean a million different things—if Ashley was even trying to send a message, and not just drunk and lonely.

She squeezed her eyes shut and screamed as loud as she could inside her mind, her entire body clenching as she thought about what she would say to the officers. If Lauren, her friend of twenty years, was questioning her and her memory loss, what were the police going to do? She couldn't blame anyone for doubting that she'd simply forgotten the night. Deep inside she was questioning herself, worried that the crucial memories—the ones that were locked somewhere deep in her conscience—were going to reveal more than she was ready for. Even though she couldn't access them, she could sense their presence, like someone hiding in the shadows. And they gave her a very bad feeling.

Where are you, Ashley?

"I just got an alert. TMZ knows." Lauren turned to her and held up her phone.

Natalie could see the headline at the top of Lauren's screen, a picture of Ashley under it. *BloMe Founder Missing in Mexico.* How had they found out? "What does the article say?"

Lauren started reading. "BloMe cofounder Ashley Green, wife of Los Angeles chef and owner of the Dinner Party, Jason Green, has disappeared in the Yucatán Peninsula area of Mexico. According to a source in the Tulum police department, she hasn't been seen since late last night, and foul play could be involved."

"Foul play? We haven't even talked to the police yet. How could they even be a source?" Natalie couldn't believe the news had leaked. She felt dizzy from the realization and shut her eyes. She needed to protect BloMe. She'd have to call Amanda, have her draft a press release. She needed to get in touch with Austin, their assistant, and make sure he said "No comment" to anyone who called the office. She rubbed the back of her neck. This was the last thing she wanted to deal with right now.

"From what I've heard, the *policía* don't play by the rules," Lauren said.

"You think the police called TMZ?" Natalie asked.

"I don't know—maybe. Who else would have?"

"I'm getting text messages, emails." Natalie held up her phone, the screen filled with alerts. She could see just the beginning of each one pop up on the screen before the next pushed it away. *Is Ashley really gone? What happened to her? Is what the police are saying true? Foul play? Was she kidnapped?* She didn't respond to any. She needed to call Ben immediately—make sure he protected Lucy and Meg from this news. She looked at the time—he could still keep them home from school. She quickly texted both him and Jason to do that. She hoped she could catch Jason before he got on the plane. Her phone kept pinging with more frantic questions from their employees, college friends, their lawyer, Arthur. He was panicked, wanting to discuss how to handle Revlon. Facebook was blowing up. Someone had posted the link to the TMZ post and tagged her. Natalie wished controlling the press was going to be the hardest part of this, but she suspected it was only the beginning. She wondered what was next. Because that twisting in her gut told her they'd only scratched the surface of what happened to Ashley.

"Ladies? The police are here." Maria's voice broke through Natalie's thoughts.

Natalie rubbed her clammy hands on her shorts. Natalie saw a dark blue pickup truck parked in front of the hotel with *"Policía Municipal"* written in white lettering.

Foul. Play.

"Can we ask you something?" Natalie looked at Lauren and patted the seat next to her. Maybe Maria could give them some insight on the police and whether they would have tipped off TMZ. And if she thought the police already had information about her disappearance or if they had just amped up the story to make money. "Have you heard of TMZ?"

Maria didn't skip a beat. "Of course. The website about celebrity gossip."

"Yes, gossip," Natalie repeated just as two men in dark blue uniforms and baseball hats that each had a shield inside of a star stitched on the front walked into the lobby. "They are already reporting Ashley is missing."

"This article says their source is someone in the police department. Do you think the Mexican authorities tipped them off, or could they have been responding to a call from TMZ?" Lauren asked.

"I'm not sure," Maria said, then pressed her lips together as if afraid to say more.

"I'm nervous to talk to them . . ." Natalie didn't finish her sentence. She looked down at her fingernails. She'd gnawed each of them to their cuticles. She worried the officers would see what she *wasn't* saying—what she had no intention of telling them. Like how a part of her worried that Ashley took off so they couldn't sell the company. And how Natalie was determined to find her so they still could. Because they might not look for her if they thought this was as simple as a spat between friends, but Ashley needed to be found. Maria squeezed Natalie's hand, and Natalie felt guilty about her thoughts.

"I wish I could tell you there is no corruption. But there is. And I hate saying that because this is my home. But it's true—not all of them are bad, of course, but many are. My brother, he fell in with the wrong people once. He didn't have the money to pay the police off, so he was jailed." Maria's eyes filled with tears.

"I'm sorry," Natalie said.

"Me too," Lauren said.

Maria inched closer to Natalie and Lauren. "To be honest, I was surprised they insisted on coming here when I called. It's not custom for the police to come to you. Usually you would have to go to the station and file a report, and the process would not be quick. It has to be because you and Ashley are well-known back home—the YouTube moms with that BloBrush, right?" she said, her cheeks darkening. "I'm sorry, I did a Google search after you said you couldn't find Ashley."

"It's okay, I get it." Nat gave her a wan smile. The BloBrush had become so much of her identity, which she'd never intended when she thought of the idea. In a million years she would have never guessed they'd have a YouTube channel, be recognized in Mexico. If she'd known that would be the outcome, would she do it all over again? She wasn't sure.

"Anyway, the police may view this as an opportunity to make money because you are famous."

They weren't famous in the traditional sense of the word, but Natalie didn't correct her. Sure, they'd been on TV, they were once in *Us Weekly* because Reese Witherspoon was spotted buying one of their brushes, and they were occasionally asked to take a selfie with someone. George Clooney was famous. They weren't.

"That's good—it will help," Lauren said.

Natalie shot her a look.

"I mean, it's not good that they will make money off it, but maybe it means they will make finding her a priority."

"She's right," Maria said, sensing Natalie's apprehension.

"As long as we can trust them," Natalie said.

Maria lowered her voice to a whisper. "My brother always told me if I got on the wrong side of the police to never offer them any information. To only answer what they asked. That's my advice to you when you talk to them. And I would definitely not ask them about TMZ. You do not want to anger them."

Natalie swallowed hard and looked at Lauren, who seemed panicked too. She wondered whether she should call Arthur first or hire a lawyer who wasn't their in-house counsel. But then again, Ashley was simply a missing person and they'd called the police to report it. To *find* her. Natalie would just answer their questions like Maria suggested and not offer any additional detail. But when she got to the part about her blank memory, would they believe her?

"It's going to be okay, right?" Lauren asked Natalie.

"I hope so," Natalie said. But her heart was doing that thing again—the beats were all over the place, like a toddler pounding on a toy drum. She put her hand up to her chest.

"I'll take you over to them." Maria smiled as if trying to calm them.

She and Lauren followed Maria. Natalie glanced at her phone again, which had been buzzing in her hand nonstop. The most recent text was from Ben with a **PLEASE CALL ME**. She fired off an OK. She felt bad she hadn't talked to him yet, but a part of her was holding off because of what he might say—the same thing she'd been thinking: that Ashley might have disappeared so she could sabotage the deal. She shook the thought away—even thinking it seemed cruel. Would Ashley really put them through this just to get her way? But if she hadn't, that thought was even worse, because it might mean something bad had happened to her. Tears pricked Natalie's eyes. She felt hopeless.

They approached the officers. "Hello, I'm Natalie Sanders and this is Lauren Davis," Natalie said.

"Good morning, I'm Officer Garcia," a tall, barrel-chested man with a broad nose said in perfect English. He introduced his partner, Officer Lopez, whose accent was thick when he said hello. He was much shorter than Officer Garcia, with wide-set eyes and a pinched face. They were both in their fifties, Ashley guessed. "We understand your friend Ashley Green has not been seen since last night?"

"Yes," Natalie said.

"We would like to take a statement from each of you," Officer Garcia said, his steely eyes giving nothing away.

Natalie and Lauren nodded.

Natalie's heart was still pounding. She'd never even had a traffic ticket. Talking to the police seemed so serious. Especially when they had guns strapped across their chests.

"Which of you was the last to see her?" Officer Garcia asked, and Natalie tried to avoid looking at his weapon.

Natalie looked at Lauren. "I was," Natalie said, something stirring inside of her. Would that automatically make her a suspect?

"Okay, we'll start with you," Officer Garcia said. "Let's find somewhere a little more private," he said, looking around the lobby.

Natalie shot Lauren another look. Were they separating them to make sure their stories lined up? Her heart felt like it might break out of her chest.

Lauren nodded at Natalie as if she understood her concern. "I'll wait over there." She pointed to where they'd just been sitting. "I'm going to post Ashley's picture and information on MissingAmericans. com. And I'll call the US Embassy too and the US Consulate," she said.

"They can help us get in touch with the local hospitals to check if she's at any of them—I'm sure she's fine, though."

Natalie nodded. "Me too. I'm sure she's fine."

Officer Garcia gestured at Natalie. "Are you ready?"

Natalie's mouth was so dry. She swallowed several times and followed the officers into the hotel's bar, which, luckily, was empty. They settled into three chairs around a high-top table, Natalie facing out toward the beach. She thought about waking up wet this morning. Ashley's text to Jason with the wave emoji. The couple hearing something in the water. Could those things be connected? Should she mention them to the police? Maria had warned her not to, but what if doing so could help find Ashley? She didn't know what to do.

"When did you last see Mrs. Green?" Officer Garcia asked, flipping open a small navy-blue notebook. He wrote Natalie's name in neat letters. Her first thought was the outdoor dance floor. Marco's hands on Ashley's hips. The dark sky with bright stars. The stage with white lights draped across it. She heard the lyrics of "Brown Eyed Girl." She heard Ashley laughing. She saw her flip her hair, which she'd worn loose around her face. She wished she could recall a single defined detail after that, but she still only had silhouettes of ideas that refused to take shape. Was that the last time she'd seen her? No, it couldn't have been.

"We were at La Cantina. We were dancing," Natalie said. She closed her eyes and saw Ashley's arms swaying high above her head, her eyes shining from the alcohol. Natalie had felt so good in that moment, the drinks she'd consumed loosening her limbs, making her wonder why she didn't imbibe more often. "To 'Brown Eyed Girl,'" she added and the officers nodded, as if they'd heard the popular American song before.

"That was the last you saw her? She disappeared off the dance floor?" Officer Lopez leaned forward.

"No, that's just the last thing I can remember." Natalie sucked in a long breath, studying their faces. She wondered which one of them was bad cop. So far, they both seemed like the good kind, but it had only been a couple of minutes.

"You lost your memory?"

Natalie nodded. "I think someone may have drugged me. Or given me bad alcohol?"

Officer Garcia and Officer Lopez shared a look.

"My husband showed me an article about a resort in Cancún under investigation for serving toxic drinks after an American tourist died. I can't figure out any other explanation." She sat up straighter and made eye contact with Officer Garcia. She needed to hold it together, to appear confident.

"When and where do you suspect this may have happened?"

Natalie folded her hands. "I don't know. We got to La Cantina around nine thirty. So sometime after that?"

"Did you ever leave your drink unattended?"

Natalie took a deep breath before responding, disappointed in herself. She didn't usually make mistakes like this. She was the person who never left her front door unlocked—even when she was home. "Yes. When we were on the dance floor. I know, it was stupid," she said before the officers could judge her. But they didn't react.

"Were you and Ashley with anyone else?"

"Yes. Lauren was also there. And Marco."

"Who's Marco?"

Natalie hesitated. Who *was* Marco? She had no idea. "He's the owner, well, actually he works at Tropical Kiss—that smoothie bowl place down the road. We'd hung out with him a lot during our trip. We met him in a yoga class the morning after we arrived."

"What day was that?"

"Tuesday." Natalie thought back to her excitement as the car pulled up to the hotel, taking that first whiff of warm sea air. Lauren snapping pictures with her phone. Ashley's jubilance when she first saw the ocean. None of them dreaming they'd end up here.

"Okay, so you were at La Cantina with Lauren and Marco. What's Marco's last name?"

"Smith. Marco Smith."

"Smith?" Officer Garcia frowned as he wrote it down. "Marco is typically a Latin or Mexican name. Is he either?"

Natalie nodded. "I think he's Mexican. He told Ashley he was born here."

"Any chance he lied about that?"

Natalie nodded. "He also told us he owned Tropical Kiss. I guess he misled us about a lot of things," she said. "And now he's gone."

"What do you mean, gone?"

"He disappeared, too. We thought Ashley might be with him, so we went to his apartment this morning, and he had cleared out of there. There were only a few pieces of furniture left." She paused. "And a dog bowl."

"Dog bowl?"

"He had a yellow Lab—Spencer." Natalie pictured him running down the beach, the fur around his face blowing backward. Marco throwing him a Frisbee. He hadn't seemed like a liar. Her radar hadn't gone off.

Officer Garcia wrote something in his notebook. "Do you think Marco might have taken Ashley against her will? Hurt her?"

Was Marco capable of kidnapping, or worse? Natalie had been wondering this all morning. The thought sickened her. Had his spirituality simply been a mask to conceal the truth? "I don't know. I hate to even think of that possibility."

"I know it's hard, but if we are going to find her, you must consider everything." Officer Garcia gave her a sympathetic look. "Think back. Was his behavior ever concerning? Were there any, as you say in America, red flags?"

Natalie went over their time with Marco. He had obviously been attracted to Ashley. Wanting to spend a lot of time with her. He'd left with her that day at the beach. But according to Lauren, it was because Ashley had asked him to. Had there been anything *concerning* about how he'd acted? Other than not seeming to care that Ashley was married, no. Not that Natalie had seen. "No. I didn't pick up on anything like that." Had she missed something? An important sign that could have saved Ashley?

"Even after spending so much time with him? There was nothing off? You're sure?"

"I suppose I could have missed the warning signs," Natalie said. "But I've thought about it. Other than spewing a lot of spiritual jargon, I thought he was harmless."

"Harmless?"

"Yeah. That's how I would describe him. But I could obviously be wrong. If he's a sociopath or something like that, he'd be charming, wouldn't he? He'd hide the dark side?" She looked at the officers.

"Perhaps," Garcia said.

"Maybe that's exactly what he did—made us think he was a good guy, but then last night, the bad part of him came out?" Natalie shivered at the thought but kept her stream of consciousness going. "Maybe he and Ashley argued and things took a turn? He knew we were leaving today, so he could have been desperate?" She shifted in her seat. "Could that all be possible? Was he conning us?"

"You tell us."

"I don't know! I'm not the expert here!" Natalie said loudly before covering her mouth with her hand. "I'm sorry. I'm just scared."

"Scared? Why?" Officer Lopez leaned in.

"Because we haven't heard from her. We don't know where she is. We have no idea if she's okay! And now you're saying maybe Marco did something to her." Natalie's eyes filled with tears. She was more than scared. She was frightened, frustrated, and mad all rolled into one—it bordered on hysteria.

"We're just trying to get some information. That's all. We aren't saying he harmed her."

"You're also not saying that he didn't."

"She's missing, and he has disappeared. It appears he is likely involved somehow. But to what extent, we don't know. Okay?" Officer Garcia said.

Natalie swallowed and gave a slight nod.

"Okay, let's move on." Officer Garcia looked at Officer Lopez.

"You don't remember most of the night?" Officer Lopez asked. Did she catch suspicion in his eyes or was she imagining it?

"That's true, I don't." Natalie hated that she might hold the information that could help Ashley and she couldn't get to it. "But I wish I could. I would do *anything* to know what happened."

"But maybe you do know. Think, Natalie," Officer Lopez said.

I have.

Her insides twisted so hard she felt sick. What if she *did* know exactly what happened to Ashley? And right now Ashley was somewhere, desperate for her to remember so she could help her.

"I really don't know," Natalie said, a tear falling down her cheek. She stared at the officers' cold eyes, slowly becoming aware they did not believe her.

"Okay, okay," Officer Garcia said. "Let's consider another possibility."

Natalie exhaled quietly.

"Could she have left with him of her own free will?"

Natalie contemplated this—that Ashley and Marco were lying on a beach somewhere laughing about how Natalie wouldn't be able to sell the company. Planning when Ashley would pop back into her life—after Revlon was long gone. Could she be capable of that? Or had she been so distraught over Jason, and that her plan to make things better with Lauren and Natalie had backfired, that she'd hurt herself? This was a thought that had crouched deep in the corner of her mind since they'd left Marco's apartment. But Ashley would never harm herself. Would she? Natalie much preferred the alternative theory—that she'd left with Marco willingly.

"I suppose it's possible she might have left with him."

"Why do you think so?"

Natalie was not going to mention Revlon or Jason. "She and Marco had grown close this week." She clasped her hands in her lap, trying to reconcile the Ashley she thought she knew with the one who might have abandoned everyone.

"But you said they might have argued last night," Officer Lopez said.

"I was just speculating on how things might have gone downhill between them. You were asking me if I thought he might have taken her. Now you're asking me if I thought she left on her own. The answer is that I don't know the answer," Natalie said as calmly as she could. It felt like they were spinning her words, trying to catch her in a lie. But was it lying if she simply wasn't telling them everything she suspected?

"You mentioned they had become close. How close?" Officer Garcia asked.

Natalie chewed on her cuticle, and it started to bleed. She sucked on it. "She spent a significant amount of time with him," she said, before backpedaling. "But it wasn't like *that*, I don't think." When the officers remained silent, she added, "She's married. She has kids." But Natalie still wondered if something had happened between them. She'd seen Marco touch Ashley possessively more than once. They had an easy rapport—an intimacy even—but there was no proof they'd been intimate. Ashley tended to be affectionate—she'd casually graze their head of marketing's forearm in conversation. Give their head of manufacturing a playful swat on the shoulder to make a point.

"Wouldn't be the first time," Officer Garcia said. "People come down here, and they act crazy. Treat Mexico like it's some sort of playground."

Was that what Ashley had done? Left the Unites States and lost her mind?

"Let's back up to the dancing. What happened next?"

"We left."

"All of you?" He looked at his notepad. "Lauren, you, Ashley, and Marco?"

"No. Just Ashley, Marco, and me."

Officer Garcia put his pen down and gave Natalie a long look. "Why didn't Lauren join you?"

"She told me earlier that Ashley asked her to, but she said no."

"Why?"

"It had been a long night—things were tense between all of us."

Officer Lopez sat up straighter. "So you weren't getting along?"

"Not really."

"Do you think the fact you weren't getting along has something to do with her disappearance?"

What was he getting at? She felt that dread inside her again. Was it because of the officers, or was it coming from her subconscious? "No, I don't."

Officer Lopez gave her a look. "Why do you remember that, but not much else?"

Natalie rolled her neck. She wished she knew why some things had remained in her memory and some had vanished. "I don't know."

Officer Lopez looked like he was going to say more, but Officer Garcia spoke first. "Okay, so what time did you leave La Cantina?"

"I'm not sure—Lauren said we left around eleven thirty."

"Where did you go?"

Natalie's face flushed. "Lauren said Ashley told her we were going to Marco's place."

"So Lauren is filling in all of your blanks?" Officer Lopez said.

"The ones she can, yes."

"And you believe her?" Officer Lopez held her gaze a beat too long.

"Why wouldn't I?"

"There are just a lot of holes from last night; we're asking everything we can," Officer Garcia said, obviously trying to soften the questioning.

Natalie thought about the harsh words Lauren said to Ashley last night. Had she told Natalie everything about their conversation? Lauren had seemed tormented about how she'd treated Ashley. Maybe there was more to the story.

Officer Garcia leaned forward. "Do you think Marco could've drugged you, then taken you to his place?"

"How could I know?" But Natalie evaluated the theory. He would have been able to get Ashley to his place without drugs, so why would there be a need to put something in Natalie's drink once they were there? Unless that had been his plan for getting Natalie out of the way so he could take Ashley. She shivered.

"Usually when someone drugs another person, it is with the intention of—" Officer Garcia started.

"Sexually assaulting them, I know," Natalie interrupted, rubbing her arms as she thought about how she and Ashley could have been violated.

"Did that happen? Did Marco or someone . . ."

"No. At least I don't think so," Natalie said, recalling how she'd taken inventory of her body this morning. Nothing seemed off—physically anyway. But what if she simply had no recollection of it? What if she *had* been raped? She shivered involuntarily again.

"We need to have you tested to see if there are any drugs in your system."

"Of course," Natalie said, but the idea scared her. What if there weren't? Would they think she was lying about her memory loss?

"We'll have someone escort you to the hospital as soon as possible. There is a private facility I recommend in Mérida. Unfortunately, it's two and a half hours away, but I would not send you to a public one. You have medical insurance, yes?"

"Yes," she said and was hit with a wave of fear. She was being questioned by the *policía*. She had to get tested for drugs. Ashley was missing. The window for a happy ending—finding Ashley safe and sound and signing the Revlon deal and fixing her finances—was closing rapidly.

"What was your week like with Ashley? You mentioned tension last night, but how were you getting along otherwise?" Officer Lopez asked.

Natalie sighed, deciding he was the bad cop. She thought about the arguments they'd all had—the tension tightening around them like a straitjacket. She should be honest. Especially if Lauren told them the truth. It would only make her look worse if Natalie pretended otherwise.

"Things were strained during the week, too."

Officer Lopez cocked his head, as if waiting for more. Natalie wasn't about to offer anything additional. "Why were things strained?" he pressed.

"Girl stuff. We've been friends a long time," Natalie said. Twenty years—a lot of history, a lot of baggage. But also a lot of good times. Why hadn't those taken center stage instead? Why was it always easier to let the bad things have the spotlight?

"Why would you leave with Ashley from the bar if things between you were as tense as you say?"

"I don't know. I wish I did. My guess is I didn't want her going off alone with Marco. Not because I thought he was going to hurt her, but because this is Mexico. And I've always looked out for her, you know?" she said, but they didn't respond, so she continued. "But my mind goes dark from that point until this morning." She wished she could explain the feeling of sheer terror that came over her every time she couldn't access that black hole in her mind—like a panic slowly consuming her, bit by bit.

Should she offer that she'd woken up on the beach? No, not after the way Officer Lopez seemed to have it out for her. Especially because it could mean she was connected to what happened to Ashley—and that idea, she could not even wrap her brain around. She needed to take Maria's advice to be careful.

"What about Lauren? How was she getting along with Ashley during the week?"

Horribly.

"Like I said, things were tense."

"Did they have any arguments?"

Natalie thought of trying to avoid the question, not sure what Lauren might disclose. But she had to be honest about everything she could be. "They did, at Chichén Itzá, but I wasn't with them—I didn't hear it."

"When was Chichén Itzá?"

"Two nights ago."

"Chichén Itzá closes at dusk," Officer Garcia said.

"We had a private tour—after hours."

"You know those are illegal."

Natalie didn't respond. She regretted not going up. Letting her conservative side win out yet again. The side of her that went back and paid for an extra Americano the coffee shop hadn't charged her for the day before. Because maybe if she had climbed El Castillo, things would have turned out differently. Maybe she could have helped Lauren and Ashley mend their relationship.

"What was the argument about?"

"I just told you—I wasn't with them when they argued."

"Where were you?"

"I stayed at the bottom of El Castillo when they climbed up. They fought there—at the top."

"They climbed El Castillo?"

Her cheeks flushed. "Yes . . ."

"I'm going to need the names of the tour guide and anyone else involved."

"Will they be in trouble?"

171

"You don't need to worry about that."

Natalie sighed. This was such a colossal mess. "I'll have to look in the room to see if I can find the names. Marco set it up for us."

"The Marco that is nowhere to be found?" Officer Garcia raised his eyebrow. "So is that why things were tense between Lauren and Ashley last night? Because they had argued at El Castillo?"

"Maybe. I don't know."

"Well, it seems odd that she wouldn't want to leave with her friends—that she'd rather stay by herself at a bar in Mexico," Officer Lopez said. "How angry was she at Ashley that night?"

Natalie regretted telling them. She should have let Lauren answer that question. "Are you accusing her of something?"

Officer Lopez frowned. "Should we be?"

"No!" Natalie said, her voice rising. "Yes, she was pissed at Ash. She was ready to go home. But she'd never hurt her," she said adamantly, even though there was a small voice inside that reminded her how incensed Lauren had been the night before. She shoved down the thought. *No way.*

"Did Lauren come back to the hotel immediately?"

"As far as I know, yes," Natalie said, thinking of Lauren's earlier confession about José. But they had only asked her if Lauren had come back, and as far as Natalie knew, she had.

"As far as you know? Well, we will be sure to ask her about that. Seems strange you can't remember, and she's not trying harder to help you fill in more holes that concern her part in all this," Officer Lopez said.

"She's doing her best. It's been a hard day." Natalie was exhausted and knew that Lauren must be feeling the same way. Like it or not, they were in this nightmare together.

"What's Marco's address?" Officer Lopez asked.

Natalie pulled the piece of paper out of her pocket and handed it to them.

"Have you notified Ashley's family?"

"Yes, her husband is on his way down here."

"Okay, we would like to talk to him when he arrives. Will you let him know that?"

"Yes," Natalie said.

"Anything else you'd like to say?" Officer Lopez looked at her pointedly.

Natalie thought of the emojis Ashley sent Jason. Maybe they'd be able to decipher them. "Ashley's husband received a text from her last night."

"What did the text say?" Officer Garcia asked.

She described the three emojis.

"What do you think they mean?"

Natalie took a deep breath. They could mean so many things. That she left. That she was taken. That she was planning to hurt herself. That last one was hard to imagine—Ashley had always loved life. Been a spark that ignited others. But according to Lauren, Ashley had begged to save their friendship. How much pain had she been in last night?

"I really don't know, I'm sorry," Natalie said, feeling sick at the thought of Ashley being so upset she'd hurt herself. She decided to keep her theories to herself. Because they were just that, theories.

"Thank you," Officer Garcia said. "We'll talk to Lauren now. And we'll send someone to escort you to the hospital for the drug tests. Be sure to stay available should we need to reach you at any point today. And please don't leave Tulum without telling us."

Natalie forced back the tears that were threatening to fall. She bit her lip hard and looked at Officer Lopez.

He stared at her, a skeptical look on his face. "Or if you suddenly remember something."

As the officers walked away, she wanted to scream after them—*Remember what? What do you think I'm hiding?* But she was already yelling those words in her own mind. At herself. She rolled her shoulders, trying to loosen the knots.

Ben's name appeared on her phone's screen, and she answered.

"Hey," he said, and she could immediately hear the concern in his tone. She exhaled, the familiar scratch of his voice bringing her immense comfort, despite their issues. None of that mattered at the moment. She was in crisis and needed him. It was strange, really, how a change in circumstances had turned her entire perspective about him and their relationship upside down.

"Hey," she repeated.

"Are you okay?"

"Not really," she answered honestly.

"I've been trying to reach you. I've been so worried. I read the link to the TMZ article you texted. What happened to Ashley?"

"I don't know," she said, then dissolved into the tears she had been holding back.

CHAPTER NINETEEN

THE NIGHT
LAUREN

They'd barely made it through the front entrance of La Cantina—a bar they'd decided to go to on a whim, after Ashley searched Yelp for popular nightspots in Tulum—when Marco came up behind Ashley and picked her up. Ashley wriggled out of Marco's grasp and playfully swatted him on the arm. "You scared me!" she said dramatically. Marco smiled, then reached over and gave Natalie and Lauren awkward side hugs. *"Hola,"* he said. "You ladies look lovely tonight." But he was looking only at Ashley when he said it.

Lauren took Natalie's elbow and led her to the bar. "Of course Marco's here," she said as she signaled the bartender and ordered three mojitos.

"What part of 'girls' night out' does he not understand?" Natalie asked.

"Some girls' night," Lauren said. "Sorry. But this evening has been brutal so far. Why are we prolonging it?"

At dinner at Hartwood, Ashley had spent more time flirting with their server than talking to them. Then she ordered another drink just as the bill came. Lauren had sighed, wanting to get out of the restaurant and somewhere she could get some space from Ashley.

The bartender set the three drinks on the bar, and Natalie grabbed one and took a big sip. "Clearly we like to torture ourselves." She laughed.

"Thank God the wine was good at dinner," Lauren said. And it had been. She had drunk until the edges of their tangled friendship had become fuzzy. But now Marco was killing her buzz.

"Is it stupid that I thought the night might get better if we came here?" Natalie said, and Lauren remembered the way she'd nodded eagerly when Ashley had suggested it, Lauren pretending to be reading something on her phone so she didn't have to answer. She hadn't really wanted to go out, but she didn't like the idea of sitting alone in her hotel room either. And although she was tempted, she couldn't seek out José. At least at a bar, she would have a chance to meet someone interesting to pass the time until she could go home tomorrow. So she had followed them out to the waiting cab and bitten her tongue as Ashley attempted to speak Spanish to the cabdriver.

"No, it's not stupid to have the expectation that Ashley would want to hang out with us tonight. But now *he's* arrived." She pressed her lips together. "I suggest we prepare ourselves for the Ashley and Marco show," Lauren said as she signed the credit card receipt. "But I draw the line at buying him drinks. I am not ordering a fourth one of these." Lauren glanced across the bar to where Marco and Ashley stood. He'd been nothing but perfectly nice, but there was something about him that bothered her. Why did he follow Ashley around like a puppy dog? And more important, why did Ashley let him—changing the dynamic of the trip she'd insisted they all come on? Natalie followed Lauren's gaze, both of them noticing Marco whispering into Ashley's ear, Ashley giggling.

"Every time I talked to him, it felt like he was just biding his time until he could be with Ashley again," Natalie said. "Tour guide, my ass. It's been all about his crush on her."

"Right?" Lauren thought of the way she'd tried to flirt with him at Tropical Kiss, him looking over her shoulder to where Ashley was sitting. At first she'd found him attractive. But now, as she studied the way his black hair carelessly hung over his oversized ears and how his eyes, small and narrow, made his nose look large in comparison, she didn't think so. His looks were much like his personality: there was something that wasn't quite the way it should be. Lauren sighed. "I'm getting drunk. You?"

Natalie shrugged. "I think that's a grand idea! Whatever makes tonight go faster."

"I guess we'll be back to our lives soon enough." Lauren looked at her phone. "In fifteen hours, to be exact."

"And what does that mean for all of us?" Natalie asked tentatively.

Lauren sipped her drink, then glanced at the third full mojito sitting there next to the two empty ones. "I really don't know, Nat," she said, her fight with Ashley at Chichén Itzá still stinging. Still racing through her thoughts so fast she could barely catch her breath, every word, every look, every tear penetrating her, still.

"Is that for Ash?" Natalie asked.

"Yes. And to answer your question, I think our dynamic is a lot like those drinks right there. You and I are often totally empty seeking to be full. Seeking to be filled by Ashley. And there's Ashley." She pointed at the untouched mojito, the rum nearly spilling over the top. "She's full, but alone. Not needing to be filled by either of us."

"True. But why?"

"Honestly, I don't know anymore. But we might want to start asking why we need *her* to fill us up." Before Geoff's death, Lauren had needed Ashley in a way that she now realized had probably been unhealthy. She'd text her at all hours wanting advice or reassurance, needing that feedback from Ashley to feel good about her choices. And sometimes, maybe even most times, just wanting her attention. Maybe there had even been a part of her that wanted Ashley to be her savior, for her to prove how much she loved Lauren. Because that was the thing with Ashley: you were always in competition with the person she loved most—herself.

Natalie tilted her head to one side. "Very good question. Sometimes I think we've been intertwined in each other's lives for so long that we couldn't untangle even if we wanted to."

Lauren wondered if she was thinking about BloMe. That it tied her to Ashley in a way she no longer wanted. She got the bartender's attention again and ordered two shots.

"Not three this time?" he asked.

"Nope," Lauren said, her eyes locking with Natalie's. "Just you and me, girl." It hadn't been a great trip, that's for sure. But maybe, just maybe, she and Natalie could walk away with their own friendship, one that didn't revolve around Ashley. Lauren held up her shot glass for a toast. "To a night we'll never forget."

"Where's mine?" Marco said as he walked up behind them, smiling widely.

"Sorry, this is a girls' night, so the shots are for *girls only*," Natalie said pointedly, before grabbing her drink and walking away.

Marco watched her before turning back to Lauren. "She doesn't like me much, does she?"

Lauren took a long sip of her drink, running back through the way Marco had wormed his way into every aspect of their trip. Would things have been different had they not met him? Maybe. "Should she?" she finally said. "Like you?"

Marco shrugged his shoulders slightly, his smile smug. "I get it."

"I don't think you do," Lauren said, her voice low and deep, Marco leaning in to hear her. "This trip has been a fucking disaster."

Marco's eyes flashed. "And that's my fault how?"

Lauren gave him a long look as she traced the rim of her glass with her pointer finger. "What do you see in her?" she asked, glancing toward

Ashley, who stood across the room, head thrown back, vividly discussing something with Natalie. She asked even though she knew exactly what he saw in her. It was what had captivated Lauren for years.

Marco followed her eyes and took Ashley in, a small smile playing on his lips. "I love the way she wraps herself around everything. She has an intense energy. She sparkles."

Lauren sighed, but she wasn't surprised to hear it. Men had often described Ashley that way: a beacon of light, a star, a force. But still, while Marco might really believe she sparkled, he still didn't seem interested in *her*. "But what is it about her? Do you even know where she was born? Her favorite color? If she needs coffee in the morning? Or are you just *attracted* to her?"

"I believe the universe brought us together. Why? I don't know yet. But I'm happy it did. And in time, I will find out the *little* things. But we have talked, a lot. She's told me what's inside her heart. And for me, that matters more than her hobbies." He touched his chest.

Lauren rolled her eyes, but before she could speak, Marco continued. "I know you think all my talk about the universe is bullshit, Lauren. And that I'm probably bullshit too. Don't think I haven't seen you roll those eyes at me all week." He smirked. "And I don't blame you. Ashley is your friend and you are protective. But there really is something out there, bigger than us. Maybe, if you could just open yourself up, the way Ashley does, you could see that."

Lauren felt her anger spike. Marco didn't have a clue who she was. Hell, he didn't even know Ashley. "You don't know anything about me."

"But I do. You lost your husband last year, yes? And you are still grieving?"

Lauren put her hand on the bar. "Stop."

Marco stepped backward. "I'm sorry. I can see I've upset you. I was just trying to help."

Lauren picked up her drink off the bar. "I think you've done enough helping on this trip, Marco. Excuse me," she said, pushing past him, back through the front entrance, to anywhere but there.

~

Thirty minutes later she returned from outside, where she'd leaned against the wood fence with the peeling paint, trying to regain her composure from her interaction with Marco. Something about the way he questioned her about Geoff had enraged her. As she walked back into La Cantina, her eyes were immediately drawn to Ashley, who was leaning into Marco, Natalie standing next to them, sipping her mojito, almost as if their conversation at the bar had never happened. *So much for being annoyed he crashed our girls' night.* She wondered how much of what Natalie said was even true. Was she really that irritated with Ashley? If so, why did she jump to her side at the first opening? Were they ever not going to be fighting for her attention?

She felt her phone vibrate in her purse. She pulled it out and put her hand over her mouth when she saw the text Annie had sent. A jolt of relief filled her chest. She couldn't wait to get home to her uncomplicated friend.

This guy says he's forty, lol. Attached was a picture of a bald man wearing small, round eyeglasses and a paisley bow tie.

Omg. Fifty. At least. But he's cute. I say go for it!
You just want me to get back out there!
Can't fault a girl for trying, right?

So, how's my favorite third wheel? Annie texted back.
More like fourth wheel, Lauren typed, glancing at Marco.
Just keep drinking. You get to come home tomorrow, Annie texted.

She walked up to the bar and blew a long stream of air out of her lips, and the bartender sarcastically asked if she wanted another. "Duh," she said, and pushed her empty glass across the bar.

I'd do just about anything to come home right now, Lauren texted as she waited, tears pricking at the back of her eyes. This trip was supposed to represent many things for her—redemption, renewal, forgiveness. With the year anniversary of Geoff's death approaching, she'd grasped on to the hope for change like a life raft, and now, without it, she was drowning.

Ashley looked over and caught Lauren's eye and beckoned her over. Lauren shook her head. Ashley made her way over to Lauren anyway, Natalie in tow.

"What's up? Having fun?" she asked Lauren.

"Do you care if I am?" Lauren shot back and felt a stab of guilt when Ashley's face fell.

"Of course I do," Ashley said, glancing at Natalie. Possibly wondering if she was going to come to her defense? Natalie looked away as if she hadn't heard. "Tell me what you want me to do and I'll do it, Lauren." She waved her hand in the direction of the small, battered stage, her voice shaking. "Want me to grab the mic and tell everyone here that I'm a terrible friend? Is that what you want?"

"I don't know what I want," Lauren said, and turned her back to Ashley so she couldn't see the tears forming in her eyes. She hated that she couldn't just wrap Ashley in a tight hug and tell her that they were okay. But if she let go of the thick ball of anger she held for Ashley, then it would mean she'd have to let go of Geoff too. And she wasn't ready to do that—they were spun together like a spool of thread. The resentment she held for Ashley had become a fabric of her being. Without it, who would she be? Lauren felt movement behind her and waited a beat before turning back. Ashley was striding back toward Marco, Natalie a few steps behind. Marco put his arms out as she approached and pulled

Ashley in, turning away from Lauren and Natalie, who stood awkwardly as they embraced.

Oh, Natalie. Can't you see that you don't need her anymore?

Ashley might have no regard for how she was acting, for what her friends might think of this man she'd opted to spend almost every second with on this girls' trip. She might not even give a shit that she was married. But someone would.

Lauren downed the tequila shot the bartender gave her, then picked up her phone and held it up so Ashley and Marco were in the frame. She pushed the red button to record video just as "Brown Eyed Girl" started playing.

CHAPTER TWENTY

THE MORNING OF THE NIGHT
ASHLEY

"What were you two fighting about anyway?" Natalie asked, and Ashley's back stiffened, her jaw tightening. She and Lauren had been silent the entire ride home from Chichén Itzá, the tension in the car as thick as smoke, Ashley breathing short breaths, trying not to cry.

"Geoff." Ashley sat down on the bed. "I said all the wrong things, of course." The conversation had been running through her mind on a loop. She knew she'd been wrong not to disclose her own abusive relationship. But she'd been right to insist that Lauren leave Geoff. What kind of friend would she have been had she just let her stay?

"I'm sure you didn't," Natalie said, comfort in her voice.

"I did, Nat. I did. And listen, I told her something. Something I thought would help her understand, and it spiraled out of control after that. It's something you don't even know."

The confession rolled off her tongue much easier this time, and she didn't stop for almost five minutes. She told her about Jason, what he'd said, how he'd pushed her. The names. Natalie stayed silent, cringing at some parts.

"Why did you keep this inside? Not even tell me?" Natalie asked.

Ashley played with the cheap turquoise ring she'd bought at the beach the day before. "I don't know. It's hard to explain. I think I was embarrassed! Me"—she pointed to her own chest—"entrepreneur and strong-minded woman, letting her own husband treat her like that? Can you imagine what people would think?"

"No one would have cared, Ash," Natalie said softly as she picked at her cuticles.

Ashley sensed Natalie was still bothered that she hadn't told her first about her problems with Jason. "And I thought Lauren would understand because she'd been through it—or something similar. If she hadn't, I probably wouldn't have told anyone. But she didn't understand. Not at all. In fact, it made her more upset."

"Can I ask you something?"

"Of course," Ashley answered, a little surprised how good it felt to tell Natalie. Up until now, every terrible thought, every doubt she'd had about Jason, she'd had to bottle up inside. Finally she had someone to confide in.

"What's going on with us? Are we the friends we used to be? Are we even close anymore?" Natalie asked.

Ashley snapped her head back. "That's your reaction to what I just told you? To make it about you? Not, 'hey, Ashley, I'm so sorry, are you okay'?" She got up off the bed and stood stiffly, the anger spiking so quickly that she knew she had to leave immediately. Before she blew up.

"Wait, Ash, I'm sorry. I . . ."

"I'm going for a walk on the beach." She turned back, gripping her hand on the handle of the sliding glass door, watching Natalie scramble to get up, to try to take back what she'd just said. "And you wonder why I don't tell you anything anymore."

She walked out, not bothering to close the slider, wondering when Natalie had stopped caring what happened to her.

When Ashley came back, Natalie attempted to apologize, but she had waved her off. But if she hadn't been sharing a room with her, she might not have returned. She would have taken the night to cool off. But she didn't have that luxury. She needed space and even thought about going to Lauren's room. But she didn't want to have to explain—to admit she'd had another fight with someone. She avoided Natalie's eyes as she pattered around the room getting ready for bed, telling Natalie she was too tired to talk about it anymore.

The next morning, Natalie got up early, returning with two ceramic mugs of steaming coffee. She sat cross-legged on the bed and tried to open the conversation once more, wanting, no, almost seeming to *need* Ashley to understand that despite their current problems, despite that she found it almost impossible to reconcile the Jason she knew with the one that Ashley had described, she was still there for her.

"It's all good, Nat," she said, blowing on the hot coffee, grabbing for her phone. "Let's just forget it ever happened, okay?" She hadn't been sure what Natalie's initial reaction would be, but she certainly hadn't been expecting that she'd question their closeness. No matter what she said now, it would be tainted by her earlier pettiness. Ashley had no desire to hear it. If she'd learned anything, it had been that her impulse to spill her inner secrets to Lauren and Natalie had been a mistake.

"How do we do that?" Natalie had asked, perplexed.

Ashley smiled and snapped her fingers. "Just like that!" And then she headed for the shower, feeling Natalie's eyes on her.

CHAPTER TWENTY-ONE

THE DAY AFTER
LAUREN

"So your friends get in a taxi with Marco, and you stay behind? Why?" Officer Garcia opened his notepad and scanned the first few pages.

Were all of those notes from Natalie? Lauren wondered what she had told them—was he checking to see if their stories matched up? She pictured Marco's hand resting on Ashley's lower back as he guided her out to the cab, Natalie trailing behind. Lauren still breathing hard from her exchange with Marco and then with Ashley. "I didn't want to go with them. Ashley asked me to, but I said no. It had been a long night, a long five days."

"What do you mean?"

"Things between all of us weren't great," Lauren admitted.

Officer Garcia found what he was looking for in his notes. "Natalie said *tense*."

"Really?" Even though it was the truth, Lauren wondered how Natalie had portrayed her. How she'd characterized Ashley. *Herself.*

"Yes. Why was it so *tense*?"

Lauren hesitated. Should she tell them about her argument with Ashley at Chichén Itzá, or would it incriminate her in some way? "We had some pretty major unresolved issues," she finally said.

"Tell us about them." Officer Lopez folded his hands in his lap, as if he had all day.

Lauren tried to calculate how much Natalie might have revealed. What if she'd told them everything? That Lauren had blamed Ashley for Geoff's death? How full of rage she'd been at the funeral?

"We've been friends a long time. Twenty years. Things build up."

"You're going to have to be more specific." Officer Lopez narrowed his eyes at her.

She couldn't tell them about Chichén Itzá. They weren't supposed to have been there. She had no idea what the consequences would be for trespassing after hours, but she did not want to find out. "We had an argument about my late husband."

"Was this at Chichén Itzá?"

Lauren swallowed hard. So Natalie *had* told them. Lauren ran her fingers through her hair. Were they going to accuse her of doing something to Ashley?

Officer Lopez tilted his chin, clearly wanting more.

"Yes. We argued at Chichén Itzá. About a year ago, Ashley insisted I stand up to my husband because he was abusive." She looked down, unable to meet the officers' eyes. The word was still so hard to say. The story still so hard to admit. "And I listened to her. He had a massive heart attack and died while I was telling him our marriage was over." Tears welled in her eyes. It was depressing how her grief still snuck up on her.

"And you blamed yourself?" Officer Garcia asked.

"No, I blamed her!" Lauren said, then instantly regretted it. "I mean, yes and no. It's complicated." She felt a chill as she tapped into the memory of how angry she'd been with Ashley at the top of El Castillo. When she'd heard Jason was abusive too. And when they'd climbed down, Natalie's confused expression, her peppering them with questions on the way home about what had happened up there and whether they were okay. Lauren had refused to speak—afraid to reopen the fight and for her feelings to be exposed again like raw skin. Ashley had probably told Natalie some skewed version of the story at some point, and that's why she'd mentioned it to the officers.

"I'm so sorry for your loss," Officer Garcia said.

"Thank you."

"So why were you fighting about this issue a year later?"

"Because we didn't talk most of last year after it happened."

"But you're on vacation in Mexico together."

"Right—it was Ashley's idea to come here and work on our friendship—try to get close again," she said, realizing how absurd that must sound. "Or at least that's what I had thought."

Lauren remembered the way she'd acted that first day. How she just couldn't let Ashley have what she wanted—an easy and relaxed reintroduction to each other. It was almost as if Lauren had wanted to punish her. That hadn't been her intention when she'd accepted the invitation, but that familiar tension had taken over once they were sitting in front of each other.

"Did you?" Officer Garcia asked. "Get close again?"

"That's also complicated."

"Try to explain it." Officer Lopez looked at her.

"We were kind of up and down. And after Chichén Itzá, I'd say we were down," Lauren said.

"How were you getting along at La Cantina?"

Lauren closed her eyes briefly, then looked at Officer Lopez. "Not great."

"Is that why you chose not to leave with Ashley?" Lauren sucked in a breath, recollecting the desperate look in Ashley's eyes. The way she'd grabbed Lauren's arm for emphasis. *Please. Let's go somewhere and work this out. We've been friends too long. I can't lose you.*

Lauren debated whether to tell them how adamant Ashley had been about working things out that night. That if Lauren had accepted the olive branch, none of this would have happened. She decided to be honest. Natalie had probably already told them anyway.

"When I declined to go with them, Ashley offered to leave with me instead. To talk things through," she said, briefly describing their exchange, avoiding their eyes so they couldn't see the self-judgment in her own.

"Why wouldn't you go with her to work things out?" Officer Garcia asked when she was done speaking.

"It just seemed pointless, you know? Like if we hadn't been able to fix things by then, I doubted we would have suddenly seen the light after several more drinks."

Officer Garcia nodded, but said nothing.

"But I wish I had," she offered, hoping they could see the sincerity in her eyes. "And there's something else," she added, deciding to tell them about the video she had recorded last night. It might not look good that she had taken it without Ashley's consent, and it would be hard to explain, but Marco was in it and maybe they could use it to identify him. She hadn't mentioned it to Natalie because she wasn't sure she was even going to tell the police. But she knew now that she had to. Anything that could help them find Ashley was more important than trying to protect herself. She knew she had nothing to do with Ashley's disappearance. But maybe she could help find her. "I recorded her and Marco dancing."

"Why?"

"I was pissed. Like, where did she get off? Bringing us here to mend, then spending all of her time with him instead of us." She narrowed her eyes. *And then playing grabass with him the whole time.* "When he showed up last night, I kind of cracked inside. I'd had it."

"What were you planning on doing with the video?"

"I had no idea. I was drunk."

"Blackmail, possibly? Threaten to put it on Facebook, show her husband?"

Lauren shook her head vigorously. "No, none of those things."

"Then what?"

"Honestly, I hadn't thought it through." Lauren immediately regretted telling them, hearing how it sounded out loud. But she quickly realized it didn't matter, that it was worth it if it helped identify Marco. "I was just mad. I thought if I showed her how ridiculous she looked, she'd see it. That maybe she'd realize she had totally dropped the ball on being here for her friends this week. I was just tired. And mad. It was stupid. Marco had come up to talk to me earlier, and that also set me off."

"You sound pretty angry," Officer Lopez said.

"What are you saying?"

"I'm just saying you sound like you were having conflicts with both Marco and Ashley, so maybe you have more to tell us about where they might be."

"I have no idea!" Lauren slapped her hand on the table. She thought she saw Officer Lopez give her a look of satisfaction.

"Let's get back on point," Officer Garcia said. "What did Marco say to you that set you off?"

"Basically that the universe had brought him and Ashley together for a reason."

"What reason?" Officer Lopez asked.

"Your guess is as good as mine."

"That doesn't sound too bad."

"It was just the fact he was there, with us, ruining our night." Lauren thought about the way Marco had tried to question her about her own life. He'd barely spoken ten words to her, blew her off when she'd tried to flirt with him initially, and now was an expert on her life, because he understood the *universe*?

"May we see the video?"

Lauren played it for them and bit down on her lower lip when she saw Ashley's wide smile light up the screen.

"I can't make out Marco. It's just the back of him. But text it to me, and I'll have my men analyze it anyway. Maybe they can get more of a visual on him." Officer Garcia didn't sound optimistic.

Officer Lopez gave her a long look. "Where were you between the hours of eleven thirty last night and this morning?"

Lauren's heart started beating harder. "You think I'm involved? That I did something to her?"

"Did you?" he asked.

"Of course not!"

"Do you have an alibi?" Lopez pressed. Her chest tightened—he didn't think she did.

"Yes. I took a taxi back to the hotel a few minutes after the others left . . ." She paused, feeling her cheeks redden. "And then I had a couple of drinks in the hotel bar with the bartender there." José had called her over as she was walking to her room; his shift had just ended. He'd offered to make her a nightcap. "And then he and I went up to my room together."

Officer Garcia frowned at Officer Lopez.

"Okay, and he can verify this?"

"Yes, but I don't want him to get in trouble with the hotel."

"We will be discreet," Officer Garcia said.

"Okay." She felt a swirl of embarrassment. What must they be thinking of her? Having sex with a hotel employee while her friend disappeared? After Ashley had practically begged her to stay with her? Guilt worked its way through her. Would Ashley still be here had she taken her up on her offer to talk things out?

"We will need you to be available if we need to talk to you again," Officer Garcia said.

Lauren started to stand up.

"Just one more thing." Officer Lopez held up his index finger, and she settled back into her chair. "Natalie told us she can't remember most of the night."

Lauren nodded.

"Do you believe her?"

"Yes," she said.

But the truth was, she wasn't sure.

CHAPTER TWENTY-TWO

THE DAY AFTER
NATALIE

Ashley had been missing for at least half a day.

Natalie stared out to the coastline, watching a cardinal diving through the air, lifting its wings. Just when she thought it was going to touch the ground, it sailed toward the sky again. *What are you searching for, little bird?* Ashley's disappearance hit her hard in the gut once more as she watched the cardinal, reminded of the sacred quetzal of Chichén Itzá. Clapping their hands together at the base of El Castillo, mimicking the sound the bird made. She wished she could go back to that moment, before Ashley and Lauren scaled the pyramid. Before they'd fought. Before Ashley had confided in Natalie in their hotel room afterward. Before Natalie had failed her as a friend.

"Drink this." Maria walked up to Natalie, who was sitting on her balcony. Maria held a glass of water with a slice of lemon lazily floating on top. "It's eleven thirty in the morning—have you had anything to eat or drink today?"

Natalie's insides felt hollow. She didn't think she had. But her stomach was rock-hard—the thought of ingesting even a drop of water made bile rise in the back of her throat. Maria's narrowed eyes made her intention clear: she wasn't going to take no for an answer. She took the glass from Maria and sipped it, the cool liquid funneling into her body, and she gagged slightly. She forced herself to swallow and felt a memory swinging low in her mind, like heavy fruit on a thin branch. She closed her eyes, trying to grasp it. It wasn't quite a vision—more of a feeling. *Thirst. Exhaustion. Nausea. Desperation.*

Not entirely different from how she felt at this very moment. She tried to distinguish the feelings from one another, but she couldn't, the emotions layered too heavily.

She looked at her cell—her battery power was at 11 percent. The stream of texts and phone calls from people back home hearing about Ashley was nonstop. Their lawyer had left several voice mails. She listened to the most recent. *Natalie, we need to tell Revlon something. I haven't heard from them yet, but I know I will. Please call me so we can strategize.*

She turned her phone over, frustrated. She knew Arthur meant well. As their attorney, he was only trying to protect them. But this was yet another reason she wanted out of this company. She didn't want to worry about what Revlon thought Ashley's disappearance would do to the value of BloMe, Inc. The room began to spin and she reached out a hand to steady herself. She felt like she was losing control. That they were all losing control.

She pulled up Ben's name.

"Hi," he said on the first ring. "Did you find her?"

"No," Natalie said, taking several deep breaths.

"I need to come down there and help."

"No, stay with the girls. Jason just texted to say his flight is about to take off. So he'll be here later. There are plenty of us looking. In fact, I should get back—"

"I can get my sister to stay with them," Ben said.

"How are they?"

"They're great. Planted in front of their iPads, binge-watching old seasons of *Survivor*."

Natalie smiled, imagining them huddled together under one of the microfleece blankets she kept in an ottoman by the couch. "Why did you tell them you were keeping them home today?" She pictured them jumping up and down, mentally mapping out their day in terms of Netflix programming, having no idea their aunt Ashley was the real reason they couldn't leave the house. Natalie cringed at the thought of having to deliver bad news. She shook it away. She couldn't think like that. Ashley had no siblings, and her parents had passed away several years ago in a car crash, leaving her alone. She'd always declared that Natalie and Lauren were her adopted family.

"I said I'd heard a bad flu bug was going around, and I didn't want them to get it. It's the first thing I thought of. But it's not like they fought me on it."

Natalie exhaled. When she woke up this morning on the beach, she had no idea the degree this would reach. Now her daughters were home from school, banned from social media. Natalie thought of Ashley's daughters, oblivious to their mom's disappearance. She prayed it would always stay that way. She knew Jason's mom was with them and in charge of keeping them off the internet, but that was easier said than done. Especially when she was upset too—probably checking her own phone for updates constantly. She couldn't imagine being in America when Ashley was missing in Mexico. "You took Meg's phone?"

"Of course," Ben said. "She thinks I'm borrowing it because I dropped mine in the toilet."

"Ben—"

"I'm a terrible liar, I know."

Not so bad that you couldn't hide what you'd done to all of our money.

"Look, I'm worried about you. I need to come—"

"I don't want the girls without both of us," she said sharply.

"Okay," Ben said, and she imagined him holding up his hands the way he did when he was admitting defeat. "I'm just uneasy sitting here, thinking about Ashley missing, you being drugged—" he said, referencing a quick text she'd sent asking him to please not be upset she was texting it, but she wanted him to know. That and she was going in to get tested. "So, Nat, I hate to do this, but we need to talk about the money," he began.

"We are not talking about that right now," Natalie said. How could he think that was a good idea?

"Okay, okay, I'm sorry. But her disappearance changes everything."

Natalie felt her blood pressure rise. "Don't you think I know that?"

"Of course. Can you just tell me what's going on?"

Pushing her anger aside, she told him the story quickly—except for the part about waking up alone on the beach—and held her breath, expecting him to launch into a safety lecture.

"I wish I was there to protect you," he said, his voice tender.

Natalie felt her throat burn. He sounded like the Ben she'd married. The one she'd known up until he revealed he'd lost their money. "I do too," she said, her voice cracking. When they'd met and he told her he was a day trader, she was apprehensive. *You gamble?* she'd asked. *No, no way. But everyone thinks that's what it is.*

He'd made a couple of bad investments. Then he'd doubled down on them. He *had* gambled. With their livelihood.

"Is Revlon willing to wait until this all gets sorted out?" Ben asked.

"Really, Ben?" she snapped. "I told you, we aren't discussing this right now!"

"Nat, it's a reasonable question. There's a lot of money on the line."

"Because of *you*."

"Look, I fucked up. But now there's an opportunity to fix it. And you'd want to sell even if we didn't need the money. So I'm just asking. What's Arthur's strategy for damage control? I'm assuming he's contacted you."

Natalie sighed. "I'm dealing with it." Before she hung up, she promised to update him the minute they had news. About Ashley. Not Revlon. Like it or not, she and Ben were in this mess together. They were still a team.

∽

Natalie needed to take a walk. She headed toward the beach, keeping her eyes trained ahead as she passed the bungalow where the honeymooners were staying. What were they doing now—swimming with sea turtles? Boating? Having sex? Maybe all three. Probably all three. She longed to be them, to have her biggest concern be whether she should do it missionary or reverse cowgirl. She kept moving forward, but hesitated when she saw the wooden table and chairs half hidden by palm leaves—where hotel guests could book a romantic dinner—and thought of something Ashley had said on their way down to meet Lauren at the beach the first day they'd arrived. *Maybe you and I should sign up.* Then she'd threaded her arm through Natalie's and leaned in, mezcal tequila on her breath. *Because I think we both know we're all the other really has.*

Natalie had laughed and felt a rush. She often wanted to be Ashley's only friend. But now the words haunted her.

The breeze picked up as she neared the beach. She pulled her sunglasses down over her eyes, the sun an orange ball of fire in the sky. She checked her phone—it was almost noon. She should be out searching for Ashley. But where? Other than the bar and Marco's place, she had no idea where to look. At the end of their questioning, she'd given the police the list of the places they'd been that week: the private beach, Chichén Itzá, downtown Tulum, Hartwood. But why would Ashley have returned to any of those places? She remembered the guidebook saying the coastline of the Yucatán Peninsula alone was seven hundred miles long. She'd almost have more luck finding her by throwing a dart at a map of Mexico and going wherever it landed. Her limbs felt shaky, her heart racing again at the thought that they might not ever find her.

She stepped down onto the beach, the granules easing between her toes with each step. A sand crab scurried across the surface, then burrowed, disappearing as quickly as he came. She thought of Ashley, how quickly she had disappeared. In the blink of an eye, she was there and then she wasn't. At least that's what Natalie's memory made it seem like. But she knew it couldn't be trusted. And that's what frightened her the most—what lay inside her mind, ready to be recaptured.

Wow! The water feels amazing!

Natalie swiveled around so fast she stumbled. That was Ashley's voice.

But Ashley wasn't standing there. No one was. She heard the taunt again, this time followed by laughter. She froze in place. A memory was there and, dammit, she was not going to let it slip away. Again.

She closed her eyes—listening to the sounds of the waves slowly breaking on the shore, of birds calling out to each other—and waited.

I. Want. Out. I. Need. Out.

It was her own voice this time.

Natalie's mind felt like a heavy door she couldn't push open. And just behind it was where the memories were locked away. She thought back to after she had her C-section with Lucy. She'd lain in the recovery room, her legs immobile from the spinal block, like two steel planks, no matter how strongly she commanded her mind to move them. The nurse had smiled sweetly and told Natalie it would be a few hours before she could feel them again. But Natalie was undeterred. As Lucy had suckled on her breast for the first time, Natalie had stared at her legs, willing her brain synapses to reconnect, despite the drugs still flowing through her body. And thirty minutes later, when her leg moved, Natalie hadn't been surprised. She knew her determination was, by far, the most interesting thing about her.

She closed her eyes again and attempted to visualize the memories reconnecting to one another. She imagined herself tethering them as they circled closer, almost within reach. She inhaled deeply and reached out once more.

And suddenly an image of Ashley materialized. She was in water, floating, the area around her blurred like the vignette filter on one of those old-fashioned photos. Natalie concentrated. Where had they been? At the beach where Natalie had woken up, soaked? She maintained her breath, afraid to move. Afraid to lose the vision.

The sound of laughter drifted into her thoughts again. It was clearly Ashley's—light and airy, like soft towels fresh from the dryer. Then she heard another voice.

It was hers. Asking Ashley to get out.

Why had she wanted Ashley to get out? And what had she wanted her to get out of? Had she been in danger? She clawed at the back of her mind for the rest of the memory. But the door had shut—the recollection no longer within reach. It was just her, on the beach, alone with her limited reflections.

The baby hairs stood on end on Natalie's arms. Natalie stared out at the ocean, wondering whether she and Ashley had been out there together last night. But the story didn't line up with the honeymooners' account. They'd heard one woman's voice. Not two.

"Where are you, Ashley?" Natalie yelled into the ocean.

"Natalie?"

Natalie turned, her cheeks flushing. Officer Garcia's thick eyebrows were squished together. "My colleague, Officer Hernandez, is here to escort you to the clinic." Natalie walked slowly toward Officer Garcia, praying the results of the tests wouldn't complicate things even more.

CHAPTER TWENTY-THREE

The Day After
Natalie

Natalie stared without emotion out the window of the police cruiser as it pulled up to the hospital in Mérida two and a half hours later.

The hospital was a large soft-peach building that advertised *"Urgencias"* in red neon, which had caught the light of the midafternoon sun. From the outside, it looked more like a hotel than a hospital, with its sharp landscaping and the palm trees swaying in the wind. But inside, babies cried, toddlers ran around, at least two dozen people crowded the waiting room. As soon as she arrived, Natalie beelined to the check-in desk and showed the receptionist Ashley's picture, asked if she'd been brought in. The woman took the phone and studied it, and Natalie felt a surge of hope. But then she shook her head and explained she'd been there since ten o'clock the night before and she would have remembered.

Her phone buzzed in her pocket. Jason had just arrived. She texted him that she'd be back around 9:00 p.m.

That would be almost twenty-four hours since she'd seen Ashley.

Several minutes later, she was led into an exam room, and the nurse pricked her arm. Natalie looked away as the dark fluid filled the vial, trying to decide which scenario would be worse: finding out she *was* drugged or that she wasn't. If she was, then it only added to the rising fear inside her, and it meant the same or worse could have happened to Ashley. If she wasn't . . . she wondered what her subconscious was protecting her from.

Then the nurse tapped her long nails, filed sharp like daggers, on the clipboard. "It says here that you are to get a medical exam as well."

"No," Natalie said, wrapping her arms around herself. "I told the police nothing happened. I'm fine." She took in the dirty linoleum floor of the exam area, the stained curtain that separated her from the next, surprised this was the private hospital. She shuddered to think of what the public ones were like.

The nurse consulted her chart once more and shook her head. "Yes. It says here. The *policía* want one."

Natalie felt sick. In America, didn't you have to consent to a rape kit? In Mexico, was it up to her? She should have contacted an attorney. She didn't want anyone to touch her. It was hot and muggy inside, the air conditioning losing a valiant fight with the outside heat. She wanted to find Ashley and go home. "No," she tried again, sick with the thought they might actually find something.

A willowy man with close-set eyes and a thick white mustache stepped into the room. "I'm Dr. Rivera," he said. "I received a call from Officer Garcia. He said this is a precaution, but it could help find your friend."

Natalie shivered despite how hot it was in the exam room.

Dr. Rivera continued. "The police need to rule out that you were sexually assaulted, okay?" he said, putting on latex gloves. "Will you lie back, please?"

Natalie hesitated, then decided for her own peace of mind to go along with it. Finally she nodded and met the eyes of the nurse, who smiled in response. She wished she'd taken Lauren up on her offer to accompany her here. She could really use someone to hold her hand. To tell her everything was going to be okay—even if it wasn't true. Long before Ben, that person had always been Ashley. And even since she'd married him, it had oftentimes still been her. They were like sisters in that way. Ashley had been by her side at everything. She'd taken care of her after her laser eye surgery—driving her home as she lay back in the passenger seat, high on Valium, the huge glasses shielding her from the sun. She'd even helped her change her C-section bandages when Natalie was so sore she could barely get out of bed. Natalie lay back on the table, missing Ashley. Even the things that drove Natalie crazy, like the way Ashley chomped her gum furiously or how she interrupted Natalie before she could finish expressing a thought, would be welcome right now. She stared at the ceiling, her eyes fixated on a spider inching its way across, trying not to imagine what the future might look like without her best friend.

Later, Natalie leaned her head back against the seat and settled in for the long drive back to the hotel, taking in the prismatic sunset to the west. Remembering the first night when they'd seen the spectacular sight, taking pictures with their phones, she shut her eyes, not wanting to see the beauty, not deserving it.

Jason was waiting for her in the lobby of the hotel when she returned. Without thinking, she hurried toward him and collapsed into his arms, the tears coming before she could stop them. Jason rubbed her back until she finally stopped crying.

"I'm sorry," she said, pulling away from him. "I'm so, so sorry."

"For what?"

"Because I don't know what happened."

"I thought you might be apologizing for something else," Jason said, stepping back from her.

"What do you mean?" Natalie's heart started pounding. The look in his eyes was unsettling. She thought of what Ashley had told her—about his darker side. One she was still trying to reconcile with the man she had known for thirteen years.

"I met with one of the officers—Garcia? He took my statement." She drew in a long breath, studying his face. "Okay."

"They wanted to see the emojis she sent me and what time they came in. They're also going to try to pinpoint where she was when she sent them. They say it's a long shot, but they'll try. They told me something else too." He stared at her for so long she finally had to look down. "Why didn't you tell me?"

Did he somehow know Ashley had been planning to leave him?

"Tell you what?" Natalie asked. She was not going to say it.

"Let's talk over here," he said, and she followed him to a couch in the corner she'd sat on a dozen times today. "I need you to stop playing dumb." He gave her a look. "Who is Marco, and why didn't you tell me about him when you called me?"

Natalie took another deep breath. "He's a guy we met the day after we arrived. We hung out with him a lot. I was going to tell you in person."

"You really expect me to believe that? I have to hear from the police that this guy is a suspect? That he may have taken my wife, or she may have left with him of her own free will?"

"I'm sorry. I thought I would talk to you before they did. But nothing was going on between them, if that's what you're thinking."

"The police seem to feel otherwise."

"They're just trying to find her."

"Was my wife sleeping with this guy?"

"No!" Natalie stopped. "At least I don't think so."

"Do you really not remember most of the night?" Jason's gaze bored into hers. She could see tiny flecks of gold in his gray eyes.

She bristled. "You think I'm lying?"

"You didn't tell me about Marco, so what else aren't you telling me?"

"I swear, I wanted to tell you when you got here."

"And they weren't sleeping together?"

"No," Natalie said firmly. Even though she wasn't completely sure.

He didn't look convinced, but his demeanor softened. "Okay, so tell me everything you do remember. And please don't leave anything out."

After she was finished, he stared at her for a long time. "You just go dark right after you guys dance? Nothing else between eleven thirty last night and this morning? That's a long chunk of memory to lose." He gave her another look that made her stomach knot.

How could she make him understand that it was more than *going dark*? That it felt like part of her mind had been stolen from her. And the missing thoughts could add up to something terrible. Something chilling. Her lip quivered as she saw him watching her. Doubting her.

"I swear to you, I can't remember."

"I don't know, Nat. You're someone who can do long division in her head. Who once put together her daughter's thousand-piece princess castle without ever looking at the directions. You're whip-smart. It doesn't make sense that your brain would fail you."

She raked both of her hands through her hair, losing faith. If her own friends weren't on her side, how could she defend herself against the police? The press? She needed to convince him. "Well, it did. It failed me. It failed Ashley!" Natalie stood up and kept her back to Jason. She took several sharp breaths, trying to calm down. Finally, she turned around. "I told you I think I was drugged. Do you think I'm lying?"

Jason sighed. "I've known you for a long time, Nat. You're like a sister to me. But you have to see it from my point of view. Wouldn't you question me if the roles were reversed? Especially if I had already withheld a piece of critical information from you?"

"Of course." *Particularly after what Ashley told me about you.* She doubted Jason had told that part to the police—how he treated Ashley behind closed doors. How his behavior might have been the catalyst for her disappearance. She rubbed her arms, wondering how bad it was. Lauren had told Natalie that it wasn't until recently, in therapy, that she'd *really* talked about Geoff's abuse—in detail. Had Ashley held back when she'd told them about Jason? She stared at him, looked into his dark eyes, trying to see the man Ash had described. Tried to imagine him saying the terrible things. She could barely come to terms with what she had been told. But what if it was even worse?

Jason softened even more. "No, I don't think you're lying." He paused. "But if you remembered anything else, anything at all, even a detail you don't think matters, you would tell me, right?"

Natalie thought of the rest of the story with Marco—the way he'd touched Ashley. Them going off alone for half a day. But she shook the thought away. She had to protect Ashley. Missing or not, she was still her best friend. "I promise I will."

"Okay." Jason stood up. "I want to go to this Marco guy's apartment." He balled his hands into fists at his sides.

"He's gone. He cleared it out."

"But maybe the police missed something."

"I was there this morning. There's nothing."

"It's the last place we know for sure that my wife was," he said, obviously trying to keep his voice steady.

"I know, but it won't help going there. We should put our efforts somewhere else." Natalie meant it, but she also didn't want to go back.

Jason thought for a moment. "Tell me you guys got a picture of him. We can give it to the police."

Natalie shook her head. "Marco always offered to take the pictures of us. He said he hated to have his photo taken." Even as she said the words, she realized how naive they'd all been.

"This guy sounds like a total con artist. You really didn't see any red flags?"

"No . . . I feel so stupid. He lied about owning Tropical Kiss, he's Mexican but his last name was Smith, and now he's gone. I think I was so focused on being irritated with him for invading our time that I missed everything else." She swallowed, feeling a burn in her throat. She felt foolish for not knowing more about him. Not getting so much as a cell phone number or friending him on Facebook. Basic things she would tell her daughters to do. Maybe it had been because she hadn't wanted to know him any more than she had to. She had considered him a barnacle on their friendship, and she had been anxious to scrape him away once they got back home, almost as if he'd never been there in the first place.

"Maybe they have a copy of his driver's license in his employee file? Because that woman did confirm he worked there, right? He didn't lie about that."

"Right. I'm sure the police are working on it." As she said it, she didn't even know if it was true. The police were now in charge of finding Ashley. She felt like she'd lost all control.

"Well, I'm not willing to wait for them to do things on Mexico time. I know they've acted faster than usual—I was shocked to find out they'd already been to his apartment, dusted for prints—but I can't leave it all up to them," Jason said, holding his hand out to Natalie. "I'm going to find my wife. You coming?"

Natalie took his hand and let him tug her forward a bit, her body feeling heavier than it had that morning, the weight of Ashley's fate like sandbags on her shoulders.

He looked intently in Natalie's eyes. "I just don't get it. It was supposed to be a girls' trip. If nothing was going on between Ashley and him, as you claim, why hang out with this guy all week?" Jason asked, grimacing, as if he were preparing himself for the truth.

"He acted as a tour guide—took us places. Showed us local fare. That sort of thing." It wasn't a complete lie, she told herself as she said the words.

Jason stared at Natalie for what felt like forever. "This guy might have my wife—and we are running out of time." He inhaled sharply and when he released his breath, his chest puffed out hard. "So you'd better not be lying to me about this."

Natalie squeezed her eyes shut. Was this how Jason was with Ashley? Turning on a dime? The reality was, she didn't know what the truth looked like anymore. There was so much she was unsure of. For now, she planned on keeping her mouth shut.

CHAPTER
TWENTY-FOUR

THE DAY AFTER
NATALIE

Natalie touched Jason's arm tentatively. "We need to stay calm. I know it's hard," she said, even though she was spinning inside. "I promise you, I've told you everything I know for sure about Marco." She deliberately chose words that were as close to the truth as possible.

"Well, I can't just stand here and speculate. Let's go to that bar you were at—see if someone remembers seeing something." He looked at his watch. "It's nine thirty, maybe the same crew is working?"

"Okay," Natalie said, her limbs aching. But she knew there could be no sleep until they found Ashley. "I'll go get Lauren."

Natalie walked quickly to Lauren's room and found her on the patio attached to her bungalow, staring down at her phone.

"Hey," Natalie said.

"Hi," Lauren said, looking up. "How did it go at the hospital? You okay?"

"I don't know. But it's done," Natalie said simply. She'd been examined a million times during her two pregnancies, but never like that. This time was different—emotionally invasive, tears spilling from her eyes as the reality of her situation hit her directly—that she had no idea what had happened to Ash, or herself, for that matter. There was no room to pretend any longer that everything was going to be okay.

"You sure? You want to talk about it?"

Natalie shook her head. "We'll hopefully have the results soon."

"I've been going crazy just sitting here. I feel so helpless," Lauren said.

"I know, it's hard. Jason just arrived. He thinks we should all go back to La Cantina—talk to people there."

"That's a good idea. Maybe you'll remember more," Lauren said. "I was just talking to Annie, and she brought up a good point."

Natalie could only imagine what *Annie* had to say about this. She could be getting a very filtered account of everything since they'd arrived in Tulum and Ashley went missing. "What's that?"

"She wondered why only you were drugged. Why not me too?"

"I don't know. I guess you can tell Annie I was the lucky one," Natalie said, unable to conceal her irritation.

"She's just trying to help."

"How is it helpful to doubt me?" Natalie asked, thinking of Jason, the police. How no one seemed to believe her.

"Maybe you only *think* you were drugged, but something else caused the memory loss? Or maybe there's more to it."

"What do you mean, *more to it*?"

"Annie did some research and sent me the link. The subconscious is capable of incredible things when it doesn't want to remember something."

"What are you saying?" Natalie pulled her head back and curled her lip, bracing herself, Lauren articulating the exact thing Natalie feared most.

"That maybe you weren't drugged at all, but rather you're suppressing something?"

Natalie inhaled and fought to keep her voice steady as a hot rage blazed deep inside her. It was bad enough that she was questioning herself—now Annie's theory was basically validating it. "Okay. I'm suppressing what, exactly?" Natalie asked, staring at Lauren, refusing to blink.

"I don't know," she said unconvincingly.

"I think you do—why don't you just say it?"

"It's just a theory. I don't have a clue what you would be suppressing. Only you would know what's in there." Lauren pointed to Natalie's head. "What did you tell the police?"

Natalie clenched her jaw. "Exactly what I've told you and everyone since I woke up. I. Cannot. Remember. I. Think. I. Was. Drugged."

Lauren jerked her head back as if Natalie had slapped her.

"What did *you* tell the police, Lauren? Did you share your *theories* about me? Did you tell them your new bestie, Annie, is an amateur sleuth and wants to come work on the case?" Natalie shot, her cheeks burning. "Did you also include how you told Ash to fuck off when she asked to leave with you?"

Lauren flinched. "As a matter of fact I did. But also, so did you. Why?"

"Because they asked why you didn't go with us. I wasn't going to lie."

"Or maybe you're lying now. Maybe you told them because you do blame me."

"I don't blame you any more than I blame myself." The reality was that there was more than enough blame to go around—Lauren for not agreeing to leave with them, and Natalie, well, she wasn't quite sure what to blame herself for yet. And that was the hardest part.

Lauren's face softened. "Look, you have to understand how helpless I feel here. You're the only one with the answers, but you can't access them. And the rest of us are playing guessing games. Don't blame Annie for trying to help."

"I don't even know this person!"

"She's been a good friend to me."

"Because I wasn't? Because Ashley wasn't?"

"No . . ."

"Did it ever occur to you that she probably doesn't trust me because of all the bad things you've said about me?"

"I haven't—"

"Oh, come on, now is not the time to lie."

"Fine, I told her what happened with all of us. But I was honest about my part in it too."

Natalie scoffed. "Helping is one thing. Accusing is entirely another."

She took the wooden stairs down to the beach two at a time, wishing she could run as far away from this hotel as possible. That she could be back at her house, lying between her two daughters on the couch watching old episodes of *America's Next Top Model*, the way she had the night before coming here. Before her entire life broke open.

"Where's Lauren?" Jason asked when she found him waiting in the lobby.

"She's not coming."

"Everything okay between you two?"

"No, everything's *not* okay. With us or with this." She flailed her hands toward the hotel. "And I worry it won't be for a long time—if ever."

Jason shook his head. "No," he said firmly, and Maria looked up from the front desk.

Natalie gave him an incredulous stare and pulled him aside. "No what?"

"You do *not* get to talk like that. I won't let you. So stop it right now. We are going to find Ashley," Jason said evenly, but Natalie could see the anger behind his eyes. She wondered if he was about to snap. Was this the razor-sharp temper Ashley had been talking about? She backed off immediately, not wanting to find out.

"Okay, you're right," Natalie said, following him out to the street, where he flagged down a cab. They rode in silence, Natalie still seething at Lauren, upset with Jason, watching the tourists on bikes navigating the same bumpy roads she and Ashley and Lauren had traveled on their first morning, wishing like hell she could go back in time. A rage started to rise in her belly, the intensity of it surprising her.

And reminding her she'd felt a similar anger last night. Only it had been at Ashley.

Natalie sat perfectly still, willing the memory to settle as a sliver of cold sliced through her. She heard her own voice.

You are more selfish than I ever realized.

The scalding words burned in her mind. She had been furious. Then Ashley's voice rang in her head.

What's wrong with you?

She remembered tears. But not of sadness, like the ones she'd shed at the clinic or when Ben called. These tears had been sharp and bitter. Natalie had felt like one of those wind-up toys that had been cranked as tight as it could go, then released, running straight into a wall, still moving until the energy depleted. She steadied her breathing and tried to lean back into the memory, but it was gone, the ire fading slightly but still there, like a picked scab. Her heart thundered inside her. What did these snippets of memories mean? If they all lined up would they provide the answer to where Ashley was or only lead to more questions? She tried to calm her breathing, to steady her racing mind. She was starting to remember; she was sure of that. But she wasn't sure if she really wanted to, because there was a thought that kept creeping back into her subconscious.

That once she got her memory back, she was going to beg to forget it all over again.

CHAPTER TWENTY-FIVE

THE NIGHT
NATALIE

Ashley leaned over the dirty bathroom sink toward the mirror, painting her lips with red gloss, then rubbing them together. She inched to the right to make room for Natalie, reaching over and wiping a smudge of eyeliner off her cheekbone.

Natalie teetered slightly as she pulled a paper towel from the dispenser.

"How many shots did you do with Lauren?" Ashley teased as she turned back to the mirror and ran her hand through her hair.

"One," Natalie said, slightly annoyed. *If you'd been hanging out with us, you would have known.*

"Excuse me." Natalie and Ashley turned at the sound of a woman's voice behind them. "I thought that was you. Carrie, come here, I told you it was them." A petite woman with sunburned cheeks and a tank top to match beckoned her friend. "We just love you guys," the woman continued. "I'm Diane and this is Carrie, and we are such huge fans. I mean, you wouldn't know it right now by the looks of it." She reached up and touched her reddish-brown hair twisted into a messy topknot. "But the BloBrush is my favorite beauty product. I have three of them!"

"I have two," Carrie said shyly, taking a few strands of her long blond hair between her fingers.

"Thank you," Natalie said, hoping she wasn't slurring her words, turning back toward the mirror, a flush creeping across her cheeks. It was embarrassing to be recognized, especially while drinking.

"You guys are so cute. Let's take a selfie!" Ashley interjected, and Natalie relaxed. She didn't enjoy these interactions. Ashley was better at handling them.

"Or I could take it of you guys," Natalie offered, not feeling like being tagged in yet another unflattering picture.

"No, let's do a selfie—it's more fun," Ashley said, and they all wedged in, Ashley holding her arm out expertly, then handing the phone back.

"This is so cute. I'm going to put it on Insta!" Diane said to Ashley as she studied the photo. Natalie looked away and rolled her eyes.

"We love your YouTube videos. The most recent one was so fun," Carrie said. "That thing you did with the green screen. That was a green screen, right?"

"Yes," Ashley said, smiling proudly. "That's how we made it look like we were surfing while BloBrushing our hair." She laughed. "It's one of our faves too."

"You guys are social media geniuses!" Diane pulled up something on her phone and turned it toward Ashley and Natalie. It was their Instagram page. "You have 800,000 followers! Amazing."

That had all been Ashley, building their following through creative content. She'd thought to hire someone to record them using the BloBrush to create different styles on them as regular women, not models. Each video received thousands of views on Facebook and Instagram and was shared even more. Their YouTube channel took it a step further—they did everything from giving tutorials to interviewing the women they were styling about their busy lives. Ashley had found a way to connect to their consumers on a natural level.

"Thanks so much," Ashley said. "We try to have fun with it." She gave Natalie a look in the mirror.

"We'll let you guys get back to your night," Diane said.

"So nice to meet you!" Carrie said.

"You too," Ashley said, watching the women through the bathroom's swinging door as they hovered over the cell phone looking at the selfies.

"Why do you always get so quiet when fans come up? You're not a shy person," Ashley asked Natalie once they were gone.

"It's just so weird—fans. We aren't celebrities. We invented a brush!"

"It's part of it, though," Ashley said.

"I know."

"You should engage more."

Natalie took a deep breath. She knew where this was going—it wasn't the first time Ashley had lectured her on how to *engage with fans*.

"I'm not trying to annoy you, but those people are our bread and butter," Ashley said. "I get that you don't mean to, but you come across kind of standoffish."

Natalie waited a beat before responding. She was so tired of arguing. "You did a great job. They didn't notice me."

"Exactly."

"Ash, this is one of the reasons I want to—" Natalie stopped. They shouldn't have this conversation now. In the bathroom. When they'd been drinking.

"Just say it—it's why you want to sell," Ashley said.

"Not the only reason. But yes, one of them." Natalie trailed off, thinking again about the financial hell she and Ben were in. That they'd have to move—yank the girls out of their school. Sell everything they had. What would become of them?

"It shouldn't be about money," Ashley said. "We've worked so hard to get this company where it is and you want to say goodbye, just like that?"

"It's not *just like that*," Nat said.

"Where's the girl who was so passionate about her cordless hot brush design that she pulled an all-nighter searching for other patents that might compete?" Ashley stared at her in the mirror, waiting for an answer.

She's older. She has two daughters who need her. And she needs the money so her life doesn't fall apart.

"Why are you giving up?" Ashley tried again when Natalie didn't respond.

"I'm not!" Natalie said, louder than she intended. A woman washing her hands in the adjacent sink looked over, curious.

"Then what? Don't you remember *Shark Tank*? That feeling we had afterward? That rush of being able to turn it down because we had something so special everyone wanted a piece of it?"

"*You* turned it down. You didn't even consult me."

"So you *were* taking digs at me the other night on the beach when it came up. I can't believe it still bothers you. If you had such a problem with how I handled it, why didn't *you* do anything to stop it? Why did you walk off that set never having opened your mouth to disagree?"

"You don't get the position you put me in—on television! What was I supposed to do? Make it look like we weren't a unified front while Mr. Wonderful scowled at us? That would have been worse. What *should* have happened is we should have discussed it before *you* told them all we didn't want a deal."

"You never complained when the checks started rolling in. When all the big-box stores came calling."

"We should have decided together."

"You don't get anywhere without taking a risk," Ashley said.

215

Natalie felt her irritation spike again. "But it should be risks that we decide on. Together. We are a team, or have you forgotten that?"

Ashley jerked her head back. "Come on, Nat. Don't you remember what a fantastic experience it was? We killed it!"

"You killed it," Natalie mumbled. "I was just your sidekick. Or have you conveniently forgotten?"

"I really thought I was doing what was best for us." Ashley grabbed her forearm lightly. "Sometimes you have to step in and do what's right, even if it seems unfair at the time."

"Are you talking about *Shark Tank*, or Revlon's offer?" Natalie asked.

Ashley paused, thinking. "Both, I suppose. In each of those instances, I felt as if I needed to step in. To follow my gut."

"But why does your gut get to override our partnership? It did then, and you're doing it again now."

Ashley hesitated before responding. "I don't know. I just knew that day that we didn't need the Sharks. Just in the same way I know we don't need Revlon."

"But what if you're wrong?" Natalie asked, shaking her head at the logic.

"What if I'm not?" Ashley said gently. "Come on. Let me buy you another drink. I think we could both use it."

Natalie knew another cocktail wasn't going to solve their impasse or yield the answers she was becoming increasingly desperate for. Yet she still allowed Ashley to tug her gently out the door and toward the bar, watching her swagger toward it as if she owned it. That was the thing with Ashley. She'd let her instincts dictate her entire life, from changing her major two years into college to breaking up on a whim with the guy she'd dated before Jason, leaving him baffled. But those were choices that only affected Ashley.

There was no way Natalie was going to let Ashley's gut decide the rest of *her* life.

CHAPTER TWENTY-SIX

THE DAY AFTER
NATALIE

Natalie stepped out of the cab and stared at the sign—the words "La Cantina" were carved into a piece of large wood hanging overhead. Her gaze fell on the mural covered in purposeful graffiti sitting in front of the bar, shining under the glow of the streetlamp. She ran her hand along another sign—this one read "Tapas, Musica & Mas." She blew out a long breath, thinking they'd all gotten *mas* than they'd bargained for last night. That was for sure.

She fixated on the shell of the Volkswagen Bug that sat in front of La Cantina. It was streaked with paint, as if someone had dipped a brush in rainbow colors and splattered it across the car. "Let's go inside," she said.

They walked in and she watched Jason take in the tattered bar-stools, his gaze resting on the bar. "Marco was here with you guys, right? Was he hitting on you guys? On Ashley?"

Natalie inhaled the faint smell of stale alcohol and took in the bar's interior—it looked so different when it was empty. She could feel Jason's eyes on her but didn't dare look at him. He'd known her a long time. He'd see what she wasn't saying. "We all hung out with him."

"And?"

She stared at the dance floor, sticky substances shining under the light of day. "And we drank and danced and then I don't remember." She finally looked at him, but his eyes were so intense, she turned her head, not wanting to see what was inside of them.

"You know what I'm asking." Jason rubbed his chin.

"I told you—"

"Listen, Nat. I need you to hear me right now. It's time to put girl code aside. Ashley is missing and if you know anything else—even something you think might hurt me—you need to say it. It could help us find her. You skirted my question earlier, but I'm not going to let you do it again. I'm not an idiot."

No, that's just what you call your wife.

Natalie hesitated, Ashley's accusations against Jason flashing through her mind. It was the logical reason Ashley had turned to another man for emotional comfort and maybe even more. She couldn't tell Jason that, but she had to tell him something. He clearly was not going to back off. "Okay, but stay calm," Natalie finally said, and eased into the same barstool she had the night before. Jason sat next to her where Lauren had been.

"Okay," he said, unconvincingly. She saw him wringing his hands under the bar.

She tried to read his face. Could he tell that Ashley had confided in her about his flares of anger? She measured her next words carefully. "Like I said, we hung out with him most of the week. He would just show up wherever we went." She paused. "Ashley didn't seem to mind."

"And," Jason said, his jaw clenched.

"And I didn't lie about them sleeping together. As far as I know, they did not. There was a connection between them—although, to be fair, Ash swore it was only friendship."

"Right," Jason said, staring at the liquor bottles behind the bar. Natalie followed his gaze, hers resting on the mezcal, sending her back to their first day in Tulum, all of them sitting stiffly around the table in the bar, reminiscing. "Did she spend any time alone with him at any point during the trip?" Jason asked.

Natalie knew he was right—that any information could help at this point, but it still didn't make it any easier to say the next words. "Yes, they went to the beach for a few hours. And they grabbed carne asada in town after." She quickly added, "It was all in the same day."

Jason put his elbows on the bar and pressed his hands into his cheeks. "Dammit, Ashley," he said under his breath.

Natalie waited for him to yell at her for withholding information from him again. But he didn't. He said something so quietly she had to strain to hear him. "I'm wondering if she left with him—willingly. If she left me? If that's what those emojis meant." He didn't look up.

Natalie chewed her lip, wondering what to say. Whether he was right. "I don't know. I don't get why, after she had fought me so hard—and you—about selling, she would just take off. Leave us all." But still, it was something she'd mulled over many times today. The one thing that kept her from accepting it as the answer was Ashley's girls. She simply could not comprehend that she would abandon her daughters.

"But what do you *really* think?" He looked at her, his eyes watery.

She sighed. "I think it's something we should consider."

Natalie debated whether to tell him she knew about their problems. But she realized there was a part of her that wanted him to know she knew. "She told me things between you weren't good."

He looked up at the starry sky before answering, his eyes somber. "So then you know we were fighting a lot. The offer seemed to be the last straw. I wanted her to sell. Move on. We were breaking under the pressure."

Natalie thought about her own marriage. How they were breaking too.

"I said some things the night before she left. Things I didn't mean. That I didn't miss her when she worked a lot. That I didn't care. It might make sense why she took off. I texted her while she was here to say we should talk, but she blew me off. I had wanted to apologize. I should have tried harder."

"But here's the thing I can't wrap my head around. How could she leave your girls . . ." Natalie knew she had to accept this as a possibility, but when she tried to put herself in Ashley's shoes and thought of never seeing her own daughters again, her heart ached.

"Maybe she would leave them if she felt like a bad mother." He rubbed his jaw, but didn't say more. And Natalie wasn't about to ask. How often had he told her she was a bad mom? Made her feel like she wasn't good enough to them?

Ashley had told her once, after she'd had a few glasses of wine, that she worried she wasn't affectionate enough with her daughters. That she questioned whether they loved her the same way Natalie's girls loved her.

"She was a great mom." Natalie reiterated now what she'd told Ashley then. She thought of Hannah's last birthday party. She'd had their backyard transformed into a carnival, bringing in animals and acrobats, a bumper-car ride, and even a food truck. She'd made sure every detail was perfect. Ashley showed her love through gifts and organizing big events—that was her way. But if Jason had triggered her own doubts as a mother, combined with his abuse, she could see how turned around Ashley might feel. How lost. How she might feel like they were all better off without her. Jason seemed to be waiting for her to say more. "I don't know, Jason. She seemed in a mindset to come back home and talk to you—figure things out."

Natalie noticed the relief on his face. She wasn't about to clarify her statement. That she was pretty sure Ashley would have gone home and left him the proper way—by telling him to his face.

"Okay, so if she didn't leave . . ." Jason pondered. "Maybe he took her. I know the police are exploring that theory."

"He really didn't seem like the kind of guy who would do that. I told them he seemed harmless."

"You guys knew him for, what? Four days? How could you really know?"

Natalie balked at his accusation. "I guess we really can't know," she said, but deep down she was sensing that memory—the one that was either taken from her or that she was hiding from herself—was going to reveal a lot more than Marco's character. It was going to reveal her own.

"Can I help you guys?" a stocky man with a long, jagged scar just below his chin asked. Natalie felt a rush. It was the bartender who'd served them.

"We were here last night."

"Oh, okay. Did you lose something?"

Yes, my best friend.

"Actually, yes, my wife," Jason said.

The bartender cocked his head. "Sorry, what do you mean?"

"I was here with three other people." Natalie described Lauren and Ashley and Marco and explained that Ashley was missing and that Natalie herself was concerned she may have been drugged. She asked him whether he remembered any of them.

"Mojitos, right? For you and your friend?"

Natalie nodded. "Lauren."

"I might forget a face, but I never forget a drink," he said. "You think someone put something in your mojito? It wasn't me!" He held up his hands.

"Oh, no, that's not what I'm saying. I left it up here when I went to dance, and I'm thinking that's when it might have happened."

"I always watch the drinks when someone leaves them to hit the dance floor. I can't be one hundred percent sure, but I didn't see anyone acting weird or anything. Usually I can spot those types."

Natalie would completely give up on her theory of being drugged if she had an alternative explanation as to why she couldn't remember. Even though the bartender didn't see anything, it didn't mean it hadn't happened.

"What about my friend Ashley?" Natalie pulled up a picture of her on her phone and showed him. "Do you remember her? Or the man who was with her, Marco? I don't have a picture of him . . ."

"I recognize her." He thought for a moment. "She sat up here with a guy who fits the description you gave me. They were drinking mojitos too."

"Anything else?" Natalie asked and looked nervously toward Jason, wondering whether the bartender would reveal how close Marco and Ashley had become.

"Yeah, I do. They were talking about her life—he kept asking her questions. Was she happy, that sort of thing." He paused, giving Jason a once-over. "You said you're the husband?" he asked, and Jason nodded. "They talked about you."

"Me?"

"Yeah, I can't remember exactly, but he wanted to know if she was happy in her marriage. I only remember because I don't usually hear that kind of deep conversation here."

Natalie imagined Ashley leaning into Marco, whispering that she was miserable. Marco taking the opportunity to tell her she should leave. Maybe even with him.

"What did she say?" Jason asked, his back stiffening.

"Oh, I don't know, man. I got busy. It's hard to recall," the bartender said, staring down at the glass he was drying.

"You can tell me. It's okay—I can handle it," Jason said.

Natalie glanced at him; he was clenching his jaw as if preparing himself for a blow. She wasn't sure she wanted to hear the answer either. Could she handle it if she'd been abandoned by her best friend and business partner?

"I really don't want to get involved. I might be wrong about what I heard." The bartender lined glasses up in front of him.

"Please." Jason tried again. "We're trying to find my wife—anything might help."

"Okay, but you have to leave me out of it with the police. I have a record. I can't lose this job."

"We will. Just tell us what you remember," Jason said.

He sighed. "All right, man. She said something like she had thought about leaving everything behind."

Jason's face fell, just as Natalie's stomach dropped. So it was possible Ashley had left. That the Revlon deal was done. She had lost her best friend and her only chance at saving her finances. A mix of emotions swirled inside her, anger, sadness, hopelessness, and then numbness. Almost as if she'd stepped outside herself, not able to process it all.

"But like I said, I might have heard it wrong. It was loud, and I was busy." The bartender tried to soften his statement. But Natalie believed he had heard exactly that.

"Do you remember anything else? Were she and Marco going to leave together?" Natalie asked.

"I didn't hear that. Hey, I'm really sorry, but I need to get the bar restocked. No barbacks here like you have in America."

They walked slowly out of La Cantina, turning right toward the main road, Natalie's heart racing as she waved her arm at a cab, trying to process what they'd just heard. That Ashley might have abandoned them. But what did that mean, exactly? She wondered again if Ashley could have harmed herself. If leaving everything behind meant she didn't want another life—she wanted to end hers. She didn't know what to say to Jason. She couldn't imagine what he must be feeling. Once they climbed into the cab, she turned to him. His face had lost its color. "Thinking about leaving and actually doing it are two totally different things." She forced the words out. Because those were the words that needed to be true. Because Ashley needed to come back.

"Are they?" Jason asked, his eyes empty. "I think it's becoming clear she may have left on her own."

"We don't know anything for sure yet," Natalie said, but Jason didn't respond.

"Should we tell the police what the bartender said?" she finally asked.

"No," Jason said, grabbing the back of the seat in front of him as the cab lurched forward. "Let's keep it to ourselves. I'm worried they'll stop looking for her."

"Okay," Natalie replied. "I still think that no matter how bad things might have been with you two, she wouldn't leave the girls."

Jason's mouth set in a tight line. "Maybe it's time to consider that you didn't know her as well as you think you did."

~

When they arrived back at the hotel, Natalie and Jason found Lauren in the hotel's restaurant sitting behind a laptop, a pad of paper next to her with several phone numbers written on it. Her hair was pulled back in a messy ponytail, blue circles under her eyes, a full cup of coffee in front of her. "I'm sorry about earlier," Lauren said before Natalie could speak. "I didn't mean to upset you."

"It's okay," Natalie said. "I don't know why I snapped," she lied. She knew exactly why—Annie's allegation that maybe something traumatic had happened bothered her because it was something Natalie had already considered.

"Hey, Jason," Lauren said, not getting up from her chair. "It's been a while—I'm sorry we're seeing each other again under these circumstances." She gave him a long look. Natalie could tell by Lauren's posture—her tight shoulders and neck—that she was thinking about Ashley's accusations against him. Like Natalie, probably trying to determine what had really been going on in Ashley's marriage. But they'd made a deal—to keep their feelings about him out of this. She hoped Lauren could stick to it.

"I feel awful about what's happening," Lauren said.

"It's not your fault," he said, and offered her a sad smile.

She and Natalie shared a quick look.

"What?" he asked.

Lauren began to wring her hands nervously. She glanced at Natalie again.

"What is it? I really can't take any more secrets." He also looked at Natalie.

"At La Cantina, Ash asked me to go somewhere with her and talk. She said she wouldn't leave with Marco—she wanted to work things out with me." Lauren looked down.

"And?" Jason pressed.

"I said no. And now I can't stop thinking—what if I had said yes?"

"Why didn't you go?" Jason asked, not unkindly.

Natalie wanted to say something to rescue Lauren from Jason's questioning. She'd just been on the other side of it, and it didn't feel good. But she didn't have the words. Because she wished Lauren hadn't been so obstinate. That she had gone with Ashley. Because maybe they wouldn't be here right now, dissecting every detail of last night.

Lauren's cheeks flushed. "We weren't getting along."

"Things weren't great between any of us." Natalie finally jumped in when she saw Lauren's eyes fill with tears. "I think we were all ready to go home."

Jason combed his fingers through his hair. "I counted on you guys to look out for her."

"We did," Natalie said, hoping that it was true. Because, truly, she didn't know.

"Obviously, you didn't!" Jason snapped, and Natalie hung her head, silent. Because he was right—they clearly hadn't.

Lauren stepped in. "Listen, we *all* have regrets about how we handled last night. But we need to stick together. Okay?" she said, waiting until both Jason and Natalie bobbed their heads up and down in response. "Let's focus on what we can do. How we can find her. The hotel loaned me this." She pointed at the computer. "I've listed Ashley missing on every website I could find. And I finally got ahold of the right person at the US Consulate, and she's contacting hospitals. There are private ones, public ones, but luckily there are only a few in this area where an American would likely end up."

"You can cross the one I was at off the list—Star Medica. I inquired there, but they said no one matching her description had come in," Natalie said, then frowned, staring at a map of Mexico on the table next to Lauren. She didn't know the population of the country but guessed it was at least 100 million. How would they find her in a place so large? If she was even still in the country. She thought about throwing that dart again. Where would it land? Where had Ash landed? Fear gripped Natalie's insides and clung to her.

"Okay," Lauren said, running a line through Star Medica. "This is like finding a needle in a haystack. Where the hell is she?" She looked at Natalie. Natalie saw the fear. She knew Lauren was thinking the same thing she was. The hours were slipping away, and they were no closer to finding her. This was Mexico. If someone wanted to make a person disappear, it wasn't that hard.

"Jason, we should see if she took any flights. I'll text Officer Garcia right now and ask him," Natalie heard herself say. But what she wanted to say was *What if we never find her?*

Jason shook his head. "We can double-check, but I sincerely hope they've already investigated that."

"Did you guys find out anything new at La Cantina?" Lauren asked.

Natalie filled her in about what the bartender had told them, Jason glowering as he heard the story again.

"Do you think this means she left with him?"

Natalie looked at Jason, wondering what he might say.

"I don't know," he said, frowning. "Maybe." He looked down and sucked in a sharp breath as if trying not to cry.

Natalie squeezed his arm, but she didn't trust herself to speak. Because every second they stood here speculating, she was losing hope that Ashley was coming back—and they had to face the real possibility she had left on her own. She found herself struggling to reconcile her feelings of relief because that would mean she hadn't been involved in her disappearance, and the frustration that she would now lose the Revlon deal, and ultimately most of her assets. Maybe even her marriage.

They sat in the empty chairs around the table. Natalie propped her elbows in front of her and hung her head.

"We have to get some sleep," Lauren said, looking up at the clock on the wall. "It's almost midnight."

"I can't sleep. Not with her out there somewhere," Natalie said, as rain started to come down in sheets without warning, pounding the sand outside the restaurant. She prayed wherever Ashley was, whomever she was with, that she was okay. That she'd found what she was looking for.

CHAPTER TWENTY-SEVEN

Two Days After
LAUREN

The next morning, Lauren found herself back at the restaurant with Natalie and Jason, a familiarity to it, as if it were the place they could find answers, a comfortable silence having set in. The laptop open in front of them. In the hour or so of sleep Lauren was able to get, she'd dreamed that Ashley had come back to the hotel with a silly explanation about getting lost without her phone. But she was fine! Lauren had squeezed her, Ashley flinching. "That hurts!" Lauren smiling. "I'm so glad you're back, Ash." She'd woken with a start, the reality hitting her hard, much like the rain that had fallen the night before.

Maria walked over to their table. "The *policía* are here again," she said. "They need to talk to all of you. Shall I direct them to one of your rooms?"

Natalie looked at Jason and Lauren. "No, it's okay, we can talk here."

Maria's lips formed a straight line. "They said they'd prefer privacy."

Jason stiffened, and Natalie became wild-eyed. Lauren was too afraid to ask Maria why they wanted privacy. It could only mean one thing: the news wasn't good. Natalie gripped her hands together to stop them from shaking. It was so odd—they were in desperate search of the truth, yet terrified of it at the same time.

"We can talk in my room," Natalie said. Silently, the two of them got up and followed her.

Natalie grabbed Lauren's arm as they climbed the winding staircase to the bungalow and pulled her to a stop. "Do you think it's bad?" she whispered.

Lauren held the railing and turned toward Natalie. Jason was behind her, blinking back tears, clearly worried about the same thing. Lauren didn't have a good feeling, but she was not about to say it. With each passing hour it was becoming harder to believe foul play wasn't involved, as the police had originally told TMZ. Lauren wondered if they'd always known more than they'd let on, even when they were interrogating them. Why wouldn't they divulge everything they had? Unless they suspected Lauren and Natalie were involved . . . She shivered at the thought of being detained here. "Let's stay positive," she heard herself say.

Natalie leaned into Lauren as they entered Natalie's room, Ashley's shorts hanging over the back of the chair, her favorite Dodgers baseball hat on the floor, her makeup scattered across the counter. Natalie hadn't moved anything—confiding in Lauren that it had felt wrong to fold her shorts or put her eye shadow in its bag. That she'd thought that if she disrupted the way Ashley had left everything, somehow it might make it harder to find her. Like it was a crime scene she shouldn't touch.

Jason looked around, seeing the room for the first time. He picked up Ashley's favorite black mesh bathing suit off the floor. "She was packing this when we argued about Revlon's offer. She tried to get me to stop talking about it, but I wouldn't relent. Why wouldn't I just back off? Let her handle it?" Jason said, more to himself than Natalie or Lauren.

Natalie reached out to console him, but he shook his head and slumped into a chair, balling the Lycra suit in his lap.

Lauren sat quietly on the bed with her thoughts. If Ashley was dead, would she ever be able to forgive herself for the last words she'd spoken to her?

A sudden knock on the glass door startled Lauren. She turned and saw Officer Garcia and Officer Lopez on the other side of it. Natalie pulled the door open. Officer Garcia asked Natalie to sit down. Lauren's heart pounded as Natalie eased next to her on the bed. She saw the color drain from Natalie's face and grabbed her hand and squeezed. Lauren tried to contain her fear. Tried to stay positive. She glanced at Jason, who was gripping the arms of his chair so tightly his knuckles were visibly white. She knew they all wanted to ask the same question: Did they find Ashley?

Officer Garcia stepped forward. "There's been a development."

She squeezed her eyes shut, bracing herself for the news.

"An American woman has come forward. She said that Marco Smith tried to get her to leave with him when she visited Tulum three months ago."

Lauren let out the breath she'd been holding. "So you haven't found Ashley?"

Officer Garcia shook his head. "No."

"Thank God," Lauren said. "I mean, I was so scared. I thought you had bad news for us." She glanced at Natalie, whose face had now regained some of its color.

"No, I'm sorry, I didn't mean to scare you. There is a leak in the police department and I am not sure where it's coming from—so I wanted to speak with you privately about this."

Lauren glanced at Nat again. She wondered who was feeding the information to TMZ if it wasn't Officer Garcia or his partner, Officer Lopez.

"This woman told us he was very persuasive but that she decided not to go with him. She said she never told anyone about it, but when she read that he was one of the last people seen with Ashley, she had to come forward."

"Are we sure it's the same Marco Smith? There's no picture of him, so maybe it's just a coincidence?" Natalie asked.

"His physical description matched," Officer Garcia said. "She also knew details that have not been in the papers. She described his dog, knew its name, and she also knew where he lived," he added, reading from his notepad. "We thoroughly vetted the story before bringing it to you. We believe it to be true."

Lauren rubbed her forehead. "So what does this mean?"

Officer Lopez leaned against the wall. "This woman, she sounds very similar to Ashley. Very successful in the United States. Wealthy. She traveled here with her girlfriends." Lauren tried to focus as Lopez explained how Marco had met the woman at a yoga class and then isolated her from her friends for the rest of her trip, asking her to disappear with him on the last night.

"Oh my God," Lauren said, breaking the silence once he finished. "But she didn't go with him?"

"No, although she said she strongly considered it. That Marco had laid out an entire plan—he gave her a place to meet him that was away from her hotel. He told her he knew how to make them disappear off the grid. He'd encouraged her to transfer money into his bank account for them to live on. She didn't, thankfully," Officer Garcia said, then glanced at Officer Lopez.

"Have you checked your bank account?" Lopez asked Jason.

"Doing it now," he said.

Lauren could see the fear etched across Jason's face, in the haunted look in his eyes—the broken blood vessels, a result of hard sobbing, no doubt. She couldn't imagine what he must be thinking. She thought of Ashley's description of his cutting words, his hot-tempered episodes. She wondered if he was planning to change if—*no, when*—they found

Ashley. She had told Ashley that Geoff would have, but she wondered deep down if that was just her heart trying to outsmart her head.

"Where did he want to take the woman?" Lauren asked.

"Belize," Officer Garcia said, holding up his hand as Lauren opened her mouth to say something. "We've already contacted the authorities there. But so far it's been a dead end. We got several sets of fingerprints from Marco's apartment, but none of them were in the system here or in the US—we've worked with our contacts there. So it's making it that much harder to locate him. He had no social media accounts. And we have been unable to find a driver's license for him because we don't know his real name, and the passport number he gave to his employer was fake. They also paid him in cash. And without a picture . . ."

"Did the woman have a photo of him?" Lauren asked, but she already knew the answer. She thought of the video she'd taken—if only she'd captured more than the back of his body. If only she'd had the foresight to know she'd need to.

Officer Garcia said no.

"Same story—about not liking his picture taken?" Natalie tilted her head.

"Yes," Officer Lopez said.

"I don't see any unusual activity with our money," Jason said. "Nat, can you check your business accounts?"

"I just can't believe she'd take from BloMe . . ." Natalie trailed off.

"Anything is possible at this point," Jason said, a pained look settling into his face.

"I'll email Janice. She'll get back to me right away."

"Check your credit card statements too, although if there's been no activity in your bank accounts, I'd be surprised if you find anything," Officer Garcia said. "This guy has done this before—or tried to—so he knows not to leave a paper trail."

"Okay, but I'm checking now anyway," Jason said.

Natalie said she would log in to their corporate Amex and Visa accounts.

Lauren watched them frantically swiping and typing on their phones, trying to find a trail to Ashley. "So this woman." Lauren looked at the officers. "Did she say why she didn't take off with him?"

Officer Garcia tilted his head. "She said there was nothing about him all week that struck her as odd, that his questioning about leaving her life had been playful, and she hadn't thought much of it. But that last day, his demeanor changed slightly. He became pushier, a little desperate, and she realized that . . ." He paused, flipping through his notepad, then read from it. "She realized that he wasn't genuine. That it was a play to get her money."

Lauren wondered how Ashley could be more naive than this other woman. Why the gut she relied on so much hadn't set off an alarm. Or had it, and Marco hadn't wanted to take no for an answer?

"And Natalie, I got your text—we had already checked all the possible flights she could have been on, and there's no record. Unless he had a falsified passport and she did too, but that I doubt."

Lauren, Natalie, and Jason sat in silence after Officer Garcia and Officer Lopez left, promising to contact them if they found anything unusual in the bank accounts or credit cards. *Or if you remember anything,* Officer Lopez said pointedly to Natalie, right before shutting the sliding door, Natalie wincing slightly at his veiled accusation.

Lauren thought back to how surprised she'd been at the way the seams of Ashley and Nat's friendship had come undone—how Natalie seemed almost desperate to sell the company, growing more and more frustrated at Ashley's refusal to sell.

Had Natalie finally lost it that night? The thought stopped her cold.

Jason finally broke the uncomfortable silence. "You guys spent time with him—you think he was after her money?"

Natalie spoke first. "She did tell me they talked about her owning BloMe. She said she'd told him that when she first met him."

"And then he lied about owning Tropical Kiss," Lauren added. "Why would he do that if he didn't have ulterior motives? I'm telling you, I did not trust that guy."

"Why didn't you mention this sooner?" Jason asked.

"I don't know." Lauren stiffened.

"Everything is relevant. Don't you guys see that?" Jason looked away as if trying to control himself so he didn't get angry. Lauren had seen Geoff do the same thing many times. Look away. Clamp down his jaw. Wring his hands. Lauren's stomach turned at the memory of how anxious it would make her. Had Ashley seen these mannerisms in Geoff, the same way Lauren pinpointed them so easily now? Was that when she'd decided she had to save Lauren, rather than herself?

"I'm sorry I didn't mention it to you," Lauren said. "But I did tell the police."

"Is there anything else that either of you want to tell *me*?"

"No," Natalie said.

Lauren hated that Jason was making her feel bad, as if she'd let Ashley down. But maybe she deserved it. She had thought confronting Marco would help. That he might leave the bar—go find another woman to seduce. But he hadn't left. In fact, he'd stood up to her. Challenged her. What if her outburst had only fueled him more? Pushed him into taking Ashley? The truth was, there was more she could tell Jason. The real words she'd said to Ashley—the ones that were so dark she couldn't bear to say them out loud to Natalie and especially not to the police. She shook the memory away; she couldn't think about that now. They would find Ashley and she would apologize.

"I didn't think he was a bad guy. He was annoying, yes. Invading our space, sure. But did I ever get the sense he was after Ashley's money? No. In fact, he paid for things," Natalie said.

"Free smoothies and a few pesos for breakfast don't count," Lauren said. "And he did seem a little off to me. I couldn't put my finger on it. Come on, Nat, you had to have felt it too."

Natalie considered this. "You know what, you're right. He was obsessed with her."

"So now the guy was obsessed? You go from harmless to obsessed in the span of a couple of minutes," Jason spit out from across the room. "Natalie, you called the police on some poor kid who was selling newspaper subscriptions in your neighborhood last year. You said he'd seemed off when he came to your door. But this guy Marco came across as harmless until Ashley disappears into thin air?" Jason hit the table, and Lauren saw Natalie flinch. "Dammit!"

If Lauren had discovered Jason's true self, what would she have done? Lauren thought back to Ashley's tears at Chichén Itzá. At the time she had been too angry to be rational. But now, being here with Jason, with Ashley possibly gone forever, she couldn't help but wonder if the situation were reversed, would she have insisted Ashley leave without revealing her own abuse?

"I don't know, Jason!" Natalie cried. "It's easy to look back and second-guess everything. In the moment we didn't see it. But I'm willing to consider it now. Especially if Lauren feels that way."

Jason glared at her. "Maybe what you should be doing is working harder to get your memory back."

Natalie spun around, her back to them.

Lauren shot him a look. Was he questioning her? She locked eyes with Jason. But then she remembered the Natalie she'd spent time with this week—the one she'd bonded with—and changed her mind.

Maria tapped on the door, holding a tray of pastries, bread, and fresh fruit. "You all must eat," she said.

Just looking at the food made Lauren nauseous. She thought of her last fight with Ashley again, her insides coiling. She tried to wave the food off, but Maria stood there until they all took a bite of something. Lauren caught Natalie's eye; she looked exhausted and pained. Lauren's legs were shaky as they made their way back down to the restaurant a few minutes later. Lauren grabbed a bottle of tequila off the bar. "José won't mind," she said.

"Why not?" Jason said, his voice soft as he accepted a glass from Lauren.

"I just heard back from the accountant," Natalie said. "No large or unusual withdrawals from the BloMe accounts."

Jason pressed his lips together. "She still could have left on her own. Knowing Ashley, she could've stashed some money on the side. In an account I didn't know about."

"Maybe," Natalie said, but she didn't sound convinced. "But I kind of hoped she had taken a shit ton of money out. Because that would've meant she was okay. It's terrible, but it would mean she was . . ."

Alive, Lauren thought. A word they'd all carefully danced around since she'd gone missing. No one willing to say that or its opposite. And no one said it now. But Lauren had been thinking it so much the thoughts kept getting louder and louder, almost as if they were forcing her to hear them. She tried to quiet the screams in her mind, but she couldn't. Instead, she picked up the Patrón and poured herself a glass and then another one for Jason and Lauren, sliding the shots over to them with a short nod.

CHAPTER TWENTY-EIGHT

THE NIGHT
ASHLEY

"Nat! It's my song!" Ashley yelled as "Brown Eyed Girl" started playing. She tugged on Natalie's hand, Marco already halfway to the crowded dance floor. She turned back and caught Lauren's eye, but Lauren looked away.

So be it, Ashley thought. She was tired of Lauren being mad at her. She leaned into Marco as the song played, one hand loosely around his waist, the other around Natalie's wrist as they danced.

She felt terrible about arguing with Natalie about their company *again.* Why was something they'd built together tearing them apart? Had they never been on the same page about it, but Ashley had been too blind to see it? Or had she not *wanted* to see it? She looked at Natalie, the lyrics from her favorite song booming from the speakers. How many times had they spun each other around to this song the past twenty years? Held on to each other as they sang off-key? The memory brought with it an urgency to solve this. Get rid of the negativity between them. One way or another.

Marco leaned into her ear, his breath hot. "Let's get out of here."

Ashley pulled her head back. "And go where?"

"I have somewhere special to take you. A place where you can cleanse away all your bad energy." He glanced in Lauren's direction, then nodded at Natalie. "It will help bring you clarity."

Once again, Marco had said the very thing she needed to hear. As if he had been reading her mind. Ashley looked over at Lauren again, who sat rigidly, purse in her lap, lips stuck together tightly. She missed the old Lauren. The one who didn't hate her. "I guess I'm willing to try anything at this point," Ashley said, gripping Natalie's hand tighter as they danced. "But not until after this song is over. It's my favorite."

"Your wish is my command," Marco said before spinning her away from Natalie, the room becoming blurry before coming into focus again.

"I'm going with you," Natalie said when Ashley laid out her plan. "You shouldn't be alone with him after drinking so much—just in case."

"I'll be fine."

"You were just lecturing me in the bathroom about how much I drank!" Natalie challenged.

"You seemed tipsy. But look at me, I'm great. Want me to walk a straight line?" Ashley laughed.

"Don't be stupid, Ash," Natalie said sharply.

Ashley gave her a look. "I might be a lot of things, but I'm not stupid," she shot back. "Now if you'll excuse me, I'm going to ask Lauren if she wants to come too." She walked over to where Lauren was standing by the bar, tapping into her phone.

Lauren looked up. "Who are you texting?" Ashley asked, trying to see the screen.

"No one," Lauren said tersely, and pushed the phone into her purse.

Ashley stood stiffly at her rebuff. "We were thinking of leaving with Marco. Want to join?"

"Honestly, there's nothing I'd rather do less."

"Wow. I guess I'll put you down as a no, then?"

Lauren folded her arms over her chest. "Put me down as a no tonight and tomorrow and basically every day moving forward. I'm done, Ash."

Ashley sucked in air as if she'd been punched. "Lauren, I know things haven't been great—"

"I think 'awful' would be a better word. Or maybe 'nightmarish'?"

"Listen," Ashley pleaded. "I get why you hate me. Believe me, I hate myself sometimes too. I screwed up on this trip. I should have spent more time with you. I should have tried harder—so much harder. But I need you, Lauren. Do you hear me? I need you, even if you don't need me anymore. I need you to be in my life. I need you to forgive me. I have been so scared to say that to you. This entire trip I have been trying to work up the courage to tell you how much I've missed you over the last year." Lauren broke eye contact, and Ashley could feel her falling away. "I'm sorry I told you to leave Geoff. I should have kept my mouth shut . . . ," she said, not meaning a word of it. But if apologizing would soften Lauren, she was willing to do it.

Lauren narrowed her eyes, clearly seeing right through her. "You don't mean that."

Ashley threw up her hands. "You're right, I don't. But I wish I did—if that counts. Because it would make you feel better. I'm just trying to find the right words that will keep us from falling apart."

"Have you ever thought that maybe this can't be put back together? That we're broken in too many pieces?"

Ashley threw a look to where Marco and Natalie waited by the door, standing next to each other but not speaking. "What if the three of us left right now, together? I could convince that guy," she said, pointing to the bartender, "to give us a bottle of Don Julio, and we could sit on the beach and drink shots until we're so drunk that we've forgotten why we were angry in the first place." Ashley grabbed her arm and pulled it slightly toward her. "Come on. Let's get Nat and go.

Give me one more chance to make this right?" she said, hoping Lauren would agree.

Lauren yanked her arm back as if she'd been stung. "We can't fix this by drinking tequila. I think this trip has only proven that we can't fix this at all. If you'd really come here to mend things with me, then you would have already." She gave her a cold stare, and Ashley could see that she was losing her.

"But I—"

"Stop!" Lauren took a step back. "No more excuses. This friendship doesn't work anymore, and I think it's time to accept that. Too much has happened that we can't recover from. Too many things have been said that we can't take back. When we get home, I think it's best if we don't see each other again. That's the easiest way for us both to finally move on. Separately."

"No, Lauren, please." Ashley's chest hurt.

"I've made my decision. I don't feel anything for you except anger."

"You can't mean that." Ashley started to cry but wiped the tears away quickly. "What about our history? Twenty years . . ."

Lauren paused, her eyes sad. "Sometimes history isn't worth repeating."

"Is this about Geoff?"

"Do *not* bring him into this."

"When has he ever not been *in* this?"

"Fuck you," Lauren spat. "If you want to know the truth, I wish you were the one who was dead."

She turned and walked away, Ashley staring at her back until she was swallowed by the crowd. She'd never felt more like a failure. She'd put her heart on the line, but it hadn't been enough.

Ashley replayed Lauren's words as Marco flagged a cab and held the door as she and Natalie slid into the back seat, littered with empty beer cans, the engine sputtering as it began the short trek to Marco's. More than once, she wanted to tell the cabdriver to turn around. That she wanted to go back to La Cantina. To Lauren. Because she couldn't have meant what she said. She was just drunk. She thought about asking Natalie's opinion. But she didn't do that either. She was humiliated. Embarrassed. She'd fucked up *again*. Why had she brought up Geoff? Why? She sat stiffly, deciding finally that she didn't deserve Lauren. That she had to accept what Lauren wanted. That's what love was, wasn't it? Setting someone free and hoping they'd return someday.

Once they arrived at Marco's, they settled into an old couch that made the back of her legs itch. Ashley sipped from a bottle of Corona that Marco had handed her, trying to shake her feelings of uneasiness. His yellow Lab put his paws on her lap.

"Finish that and we'll go," Marco said.

"Go where?" Natalie asked. She was slumped in a worn leather recliner in the corner, her eyes glassy and half open. Ashley tried to remember the last time she'd seen her this drunk. Her thirtieth birthday, maybe? They'd rented a party bus, and she, Lauren, and Natalie had danced to eighties music under a strobe light. Ashley remembered thinking she wished the night would never end, their bond feeling impenetrable.

How far they had fallen.

"Somewhere amazing, I promise." Marco winked at Natalie. "But you're going to have to wake up!"

"Will they have food there? I'm starving."

Marco walked over to his pantry and pulled out a bag of chips. "Here, eat these."

Natalie looked at the bag. "Duos?"

"Doritos," Marco said.

"I haven't had these in so long!" She tore open the bag and began to eat, her crunching echoing through the small space. "So, I still don't get it. Why do we need to go to this place? Right now?"

"You don't have to go with us, Nat," Ashley said, half hoping she'd just pass out here. After her confrontation with Lauren, she really did want to see this place that Marco said would help on her journey for clarity. For her company. For her friendships. For her marriage. Because at the moment it felt as if they were all on a collision course with one another.

"You can't get rid of me that easily," Natalie shot back, her mouth full. "If you're going to some magical place, then I'm sure as hell coming too."

"Fine," Ashley said, pulling herself up off the couch and dropping her half-drunk beer in the garbage can. Marco tossed his and Natalie's empties in after it.

"Here." Marco reached into a coat closet. "Take these," he said, handing them each a flashlight. "It's going to be pitch-black where I'm taking you," he said, locking eyes with Ashley.

Pitch-black? She shivered slightly and wrapped her arms around herself, letting her appetite for change propel her forward.

CHAPTER TWENTY-NINE

THREE DAYS AFTER
NATALIE

Natalie looked around her hotel room. It was a mess, but she still wouldn't let them clean. She believed she might find something—a clue that would lead her to Ashley. Her cell phone rang. She was going to ignore it, assuming it was another reporter. They'd been calling all morning, somehow tracking down her phone number. But it was Jason. The hotel had a cancellation, and he had gone to check into his own suite a few minutes ago.

"Hey, how's your room?" Nat asked.

"Hey . . ." She could barely understand him. "They . . ." He was sobbing so hard he couldn't talk.

"What is it?" Natalie asked as her gaze fell on Ashley's pink suitcase, splayed open like a butterfly's wings. She physically ached for Ashley as she took it in, a deep pain that vibrated through every limb.

"Officer Garcia called. They think they found her body. They think they found Ash."

"Oh, Jason," Natalie said as her head began to pound, staring at her hand until she saw three of them. It felt like everything was moving too quickly. That she couldn't process it.

"They think . . . Oh God, I can't even say it . . ." He tried to talk through his tears. "They want us to identify her. Her body." He let out a guttural sound.

Natalie couldn't breathe. She could barely see through her tears.

"Garcia described her and the outfit she had on. I know that top she was wearing. It was her favorite . . ." He trailed off.

They sat in silence for a moment, Natalie unable to speak. What was there to say? No words could possibly make this better—there was no changing the tragedy they'd found themselves in.

"He said they still needed a positive ID. Nat, I can't do it. What if it is? What if it's her? The kids. I can't even think straight."

Natalie sucked in a long breath. "Let's just take it one step at a time. I'm coming with you," she said, even though the thought scared her out of her mind. If it was Ash, Natalie would never be the same again after seeing her. Nothing would be. And the worst part? She didn't have any real answers to that night. Whether she'd helped Ashley.

Or if, God forbid, she'd been the one to hurt her.

She shoved that crazy thought away.

"Garcia said the morgue is in Cancún," Jason said, his voice cracking. "Something about overcrowding in the closer ones." He let out another sob. "How is this happening?"

"I don't know, Jase. But we'll figure this out together, okay?"

"Thank you," Jason said, his voice barely audible.

"Are you in your room?"

"Yes."

"Give me five minutes and I'll be there."

She walked quickly to Lauren's room. When she saw her friend's face, she paused. Her mouth was suddenly so dry. She would give anything to not have to deliver this message.

"Nat?"

"Hey."

"What's wrong? Oh God."

"The police found a body."

Lauren made a noise that Nat couldn't identify. A cross between a cry and a gasp. "Do they think it's her?"

"They don't know. But Lauren, what if it is?" Bile rose to her throat as she said the words.

"It's not. It's definitely not. Ashley's supposed to outlive all of us." Lauren smiled through her tears.

"You're right. I need to stay positive. It can't be her." Natalie's voice shook. "The morgue is in Cancún, so we'll be gone awhile," she said, trying not to cry. She had a picture in her mind she couldn't shake— bodies everywhere as they searched for the one that might be Ashley's.

"Cancún?"

Natalie swallowed. "Overcrowding in the local ones."

Lauren made a face. "I'm coming with you."

"No, you should stay here—in case she comes back." Natalie said it, but she wasn't sure it was even a possibility. Not now. Garcia wouldn't bring her and Jason to a morgue that was two hours away on a whim. Would they?

"Okay," Lauren said. It sounded like she had more on her mind, but she stayed silent, her mouth tight. Natalie wondered if she was doubting the possibility of Ashley walking through the door as much as she was.

"I'll update you as soon as we know something."

"It's not her," Lauren said and hugged her.

Natalie could feel Lauren's small body shaking. "I know. It's definitely not," Natalie said as they parted, and she turned toward the door. Despite the fact that something in her gut told her that it definitely was. Almost as if the memories locked in her head were whispering to her from beyond the wall they were hiding behind.

$\sim$

She moved as quickly as she could toward Jason's room, but she felt like she was pushing against the wind, her feet heavy like cement blocks.

She found him on the edge of his bed, cradling his head in his hands, his shoulders shaking uncontrollably. She sat next to him and wrapped her arms around him and held him. She saw images of Ashley from college—running across the quad to tell Natalie about a test she'd just taken. She saw her eyes light up when they went to Bed Bath & Beyond and saw the BloBrush on an endcap display for the first time. She saw her on her wedding day, her skin glowing as she walked down the aisle. She realized, now, more than ever, that she needed to see her again. Her huge brown eyes when she had a creative spark. Her twisted lips when she had a surprise. The face she made when she smelled onions. All of it.

"It's not her, right? Tell me it's not going to be her," he finally said.

"It's not going to be her," Natalie said, wiping the tears from under her own eyes.

"Garcia is on his way to pick us up. I don't even want to ride with that corrupt fucker, but I guess we have no other choice."

Natalie thought of all the stories that had hit the press since he arrived, about nearly every private detail of the investigation. It had to be someone at the police department feeding the information.

They turned when they heard a knock on the sliding glass door. Natalie forced herself up from the bed and opened it.

Maria frowned, her eyes welling with tears. "The *policía* are here to escort you to the morgue."

"Thanks—we're coming in a minute."

"It's not going to be her," Maria said with so much confidence that Natalie believed her. The woman reached out and hugged Natalie, catching her by surprise.

Natalie pulled away gently. Maria half smiled and slid the door closed behind her.

"Are you ready?" Natalie asked.

Jason peered up from his hands, and the look on his face sucked all of the air out of Natalie's lungs. He looked like a little boy, his eyes full of fear, his lip quivering. She wanted to help him, to reach out and tell him it definitely wasn't going to be Ashley. But something deep inside her told her it was. She hated herself for thinking it. She tried to push the thought away, but it kept creeping back like an itch.

"No," he said, his voice shaky. "But we'd better go."

Natalie grabbed his hand, ice cold to the touch, and they walked in silence to the police car.

Officer Garcia opened the door. They slid across the back seat, and Natalie rested her head against Jason's shoulder, both of them crying silently off and on. After about an hour, Jason fell asleep against her. Yes, he had been terrible to Ashley while she was alive. But right now, in this hot and dirty squad car, he was all Natalie had.

When they arrived, Officer Garcia woke them. She must have dozed off after Jason did. They followed him into a small room.

"Coffee? Water?" he offered.

Natalie could barely breathe. She couldn't imagine drinking anything. She shook her head. Jason also declined.

"So like I said to Mr. Green on the phone, a group of tourists—scuba divers—found the body in a cenote just outside Tulum early this morning. We have reason to believe it is Ashley because it matches her physical description, and the clothing is consistent with what you told us she was wearing. But we are going to need you to make a positive ID," Officer Garcia said.

Natalie flinched as a rush of heat surged through her, and gripped the edge of the table reflexively. She could feel the tip of a memory—knew it was there, the way you know when you're about to throw up. Her heart raced in anticipation. Jason reached over and wrapped his hand around hers.

Natalie stared at Officer Garcia, wondering if he or someone in the police department had already called TMZ about the body. On the way to the morgue, she had seen another post on the gossip site about how Natalie had gone in for testing yesterday. Sources at the hospital in Mérida said she was being drug tested, but didn't know why. Natalie had almost thrown her phone out the window, anger boiling inside her as she imagined Dr. Rivera selling her story. How could the media be so cruel? Instead of coming down here and aiding in the search, they were sitting in their offices in Hollywood writing articles with cheap clickbait titles. She vowed never to click on one ever again.

"Will you come with me, Nat?" Jason asked. "I don't think I can do it alone."

If it was Ashley's body, Natalie wasn't sure she could handle seeing it. Her best friend. Her sister. Lifeless. She already felt a deep pain in her heart just from imagining it. But if it was a reality. If it was her . . . if Natalie's memory came back . . . if it revealed she had been the one to hurt Ashley, she would break in half, never be the same again. But as she stared into Jason's vacant eyes, she knew she had to find the strength to get past her own fears. She had to face what she might have done. "Of course," she said, her insides running cold.

"I'm sorry, I know I'm supposed to be strong, but I just . . ." He put his head in his hands again. "I can't go in there by myself."

Natalie turned to Officer Garcia. "I know you said the description and clothing match, but what if you're wrong? What if it isn't Ashley? Has that ever happened before?" Natalie remembered the crisp white top Ashley had worn, the way it glowed under the lights when she'd danced. The cutoff jeans shorts and how they hugged her hips. A white shirt and jeans shorts was a common outfit. Surely Ashley couldn't have been the only woman wearing it that night.

Garcia took a long pause before speaking and gave Natalie and Jason a look she could only liken to pity. Her heart sank. "It has, yes, and I sincerely hope I'm wrong about this, but it's not just her physical description and clothing that prompted us to call you. According to the physician who certified her death, the deterioration of the body fits the timeline of when Ashley disappeared based on what we know so far. And no one else has reported a Caucasian woman of her age—or even within ten years of her age—missing." He paused for a moment as if giving them time for his words to sink in. "When you're ready, please follow me."

Natalie would never be ready. She looked at Jason and swallowed her tears. Finally, they both stood and followed Officer Garcia down a series of hallways until he came to an unmarked door.

He paused, his hand on the doorknob. "I have to warn you that because of the overcrowding of unidentified bodies from drug war victims that I mentioned earlier, this isn't going to be like what you'd see in America. This location doesn't have as many deceased, and we did pull the body away from the other stacks, but still."

Natalie couldn't breathe. She stared at the door and watched Officer Garcia pull it open in what felt like slow motion. Her heart rammed against her rib cage. Was her best friend of twenty years going to be in that room—the girl who taught her how to shotgun a beer, the one who surprised her on her twenty-first birthday with a homemade cake, the one who crocheted Meg a tiny hat when she was born? She prayed it wasn't her. She wanted decades more of those moments.

It was the smell that hit Natalie first. Her hand flew to her mouth. Piles of what must be bodies wrapped in sheets were stacked on top of each other like sandbags. She gagged and bent over a trash can, spitting into it. Jason rubbed her back. "Shit," she said, still hovering over it.

When she stood up, she saw that Officer Garcia was watching her, expressionless.

"Do you need to step outside?" Garcia asked.

Yes, I need to step outside and never come back.

"No, it's okay," Natalie said, the putrid smell engulfing the room. She fought the urge to gag again.

Officer Garcia said something in Spanish to a small man wearing square eyeglasses—whom he identified as the morgue technician—who walked over to a table where a body lay under a sheet.

Natalie grabbed Jason's hand. He squeezed hers so hard she flinched but didn't move it away. The technician looked at Garcia; then he pulled back the sheet. Natalie screamed. Jason let out a deep cry.

Ashley's face stared back at them.

CHAPTER THIRTY

THE NIGHT
ASHLEY

Ashley stood in front of a wall that appeared to have a mural painted on it. She pointed her flashlight at it, the beam illuminating the design—three yellow skulls that seemed to be smiling. She directed the light across a small white sign with *"cenote"* written on it in black letters, an arrow underneath pointing in the direction of the sinkhole Marco was leading them toward. She glanced up at the archway and thought that it looked more like an entrance to a private residence than a tourist attraction. She said a silent prayer that this place would help her—give her the clarity she needed to make some important decisions about her future.

She looked at Natalie, swaying slightly as she stood next to her. She grabbed her arm to steady her. "You okay?" she asked, wondering what it was going to take to pull Natalie back to her, to make her understand she needed her in her life—not just as her business partner, but as her best friend. Her sister. She'd already lost Lauren. She'd been sure of that when she'd seen the look in her eyes at La Cantina—vacant, cold. As if she were looking at a stranger. She couldn't lose Nat too.

"I'm fine," Natalie said, and yawned. "What time is it?"

"It's twelve forty-five. Nearly one in the morning," Ashley said after checking her phone.

"We should get going," Marco said. "The cenote is this way." He pointed his flashlight beam toward a thick patch of palm trees and bushes. Ashley tried to see what was beyond it, but the tropical forest was too dense.

"You sure you want to do this now?" Natalie asked, her forehead knotted.

"Yes. We leave tomorrow—this is our only chance. And I really need this."

"You coming?" Marco asked, already a few steps ahead. "It's so beautiful—I can't wait for you to see it."

"He seems so anxious," Natalie said. "Don't you think?" She grabbed onto Ashley's arm and pulled her to a stop.

Ashley gently loosened her wrist from Natalie's grip. "He's just excited to show us. Come on," she said.

Natalie fell in step with her silently as they followed him down a path to a sign with another skull. "The Temple of Doom."

"Why is it called the Temple of Doom?" Natalie stared at the sign. "And what's with all the skulls? I thought you said this place was peaceful."

"The cenote gets its name from the three circular openings in the roof of the cave that resemble the eye sockets and mouth of a skull when viewed from above. The official name is Cenote Calavera. It's known as the Temple of Doom only because that is the name of the cave system it used to be a part of. I assure you, there will be no doom here." Marco smiled. "Come, I will show you."

"Do you really think this is a good idea? Being out here in the pitch-black night alone with him?" Natalie whispered to Ashley as they walked. "We barely know him."

Ashley sighed. Natalie was always so practical. Such a rule follower. Skeptical to a fault. She slowed down and dropped her voice. "I get how it looks—we're in the middle of nowhere. In Mexico. And it's late. But I trust him. So even if you don't, can you trust me that I know what I'm doing?" Ashley asked.

Natalie didn't answer. She started walking again. Ashley decided to take her silence as agreement. "Thank you," Ashley said quietly.

They made their way through the brush, the only light coming from the full moon and the beams of their flashlights flickering through the coconut palm trees.

Suddenly Natalie screamed.

Ashley grabbed her chest, her heart beating hard. "What is it?"

"Did you see that scorpion?" Natalie shone her light down on the jungle floor. Ashley moved back, squinting into the darkness.

"There are a lot of creatures out here, but if you stay away from them, they'll stay away from you," Marco said lightly.

Natalie stood, frozen.

"There is also much beauty that is hard to see because it is so dark." Marco moved his beam around the vegetation. "Like this—the pitahaya—it's the fruit of a cactus which flowers at night." He directed his light to a pink-and-green plant.

"It's beautiful," Ashley said, reaching out to touch it, rubbing the waxy flower between her fingertips.

"You might know it as dragon fruit back home," Marco added. "If you sliced it open, it would be white with many seeds. Very sweet. Shall we continue?" he asked.

Natalie scratched at her arms. "I'm getting eaten alive by mosquitoes all of a sudden. What other creatures do I need to be aware of?"

"Nothing to be concerned about," Marco said. "I would rather show you more of the beauty—there are exotic flowers and many medicinal plants used by Mayan healers. Harmless."

"Like you?" Natalie asked, her tone sharp.

Ashley snapped her head in the direction of her voice.

"Yeah, just like me," he said evenly.

"Why should we trust you?" Natalie pressed.

"Natalie!" Ashley called out. "She's just drunk," she said to Marco.

"Drunk or not, we're out here—somewhere in Mexico, I have no idea where. I can barely see my hand in front of my face. There are little creatures running around." She patted her purse. "I don't even have my phone to send my location to Ben in case . . . So I think Marco can answer me on this one. Why should we trust you?"

Ashley shot a look at Natalie. What was she doing? She was going to ruin this opportunity. Any second, Marco could tell them to forget it. Drive them back to their hotel and she'd never see him again. She wouldn't blame him. "Natalie, please . . . ," Ashley tried. This trip to Tulum needed to have meant *something*.

"It's okay, Ash. I've got this," Marco said, his tone confident.

"'Ash'? She's *Ash* to you now?" Natalie's eyes were bulging.

"Okay." He held his hands up. "Ashley," he said gently, giving Natalie a warm smile. "You *can* trust me. Haven't I shown you that already this week?"

"Yes, you have," Ashley jumped in, to try and calm Natalie down.

"I assure you I didn't bring you out here to kill you." He laughed and looked sideways at Ashley, who smiled at him.

Natalie's shoulders slumped, but she didn't respond. Ashley walked over and stood next to her. "It's going to be fine."

"Please just relax," Marco coaxed. "I'm just here to guide you guys, to help you find your own peace, whatever that may be."

Ashley held her phone out to Natalie. "Here, do you want to text Ben and tell him where we are and who we're with? Would that make you feel better?"

Natalie shook her head stubbornly. "But you can see how this looks, right? Two women. One man. Middle of nowhere—"

Ashley grabbed Natalie's elbow, seeing that they weren't making any progress with her. She was repeating herself now, a sign of all the alcohol she'd consumed. "Can you give us a minute, please?" Ashley asked Marco.

Marco shrugged, then walked farther down the path, his flashlight beam guiding him.

"What's your problem?" Ashley asked, once they were alone.

"*My* problem?" Natalie said, sounding shocked. "How can you not see everything that is wrong with this situation?"

"Why are you questioning him? Marco got us special access to this cenote. He's trying to *help* us." Ashley could feel her irritation bubbling inside of her, working its way up. "You talked about feeling disconnected from me and wanting things to be better, but you only seem angry."

"I went back to his apartment with you because I couldn't let you go off alone with him," Natalie said, making a face. "And I did want to reconnect—I tried at Ziggy's earlier in the week, but you stormed off with Marco to eat carne asada! And when you came back, you gave us a halfhearted apology but really didn't try any harder after that."

Ashley fought against her tears. Lauren had accused her of the same thing earlier. When Natalie had come with her tonight, she had hope that she hadn't lost her too. But if she had lost both of them, she wasn't sure she could live with that. She thought she had made choices in both of their best interests. If she had been that far off, what did that say about her? "Can you try harder now?" Ashley asked in a small voice. "Please?"

Natalie followed her gaze. "I hope you're right about him. And that he's worth it."

She didn't elaborate on what she meant, and Ashley didn't ask. Sometimes it was better to not know.

CHAPTER THIRTY-ONE

THREE DAYS AFTER
NATALIE

Natalie's loud sobs echoed off the stark mortuary walls. The room began to spin—a blur of dead bodies covered in sheets spiraling past her. Her heart hammered in her chest, threatening to burst through. She put her hand over her heart and fought the urge to pass out. To not see Ashley's face—her blue lips and paperlike skin—lying on that table. Natalie drew short, sharp breaths. Her body tingled. Her legs buckled beneath her; Jason grabbed for her, and he caught her arm, but her knees still hit the floor. She didn't move, sobbing into the linoleum. Jason picked her up and wrapped her in his arms. He sobbed into her shoulder. She cried hot tears into his chest.

She finally turned, willing the body to belong to someone else when she looked again. But it was still Ashley—or resembled her. Her brown hair was no longer hanging in bouncy curls like she'd styled it, but matted against her head. "Oh my God."

A dense forest.

Darkness.

She heard herself scream.

A stab of fear shooting through her body.

Natalie's head began to pound, the fragmented thoughts bringing with them more questions than answers.

"What happened to you, Ash?" She reached out and touched Ashley's arm through the sheet. It was rigid. But she kept her hand there anyway. She didn't want to let go. "What happened to her?" she yelled toward the mortuary technician, who winced.

Officer Garcia stepped forward. "The examiner showed me a contusion on the back of her head. It could be consistent with a fall if she hit one of the jagged rocks that surround the Cenote Calavera as she dropped into the water. Or she may have been hit with something first and then pushed, or she fell. But we will need permission to do an autopsy to be sure. Either theory is consistent with the fact she was found floating at the top of the cenote rather than at the bottom. If she had drowned or . . ." He paused as if realizing who he was talking to. "Or if someone drowned her, her body would have sunk to the bottom."

Natalie's stomach cramped. She covered her abdomen and pressed, trying to make the pain stop. She winced. There was something about the cenote. But what? Another sharp sting rippled through her stomach. She tried to breathe.

Why is it called the Temple of Doom? Natalie had stared at the sign. *And what's with all the skulls? I thought you said this place was peaceful.*

The cenote gets its name from the three circular openings in the roof of the cave that resemble the eye sockets and mouth of a skull when viewed from above. The official name is Cenote Calavera. It's known as the Temple of Doom only because that is the name of the cave system it used to be a part of. I assure you, there will be no doom here.

Natalie jerked her head back at the memory. She and Marco had been at the cenote with Ashley. She started shaking. What did that mean?

"Natalie?" Garcia said her name as if he wasn't sure he had it right. "Are you all right?" He frowned at her.

She knew she had to pull it together—to not look suspicious. "No, no, I'm fine. Sorry, this is all so hard to hear." What happened at the cenote? The tiny memory that just resurfaced made her feel like her body was being consumed by a virus.

"We need to find who did this to her or knows what happened to her," Jason said sharply.

"We are trying to find Marco. At this point, he is our lead suspect because of the timing of his disappearance. But we don't have much to go on other than he was one of two people last seen with her." Garcia hesitated briefly, staring at Natalie for a beat. "And because you were the other person who was last seen with her, we're going to need to collect your passport."

"What?" Natalie asked, that feeling she'd been trying to ignore threatening her again. That feeling she *had* been involved.

"We can't let you leave Mexico until we complete our investigation."

"But I told you, I don't remember."

"Right. But what if you don't remember hitting her over the head with something? Or pushing her over the edge of the cenote?" Officer Garcia asked.

"I would never do that! Jason, tell them I would never do that." Natalie felt frantic. Trapped.

Jason turned to her. He stared at her for a long time. Finally he spoke. "There is no way Natalie would hurt my wife. She's been her best friend—practically her sister—for twenty years."

Natalie felt herself breathe.

"Sometimes it's the people closest to us that do the very worst things, yes?" Officer Garcia said, holding Natalie's gaze.

Natalie couldn't have hurt Ashley. She loved her. She thought again about Ashley's accusations toward Jason. His abuse. Then again, Jason loved Ashley too.

"Please just understand we have a job to do," Garcia added, a little softer this time. "I am going to collect everyone's passports, not just yours. Lauren's. And Jason, I will need yours too."

Natalie looked at Jason, but he either hadn't heard Garcia or was ignoring him. She couldn't be sure.

"I would like you all to stay in Mexico until we have more information. And Jason, do we have your permission to perform an autopsy?"

There was a long silence. Natalie strained to remember more. To reach the answer of what happened to Ashley. Because she was sure of something now: She knew. Somewhere inside of her, she knew.

Finally, Jason spoke. "Yes, you have my permission. But then I want to take her home. I want to get her out of here."

"Of course. After the autopsy, we will need you to provide us with her birth certificate and sign some papers."

"Birth certificate? Why? You know it's her." Jason rubbed his eyes. "I have no idea where it even is—in some box, somewhere."

Natalie thought about her own birth certificate, meticulously filed away in a cabinet at home, along with everyone else's in her family. She had no clue where Ashley would have put hers, or if she even had a copy.

"I am sorry, but it's standard procedure. I did not make the rules. I'm sure you'll be able to get a copy quickly if you can't locate yours. But we will need to keep her body here until we finish our investigation. Now if you are ready, I can escort you out."

"Wait, what?" Jason asked.

"As I said, our investigation is not yet complete," Officer Garcia said.

"Didn't you say we'd get the results of the drug testing today?" Natalie asked, feeling desperate to be absolved. Now that they knew Ashley's fate, she couldn't stop wondering if Officer Lopez was right—if she'd been a part of it. Because she *had* been there. What had been so bad that her mind would block it? The thought terrified her.

"Those tests should come back very soon," Garcia said, checking his watch.

"We just all want to get back to the States now—which I'm sure you can appreciate." Natalie looked at him. "Won't it help you to confirm I was drugged—move the investigation along?" *Rule me out.*

"Yes, *if* it turns out you had drugs in your system, depending on what they were, it could help support the story you are telling us. And it will move things along in that regard. But we still won't know what really happened. As I said, just because you've lost your memory doesn't mean you weren't involved in her death. Also, we haven't ruled out the possibility that you could have drugged yourself after harming Ashley—as an alibi."

Natalie tried to process his words. "Drugged myself?" She stepped away from him as if it would make his accusations weaker. Would she have done that? And why? "Why would I do that?"

"You tell me," Garcia said.

"This is ridiculous," Natalie said, trying not to show the intense fear that was radiating through her. She needed to call Ben immediately. She needed a lawyer—now.

"I'm sorry, but we have to consider *all* options," Garcia said sharply.

Jason stood over Ashley's body, weeping. He was a million miles away, not paying any attention to Officer Garcia's accusations. "I can't leave her," he cried. "I cannot leave her here."

Natalie stood over him and rubbed his back, tears streaming down her cheeks as she listened to him moaning. Here she was, worried about clearing her name when Ashley was dead. Petrified she might be thrown in a prison in Mexico for the rest of her life. What kind of friend did that make her? She forced herself to look at Ashley's face. She couldn't be responsible for this—she couldn't have done this to her friend. Officer Garcia's phone started ringing. "That's Lopez. He's at the Cenote Calavera now. Maybe he has more information."

Jason was still staring at Ashley's body. "Jase," Natalie said. "Come on, let's get some air."

"I can't, Nat. I can't leave her."

"I know. But that's not her. She's not in there. She's already gone."

"I know, but the thought of leaving her here. I can't imagine." Jason looked up at Natalie, his skin blotchy.

"I'll call Ben and have him work out the details of how we bring her home, okay? He'll collect all the paperwork Officer Garcia needs." Jason's hands were visibly shaking, and Natalie's heart ached for him. How would he survive this? *How would she?* "Let's take a walk."

He hugged Ashley and kissed her forehead, and Natalie started to cry again. She opened the door and guided him down the hall.

"I need a drink or a sedative. I don't want to feel anything," Jason said.

"I know," she said, putting her arm around him. "I want to be numb too."

$$\sim$$

"I have to call the girls," Jason said when they arrived back at the hotel.

Natalie cringed, thinking about all the people they would have to tell—including Lauren. "You should tell them in person."

"I can't go home. They can't come here. And I'm scared out of my mind they're going to find out from some dickhead reporter. I can't, I . . . can't let that happen," he stammered. He paced the lobby. Finally, he stopped and stared at her hard. "How do I explain to my daughters over FaceTime that their mother is dead?"

Natalie's heart cinched shut. She pressed the corners of her eyes to hold the tears in. She couldn't imagine that conversation. It would break them. And him. All over again.

"I don't even know what happened to her," he said. "Just that she has a huge gash on her head, but she didn't drown even though she was found in water. I just don't get it. Are we ever going to know the truth?"

Natalie knew what he wasn't asking. Was she ever going to remember? And if she didn't, then what?

She peered into the large hole in the ground.

She saw a ladder that led down to the water.

It was dark as ink.

She shone a flashlight toward it, wondering how deep it was. Her light catching the jagged rocks around the edge.

Natalie's pulse quickened. More snippets of memories. What were they leading to? "I hope so," she finally said, watching him walk to his room to make the worst call he was ever going to have to make. In just minutes, the life Jason's daughters knew would never again be the same. None of their lives would. Because one moment would define the rest of all of their lives: the moment when they each found out Ashley was dead. Natalie shuddered—seeing Ashley's stark white face on the gurney at the morgue. She had no idea what the rest of her life looked like. It could be behind bars in a prison in Mexico. It could be discovering the awful depths of what she might be capable of. It could be back home with her family. It could be a million different things. But it would never include Ashley.

And that thought was sadder than any other.

CHAPTER THIRTY-TWO

THE NIGHT
ASHLEY

Ashley and Natalie followed Marco in a single line through the thick tropical forest, along a man-made path, the only sound the palm leaves and branches that had fallen from the trees crackling below their feet, the only light coming from the beams of their flashlights and the full moon.

A clearing opened up, and Ashley drew in a sharp breath as she saw the cenote. She and Natalie peered over the edge—shining their lights toward the water. "It looks like dark ink," Natalie said. "How deep do you think it is?"

"It's fifty feet deep right there. But it connects to underwater caves where it's even deeper in places," Marco said.

"It's pretty far down," Ashley said.

"About fifteen feet, maybe more," Marco said. "You definitely want to use that to get down." He shone his beam over to the side where a wooden ladder was attached to the top and disappeared into the sink-hole below. "Jumping or falling would both be very bad." He pulled Ashley by the elbow so she wasn't standing so close to the edge.

Ashley shone her light across to the other side—she couldn't tell how wide it was, but guessed maybe twenty to thirty feet. There was something both eerie and beautiful about this place—as if it could save you or break you, depending on what you wanted from it. Ashley felt drawn to it, still thinking about Lauren, not sure how she was going to survive without her in her life after she'd stripped away any hope of reconciliation. There was a look in her eye when she'd said the awful words that had stabbed Ashley in the heart—she had meant them. How had Ashley lost control over her friendships, her career? Her marriage? How had she lost her grasp so easily on the most vital of things?

She kicked off her sandals and put them next to her phone, then she started to climb down the ladder toward the water she prayed would bring her answers. The wood was slippery, and she tightened her grip on the rung with her one hand, and held her flashlight in the other.

"Where are you going?" Natalie asked, shining the light directly in Ashley's eyes, causing her to lose her balance momentarily.

"Whoa! That's bright. Are you trying to kill me by making me fall?" Ashley asked, flinching.

"Sorry," Natalie said. "But it's so dark down there. It's scary."

"I just want to feel the water. I'm not going all the way in—yet," Ashley said, shining her light up at Natalie, careful not to point it in her face.

Marco followed her down the ladder. He stood just above her. "It's amazing, isn't it?"

Ashley turned and looked up at him. "You were right. I can already feel the energy, and I'm not even in the cenote yet. My entire body is buzzing, like the spirits are inside me." She took a deep breath, the knots in her stomach finally coming undone.

"Well, in order to truly feel the energy, I have something for you." Marco leaned back against the ladder and removed two clear bottles from his pocket. Ashley was so close she could see that there was a green liquid inside them.

"What do you have?" Natalie peered over the edge of the cenote, looking down at them.

"This is balché."

"It's what?" Natalie called down. She shone her flashlight on the bottles.

"It's called balché," Marco answered. "An ancient drink made from the gum tree which can be found at the ruins of Chichén Itzá, among other places in the Yucatán. High priests and shamans have been administering it for centuries. Drinking the amount I've brought will help clear your mind so that your soul can communicate with the gods. To find your center. It will help you resolve your conflicts."

"So we drink *that* and suddenly we know what to do about Revlon? We're in perfect agreement? We're all best friends again? Our marriages are perfect? God, who knew it was all so simple?" Natalie's voice was mocking. "Why stop with us, why don't you sell it to the leaders of the US and North Korea! Why not broker world peace too?" She let out a short laugh.

"Natalie—" Ashley started.

"I told you we couldn't trust him," Natalie said. "Why didn't you tell us about the drugs back at your place?" she asked Marco. "You said it would be magical and conveniently left out that we'd need to get high to see the magic."

"I didn't want to overwhelm you with information. I wanted you to see the cenote first. Take it all in."

"Do you think I'm an idiot?" Natalie asked, her eyes protruding. "Is this some kind of sick game—get women to go with you to a forest in the middle of the night and take your drugs? How do we know what that really even is? It could be anything!"

"Let's go back up," Ashley said to Marco. She climbed up behind him. He stepped to the side so she could pass.

"Natalie, will you stop!" Ashley said as she approached her, Marco close behind. "Marco means well. Why can't you just trust him?"

"I can't understand why you trust him—you've known the guy for four days!"

"Please," Ashley said, her voice light. She needed to convince Natalie this was a good thing, that the liquid in those bottles could help them. That the universe wanted them to heal.

Natalie stood, her gaze darting back and forth between Ashley and the bottles Marco was holding. Ashley saw an opening as she studied Natalie's face. She was softening, just slightly. "Come on. I don't want to do it alone. I need you."

Natalie's eyes widened at her confession. Ashley typically didn't say such things. "Do you really believe it will help?"

"I do." Ashley reached out her hand and exhaled deeply when Natalie took the bottle.

CHAPTER THIRTY-THREE

THREE DAYS AFTER
LAUREN

Lauren heard the light knock on the door—so faint she almost told herself she'd imagined it. That it wasn't Natalie standing on the other side of the glass about to give her the news she suspected she was about to hear: that Ashley was dead. Because if it hadn't been her body at the morgue, Natalie would have called her immediately and said so. Right? Lauren walked slowly, her legs shaking.

"It wasn't her. It wasn't Ashley," Lauren said out loud. She pulled back the sheer curtain and opened the door, staring into Natalie's eyes. They were red and puffy from crying. The room started spinning. She grabbed the edge of the bed. "No!"

Natalie wrapped her arms around Lauren and held her as she cried. Lauren's shoulders shook hard. She couldn't stop gasping. After several minutes she caught her breath. Natalie brought her a box of tissues, and she blew her nose repeatedly. Her throat burned.

"Not another person I loved." Lauren was hit with a terrible realization that she'd told Ashley she wished she were dead—and she was.

"I'm so sorry," Natalie said.

"She didn't deserve this."

Lauren could see Ashley standing at La Cantina, begging her to change her mind—to think about their twenty-year history. To give her another chance. And then she'd wished her dead. Those would forever be the last words she'd spoken to Ashley.

"I know," Natalie said. "She didn't."

Lauren's chin trembled, and she started to cry again. "What happened to her? How did she—"

Natalie explained what Officer Lopez told them. She ended on the fact that she was a suspect.

"What?" Lauren's eyes widened.

"He thinks I'm responsible. That even if I did lose my memory—which I think he doubts, too—I might not recall hurting her," Natalie said, obviously trying to hold it together. "Kind of like what your friend Annie said."

"She didn't mean—" Lauren felt horrible. Why had she said anything about Annie's theory?

"Yes, she did. She didn't believe me. Nobody believes me. My best friend is dead, and now I'm a suspect." Natalie started to cry. "I didn't kill her."

"I know you didn't," Lauren said, pushing away the guilt that she'd also suspected Natalie earlier. But there was no way she could have hurt Ashley. Seeing her now, distraught, broken, she couldn't imagine she had anything to do with it.

"Do you really believe that?" Natalie asked, wiping at her tears.

"I do. And I'm sorry I questioned you," Lauren said, putting her hand over Natalie's, thinking again about the terrible words she'd said to Ashley. Had she driven her to harm herself? "Do you think she might have jumped?"

Natalie took a long pause before responding. "It crossed my mind today when we were searching—could she hurt herself? The Ashley I knew would never do that. But she didn't tell me about Jason. Maybe there were other things I didn't know."

Lauren folded her arms over her stomach as if to protect it. "I just can't believe she's gone."

"I know," Natalie said quietly. "What if we never find out what really happened?" She choked back another sob. "And I rot in prison here."

"That is not going to happen. They still have to find Marco. Why would he take off if he were innocent?"

"I have no idea. And we probably never will," Natalie said.

Lauren couldn't imagine what it must be like for Natalie to be hit hard with two pieces of horrible news. Ashley was gone and Natalie was a suspect. How could the cops be so cruel as to accuse her while she was identifying the body? Had they no shame? "Are *you* okay?"

Natalie squeezed her eyes shut, tears spilling out from under her lids.

"Sorry, that was a terrible question. Of course you're not."

Natalie opened her eyes. "It was beyond anything I could ever describe, being there. Seeing her. Jason is in so much pain. He's calling Hannah and Abby now." She lay on the bed. "My heart hurts. I literally feel a burning in my chest."

"It's going to hurt for a very long time," Lauren said, then added, "Maybe always." She lay back next to Natalie and stared at the ceiling fan, her insides feeling as if they were being wrung like a wet towel. She couldn't believe Ashley was gone—and not just gone, but *never coming back*. Tears slid down her cheeks. She clenched the sheets between her fists, images of their final terrible fight at La Cantina playing in a loop in her head. She'd let her grief become an uncontrollable anger when Geoff died. And what had it helped? Now, here she was, a year later, with more death. More remorse. More anger. And nowhere for any of it to go.

"I hate how things were left so unsettled with her," Natalie said.

"I was just thinking that," Lauren said. "I feel sick for being so stubborn. For not just forgiving her. That's all she wanted, and I just wouldn't do it. Not at El Castillo, and then again I refused her at La Cantina. God, the things I said to her, Nat!" She stifled a sob. "Did Ashley tell you what happened up at El Castillo?"

Natalie nodded.

"I figured she had. She told me about Jason's abuse, and I just snapped. She was being so hypocritical, or so I thought at the time. Now I wish I could go back, give her a hug, and tell her I'm sorry he was such an ass."

"It was hard to find that out. I had no idea it was going on. And honestly, I got a little caught up in her telling you before me. How stupid was that?" Natalie said.

"When were we ever going to grow up? We were always begging for her to like each of us better. Like two puppies wanting to be adopted by the same person."

"I know," Natalie said sadly. "I hate that we were like that."

Lauren felt disgusted by all the time they'd wasted, jockeying for position within their own friendships, rather than just enjoying them.

Natalie turned toward her. "I need to tell you something."

Lauren felt a rush of dread flood her body. She didn't want to hear more bad news. "Okay," she said.

"She wanted to apologize to you the night of the funeral." Natalie closed her eyes briefly, then opened them. "And I told her not to."

Lauren let herself swallow the information slowly. Let the news work its way through her. Let her heart and mind process it, forcing away the angry thoughts. She could not allow herself to do what she did when Geoff died—to let her rage settle on someone who could still feel it—like Natalie. But she didn't know if she could control it. Her anger always had a way of working its way out of her. Finally, she spoke. "Why?"

"I told myself that I was being protective of Ash, but I should have stayed out of it. I'm sorry. You two might have mended things then, and we wouldn't have even come here on this trip. So many things would be different."

"Why couldn't you have stayed out of it?" Lauren's chest tightened. She breathed slowly—in and out, in and out. She didn't want to explode, but Natalie was right. Everything could have been different. Ashley would still be alive.

"It's going to make me sound awful if I tell you," Natalie said.

Lauren looked at her sallow face. She wasn't sure she wanted to hear it. She took a deep breath. Finally, she spoke. "You can tell me." The cycle had to stop. Somewhere, somehow, they needed to figure out how to be the friends to each other that they hadn't been to Ashley. So whatever she was about to say, Lauren would just have to accept.

"I wasn't sure I wanted you guys to make up. I was upset with you for how you treated her, and I saw it as an opportunity to have her all to myself." Natalie rubbed her eyes. "It sounds so bad when I say it out loud."

Lauren's instinct was to scream at Natalie for what she'd done. But she was tired. Tired of all the arguing, the negativity. "It's okay," she forced out, even though it really wasn't. But she'd get there eventually.

"I'm sorry," Natalie said. "If I hadn't—"

"We can't play the what-if game. We just can't. Please don't beat yourself up over it." They could drive themselves mad going over those scenarios. She'd already done that with Geoff, for months. She still did. If she hadn't seen Ashley at lunch that day. If she hadn't flinched when Ash touched her bruise. *If, if, if.*

"Lauren?" Natalie said. "I am so sorry. About everything. I promise, moving forward, to be up-front about everything."

Lauren drew in a long breath. "I agree. We have to be." She looked at Natalie. "We need to be strong. For Ashley. For her girls. Even for

Jason." Lauren looked away. "He will have to live with how he treated her. And honestly, so will we."

"I'm sorry, Lauren. I'm sorry that I've always kept you out here." Natalie stretched her arm over the side of the bed. "When you should've been here." She touched her chest. "She had such a power over me," she said, her voice breaking.

"She had a power over everybody," Lauren said. "When Geoff died, I just could not get over the fact that I hadn't made the decision to confront him on my own. That *she* had to tell me to do it. And I resented her for it. You know? And then holding on to that rage toward her became my power over her. Or so I thought." Lauren choked on her sobs. "Now I realize none of it really mattered. He was gone, and I should have been concentrating on the people who were still here."

Natalie bowed her head, tears falling down her cheeks. "I got to the same place with her—finally tired of letting her call all the shots for us, our business, and in many ways, for me. My life ended up looking like it did because I listened to her every step of the way about BloMe. And that made me so upset. But really, it was my own fault that I let it get that far. That I let her control me." Natalie quieted for a moment. "I'm going to miss her. Controlling or not, I loved her. She was my best friend."

"Me too."

"What do we do now?" Natalie whispered.

Lauren felt the same dull ache in her chest as when Geoff had died. The disbelief that turned to realization and then into despair, time the only path to healing. "We take one breath at a time," she said, and pulled Natalie in, letting her sob into her shoulder until there was nothing left.

CHAPTER THIRTY-FOUR

THE NIGHT
ASHLEY

Natalie pulled her hand away. "I can't do it. I have no idea what's in that bottle. And neither do you!"

"He just explained it," Ashley said, exasperated. It reminded her of the time they'd been passing around Jell-O shots at a party in college and Natalie refused to take one off the tray until the guy with the handlebar mustache and beer belly stated exactly what was in them.

"That it's made from a gum tree or whatever doesn't tell me anything. How are we going to react? What if we overdose?"

"We're not going to OD. Come on, this could be the solution we're looking for," Ashley appealed again.

"I can give you more detail about the drug if you'd like," Marco said.

Natalie glared at him. "Will you stay out of this? I think you've given me all the detail I need."

He shrugged, but said nothing.

She turned to Ashley, her voice fiery. "I don't get it. You're ruining my life, and you want me to do drugs with you as a solution?" Natalie's angry words echoed off the trees, landing in Ashley's chest. First Lauren, and now Natalie. Her oldest friends, both ready to walk away from her.

"You're drunk," Ashley said calmly. But her heart hurt. How many hurtful words would be hurled at her tonight? Because she felt like a fragile piece of china—one wrong move and she might break into a million tiny little pieces.

"You're right, I am," Natalie said. "But that doesn't make what I said any less true."

Ashley didn't answer. She turned and walked to the edge of the cenote, staring down at the water. What was that thing people said? That if you are the common denominator in fights, then the problem must lie with you? First Lauren. Then Natalie. Clearly, she was the one doing something wrong.

"You have nothing to say?" Natalie asked.

"What do you want to hear?" Ashley turned around, her voice hoarse.

"That you'll sell the company," Natalie said, her voice firm.

"I can't say that."

"But you promised me that first night here that you'd think about it," Natalie pleaded, walking toward her, slipping and then catching herself.

Marco stood beside Ashley. It looked as if he wanted to say something, but Natalie had already shut him down.

"And I did. I really did. I need you to know that."

"When, exactly? While walking on the beach with Marco? Or in between bites of your beloved carne asada tacos?" Natalie curled her lip.

"Yes—and no. I did talk to him about it. He actually agrees with you, believe it or not." Ashley turned her body to face him. "He thinks starting over would be a good thing."

"I knew I liked you." Natalie looked his way and deadpanned.

"But my answer is still no," Ashley added after a beat. Her heart fell when she saw the pained look on Natalie's face. But she couldn't change her mind. She needed to be strong—hang on to what was rightfully hers. Even if that made her the common denominator here too.

Marco took the opportunity to speak. "What's going on between you two now—this negativity. This toxicity. This is the exact reason you both need to drink this." He held the bottles up. "It's clear you *both* need some peace. Give your problems to the gods. The Maya worshipped both the upper- and underworld to achieve balance. To them, death was not the end of life. Rather, it was an opportunity to be reborn. They believed that when you are sacrificed, you go underground for five years and then your soul comes back in different ways—that your soul had to pass a series of tests in the underworld to achieve a rebirth in the middle world."

Natalie let out an angry snort. "Not happening."

Ashley eyed Natalie, searching for a trace of the girl who would forgive her for almost anything. Like when she'd borrowed and then lost the beloved gold hoop earrings Natalie's grandfather had brought back from Italy. Or when she'd accidentally sent a text to their most important vendor, calling her a whorebag, thinking she had been firing it off to Natalie. That's what they did—made mistakes and then forgave each other for them. But had it become too lopsided—Ashley doing more hurting than Natalie had capacity to forgive?

Ashley exhaled, knowing she had partially created the person she was looking at. That she'd worn Natalie out, in that way she knew she could. Jason had been right—she'd manipulated her into taking on more responsibility than she should have in the last year. She'd played on Natalie's emotions, complimenting her on her strengths in cutting manufacturing costs, in targeting vendors, in developing sales strategies, knowing the exact words to use to get her to agree. To get her to understand that she wasn't replaceable. For her to feel the enormous pressure that came with knowing they'd never find someone who could fill her shoes. She did this even though she knew Natalie was already maxed out.

She had listened as Natalie vented that she was so stressed she had to take Ambien to sleep each night. But had Ashley really heard her? She looked the other way when she saw how the long hours were affecting Natalie's relationship with Ben. Because Ashley knew she couldn't run BloMe without her. That she didn't *want* to run it without her. Their partnership was the catalyst for their incredible success. Break it apart and they were no longer special. How could Natalie not see that? How could she walk away from their company? From Ashley? She tried again. "Please, Nat, take the balché with me. Let's see if it helps. At this point, what could it hurt?"

"I never even tried pot in college. Remember? And I'm certainly not going to drink some mysterious green liquid now. You go right ahead. And I'll stay here, making sure you stay safe, like I always do." Natalie gave her a flat look.

Ashley swallowed her tears, frustration, and anger, then wordlessly took one of the bottles from Marco. She held it carefully as she climbed back down the wooden ladder to the warm water, and Marco followed close behind. She swam over to the side of the cenote, grabbed onto a branch growing out of the limestone rock, and drank the liquid slowly, trying not to gag as she swallowed. She needed answers. Now.

She floated on her back in the water, closed her eyes, set her intention, and waited.

CHAPTER THIRTY-FIVE

THREE DAYS AFTER
NATALIE

"Natalie?"

She tried to talk when Ben answered the phone, but the words were caught in her throat, only sobs escaping through her lips. She saw Ashley's sheet-white face again and started to cry harder.

"Honey, are you okay? You're scaring me," he said, his voice rising.

"She's dead," she managed, trying to catch her breath in between her heavy tears.

"Oh my God," Ben said. "I'm so sorry."

Natalie could hear Lucy and Meg in the background, asking what was wrong, Ben sucking in a sharp breath, telling them he needed a minute. She heard the familiar creak of their back door, and it made her heart ache not to be there with her family. Her marriage had suffered a huge blow, but was it too big to overcome? She didn't think so. She had to hope that if Ben found out she'd made a horrible mistake, he'd stay by her side.

"What happened to her?" he asked, once he was outside.

Natalie told him what she knew in fits and spurts, her voice breaking every few sentences. "I need an attorney," she said at the end.

"You have Arthur."

"No, I need a Mexican attorney. Preferably one who specializes in criminal law. I did a little research on the way back from the . . ." Natalie stopped, not wanting to say the word. "Anyway, I don't think I should talk to the police again without an attorney present."

"This is crazy. How could they think *you* had anything to do with it? Do they know you're her best friend and business partner? That you guys are practically sisters?"

"They don't care about any of that. They don't believe anything I've said because I can't prove I lost my memory. Officer Lopez actually said maybe I don't remember bashing her head in!"

Since he'd said the words to her at the morgue, Natalie had been trying to remember, trying to recall whether she had hit her.

"Fuck," Ben said. "He really said that?"

"He did." Natalie rubbed her sternum. Her chest felt like it was on fire. "And not just that, but also that I might have drugged myself as some sort of alibi—"

"What the hell?"

"Ben, I'm scared. I was probably the last one to see Ashley alive. *Of course* they're looking at me—accusing me—thinking I killed her!" Natalie panicked, terrified by the notion that she could have snapped, that the reason she could've woken up wet was because she'd been in the water with Ashley.

"They're looking at you because that Marco guy is gone and there is no one else admitting to being with her. But they can't prove a thing. If they could, they would have arrested you already."

"What if they're right?"

"What do you mean?"

"What if I did do something to her? What if I buried the truth about what happened because it's too horrible to remember?" she asked.

"Couldn't that be a possibility? What if I did bash her head in?" She felt relieved to finally say it out loud. She waited for Ben's response. He knew her better than anyone in the world. She needed him to defend her—now, more than ever. If her husband didn't believe in her, that would be it. Because she certainly didn't believe in herself right now.

The silence on the other end of the phone while she waited for his answer felt like forever as she teetered between her anger at what he'd done with their finances and the need for his unwavering support.

"No way—you did not hurt Ashley. Do you hear me? You did not suppress some violent act. You can't even kill a spider. Remember when Lucy was freaking out about the one in the bathtub? She was saying, 'smash it, kill it!' And you refused. You put him in a cup and released him into our backyard."

Natalie started weeping at the memory. What she wouldn't give to be there right now saving her children from eight-legged creatures. "Thank you, Ben. I needed you to say you believed me."

"Of course I do," he said. "Have you remembered anything else?"

I am so done. Done letting you control my choices. Letting you control me. Her own voice in her mind was shrill and tight. She almost didn't recognize it as her own.

Natalie pushed down the memory. "No," she said, rubbing her temples. Even though fragments of the night were coming back, none of them made sense. Like a puzzle missing most of its pieces. And she wasn't about to say she'd been at the cenote—not until she had more context. The last thing she needed was her own husband losing faith in her innocence. Even though she might doubt herself, she wouldn't be able to handle it if he did too.

Her limbs were heavy from exhaustion. "Ben, can you take care of getting a lawyer for me? I just can't. I feel like I'm going to have a mental breakdown."

"I'll call Arthur and get a referral. And I'm going to catch a red-eye there," he said, then paused. "I'll charge it on the Mastercard—it has a little room left," he finally said, so quietly Natalie barely heard him.

"No—" Natalie made a feeble protest, ignoring the reference to their money problems. She couldn't think about that right now.

"I'll call my sister and see how soon she can get here," he said.

Her hands were trembling. She needed him.

"What the hell do I say to the girls? They just saw me start to lose it."

"I don't know. I don't know anything anymore." She felt so empty—she hoped he could find the words for them on his own.

Head pounding, she forced herself to work out the details with Ben before hanging up, then sank into the bed she'd shared with Ashley only four nights ago, which now felt like forever ago. Almost like she'd never been here at all. She fingered the little white pill Maria had forced into her hand earlier. "To sleep," she'd whispered in her ear. "You need rest." Natalie placed it in her mouth and swallowed it without water, staring at the ceiling until her eyes could no longer stay open.

CHAPTER THIRTY-SIX

THE NIGHT
ASHLEY

Ashley lay back in the warm cenote water and let it envelop her body and her spirit. Marco swam toward her, his movement causing the water to lap around her face.

"Take your power back," he said as the sound of her breath pounded in her ears. "Ask for forgiveness," he reminded her, every inch of her tingling as the balché flowed through her limbs. "Let the water heal you," he said as she opened her eyes and stared up at the pitch-black sky. She focused on a lone star shining brightly.

She felt Marco's arms underneath her back and relaxed into him, her body feeling light. She imagined her mind as a chalkboard that had been wiped clean, the dusty eraser sitting nearby. *Please forgive me,* she repeated to herself over and over, even though she wasn't totally sure whose absolution she wanted most. Lauren's. Natalie's. Jason's? Hannah and Abby's? Her own?

Natalie's voice pulled her out of her meditation. She eased away from Marco and craned her neck toward the top of the cenote where Natalie stood. Natalie shone her flashlight into Ashley's face again, and she flinched in the light. She tried to make out Nat's image, but the light had temporarily blinded her. She was telling Ashley to get out, that she wanted to go back to the hotel.

"Get out now," Natalie said again.

Ashley was finally able to focus, the splotches of light that dotted her vision fading. She saw Natalie stumble, the flashlight falling from her hand and rolling over the edge of the cenote. She heard it crash against something on the other side of the cenote.

"It hit the rocks," Marco said.

That could have been Natalie. Ashley felt heavy, but she forced herself to swim back toward the ladder. She needed to get Natalie away from the edge. To keep her safe. "Stay here. She's fine. You need to relax for the balché to work," Marco said, but she continued toward Natalie.

"You need to be careful up here. You saw what just happened to your flashlight. I couldn't handle it if it had been you, Nat," Ashley said when she reached the top of the ladder and climbed out.

Natalie didn't respond—she stared straight ahead.

"Hey," Ashley said, her tongue suddenly thick. "I care about you." She reached for Natalie's arm—she was still standing too close to the edge. "Here, let's move away from there."

"Come back in," Marco called from below, but Ashley didn't respond. "You should be meditating." He'd pulled her aside at his apartment and asked her to leave with him tonight—to not go back to her home in Santa Monica but instead to go away with him, an idea he'd been bringing up all week. *Think of the life we could live together,* he'd said over and over. *When you leave everything behind, you will truly become free.*

But freedom had a large price tag. To leave everything behind would mean her girls, her company, Natalie. But in moments like now, when it didn't seem like she could pull Natalie back to her—literally or figuratively—when she'd already lost Lauren, she wondered. *Could she go through with it? And would anyone even miss her if she did?*

"I said I cared about you. Did you hear me?" Ashley said.

"I did," Natalie said.

"I want to make things right between us."

"Can we not do this now?" Natalie sighed. "I'm tired. I want to go back to the hotel. We have an early flight."

"Soon, I promise. But he's still guiding me through it," Ashley said, her head feeling foggy. She was starting to wrestle with the idea that maybe she should go away. Was that what the universe was telling her to do? Was that the clarity that was going to take shape?

"So how do you feel? Like all of your problems have, whoosh, disappeared?" Natalie flicked her fingers.

"I don't know yet—it's just starting to take effect," Ashley said, feeling strangely liberated. Like any choice she made would be the right one.

"What is it about Marco?" Natalie whispered. "I feel like you're on a reckless path."

"That's why I took the balché, Nat. Because I don't want to be," Ashley said, but her words were echoing in her head. She took a deep breath so she could focus. "Why don't you drink the other bottle? Or even just half? Look, I'm fine."

Natalie hesitated. Ashley watched as she glanced over to where Marco had left the other bottle, on a rock not far from where they stood. Natalie walked over and picked it up, running her thumb over the glass.

"I told you, I don't feel comfortable if both of us are high; then we'll both be vulnerable to—"

"Forget Marco—look at him. If he wanted to rape us or hurt us, he's strong enough to do so. And it would have happened by now. He could have drowned me down there. What would you have done from up here?" She smiled.

"Has something happened between you two? Is that why you defend him so much?" Natalie twisted her mouth into a frown.

"No," Ashley said. She needed her to know that. She had felt something this week, but she realized now it wasn't a physical attraction to Marco. It was the pull toward a different reality. He had so many promises of good things, of changes, of a life where stress wasn't the headliner. "We're just friends." She waited for Natalie to respond, but she didn't. "Do the balché with me, Nat. Let's be vulnerable together, let go of control. Let the universe weigh in." She thought about what she *really* wanted from Natalie—to know honestly what was in her heart when her walls were torn down. Would she tell Ashley she still cared about her too? That it hadn't all been destroyed, like a sandcastle after high tide?

"I don't know. I feel like you're not being honest with me about Marco—that you're holding something back."

"Okay. Hanging out with Marco has given me a new perspective. Maybe what I like about him is that he's given me the courage to think about leading a different life," she added, trying out how it felt to say the words. She suddenly felt brave. Was it the balché?

Natalie brightened, clearly misinterpreting her. Taking it as an olive branch, rather than what it was: a confession. "Does that mean you're thinking of selling? Has the balché given you clarity to see that it's the right choice?"

She looked at Natalie's face—how in just a split second it had gone from a scowl to a grin. How the color had rushed back to her cheeks. Even though the mere idea of selling was like a vise grip clamping down on Ashley's chest, pressing the air out of her, she wanted her friend to be happy. She looked at Natalie and smiled.

"This calls for a celebration!" Natalie opened the top of the bottle and drank the liquid before Ashley could respond.

They sat together in silence for several minutes.

Finally, Natalie spoke. "I think I can feel it already. Wow, it's so strange and incredible all at the same time."

"Isn't it?" Ashley said. "See, I would have never been able to explain it to you."

"Do you feel like you're vibrating?" Natalie held out her arms.

"Yes, that's the energy of this place—it's inside you now."

"Amazing," Natalie said. "I can feel it in every muscle—every inch of me. Is this what pot is like? If so, I should have tried it."

"Ha. I don't remember. It was so long ago. But I suspect this is much better than that," Ashley said, feeling as if she were seeing the Natalie she'd missed for so long finally coming out. The Natalie who didn't have her guard up all the time. The one who laughed easily. Who didn't take everything so seriously. It had been months since she'd seen her.

They stood up and looked at the moon for what felt like forever, Marco floating on his back peacefully below them. Ashley was just about to suggest they go into the cenote and join him when Nat spoke. "So what made you change your mind?" she asked.

"About what?" Ashley asked. But she knew exactly what.

"Revlon, silly." Natalie elbowed her.

Ashley sighed. "Let's not talk about it right now; let's talk about us. I want you to know something—I really want things to be good between us again. I want to be how we used to be. Before Revlon."

"So do I. And maybe now it can," Natalie said. "We can spend more time together. I have plans to get involved in some charities, if you're interested."

"Nat—" She had thought that she could let her believe she'd reconsidered. That they'd have a fun night and bond and then tomorrow she'd correct her—tell her what she really meant by starting a new life.

Natalie turned, then recoiled, obviously reading the expression on Ashley's face. She stepped backward and lost her balance again slightly, a few rocks falling over the side of the cenote. She righted herself.

"Please step away from there. You could fall. There are sharp rocks all around the edge at the bottom."

"I can take care of myself." She gave Ashley a hard look. "I can't believe you lied to me."

"I didn't lie, exactly. You just looked so happy, and I wanted that for you. I wanted to spend time with that Natalie. I was going to talk to you tomorrow and—"

"Shatter me all over again?" Natalie clenched her jaw.

"I just wanted *you*—the old you. Can't you see I'm desperate for that?"

"Then sell the company, and I promise you that carefree Natalie will hang out with you twenty-four seven." Natalie stared at Ashley but she couldn't respond. "She'll meet you for coffee and spin class and PTA meetings wearing those overpriced yoga pants you love so much. Sell, and I'm yours."

"So you only want our friendship if I acquiesce to what you want? Because you're not willing to give up what you want for me," Ashley accused.

"And neither are you, despite the fact that I've been doing it for years. When you wanted to hire that flighty web designer who never finished our website? Remember, you said she had a *great energy*, so we didn't need to call her references? Or how about the time you browbeat me until we chose the logo you wanted for the BloBrush?"

Ashley stood very still, staring. "That's not fair."

"Isn't it, though?" Natalie scoffed. "Name a time *you've* acquiesced! Just one!" When Ashley didn't answer, she said, "You can't, can you?"

Ashley took a deep breath and tried to mentally push Natalie's accusations away, the water from the cenote dripping from the hem of her jeans shorts. She wiped at her legs. She felt as if she were floating above her body. Finally able to see her life and what she wanted, objectively. She understood what Natalie wanted, but she also knew what she needed. Selling the company wasn't a compromise. It would just be gone—never again theirs. But Natalie making changes to her involvement in the company, that was the logical solution. "Can I just explain? Explain why I don't want to sell. I really did think about it. I did. Just like I promised."

"No," Natalie said. "No," she repeated louder.

"You guys okay?" Marco called out. They both ignored him.

"What's wrong with you?" Ash stepped closer to Natalie so she could see her face better. "Why won't you let me explain?"

"I just know what you're about to say, and I'm tired of hearing it." Ashley pressed on anyway. "I'm sorry, Nat. I love you, but I can't sell the company. I just can't."

Natalie twisted her face. "Well, I'm super happy for you, Ash. I really am. But you know where that leaves me? With a shitload of very serious problems," she spat. Her eyes were wide and glazed. Anger danced in her pupils.

Ashley felt like she could actually see a flame reflected in Natalie's eyes. She shook her head hard, trying to refocus. "What are you talking about?"

"Selling BloMe is about more than me wanting more time with my family and being burned out. If we don't agree to Revlon's offer, I'm going to lose everything," Natalie said, staring hard at Ashley without blinking.

"What?" Ashley's mouth fell open.

"I'll lose my house, every asset, everything I've worked so hard for. Maybe even my marriage. I can't imagine Ben and I could survive it." She looked away.

"But what happened?"

Natalie flapped her hand in dismissal. "It doesn't matter. What should matter to you is my life is basically over if we don't sell. So tell me, Ash, is your mind still made up?"

CHAPTER THIRTY-SEVEN

FOUR DAYS AFTER
NATALIE

"Natalie?"

She heard her name, then a pounding on the door of her suite.

Natalie tried to open her swollen eyes—her lashes sticking together as she pulled them apart.

Ben? She glanced at the clock on the bedside table. It was 9:00 a.m. She'd been asleep for more than sixteen hours. She still felt like she was dozing, standing at the doorway of dreams and reality. Raising her head off the pillow, she willed herself to move toward Ben's frantic voice. "Coming!" she tried to call out, but her mouth was so dry, the words seemed to disappear.

She slowly made her way over and unlatched the lock. "You scared me," Ben said, his eyes shining.

Natalie's chest warmed as she stared up at him. She hadn't realized just how much she needed him here, next to her. Just his body filling the doorway was easing her. His light brown hair was sticking out from under a baseball hat. He was wearing a faded pair of cargo shorts, the scar from his ACL surgery peeking out. He had on his favorite Metallica

T-shirt from a concert they'd seen together a million years ago, the cotton soft and worn. She reached out and hugged him tightly, her cheek brushing against his broad chest.

"I'm so glad you're okay. I've been calling you since I landed in Cancún two hours ago. And I started imagining all of these scenarios. After Ashley . . . I just . . . my head went to the worst places," he said into her shoulder.

Natalie smiled sadly. "I'm sorry I worried you." She pulled back to face him again. "I'm so glad you're here." And she was. It didn't mean what he'd done was okay. And the truth was, it could very well still destroy their marriage. But in that moment she needed him urgently. She started to cry. She was surprised she still had tears left.

"Me too," he said, brushing a strand of her hair out of her eyes.

She glanced at her phone plugged in next to the bed. "I think I had it on silent," she said. "And Maria from the front desk gave me a sleeping pill. She's been a godsend, taking care of me."

"I met her downstairs; she's worried about you," he said, kissing her softly on the lips, the taste of his coffee lingering. She turned to let him in and stumbled, she held out her arms and Ben grabbed them and steadied her. Something about the movement felt familiar. She leaned against him again and closed her eyes, sensing that the memory of what happened to Ashley was close, willing the door to her subconscious to swing open wide. She pressed to remember, but nothing more would come. She studied Ben, wondering suddenly how the girls were. How they'd taken the news of Ashley's disappearance.

"How did the girls react when you told them?" she asked.

Ben's face darkened. "They took it pretty hard. I felt terrible leaving them, but I told them you needed me here. They understood. My sister is keeping them home from school again today."

Natalie bit her lip to keep from crying again, but she began to shake, thinking of how scared Ashley's children must be, what they were going through. Jason said they were in shock—his entire family had descended on their house, trying their best to shield them from the media that showed up at their door when the story of her death hit the news.

"Here, come, sit down," Ben said, leading her back over to the bed. "Maria told me the police are on their way. The lawyer I hired is also here and is anxious to talk with you. I filled him in on the phone, and he's read and heard the news coverage, but he obviously wants to interview you directly. Want to get changed and I'll bring him up?"

Natalie barely heard him; the night she'd thought she lost was now downloading into her head in bursts, the pieces tying together to tell the story of Ashley's final moments, the feeling of desperation she'd experienced that night leaping into her chest, almost knocking her over.

Trying to convince Ashley to sell the company.

Ashley refusing.

A heated argument.

A cenote far below.

Jagged rocks lining the bottom.

"Did you hear me?" Ben asked, rubbing his jaw. "The police are coming. I presume they have your test results. I hope so anyway. And the lawyer is here. You should probably meet with him first, and we can come up with a game plan."

Natalie massaged the back of her neck. "No, wait until the police arrive; then bring the lawyer up with them."

"I don't think that's a good idea."

"It's okay." Natalie gripped his arm, a mixture of relief and panic swirling inside of her.

Ashley had stood there, soaking wet. Water running down her legs. *I'm sorry . . . but I can't sell . . .*

Natalie scowled. *My life is . . . over if we don't . . . ?* She had felt her chest burn with rage. She was going to lose everything. She had stepped closer to Ashley.

What's wrong with you? Ashley had asked, her eyes registering fear.

"Why is it okay?" Ben stepped closer and studied her face. "What is it? You look like you've seen a ghost."

In so many ways, she had.

"I know what happened to Ashley."

CHAPTER THIRTY-EIGHT

THE NIGHT
ASHLEY

Ashley was stunned as she stared at Natalie, her emotions fighting one another. Her heart ached for Natalie—she didn't want her to lose everything, but Ashley also didn't want to give up everything. Did that make her a terrible person? She fought to focus, her eyelids becoming heavy from the drug. "Why didn't you tell me what was going on?" Ashley finally asked.

"Probably for the same reason you didn't tell me about how Jason treats you." Natalie's eyes were vacant. She'd lost her again. "It's hard to say out loud, isn't it—even to your best friend?"

Ashley crumbled inside. How had both of their lives turned upside down without the other one noticing? What did that say about them? That their friendship would disintegrate so easily when pressure was applied?

"Ashley, you really need to come back to the water before the balché wears off," Marco called out.

Marco—what a presence he'd been. What a source of conflict between her and her friends. She didn't respond. She tried to crystallize her thoughts. She needed to help Natalie. Figure out how they could both get what they wanted. "Can I loan you money?" Ashley asked. She had some stashed away that Jason didn't know about. Savings. Just in case.

"It's more than you have. Ben says we have nothing left." Natalie squeezed her lips into a tight line.

"What happened?"

"He lost it. He fucking lost it all."

"What? How could he—"

"No, it's my fault too. I knew some of what was going on, but I thought he was going to fix it with his last investment."

"So then let me help. I'm sure my money can get you started . . . get you guys on solid ground, and then we can go from there?" Something caught her eye above Natalie's head. A pod of gold and black butterflies danced above her. She pointed. "Do you see that?"

Natalie looked up and shook her head. "Come on, Ashley, it's not just about writing me a check. But even if you had enough money, then what? I'm back at work, miserable. I need my family back. I want out." Her voice shook. "I can't do this anymore. Can't you see that? It's literally breaking me."

Ashley pictured them signing the company over to Revlon. Part of Revlon's proposed deal was they'd want to keep only Ashley and Natalie on as consultants for six months and give severances to everyone else. After that, they planned to fold BloMe into *their* company. Ashley pictured herself clearing out her office, putting her things in a cardboard box. Driving home. Sitting in her living room on her stiff sofa and looking around. What would she do with herself? She shivered at the thought of volunteering with Natalie and a bunch of bored house-wives who had nothing better to do. She was proud of her career—of their success. She loved talking about it with people. She wouldn't have an answer when someone asked her, "So you sold. Now what?" She'd shrivel up. She knew she could never give Natalie what she wanted. "I'm sorry," Ashley said quietly. "I will give you every extra penny I have to help you out of your financial troubles. You can even borrow against the company if you need to. I'll make sure you don't lose your house."

Natalie clenched and unclenched her hands. "You are more selfish than I ever realized."

Ashley felt like she'd been slapped. Jason had said almost the same thing when they'd argued right before she came here. When Jason accused her of it, it hadn't had an impact. But Natalie's words held weight.

"You asked me earlier why I haven't told you about all this. The real answer is because I knew you wouldn't give a shit," Natalie said.

"It's not that I don't give a—" Ashley struggled to speak. She glanced down toward the water. There was a beam of light shooting up to the sky. Had that been there before? It was so beautiful. So inviting.

"Bullshit! I just told you I could lose everything, and you stood there all pious and offered me money. Like that was the only option." Natalie's nostrils were flaring.

"I want to help you. I'm not trying to be selfish. I'm trying to compromise. And I'm offering a viable solution."

"You aren't getting it. You're never going to get it! I. Want. Out. I. Need. Out." She screamed, her veins visibly straining against the skin of her neck. She teetered again.

Ashley tried to reach for her, but she moved to the side, more rocks sliding over the edge. "Come on, Nat, please move away from there."

"No," she said. "How does it feel to hear that word? No." Natalie's face was slightly veiled in the darkness, but Ashley could hear the desperation in her voice.

Marco climbed out of the cenote. "Listen, you've both had a lot to drink. This isn't going to get settled tonight, even with the balché. And Ashley is right; you should both move away from there."

Natalie stepped to the other side of Ashley and moved toward her. Now Ashley was the one closer to the edge. How had that happened?

"This is *never* going to get settled, Marco." Natalie looked at him, then turned back to Ashley. "Because if you won't sell, we can't sell, which leaves me, well, *fucked*."

"You're not fucked. We can work this out. There has to be a solution we can both live with," Ashley said, pushing to be more alert. But she was so tired. Her eyelids fluttered. She wanted to see where that beam of light led. She looked back at Nat and finally felt the courage to say what she realized at that very moment had been sitting in her heart all along. "Nat, don't leave me. I need you. I need BloMe."

Natalie's eyes narrowed. "Are you serious? I tell you I'm going to lose my house, everything, and you make it about you?" She threw her hands up in the air. "Why am I not surprised?"

Ashley looked down. She had failed miserably tonight. On this trip. All of her good intentions stomped into the ground. Lauren's face when she'd pleaded with her to reconcile earlier had said it all: it's too late. And now, here, with Natalie, failing once more. How could she make her understand that all the material things she was terrified to lose were just things? They were replaceable. But their partnership, the things they could accomplish together? Their friendship? That was priceless. And she wouldn't just let her throw it away.

Marco picked up his flashlight and turned it on. "Come on, you guys."

"Please," Ashley pleaded, feeling her throat burn. "I need you. I need this company. Now more than ever. Why can't you see that?"

"You don't need my friendship. What you want is my fucking devotion, which I've given you for years. And you know what? You don't deserve my friendship. You use people, Ash."

Ashley's heart sank. "Is that what you really think of me?"

"I don't even think you realize you do it anymore. But it stops right now, right here. We are selling this company. You are going to do something for me, for once! You are going to put my needs above yours!"

Ashley's limbs felt so tired. How could she make Natalie understand that their company was important? If they let it slip away, they'd have nothing. She wasn't just doing this for herself; she was protecting the company for both of them. For their legacy. Her mouth felt thick, the words she knew Natalie needed to hear not coming to her. So she shook her head. "No."

Natalie's cheeks were flushed a dark red under the moonlight. She jabbed her finger at Ashley. "I am so done." She thrust out her chest. "I am done letting you control my choices. Letting you control me. Manipulate me. Doing the right thing all the time. That ends tonight. I wish I had never met you!" Natalie's lip curled. She took another step toward her, her face within inches of Ashley—she could see the whites of her eyes. Ashley glanced over her shoulder; she was too close to the edge of the cenote, Natalie now blocking her exit.

Ashley's heart pounded hard as she looked into Natalie's eyes. It was as if something had broken inside Natalie. As if Ashley had been the one to shatter it.

"Tell me, Ashley, why did you really say you wanted to try another life?" Natalie asked. "Because keeping the company sounds exactly like the life you have now."

Ashley looked at Marco. Thinking again about their conversation. About leaving. If she didn't sell BloMe, Natalie was going to hate her. They'd never be the friends they once were. And Jason? Would they be able to settle things amicably? Without the girls hating her? She really didn't know. There would be no guarantees when she arrived back home.

"What? You didn't really mean you'd sell? Was it another lie?" Natalie asked. "You were just baiting me to get me to take the drug."

"No, I wasn't, I swear." Ashley stepped backward, rocks sliding over the cenote. She glanced over her shoulder. She hadn't realized she was this close to the edge.

"Ashley, tell her the truth that's in your heart," Marco said, stepping toward her.

"There's no truth in there—she's just a liar," Natalie shouted. She pointed at Ashley and moved closer to her. "Aren't you, Ashley? Just admit it."

Ashley stared into Natalie's eyes, which burned with fury. There were only inches between Ashley and Natalie and Marco; they were blocking her in. The only way out—down to the cenote or pushing through them. Her heart thumped hard. She felt like a caged animal.

"I'm not lying," Ashley said, but she wasn't sure if she'd spoken the words aloud or if they were only in her head. She closed her eyes for a moment, trying to think what she could say to convince Natalie she wasn't a fraud. In a flash, she felt movement, then heard her name. She flinched as she opened her eyes, the solid ground underneath her slipping away quickly. She heard herself screaming. A shrill sound that echoed in her own ears and through the night.

She saw Natalie reach for her. So did Marco, his strong arms shooting out from his sides like bullets, just missing Ashley's fingers. But it was too late—she was already plunging into the darkness.

CHAPTER
THIRTY-NINE

Officer Garcia stepped onto the veranda, Officer Lopez in tow. Natalie studied their faces—looking for signs of what the drug test might have revealed. But as usual, she could not read them. She closed her eyes briefly, the smell of the hotel's signature chilaquiles wafting up from the restaurant below. When she opened her eyes, Jesús Campo, the small and wiry attorney with a shiny bald head and a long nose, whom she'd met only a few minutes before, gave her a look. He hadn't hidden his frustration that she would not tell him what she'd remembered about the night prior to the officers' arrival. He wanted to properly vet the information. Barring that, he had strongly recommended against speaking to them and told Natalie he could not protect her and could not guarantee she wouldn't be arrested if she incriminated herself in any way.

But Natalie had been waiting for this—for the memory of what happened to Ashley to come back. She wanted to tell Lauren and Jason first, privately. There wasn't time, though—the officers were here; they wanted answers. So she'd tell Lauren and Jason afterward, when she could sit with them as long as they needed. Natalie greeted Officer Lopez and Officer Garcia and introduced Ben and Jesús Campo to them. She didn't miss Officer Lopez's raised eyebrow, clearly surprised she'd hired an attorney. They exchanged pleasantries in Spanish.

"May we reveal the results of the drug testing in front of everyone here?" Officer Garcia asked after they all settled into the wooden deck chairs.

"Yes," Natalie murmured, already knowing what the results were going to be. She'd finally remembered. The memories unsettling as they became clear in her mind. As the missing pieces of the night finally came together, she was hit hard with feelings of extreme regret and a deep sadness. She'd run to the bathroom and dry heaved, wondering if subconsciously she was also trying to purge the thoughts she'd just regained. She noticed Jesús grimace slightly at her assent, probably wondering how Arthur knew this crazy American woman with no regard for the importance of lawyers.

Officer Garcia cleared his throat and flipped open his notepad. "There were large traces of Xanax in your system, also balché. Mixed with the alcohol, we have concluded that those two drugs could have caused you to black out."

Natalie let out the breath she'd been holding and met Ben's eyes. Even though she'd felt strongly that she knew how the Xanax got into her system, there was still that chance she'd been wrong.

"So the question is, who drugged you—and why?"

"I can tell you that," Natalie said.

"You remember?" Officer Garcia straightened in his chair.

"I do," Natalie said, scooting to the edge of her seat. "It's still foggy—kind of like a bad dream that you remember in pieces." Officer Lopez and Officer Garcia nodded as if they understood. "But I'm certain I know what happened."

"Start at the beginning," Officer Garcia said. "May I record this?" He tapped his smartphone and looked at Jesús, who frowned.

"Yes," Natalie said anyway.

Ben looked at her, his eyes asking again, *Are you sure about this?* Earlier, he'd tried to talk her out of it, worried the officers would twist her words or trap her in some way. Telling her it was crazy she didn't want to protect herself, that she had asked for a lawyer and now she wasn't taking advantage of his help. He'd stood outside the shower, his back against the wall, pleading with her. But she'd told him he would have to trust her—that she knew what she was doing. That having a lawyer talking for her and telling her what she could and couldn't answer or say would frustrate the police. And probably make her appear even more guilty. She'd let the lawyer sit in on the meeting, but she needed to tell her own story. As the lukewarm water washed away the soap she'd lathered on her body, she'd hoped she was right.

Officer Garcia started recording.

"After we left La Cantina, we went to Marco's apartment. That's where we decided to go to the cenote. Well, they decided, and I didn't want Ashley to go there alone with him." Natalie recalled how Marco had massaged Ashley's shoulders as he spoke of the healing properties of this particular cenote, Ashley listening intently. "We drove to Cenote Calavera in his car."

"What time was it?"

"I'm not sure. I can remember chunks of what happened, but I'm not sure of the time frames."

"So Marco drove you to the cenote," Officer Garcia prompted.

Natalie closed her eyes, she could see Ashley floating on her back in the black water. "It was Marco's idea—he convinced Ashley that if she swam in the cenote, it would cleanse her soul. He'd been feeding her head with this spiritual bullshit all week. She'd totally bought into it."

"Why did she feel like she needed to cleanse her soul?"

"I think she just wanted to clear her mind. She'd had that huge fight with Lauren at Chichén Itzá. None of us had gotten along great during the week. We had some big things going on at work, and she wanted clarity." Natalie glanced at Ben.

"Okay, so she wanted to clear her mind. What happened next?" Officer Garcia asked.

Natalie thought about the way Ashley had kicked off her sandals and climbed down the ladder and dropped into the water. How she'd tilted her head up and drunk from the glass bottle Marco handed her. It was so dark, Natalie had to shine her flashlight to see them nearly fifteen feet below. She could still feel the anger that had welled inside her as they swam. "Marco gave her something called balché."

"What is balché?" Ben asked.

"It's an ancient drug. A very mild hallucinogenic," Officer Garcia said.

"I refused to take it at first," Natalie said. "Anyway, after she drank it, I told her she should get out, that it was late—we should go back to the hotel."

"And then what happened?"

"I stumbled a little bit from being drunk. I was by the cenote. Ashley climbed out to check on me—told me to move away from the edge. Then we got into a heated discussion."

"What about?" Garcia asked.

Natalie glanced at Ben again. He gave her a look like he was sorry—for pushing her so hard to get Ashley to change her mind.

"Our company. Revlon wanted to buy it. They offered us eight figures. And Ashley didn't want to sell."

"And you did?"

"Exactly." Natalie remembered standing next to the cenote—pointing her finger at Ashley. Her anger boiling. She couldn't recall ever being that furious with anyone. "We'd been going around about it all week. But after she took the balché, she seemed to change her mind about selling. Begged me to take the drug with her." She shot an apologetic look at Ben. "So I did. I drank it."

"And then you pushed her?" Officer Garcia sat up taller in his chair.

"What? No." She looked at her lawyer. Wondering if she should have consulted with him.

"She would never hurt Ashley," Ben said.

"I would never hurt Ashley," Natalie repeated.

"But you'd been arguing. She wasn't going to give you what you wanted. You said eight figures was at stake. With her gone, they'd still sell to you, right?"

"I don't know. I never thought about it like that." Natalie's hands were suddenly clammy. She rubbed them on the chair. "I would never hurt her. That's not what happened. Yes, I wanted to sell the company, but I wouldn't have killed her over it!"

"Do you want to talk to me privately?" Jesús asked.

"No, listen." She stared at Officer Garcia. "I didn't push Ashley. She slipped."

"How?" he asked.

"It was a terrible accident. Marco came over to us—he was trying to help. He . . ." Natalie started to cry as she remembered Ashley's eyes wide, blinking rapidly. She had let out a primal scream.

"He was trying to get us to stop arguing, and he stepped toward her to try to get her to move away from the edge. She was closer than I was, and she lost her balance." Natalie stopped, her tears falling hard. She didn't bother to wipe them. "So yes, in that way, I'm responsible. Because if we hadn't been arguing, then Marco wouldn't have tried to break it up, and then she wouldn't have fallen." She sucked in too much air and coughed.

She remembered Ashley's hands flailing in the air, trying in vain to hook on to anything. It had seemed to happen in slow motion, her fall. Her screams echoing through the dark night. Neither of them able to get to her in time. "I tried to help her. So did Marco, but she was already falling." Natalie covered her face, crying into her hands. Finally, she looked up, meeting Ben's eyes. "She fell down into the cenote. There was a crack. It was so loud."

The room was silent as Natalie tried to find her next words. She struggled, feeling sick. They were harder to say than she could have ever imagined.

We need to get her out! Save her! Natalie had screamed, her pulse racing. She had broken into a cold sweat.

Marco had raced down the ladder and jumped into the water, frantically searching for Ashley. Natalie shone her flashlight to help him.

I have her, he had yelled.

Natalie's heartbeat had pulsed in her ears. Maybe Ashley was still alive. *Please God,* she had prayed, *let her be breathing.*

"He pulled Ashley up the ladder. I don't even know how he did it, but he did. And laid her down on the ground. He performed CPR. Finally, he stopped pressing his palms into her chest. He pulled his mouth away from hers." Natalie couldn't say more.

There had been so much blood gushing from her head. Natalie pressed her hand on it, but it kept coming.

Oh my God, Marco had said. *She's dead. I can't believe she's dead.* His eyes had bulged. He had rocked back and forth on his knees. *This is all my fault. It's all my fault.*

We have to get her to a hospital. Maybe they can still save her, Natalie had yelled over the sound of her heartbeat.

It won't do any good, she's gone, Marco had said.

Natalie had checked Ashley's pulse again, put her head on her chest. Maybe he was wrong. He had to be wrong.

"I wanted to call the police, take her to the hospital. I wanted to get more help."

"But you didn't," Officer Garcia said matter-of-factly. "Why not?"

Natalie shook her head, her cheeks burning. Jesús handed her a box of tissues. She blew her nose. "I didn't have a phone. And Marco wouldn't give me his. I searched for Ashley's, but couldn't find it either.

Marco said the police wouldn't believe us. That we'd be arrested, or worse." She looked at Officer Garcia, whose jaw tightened. Something told her he was one of the good ones, that he always played by the rules.

The ground was cold underneath her as she had cradled Ashley's lifeless body in her arms.

Marco had been pacing. *We need to get out of here—now.*

"He wanted to leave. To protect ourselves. I refused. I told him that I was going to the police with or without him. That there was no way I was leaving her there, like an animal." Natalie's voice cracked again.

Natalie had pulled her knees to her chest, everything around her spinning. She pressed her eyes shut, praying that when she opened them, Ashley would be alive again. That it was all just a bad dream.

"I finally managed to convince him. We were going to take her to the hospital and then call the police."

Natalie's vision had been blurry from the tears that wouldn't stop. She didn't care if the police arrested her. She didn't care what happened next. She needed to get Ashley's body somewhere safe.

"But you didn't take her there? Why not?" Officer Lopez asked.

"Clearly Marco must have given her something besides the balché," Jesús cut in, looking at Natalie. "Right?"

Natalie held the officer's steely gaze. "Yes." Ben shook his head, his fists balling at his sides. She wondered what it must be like for him to hear this. "As we were walking back to the car, he was carrying Ashley, and he stopped and told me I needed to hydrate. He bent over his backpack for a minute, and I thought he was trying to find a water, but that must have been when he crushed the Xanax into the bottle. He told me to drink it all. That I was in shock." Natalie could still feel the water as it coated her dry throat. "I didn't think anything of it—why would I? We were on our way to get help—or so I thought. But maybe if I hadn't drunk so much tequila and God knows what else, I would have noticed something about his demeanor."

Marco had stood beside her as Natalie closed her eyes. *I'm so sorry, Ash. I'm so sorry,* she'd said as she'd stared at Ashley.

"He just had Xanax in his pocket?"

"Both balché and Xanax are legal here in Mexico," Jesús interjected. "Not that hard to believe."

"So, after the Xanax, you passed out and Marco presumably took Ashley's body back and put it in the cenote and then drove you back to your hotel?" Officer Lopez said, his eyebrow raised as if he wasn't sure this was plausible.

"I became drowsy after I got into Marco's car. The last thing I remember is Marco carrying her body back toward the cenote. And then I must have passed out." Natalie started to cry again, staring down at her gnawed fingernails. "I don't see any other way I would have ended up back at the hotel." Natalie glanced at the officers, wondering if they thought this was another lie.

Officer Lopez gave Natalie a long stare. They all sat in silence for a few moments.

Finally, Natalie took a deep breath and spoke the words that had been circling inside her head. "So now what?" Officer Lopez's gaze unnerved her. She turned to Officer Garcia. "Are you going to arrest me for having an argument with her?"

Officer Garcia took a moment before responding. She wondered what he was thinking. Did he believe her? Did he want to keep investigating? Did he want to find Marco first? "We need to get the autopsy report back and see if it is consistent with a fall. They conducted it yesterday after you left the morgue, so we should know soon—although this is Mexico. We are on our own clock, as you Americans know." He paused, consulting his notebook again. Natalie wondered how many he had—if there was one for each case he worked on. What he did with the notebooks for the cases he couldn't solve. "Although there is always the chance you drugged yourself, as I mentioned to you the other day. You could have done that to create an alibi. After you concocted this story."

"I didn't concoct this story." Natalie's eyes flashed to Jesús. She now officially needed his help.

"Are you accusing my client of killing Ashley Green?" Jesús asked. "Because if you aren't—if you aren't planning to arrest her—then she does not need to sit here and listen to your accusations. Which is all they are, accusations. That are clearly unsupported. You have no evidence of a sign of a struggle at the cenote. You have no way to prove Ashley was pushed. You have no eyewitnesses. You only have a body, which shows a laceration to her head that you stated *could be* consistent with a fall. But you don't have the autopsy report back yet. I know you'd love to make a quick arrest to please your superiors and get the press to move on, but arresting the wrong person will only make it worse."

"We have motive. And opportunity."

Jesús didn't hesitate. "We both know you can't prove Natalie pushed her. Ashley had been drinking and had done drugs. Have you considered the possibility she committed suicide? That she jumped?"

"That would be almost impossible to prove," Officer Garcia said.

"It sounds like you have your answer then—my client's account of what happened. She has cooperated with you every step of the way. You have nothing else except theories. My client was an eyewitness to what happened. I suggest you take her statement officially and close the case so everyone here can move on."

Natalie bit down on her lip hard. She wondered if the officers would ever believe her. Or if they would continue to try to find her at fault—to try to put the puzzle pieces together in a way that made Natalie responsible. She knew in her heart that Ashley hadn't jumped, but she wasn't going to say that now. It seemed to her that the more theories that were in the mix, the better. It meant they couldn't prove anything. That they could take Ashley's body home. That Natalie could get back to her girls.

Officer Garcia cleared his throat. "Let us complete our investigation—in due time. We will not be rushed because your American client wants to go home."

"I will ask you again, are you planning to arrest Natalie?" Jesús asked.

Natalie's heartbeat raced. Her nerves felt raw. Was this it? Was she going to be arrested? Should she have left out the part where they'd argued? She looked at Ben, her eyes full of fear. She should have listened to him. And to Jesús. What was she thinking?

"At this point, no," Officer Garcia finally said.

Natalie let out a long breath.

"But I am going to continue to hold your passport until the autopsy report comes back. And we'll scour Cenote Calavera to see if we missed anything. Make sure there were no eyewitnesses. And we are going to continue to look for Marco. Only after all of that will we *consider* clearing you to leave Mexico." Officer Garcia looked at Natalie. "Unless you have something else you'd like to say."

"Only that I did not push Ashley. I swear to you." She looked down at her shredded cuticles and nails bitten down to the beds. She wanted to be alone with her memories of Ashley. With the guilt that she was sure would haunt her for the rest of her life.

As terrible as they both were, they were all she had left now.

CHAPTER FORTY

ONE WEEK AFTER
LAUREN

Lauren walked heavy-footed through Cancún International Airport. The police had finally cleared them to go home that morning—Officer Garcia handing them back their passports. He'd seemed like he'd wanted to say more as he held out the small blue books, but he didn't. He simply wished them well in their journey home. Lauren had been at a loss for words when she'd heard about how Ashley had died. Natalie had sat her down in her hotel room, tears streaming down her face, trembling as she told her the story, stopping frequently to catch her breath. Lauren's heart was crushed. God, how she wished she had agreed to leave with Ashley. To talk things out. But she'd been too angry and selfish to step outside and see Ashley for what she had been—a woman, much like herself, who was desperate for her friends to understand her. And now, in her death, Lauren did finally understand. Ashley had been trying to protect her. But when she'd been the one needing protection, Lauren and Natalie had failed miserably. And she could only imagine how Natalie must feel. She had been there. Standing next to her as she'd fallen, unable to save her. How Natalie was going to live with that, Lauren did not know. But she could understand living with her own guilt. Over telling Ashley she wished she were dead. Those final words would haunt her forever.

For the three additional nights they'd been required to stay in Tulum, Lauren had refused to turn to José. He'd offered, but she had politely declined. She knew it would help her escape the pain, but only temporarily. She'd already deleted her Tinder app and had confessed to Annie that she had a sex addiction. Annie said to call her anytime she felt the urge to have a random hookup and she'd remind her of all the ways she could get nasty STDs. Lauren had laughed quietly, both wanting and not wanting to feel better.

Lauren found herself in the gift shop now, passing by the bottles of hot sauce and tequila, the bright T-shirts and woven bracelets. She watched a curly-haired woman deliberate over which wooden picture frame to buy—the one with the dolphin carved into it, or with the flip-flops? She looked up and caught Lauren staring at her, and Lauren turned away quickly. She was sure she'd been scowling at her, finding her souvenir dilemma trivial.

Her insides went cold when she saw Ashley on the cover of *People en Español.* Even though she'd been living through the media storm for the past seven days—her voice mail full of messages from reporters wanting a statement, some even finding them at their hotel and accosting them for a comment—it still felt surreal. Lauren couldn't believe Ashley was gone. That she'd never again hear her throaty laugh after listening to a raunchy joke. She'd never again watch her eat her favorite dessert—dairy-free coconut chocolate-chip ice cream—licking the spoon as if it were the greatest thing she'd ever tasted. And she'd never again see her lift her chin in anger—determined to convince you she was right. What Lauren wouldn't give to go back to El Castillo and see that chin again—to hug Ashley tightly after she confessed what Jason was like, instead of pushing her away. She would have unraveled the intertwined feelings that tied Ashley and Geoff together. Maybe that would have saved them. Saved Ashley.

She'd made the decision yesterday to apply to go back to school—to stop letting the past hold her future hostage. Annie was picking her up from the airport, and they were going straight to a grief meeting where, for the first time, Lauren was planning to tell her story to the group. Every last word of it. Including the most important words of all: *I forgive you, Ashley. And I forgive myself.*

CHAPTER FORTY-ONE

ONE WEEK AFTER
NATALIE

She had told as much of the truth as she could. It was the best she could do for everyone involved. At least, that's what she kept telling herself. As she'd packed Ashley's clothes, carefully folding each item and pressing it into her pink roller bag, her chest ached from crying. Lauren passed her Kleenex until the box was empty. They'd sat on the beach last night as the glowing pink sun set on the ocean and told their favorite stories of Ashley, but Jason was unable to finish the one about their wedding night. When they had gotten into the shuttle for the airport, Natalie squeezed her eyes shut, wishing she could leave the memory of what had happened behind, but she knew it would follow her home and through her life, like a shadow.

The pain would chase her too. Because she would never stop grieving, even though it couldn't change what had happened. Nothing could. Ashley would still be at that cenote with Marco because she believed it would somehow be her salvation—that the water would cleanse her, that the balché would bring her clarity. Natalie would still be there too, bitter and looking for an outlet. Ashley would still end up dead.

Natalie glanced over at Jason in the airplane seat next to her. Ben had given up his seat and taken one in the back of the plane; he didn't want Jason to sit alone. His eyes were closed, but she knew he wasn't sleeping—that he was afraid to fall asleep. He told her the pain of waking up and remembering was almost worse than living with it while he was awake. Natalie wished she could do something to make him feel better, but there wasn't a single gesture or word that could help. The truest words inside her would only make it worse.

She wasn't quite sure how to live with that.

The email from Arthur had come in right before they boarded the plane. Revlon had told Arthur, off the record, that they were so sorry about Ashley's passing, but they had to retract their offer. Even though Natalie had already prepared herself for this, the news had hit her hard.

The story had become an absolute firestorm in the last week—a mixture of truth and lies about Ashley and the investigation splashed across magazine covers and newspapers—some saying she had been having an affair with Marco and painting her as a careless party girl who'd gone to Mexico to break all the rules. The speculation stabbed Natalie in the heart. She hated anyone believing bad things about Ashley. The truths tore her insides too, each time she read them, her wounds reopened. All of it scared Revlon away.

It turned out the police department leak had been Officer Lopez. Officer Garcia had told them as much the day before they left, when he'd stopped at the hotel to return their passports. Officer Garcia had suspected him, so he'd fed him an innocuous lie and it appeared in one of the stories. Lauren had been shocked, but Natalie wasn't. Nothing would ever shock Natalie again.

Officer Garcia had pulled Natalie aside before he handed her passport back. He'd said the autopsy had come back, and the head wound was consistent with a fall. The medical examiner agreed that the laceration could have been caused by Ashley's head hitting one of the jagged rocks below. Traces of Ashley's blood were also found on the wall of the cenote. They had theorized that it had to have been Marco who sent the emojis to Jason, no doubt buying himself time to get out of town, terrified that he would have been blamed for Ashley's death. He'd then leaned in close and gripped her arm. *But I don't think she stumbled and fell. I think she was pushed. And I think you're the one who pushed her. Once you knew Marco had disappeared, you could tell any story you wanted. Maybe the two of you even planned it out before he left—when he dropped you off at the hotel?*

Natalie had pulled back, wide-eyed, and denied it. Told him he couldn't prove a damn thing. And that was when he confessed that was exactly why he was letting her go home—because he didn't have the evidence to support what he called his gut.

Natalie's gut had been right too—that he was a damn good investigator.

She looked out the window, the jagged edge of the Yucatán Peninsula disappearing behind the clouds. Her best friend was never coming back. And the company Natalie had been dying to break free from was now hers to keep, whether she wanted it or not. She considered this karma—to now be handcuffed to the business she had grown to hate. To be forever tied to the memories—*all* of them. BloMe would become her own personal prison, the penance she'd have to pay for her part in Ashley's death. For the secrets she'd kept to protect herself.

Arthur said they could try to dredge up interest next year once everyone forgot about Ashley—after she'd became a footnote in the public's memory.

Ashley would have hated everyone moving on without her permission.

Natalie had heard Ben on the phone with a real estate agent that morning, talking in a hushed tone to spare her, but she'd known. They'd discussed it this morning—Natalie couldn't get any money out of the company, not for a long while. Jason was Ashley's beneficiary, so he had signed a spousal agreement that, should she ever die, he would sell back his shares to the company. Ironically, after Ash had been so adamant that he not profit from BloMe, Natalie would have to pay him out. And it would take time. A lot of time, especially because most of their cash was tied up in inventory in long payment terms. Natalie pushed her feelings away about losing their house and moving in with Ben's sister in Pasadena. She didn't have a right to be sad about losing her home. Ashley was dead. Her body beneath them now in the cargo hold.

Jason made a sound and Natalie turned to see tears falling down his face, splashing on the airline magazine on his lap. Natalie said nothing but grabbed Jason's hand and squeezed it. Before she could say anything, he spoke.

"You were an amazing friend to her, Nat."

"Thank you," she said, loathing herself as she said the words.

After she told the police what happened to Ashley, she'd taken a long walk on the beach, then gone to find Jason. He'd cried silently as she told him her memory of how she'd died. The same version she'd given the police. And then she'd found Lauren and done the same. Natalie had found herself thinking back to the honeymooners who'd heard the screams in the water. She could never be sure, and the police had written it off because Ashley had been found at the cenote, not in the ocean. But Natalie had a feeling it had been her, not just because her dress was wet, but because she would have been letting out the anguish of losing her best friend. And then she'd gone to the beach chair and passed out. At least, she wanted to believe that's how it had happened.

"I need you to know something. It's been eating away at me, ever since the bartender told us what he heard Ashley say." He dropped his chin to his chest. "I wasn't a good husband. I could get really angry. I said things, awful things, especially after the offer, and maybe this wouldn't have happened if—"

"It's okay." Natalie stopped him. His chin was quaking, and she knew he was on the cusp of breaking down completely. She couldn't let that happen. "It's not your fault."

Because it's mine.

"I just keep thinking that if she hadn't slipped, then maybe she would have left with him. And at least she'd still be alive. Or if we'd had a better marriage, she wouldn't have been at that cenote in the first place. Because she wouldn't have given that douchebag the time of day."

Looking at Jason, she decided to tell one more lie—convincing herself that it would give Jason the peace that she knew would elude her for the rest of her life.

"She never would have left you," Natalie said.

"But how can you be so sure?" Jason asked, but she could tell by his pained stare that he was desperate for it to be true.

Natalie held his gaze tight. "Because I was her best friend. I knew her better than anyone."

Jason looked back toward the window, and Natalie followed his gaze. The chalk-white clouds created a barrier between their plane and the real world below, giving Natalie the false sense that she was free. When in reality, she would always be anything but.

"Ashley was lucky to have you," she heard Jason say.

Natalie swallowed hard, a thickness in her throat. She heard her scathing tone from that night, saw the spittle flying from her mouth and her fists shaking in the air. The hateful last words she'd shouted at Ashley while at the cenote ringing in her head. *You're ruining my life. She's just a liar. Aren't you, Ashley? Just admit it. You are more selfish than I ever realized.* The way Natalie had moved toward Ashley, so consumed with anger that it blocked out all reason. Realizing too late how precarious Ashley's position on the edge of the cenote was, not calculating how the balché had affected her balance. Reaching out for her and missing, Ashley's arms flailing as she fell backward. And then the sound of Ashley's screams. The crack of her skull on the rocks. And then silence.

She had lain awake the entire night before, listening to the waves crash against the sand and wondered whether there was any path that would lead her back to the person she was before Tulum. She knew she'd have to find a way to live with the constant echo of her own thoughts whispering that she'd been responsible for her best friend's death. The memory she'd fought so hard to regain was now becoming her prison. Ashley, who had oftentimes seemed larger than life, was now lifeless.

The very worst part? That as Arthur delivered the news that Revlon no longer wanted to buy BloMe, Natalie couldn't help but think of the terrible irony.

That Ashley, even in death, had gotten what she wanted.

CHAPTER FORTY-TWO

THE NIGHT
ASHLEY

Ashley was falling, hard and fast, yet her thoughts paced in slow motion, as if she knew they were her last.

Hannah. Abby. Natalie. Lauren. Jason.

Holding Hannah's hand tightly on the first day of kindergarten, her bright yellow dress making her look like a beautiful sunflower. How she gazed up at Ashley with her wide brown eyes. Abby, arms folded over her chest just last week, angry with Ashley because she'd missed her back-to-school night. Natalie, so desperate that she'd become a person that Ashley didn't recognize. Lauren, glaring at her with narrow eyes and tight jaw at Chichén Itzá, so angry that she couldn't see how much Ashley needed her. And Jason. Loving her and hating her in equal measure, both emotions spilling into one another until it was impossible to determine where one ended and the other began. It all came to Ashley in that moment, in the shock that her body was actually flying through the air and the realization that she had stepped off the ledge intentionally, almost instinctually. The choice she'd made to let herself go. To head toward that other life—whatever that might be. Flashes of regret layered with hope, fear, and then, in her very last moment, the peace and clarity for which she had been searching.

ACKNOWLEDGMENTS

There are so many people to thank. But first, a confession.

Girls' Night Out broke us open, hard and wide, before putting us back together again. Our friendship and our partnership were put to the test in a way we'd never experienced before. The pressure of writing a follow-up that could rival *The Good Widow* hit us hard. We argued. We cried. We wondered if this book would ever make it to you.

Girls' Night Out took us on a year-long journey from the beautiful beaches of Tulum, where we excitedly developed this plot while drinking margaritas and touring ancient ruins, to the magical city of New Orleans, where we fought and struggled with our developmental edits, our thirty-year alliance crumbling. Would the book make it? Would we?

What had started as a *wink, wink* storyline about two longtime best friends whose connection begins to fragment when the business they founded takes off, slowly began to acutely resonate. We were also lifetime friends. We too ran a business together. Under time constraints and rigorous rewrites, we started bickering more than ever, wondering how and why life had begun to imitate art. We'd never had these problems before. Maybe a testy voice here or a curt email there. But nothing like this. Why now? We plunged into a dark ravine. We felt hopeless.

Thankfully, the elasticity of our friendship remained durable, our strong bond pulling us back together and forcing us to learn from our mistakes. From each other. And interestingly enough, this novel began to come back together too, almost as if the fate of our friendship and the book were intertwined. And maybe they were, because both are stronger today after the pressures they endured.

This challenging but important experience is why we've dedicated this book to friendship—something that isn't always easy. That is both delicate and strong. That is worth fighting for. Go hug your best friend. Or give her a call. (Maybe not a text this time!) Remind her why she's important to you—even if you think she already knows! And most important, never be afraid to utter those two magical words: *I'm sorry.*

And now, on to the thank-yous.

To the lovely and generous people of Tulum, Quintana Roo, in Mexico, your smiles and pleasant attitudes are infectious. To the staff at Encantada, the boutique hotel where we stayed while researching this book, your hospitality and kindness are unmatched. And your patience as we asked question after question will not be forgotten. We hope we channeled all of your wonderful qualities into our fictitious characters, Maria and Ishmael.

To Fernando, our guide at Chichén Itzá, we are appreciative of your incredible knowledge of the Mayan civilization and city and your willingness to stop your tour as we took copious notes and to answer each of our one million questions.

Tulum is a wonderful city, one we will visit many more times. Unlike the characters we created, we felt very safe while there. (Even when we took a wrong turn and walked two miles the wrong way in triple-digit heat!) We highly suggest visiting. Stay at Encantada! Be sure to take a yoga class at Maya Tulum. Have a meal at Hartwood, Ziggy's, La Zebra, and Posada Margherita. Have a smoothie at Playa Canek or a smoothie bowl at Raw Love. Be sure to go to Batey—the best nightlife in Tulum! Bike around the city! Take the time to visit Chichén Itzá. And don't forget to order a mezcal margarita.

To our incredible agent, Elisabeth Weed at The Book Group, we love you more with each passing year. How is that even possible? Thank you for your smart and savvy guidance. And for your visit to Tulum, which gave us the idea to travel there. Hallie Schaffer, thank you for all that you do.

Danielle Marshall, editor extraordinaire, thank you for bringing us into the Lake Union family. Your unflinching support means more than we could express here. And your southern sayings make us so very happy. Dennelle Catlett, we love your unflappable nature. Your unwavering dedication to getting our books out there. Gabriella "Gabe" Dumpit, girl, you are da bomb. Much love to you. And everyone on the Lake Union author team, huge thank-yous all around. From cover design to congratulatory surprises in the mail, we appreciate you.

Tiffany Yates Martin! We don't want to gush too much for fear you might make us rewrite it! Ha! In all seriousness, we do appreciate when you push us to be our best. You are a talented and insightful editor, and we're lucky to work with you. And know that we will forever think of our characters' inner lives as we write.

Kathleen Carter! Your love of publicity and the authors you support is inspiring. Congrats on your new endeavor at Kathleen Carter Communications. You deserve it! (Did you like that plug we just gave you? We learn from the best!) We look forward to a long relationship.

To all the readers' groups out there, we are so grateful for you. For getting the word out about books. And not just ours—everyone's. Thank you for fostering and perpetuating a love of reading. Great Thoughts, Great Readers, Bunch of Book Baristas, Literary Love, Readers Coffeehouse, RW Book Club, Bookworms Anonymous, and Kristy Barrett of A Novel Bee—we adore you all. And a shout out to our favorite Bookstagrammers—Natasha Minoso (@bookbaristas), Vilma Gonzalez (@vilmairisblog), Abby Endler (@crimebythebook), Chelsea Humphrey (@suspensethrill), Jen Cannon (@literarylove), Samantha "Sam" Ellen (@cluesandreviews), Kate Olsen (@theloudlibrarylady), Athena Kaye (@athena.kaye), Suzanne Leopold (@suzanneleopold), Kayleigh Wilkes (@bookish.mama13), Uma Kayla G (@booklover12),

Bethany Clark (@blclark513), Courtney Marzilli (@blissbeautybooks), Julie Caldwell (@juliejustreads), and Jaymi Couch (@bookfairies_oc). And to amazing book champions Jen Lynette, Deborah Blanchard, Barbara Khan, Bianca O'Brien, Sharlene Moore, Cindy Burnett, Marilyn Grable, Linda Zagon, and Jenny Collins Belk. And so many more! We appreciate every one of you.

And always, special love to Jenny Tropea O'Regan (@jenny_oregan).

Andrea Katz, you are amazing. Thank you for the sharp beta read and invaluable advice. For founding Great Thoughts, Great Readers. For your ninjas. For your love of books. For your refusal to send emojis in your texts. (Stay true to yourself, girl!) For all of it, we adore you!

And to Brenda Janowitz, author and book champion extraordinaire, thank you for the huge love you give so many books as a PopSugar Books correspondent.

George Piner, thank you for sharing your experiences from your trip to Tulum and Chichén Itzá. The information was invaluable!

Stephanie Herbek, thank you for clarifying the difference between the ruins in Tulum and Chichén Itzá. Our chance meeting in the grocery store just days before the trip to Mexico changed our entire trip and helped shape this book.

To Cristine and Matt, thank you for reading and loving the initial draft of this book. We needed that early support more than you know!

To our families, whom we ignored for days at a time to finish this novel, thank you for understanding how important it is to cultivate not only our writing, but also our friendship. We love you all so much.

ABOUT THE AUTHORS

Photo © 2016 Debbie Friedrich

Liz Fenton and Lisa Steinke have been best friends for thirty years. They've survived high school, college, and the publishing of four novels together, including the bestselling novel *The Good Widow*. Liz lives in San Diego, California, with her husband and two children. Lisa, a former talk-show producer, now lives in Chicago, Illinois, with her husband, daughter, and two bonus children. They're huge animal lovers—between them, they have seven rescue dogs. Visit Liz and Lisa at www.lizandlisa.com.